Sa

Would you g

Two sizzlingly sensational stories about
women turned seductresses who satisfy their
desires as passion takes over...

The final thrilling instalment of the sexy
Seduce...Surrender...Satisfy trilogy,
Satisfy is wickedly hot!

CARA SUMMERS

The Favour
"What an extremely sexy and exciting story!"
—*Freshfiction.com*

KRISTIN GABRIEL

Good Night, Gracie
"A heated tale"
—*The Best Reviews*

SEDUCE...SURRENDER...SATISFY

Satisfy

How far will you go?

Cara Summers

Kristin Gabriel

*M&B™ and M&B™ with the Rose Device
are trademarks of the publisher.
Harlequin Mills & Boon Limited, Eton House,
18-24 Paradise Road,
Richmond, Surrey TW9 1SR*

Satisfy © by Harlequin Books S.A. 2006

The publisher acknowledges the copyright holders of the
individual works as follows:
The Favour © Carolyn Hanlon 2005
Good Night, Gracie © Kristin Eckhardt 2005

ISBN 0 263 85077 3

055-1006

*Printed and bound in Spain
by Litografia Rosés S.A., Barcelona*

The Favour

CARA SUMMERS

Dear Reader,

I love to write stories about strong women who find the courage to take risks. And *The Proposition, The Dare,* and *The Favour* have allowed me to do just that.

Psychologist Sierra Gibbs, the youngest of triplet sisters, has lived all of her life on the sidelines. Up until now, romance and adventure were things she experienced only vicariously in books and films. As for great sex – well, so far she's been researching that instead of getting any.

However, all that is about to change! Sierra is about to change. Inspired by her own curiosity and her sisters' recent experiences, she's determined to break out of the cocoon of academic life and embark on a sexual adventure of her own. How hard can it be? Using the same technique that has earned her two PhDs, Sierra makes a list – a five-step plan to initiate a sexual adventure with a man.

But before she can even implement step one, she runs into a sexy, rugged stranger in a bar who kisses her senseless. Then she shocks herself by kissing him right back. Even more shocking, she's tempted to toss out her list and cut straight to step five! That isn't like her at all.

I hope you get a kick out of reading Sierra and Ryder's story. For excerpts from these stories, contests and news of upcoming books, be sure to visit my website, www.carasummers.com.

Happy reading,

Cara Summers

To my editor, Brenda Chin. This is the seventeenth book we've worked on together. You make me a better writer. Thanks for everything! To my sister Janet. I can't imagine my life without you. And to sisters everywhere.

Prologue

Summer 1999

STEALING THE O'Malley necklace was going to be a challenge that would require all of the skills Harry Gibbs had honed to perfection over a long and successful career. The way Harry saw it, the risk itself was almost more important than whether or not he'd pull off the heist of what many in Ireland believed to be a national treasure.

Harry had done extensive research on both the family and Arden Castle, their ancestral home. The O'Malleys claimed they could trace their roots back to the Celts. The castle didn't date back quite that far, but it was built like a fortress with high stone walls on three sides and a drop to the sea on the fourth. Harry planned to gain access by climbing up that cliff. He smiled at the thought.

When his horse shifted nervously beneath him, Harry lowered his binoculars and patted the animal's neck, "Easy, Dracula."

"That's a nice horse."

Startled, Harry turned to see a young woman with the greenest eyes he'd ever seen studying him through large, wire-framed glasses. She was slim, with a boyish build, and her long, straight hair was the rich shade of red that had been captured in all of the portraits Harry had found of the O'Malleys. He guessed her age at fourteen or fifteen, which meant she was probably Bridget, the youngest daughter of the current residents of the castle. And she'd sneaked up on him like a master thief. He couldn't help but admire her for it.

"Dracula is a very nice horse," Harry agreed with a smile. "Do you ride?"

The hand that she'd raised to pat the horse dropped without making contact. "No. I have asthma. I'm not even supposed to be out here on the hill. Too many allergens in the air."

"Ah." Harry nodded in understanding. "You've gone AWOL."

"Yes." She sent him the barest hint of a smile. "I do it quite a bit. You're not supposed to be here, you know. The land is posted."

Harry had thought that they'd get to that sooner or later. The sharpness and directness of the girl's gaze reminded him a bit of his youngest daughter's. Of course, Sierra was taller and her hair was Alice-in-Wonderland blond, but Sierra too had suffered from asthma, and her approach to life was as serious as this young woman's seemed to be.

He tried his most charming smile. "I'm Harry Gibbs."

She studied him for a moment and then moved closer to take his outstretched hand. "Bridget O'Malley."

Harry lifted his brows. "One of the owners. I hope you aren't going to report me to the authorities. There was a fence a ways back. Dracula and I were both irresistibly tempted."

She met his gaze steadily. "I won't tell. If I did, I'd have to admit I was here, wouldn't I?" The small smile appeared again. "And if I could ride, I probably would have done the same."

Harry tapped one finger to his riding hat. "Thank you, Bridget O'Malley. It's been a pleasure meeting you."

Her smile blossomed slowly, beautifully. "One favor."

"Name it."

"When you take that fence this time, think of me."

"That I will."

HARRY WAS still thinking of Bridget O'Malley that evening. He told himself that she'd stayed in his mind because she'd reminded him so forcibly of Sierra, and his youngest daughter had been weighing on his mind lately. He raised his snifter of cognac and took a sip, staring into the flames of the fire that he'd built. The cottage outside of Dublin was one of three places he kept, but it was the one he thought Sierra would like the most.

She was the youngest of his triplet daughters and the one he worried about the most. Spread around him on the floor were his plans for the O'Malley heist. To his right were the architect's drawings of the latest renovations to the castle. They revealed the exact location of the safe. To his left were photos and sketches of the wall he'd have to scale, and in front of him was the plan, with the steps neatly listed on blue note cards. Since he suffered from color blindness, he'd always used blue so that his plan would stand out from the other papers.

The cards made him think of Sierra too. As a child, she'd imitated his habit of jotting things down on blue cards, and as he thought of her, his heart twisted a little. Each of his daughters had inherited something from him. Natalie, the oldest of the triplets, had inherited his gift for opening safes and his talent for disguise. Rory, his middle daughter, had inherited his love of risk-taking—for better or for worse. And Sierra—well, his wife claimed she'd inherited her father's curiosity and analytical brain, and Sierra had definitely inherited his love of making lists.

Harry took another sip of his cognac. Lately, he'd been missing his family more and more, and he'd been feeling an urgent need to talk to them. But contacting them in any way would violate the promise he'd made to his wife, Amanda.

The girls had been ten when he and Amanda had separated. She'd wanted a normal life for the girls, and he'd agreed. When they'd been born, he'd retired from his profession and tried his best to provide his family with as normal a life as possible in the suburbs of DC. But it hadn't worked out. He'd missed the risks, the adventure, the thrill of pulling off the perfect heist.

His wife had refused to go back to that life. The girls already idolized him, and she didn't want them following in his footsteps. Neither did he. So they'd agreed that he wouldn't contact them in any way until their twenty-sixth birthdays.

They were twenty now, and Harry was beginning to think that he wouldn't be able to wait six more years. That was why he'd decided to write to them. He'd already written to Natalie and Rory. His attorney would deliver the letters to them if he couldn't be there himself.

He glanced over at the photos he'd taken of the wall he'd have to scale to gain access to the O'Malley castle. Could be he wouldn't have six more years. One misstep while climbing that wall would end his life.

Of course, that was part of what had drawn him to the caper—the risk. Natalie and Rory would understand that, but he wasn't sure that Sierra would. Of his three daughters, he figured she was the one who would judge him the most harshly for the decision he'd made to leave them behind. That was why he'd put off writing her letter.

Rising, he took his cognac with him to the desk where he kept his collection of photos. Earlier, he'd taken out his three favorites of Sierra. Although she'd been unaware of his presence, he'd taken them himself. His promise not to contact his daughters in any way hadn't prevented him from secretly being there at the important events in their lives.

In the first picture, she was giving the valedictory speech at her high-school graduation. What he hadn't captured in the photo was the fact that beneath the podium, she'd held blue note cards in her hand—just in case she forgot her speech. In spite of her academic achievements, she'd never had the kind of confidence she should.

In the second picture, he'd captured her poring over books in her college library. From the time she'd been tiny, she'd loved books, and he'd read to her often.

The third one had him frowning. He'd taken it less than a month ago, and he'd very nearly broken his promise when he'd snapped it. She was sitting on a bench in Rock Creek Park watching the never-ending flow of runners, bikers and in-line skaters along a jogging path. The longing on her face had tightened a band of pain around his heart. It was the same expression that he'd seen on Bridget O'Malley's face that morning when she'd looked at Dracula.

If there was one piece of advice he most needed to give to Sierra it was that she had to stop hiding away in her books and studies and take the risk of really participating in life.

Pulling a piece of blue paper out of his desk, he sat down and began: Dearest Sierra, my beautiful dreamer…

1

WHY DID SHE always have to be such a coward?

As she threaded her way through the other pedestrians on a busy Georgetown street, Sierra Gibbs pondered the question that was currently number one in her mind.

Of course, when it came to questions, there were bigger, more important ones. She supposed that Hamlet's "To be or not to be?" had been more fundamental, hitting as it did on the issue of existence. But the Danish prince had also worried about personal cowardice and he'd certainly suffered from acute paralysis when it came to taking action.

Realizing the direction her thoughts had taken, Sierra let out a disgusted sigh. Since today was the day she was going to change her life, Hamlet was a lousy role model.

On the street horns blared, pedestrians flowed around her, but Sierra didn't let her focus waver as she continued on her way down the sidewalk. During the past month, ever since her sisters had opened their birthday letters from their father, she'd become more and more dissatisfied with her life. Not her professional life. That was humming along quite smoothly. She'd recently been appointed to a tenure-track position at Georgetown, and she'd also signed a book contract for her research on the sexual habits of single urban dwellers.

Sierra paused in front of a traffic light. The cars moved at a determined pace through the intersection. She ignored them.

It was her pathetic personal life that was the problem, and that point was driven home to her each and every time she met with her sisters and saw the contented expressions on their faces.

In the process of following their father's advice, Natalie and Rory had both become involved in very satisfying sexual relationships with men.

Sierra's own personal life, and indeed her sex life, hadn't changed much since she was a child. As she had back then, she spent most of her waking hours reading books or watching movies. As an adult, in addition to that, she buried herself in her academic work. Bottom line—she researched sex instead of having any.

As a child, she'd had some excuse for letting life pass her by. She'd suffered from severe asthma, and she'd constantly battled high fevers and sinus infections. But at twenty-six, her only excuse was that she was a coward. If you remained on the sidelines, you never had to risk a thing. Or lose anyone.

Well, she was sick and tired of being Jane Eyre, the mousy little governess, content to observe life and never participate in it.

Jane, along with Hamlet, was another lousy role model. Closing her eyes, Sierra banished all images of each of them from her mind. She needed to be imagining herself as someone much more assertive, someone like…like Buffy the Vampire Slayer. The TV series had become one of her favorites. Now there was a woman to be reckoned with. Sierra pictured the feisty blonde with her kickass attitude. And Buffy probably always had great sex, too.

And Buffy's nerve would come in handy, too, if Sierra was going to ride over the objections her sisters were sure to make when they heard her plan. Even though she was only fifteen minutes younger than Natalie and a mere seven and a half minutes younger than Rory, her family had always treated her as the baby. And despite that she was an adult now, her sisters still felt it was their duty to protect her.

Opening her eyes, Sierra let out another disgusted sigh when she saw that the little white man on the pedestrian traffic signal had changed to a blinking red hand. Not even Hamlet would have hesitated at crossing a street. And Buffy would have been at the Blue Pepper by now. She hurriedly stepped off the curb, but halfway across the street, paused and drew a blue note card from her canvas bag. Then she reread the heading. Five steps for initiating a sexual relationship with a man. For the first step in becoming a full-fledged participant in life, she'd decided that she wanted to learn more about her own sexual side. Her curiosity about that no doubt had grown out of her current research into the sexual practices of modern single urban dwellers.

Her decision to kick off her plan with a sexual adventure would not only satisfy her curiosity, but it was also very practical. After all, her research so far had provided her with some expertise—even if it was totally vicarious.

She'd collected hundreds of case studies, and completed nearly as many interviews. Plus, she had a five-step plan. If there was one thing that she could do in her professional life it was to stick to a plan once she'd mapped it out.

The sharp blast of a horn made her jump, and a quick glance around informed her that five cars were waiting for her to get out of the pedestrian walkway.

"Lady, could you hurry it up?"

Rush hour in Georgetown was not the best time to dawdle. Stuffing the blue card back into her bag, Sierra waved apologetically to the man in the silver convertible. The black sedan next to it revved its motor. She dashed to the curb.

Once she was safely on the sidewalk, she dug in her canvas bag for her inhaler. After using it, she dropped it back in her bag, then drew in a deep breath and continued up the street.

The Blue Pepper was only a block away, and her sisters had agreed on very short notice to meet her for the grand opening of Harry's letter to her. She rubbed the heel of her hand against the little ache that always settled around her heart when she thought of her father.

She and her sisters had lost Harry Gibbs twice—once when they'd been ten and Harry had decided to follow the call to adventure and resume his career as a master jewel thief. That was when they'd made a pact to call him Harry. Then when they were twenty, he'd died in a climbing accident, and they'd lost him permanently.

Sierra had always blamed herself for the fact that Harry had left them behind. If she hadn't been so prone to illness, her mother surely wouldn't have been too worried about her youngest to go with him. Amanda Gibbs had loved her husband deeply, and she'd passed away within months of Harry's death.

Then suddenly, on the day that they'd turned twenty-six, the letters from Harry had arrived. Of course, Natalie had read hers the night she'd received it. If there was a gene for courage, Natalie had inherited it. Her job on a special task force with the DC Police Department testified to that.

Rory who always met life head-on had only needed an

extra two weeks to open hers. Then she'd been off and running, putting their father's advice right into practice. If there was a daredevil gene, Rory had gotten it in spades.

The way Sierra figured it, she'd inherited nothing from her father. The one thing Harry Gibbs had never been was a coward, and she'd postponed reading his letter for almost a month because she was a chicken. She was sure that his advice to her would be different. Harry had always treated her differently than he'd treated her sisters.

Sierra stopped short when she realized that she'd walked half a block past the Blue Pepper. Nerves bubbled in her stomach. After reaching for her inhaler, she used it again and drew in several steadying breaths before she turned and walked back to the restaurant. Then she pulled out her blue card once more and began to pace. Five steps—she could do this. When she finally glanced up and caught her reflection in the glass door, her confidence wavered. The woman looking back at her had her hair twisted into a bun and wore a loose-fitting, drab-colored jacket and skirt. And sensible shoes. Sierra Gibbs—academic nerd.

Think Buffy, she reminded herself.

The moment the image of the vampire slayer was clear in her mind, she squared her shoulders. "I can do this."

Sierra Gibbs was sick and tired of being a coward. If she had to imagine herself as someone else to find some courage, so be it. Striding forward, she pushed through the door of the Blue Pepper.

IN RYDER KANE'S mind, the Blue Pepper was a yuppie haven. And the kick of it was he fit right in. Fifteen years ago when he'd been fighting for survival on the streets of Baltimore, he'd never have imagined ending up in a trendy Georgetown bistro drinking a designer label beer and wearing the kind of finely cut clothes that allowed him to blend in perfectly with the other well-heeled clientele.

If his Aunt Jennie could have seen him now, she would have been proud. And if his mother could have pictured this kind of a future for her son, she might have thought twice about abandoning him when he was twelve.

With a wry smile, he lifted his beer and toasted his high-tech security business, Kane Management; it had played a major role in his transformation. And thank God that computer security wasn't the only business that he dabbled in. While it had put a great deal of money in his pocket, it was his other business, Favors for a Fee, that was his real love. It provided the kind of adventure and excitement that was lacking in a lot of the security work he did. Not to mention that doing "favors" for a select clientele allowed him to use some of the skills he'd picked up when he'd served for two years in a Special Forces unit.

But tonight wasn't about work. Ryder was meeting up with Mark Anderson, an up-and-coming investigative reporter for *The Washington Post*. He was looking forward to seeing Mark. His friendship with Mark went back to his early days in Baltimore. They'd been fifteen or so. Of course, neither of them had worked in legitimate professions then. They'd both had close brushes with the law and survived mostly on street smarts. But they'd been friends. In addition to that, the cryptic message Mark had left on his voice mail had intrigued him: "I've got something hot and political that I need your perspective on. Meet me at the Blue Pepper at five."

Turning slightly on the bar stool, Ryder scanned the entrance area and the upper dining level. Then he checked the crowd in the bar again. In the half hour that he'd been waiting, the area had filled so that patrons were standing

three-deep, and conversation, thanks for the most part to
a group at the far end of the bar, now drowned out the TV
set that was carrying the final inning of an Orioles game.

"Hey!" a large man waved a hand at the bartender. "Another round over here."

It was the third round the rather obnoxious man had ordered since he'd taken his seat. Ryder glanced at his watch.
There was no sign of Mark Anderson, and it was nearly
five-thirty.

He was lifting his glass for another sip of beer when he
spotted the tall blonde through the glass entrance door. She
wore her pale, straw-colored hair fastened into bun, and
even though she wore a loose-fitting jacket and long skirt,
he could see that she had that slender, Audrey Hep-
burn/Nicole Kidman kind of body. Sexy.

Tall women with mile-long legs were one of his weak-
nesses. Twisting his chair a little further, he watched as she
used an inhaler and then paced back and forth in front of the
restaurant while she studied a blue paper. A true nervous
Nelly, he decided. Finally, she paused, stuffed the paper
into her bag, squared her shoulders and approached the door.

His curiosity piqued, Ryder narrowed his eyes. She
looked as if she were preparing to face a firing squad instead of joining friends for a drink in one of Georgetown's
most popular watering holes. Was she meeting a man? If
so, she surely didn't look as though she were looking forward to it. The thought had him frowning.

She crossed the entrance area and climbed the short
flight of stairs to the bar. As she drew closer, he could see
a shadow of a frown marring what appeared to be a perfect face. His own frown deepened when he saw that one
of her hands gripped the large canvas bag she wore slung
over her shoulder as if it were a lifeline.

He had a sudden urge to go to her, take her hands, and ask her what he could do to help. The realization, and the effort it took to remain on his stool, surprised him. Rescuing damsels in distress was not the type of work that either Kane Management or Favors for a Fee regularly engaged in. He might like women in all their various shapes and sizes, but he didn't often find himself with an urge to do the knight-in-shining-armor thing.

He was bored. That's what it was. Mark Anderson had piqued his curiosity and then kept him waiting for over half an hour. Swivelling back to the bar, Ryder took another sip of beer and checked on the score. The Orioles were tied at the top of the seventh. He didn't turn when she passed behind him. That was why he only glimpsed what happened out of the corner of his eye. The loud obnoxious man who was working on his third beer shoved another man and that man plowed into another in a domino effect that sent the blonde stumbling backward.

Fate, he thought, slipping from his stool and catching her elbows as she struggled for balance. For one brief moment, as he steadied her, he caught her scent—something that reminded him of tart lemonade on a hot afternoon. Surprising. And certainly not sexy, at least he wouldn't have thought so. But his body had different ideas. If he'd followed his impulse, he would have turned her around and pressed her close, just to see what that would feel like. But Ryder Kane could be cautious when the occasion called for it. And the intuition that he'd come to rely on in his work told him something about this fragile beauty spelled trouble.

"You all right?" he asked as he turned her around and carefully set her away from him.

"Yes." Then she gasped. "My bag."

Ryder saw the canvas bag on the floor, its contents spread about. As he dropped to his knees, he picked up the nearest item—the inhaler she'd used. He reached for the objects that had slid beneath his bar stool—a pack of blue note cards and a plastic bottle that held prescription pills. Sierra Gibbs was the name he noted and she was to take two as needed for migraines. A definite nervous Nelly.

"Thanks." The voice was deep and just a little breathless. When he turned, she was on her knees facing him, and for an instant as he gazed into her eyes, his mind went blank except for one word. *You.*

Ryder couldn't put a name to the feeling that raced through him. It didn't feel like the flashes of intuition he sometimes got. And it couldn't be recognition. The first time he'd laid eyes on this woman was a few moments ago.

This close, her face wasn't quite as perfect as it had seemed from a distance. Oh, the skin made him think of pale and delicate porcelain—the kind that you were almost afraid to touch. But the sprinkle of freckles across her nose and the faint scar on her chin made it more interesting.

The hair wasn't quite perfect either. Several long strands had come loose. Reaching out, he resisted the urge to pull the rest loose and instead tucked one of the stands behind her ear. He heard her quick intake of breath and felt the instant tightening of his body as his fingers touched her skin. When she bit even white teeth into her bottom lip, heat shot through him. He wanted *very* much to replace those teeth with his own.

Okay. Now he could name exactly what he was feeling. Lust. That was familiar. He might have even relaxed a bit if it weren't for the fact that he couldn't quite free himself from her gaze. Her eyes were the deep-blue color of lake water—the kind that tempted you to jump right in even though there was no telling what lay below the surface. From the time he'd been a kid, he'd been fascinated by the water, by the secrets it held, the adventures it promised.

"You remind me of someone," she said in that same breathless voice that sent ripples of awareness along his skin.

"Really?" He watched her eyes narrow until she was looking at him as if she were determined to see everything.

She took a deep breath. "Have me met somewhere before?"

He smiled. "Isn't that supposed to be my line?"

WHEN SIERRA caught his meaning, she felt color flood her cheeks. In a moment, she'd be beet-red. Her skin was already flushed from that arrow of heat that had shot through her during the moment when he'd held her against him. His chest had been hard as a rock, and the warmth of his breath at her temple had made her insides melt. She'd never reacted quite that physically to a man before. She'd never talked to a stranger in a bar before.

And he thought…he thought she was coming on to him.

"I didn't mean…" she began. "I'm not trying to… It's just that… I mean…" How was she supposed to explain that strange feeling of recognition she'd felt just seconds ago when she'd looked into his eyes? "I—"

"Stop." He held up a hand. "I'd rather you didn't tell me that you're not trying to pick me up. My ego is very fragile."

The glint of humor she saw in his eyes settled some of her nerves. "Somehow, I don't think so."

Competent and *confident* were the two words that came to mind as she studied him. He was different from the men who frequented the Blue Pepper—they were either local merchants or the up-and-coming movers and shakers of DC. He was also different from the men she ran into in her field of work. They were slow-moving academics. Cautious book people who seldom took risks. Just like herself.

This man, in addition to having classic Adonis-like good looks, was…what? *Real* was the first word that came immediately to mind. His skin was a golden-brown that came from working in the sun rather than a tanning salon, and she bet the muscles she'd felt came from something other than a tri-weekly appointment with a personal trainer. And there was a hint of danger about him.

He smiled at her then, and her gaze shifted to his mouth. For a moment she thought of nothing at all, except how those lips might feel pressed to hers. The thought startled her. She'd never before wanted to pull a man's mouth to hers.

"Why don't we start over?" He took her hand, and though his fingers only gripped hers lightly, she felt the sensation right down to her toes.

"I'll say I'm sure I've seen you somewhere, I'll introduce myself and I'll offer to buy you a drink? And you'll say…?"

She couldn't say a thing. They were squatting down, leaning toward each other, their fingers linked, their knees nearly brushing, and she'd never felt this kind of intense connection with anyone in her life.

In the part of her mind that hadn't shut down, she realized that she wasn't feeling like herself at all. Around them, people edged past. Above them, faint noises swirled—glasses clinking, people talking, laughing. She barely heard them. All she knew was that she wanted this man—this perfect stranger—to kiss her. She couldn't recall ever wanting anything quite this much. What would happen if she just leaned a little closer, reached up and drew his mouth to hers?

Her sister Natalie would do it. And her sister Rory wouldn't be the least bit afraid. What about the Sierra she wanted to be? She would do it. Suddenly, the wanting, the need was so strong that she felt herself swaying toward him.

As if he'd read her mind, he tightened his grip on her fingers and his free hand moved to the back of her neck, steadying her. "I want to kiss you," he said.

Startled, she raised her eyes to meet his, and the old Sierra suddenly reasserted herself. "You…can't."

His brows lifted. "If you don't want me to, offering a challenge isn't the best strategy."

She'd known he would be a bit dangerous, but she hadn't expected the thrill that moved through her. "I'm not offering a challenge. But we're in a public place. We don't even know each other."

His lips curved again. "And your point is?"

She moistened her lips, and tried to focus her thoughts. What was her point? If she truly wanted to initiate a sexual relationship with a man, she had to start somewhere. It would be good practice. "Never before in my life have I wanted to kiss someone that I didn't know."

Something flashed into his eyes then, and it made her breath hitch.

"That makes two of us," he murmured as he took her mouth with his.

A riot of sensations moved through her. His mouth was just as strong, just as competent as she'd anticipated. It terrified her. It delighted her. The scrape of his teeth on her bottom lip, the clever slide of his tongue over hers sent tiny explosions of pleasure shooting through her.

She'd never been kissed like this—as if he had all the time in the world to take and take and take. She'd never felt this alive. Her blood pounded, her body heated until all the worry, all the anxiety that had been plaguing her for weeks seemed to evaporate. She should think. But how could she when her whole being seemed to be filled with him? No one had ever made her feel this way. So wanted. So wanton. So free.

You. The word repeated itself over and over in her head as she gripped his shoulders and felt those tensed, hard muscles. Greed erupted in her. She wanted to touch more of him. She wanted to run her fingers through that dark hair. She wanted to press her palms against his chest, his back, his waist. And she wanted his clothes out of the way.

With a moan, she moved her hands to the back of his neck and pulled him closer.

RYDER FELT as if he were going under for the last time. Worse, he felt as if this time he'd be sucked into a riptide that would drag him places he'd never been before.

Oh, he'd experienced the sparks from the moment that he'd touched her. Those he'd been familiar enough with. And he'd known that he was skilled enough to fan them into a flame. That had been his plan. He would coax until she offered and then take a real taste of her.

But she wasn't at all what he'd expected. Her mouth wasn't soft and warm as he'd expected. Instead, it was hot and avid and as demanding as his own. She was so alive. So responsive. He felt the beat of her pulse against his fingertips, the moan vibrating deep in her throat. And beneath the passion, he could sense innocence, too.

Greed—his, hers, or a combination—rocketed through his system, tearing at his control. This was a first for him.

No woman had ever set off this fevered combination of sensations and needs.

Needs? Even as a little alarm bell went off in his mind, Ryder felt a flash of intuition—the kind he often got when he was working on a case. This woman could have the power to shake up a life he was perfectly satisfied with. That uncomfortable possibility, along with the fact that they were kneeling on the floor of a very public place, had him grasping the reins of his control and pulling tight.

Slowly, he set her from him. Her eyes were huge and that blue color had turned smoky. Her hair had tumbled to her shoulders, and she looked every bit as stunned as he felt.

"Are you all right?" His voice was ragged, and when he drew in a deep breath, his lungs burned. He'd forgotten to breathe. Another first. Just who was this woman that she could do this to him?

It had been years since he'd allowed himself to need anyone or anything. No one could be depended on. He'd learned that lesson the hard way when his mother had walked out on him, and later, when his aunt had left him too. He was always careful to keep his relationships with women uncomplicated and mutually satisfying. This woman had complications written all over her.

Despite all that, he wanted to kiss her again. He was going to have to give that some thought.

When she closed her eyes, and sagged, he felt a sprint of fear. That was a first too. How could he feel such a concern for a woman he didn't even know?

"Are you all right?" he repeated as he tightened his grip on her.

No, SHE WASN'T all right. And she wasn't feeling like herself at all. Clenching her fists, Sierra stiffened her spine, and wished for her inhaler. If she'd had any strength in her limbs, she might have tried to find it. Instead, on a count of ten, she drew in a breath and let it out.

"Fine. I'm fine." She would be in a minute. What had she been thinking? She'd kissed him. She'd let him kiss her back. And there was something, someone, inside her who wanted very much to repeat the experience.

She drew in another breath and pushed down the little ripples of panic that threatened to turn into huge waves. The problem was she hadn't been thinking at all when he was kissing her. For those few moments, she'd felt so extraordinary, so…wild, and so incredibly wanton. It was as if she were a totally different woman. She took yet another breath.

"Here," he said, pushing something into the hand he'd been holding. "Do you need this? Or this?"

Once he released her hand, her brain started to clear. Sierra glanced down to see that he was offering her inhaler and the prescription pills she carried with her at all times. Reality check. This was the old Sierra Gibbs, she thought, a woman who suffered from asthma and migraines. That Sierra wasn't a woman who kissed strangers in bars. So who was the woman who *had* kissed this man?

It was a new question and her desire to find the answer to it had her fighting off another onslaught of panic. She used her inhaler. Then feeling a bit steadier, she said, "Thanks." Steeling herself, she met his eyes.

Concern was all she saw. There was nothing of the desire she'd seen earlier. Sierra swallowed her disappointment. All of her life she'd managed to bring out the protective streak in men. Even Bradley Winthrop, the man she was currently seeing, treated her as if he were her caretaker.

Wasn't that one of the reasons that she'd come up with her five-step plan? She didn't want to be the baby who was taken care of anymore. And she wanted to be a take-charge woman in the bedroom as well as out. In short, she wanted to be the woman she'd just been in this man's arms.

She'd do well to remember that she had a five-step plan. But while she was gazing into his eyes, it was difficult to remember the steps. His eyes were as gray as smoke, the kind that could swallow you up in a heartbeat. For the first time in her life, the thought of losing herself that way sent a little thrill through her.

Oh, she was definitely not the same woman who'd walked into the bar a few minutes ago. But she wasn't at all sure that she was ready to be the woman she'd felt bloom inside her during that kiss. She had to think…she…

"At least let me buy you a drink. You look as if you could use one. I know I could."

"Yes. Okay." The words were out before she remembered. "Oh no, I can't. I forgot." She tore her eyes from his and glanced around. How could she have forgotten her sisters, not to mention her father's letter?

"You have a date?"

"Yes." She grabbed her canvas bag and stuffed the pills and the inhaler into it. "Sort of." Spotting her day planner under a stool, she reached for it, but he was quicker.

"Sierra Gibbs, Ph.D." He read the name off the card that had slipped out of the plastic slot on the cover. "What's the Ph.D. in?"

"Psychology and Sociology." She glanced around, but didn't spot the letter from her father.

"Two Ph.D.'s. I'm impressed, Doc. And you're a shrink?"

In spite of the interest in his voice, she kept her eyes

averted. "Not in the way you probably mean. I don't have a private practice or anything like that."

"No couch?"

"No. Only psychiatrists use those." He was smiling, she was sure of it, but she didn't dare risk another look at his mouth. She wouldn't be able to think if she did. "I teach at Georgetown in the graduate school. Mostly, I do research and write. I just finished a book." She was babbling. And no wonder. Her lips were still vibrating from that kiss.

In spite of her resolve, she found herself looking at his mouth again. Immediately, curiosity began to war with common sense. If she just had the courage to lean forward and close the distance, would she experience that same whirl of sensations again? The thought slipped into her mind so easily, as if the man who'd just kissed her was simply some experiment that she wanted to run through again.

But he wasn't a lab experiment, and she should really get a grip. Her sisters would be waiting for her, she reminded herself. She was never late for an appointment. And she had her father's letter to read.

Scrambling reluctantly to her feet, she said, "I really have to go."

She made it halfway to the stairs that led to the upper dining level when she remembered the letter. With a flutter of panic, she whirled around and saw that he was right behind her, the envelope in his outstretched hand.

"It was under one of the stools," he said.

"Thank you."

"My pleasure."

Ryder grabbed her wrist before she could turn and used a finger under her chin so that she had to meet his eyes.

"The kiss was my pleasure, too, Dr. Gibbs."

"I…it was…I don't think…I…"

Ryder smiled at her. This blushing, flustered woman was the nervous Nellie he'd first spotted pacing in front of the restaurant. This side of her contrasted sharply with the determined-looking Joan of Arc who'd strode so purposefully into the restaurant. And then there was the woman he'd held in his arms a few minutes ago. "Kisses are best when you can't think at all—don't you think?"

Color flooded her face, and Ryder saw once again the innocence that he'd sensed in the woman who'd kissed him so passionately. How many other women lurked below the surface? Curious, he felt the strong pull of desire. Oh, there were complications here all right.

"That kiss was…" she began.

"Incredibly exciting."

"Yes, but I think…I'm sure…."

Later, Ryder would wonder if he might have given into impulse and kissed her again right then and there, but his cell phone vibrated in his pocket. The high-tech version of "saved by the bell," he supposed as he took it out.

"I'll be in touch," he said to Sierra Gibbs before, with some effort, he turned away and took the call.

"Ryder, it's Mark." Static rattled in his ear for a second. "…delayed…not going…make it."

Right. Mark Anderson, the man he was supposed to meet. And the man who'd slipped right out of his mind for the past few minutes. "Where are you?"

"I've been…think it was worth it."

In spite of the choppy connection, Ryder could hear the excitement in his old friend's voice, and something else that he recognized as fear. "Are you all right?"

"…can't talk…on the phone. Not safe…they can trace the location…?"

"If they have the right equipment," Ryder said. And just what was Mark involved in that he'd have people tracing his cell? "Are you in trouble?"

"...tomorrow...same place?"

"Sure. Blue Pepper, five o'clock?" Ryder frowned when he realized that the call had ended. He hoped that they had the time straight between them.

He was about to climb back on his stool when he spotted the blue note card beneath it. It had to have fallen out of the doc's bag. He bent over and picked it up. He was turning, intending to take it to her, when his gaze fell on the neat little list.

A five-step plan for initiating a sexual relationship with a man.

Intrigued, he read further.

1. Attend speed-date night at the Blue Pepper and collect data. 7/28.
2. Study data. 7/29.
3. Select a lover. 7/30.
4. Review and select appropriate sex techniques. 7/31.
5. Initiate sexual relationship.

Could this possibly be what it seemed to be? Eyes narrowed, Ryder read the list again.

What kind of a woman set out to have an affair with a to-do list in hand?

2

As Sierra made her way up the stairs to the dining room, she felt two different women warring inside of her. One of them wanted to turn around and kiss that man again. The other one was much more cautious. The second was the one who currently had the upper hand.

Still, she'd kissed a stranger in a bar and part of her had enjoyed it. She hugged the knowledge to her, hoping that the experience would give her the confidence she needed to go forward with her plan.

She spotted her sisters the minute she entered the dining room. They were already seated and Rad, one of the owners of the Blue Pepper, was emptying a tray of drinks and an hors d'oeuvres platter onto their table.

She was late. Just how much time had she spent kneeling on the floor with that man?

Too much time, a little voice in her head lectured.

Not enough time, another voice taunted. *Not nearly enough.*

Stopping short, Sierra straightened and drew in a deep breath. It just wasn't like her to think that way. She dug though her bag and then closed her fingers around the inhaler, just in case she needed it. She had to put the man and the kiss out of her mind until she accomplished her mission.

Drawing in another deep breath, she headed toward the table.

Rad spotted her first and hurried toward her, surprise lighting his features. "Dr. Gibbs! You look absolutely ravishing tonight."

It was Sierra's turn to be surprised as Rad hugged her and rose on his toes to kiss the air on one side of her head. Rad and his partner, George, ran the Blue Pepper. George, a huge bronze giant of a man, handled the bar while Rad greeted the customers. A small man, Rad changed his hair color nearly as frequently as he changed his ties. Tonight, the white spikes matched his shirt and the tiny dots in his fuchsia tie. As a dues-paying member of the fashion police, Rad was not given to hyperbole. His usual greeting to her was a sigh.

Holding her at arm's length, Rad studied her carefully. "It's your hair. That's what it is. You've finally taken my advice to wear it down."

Her hair. Sierra ran a hand through it. Sometime during that all-consuming kiss, the man in the bar must have loosened her hair. She risked a quick glance over her shoulder, but she couldn't see him.

Rad gripped her arms and turned her to face her sisters. "Tell her she looks ravishing with her hair down."

"Ravishing," Natalie agreed, winking at Sierra.

"Totally," Rory said. "We've been telling her that for years. But does she listen to us? No. We're just her sisters. We owe you big-time, Rad."

"Just part of the service," Rad said, sweeping them a bow before he turned and hurried away.

"This is a major coup," Rory said as she snagged a shrimp off the hors d'oeuvres platter. "You're usually immune to Rad's advice. What's up?"

She'd just kissed a stranger in the bar, Sierra thought. From her seat, she was able to scan the bar again, but he wasn't in sight.

"Sierra?" Natalie asked. "Is something wrong?"

Sierra gripped her inhaler more tightly as she drew in another deep breath and refocused her thoughts. "I'm just a bit nervous about opening Harry's letter." That was the truth, just not the whole truth.

"Have a shrimp," Rory said, pushing the platter closer. "Food always soothes my nerves."

"Thanks, I'll pass," Sierra said.

"At least take a drink of the martini we ordered," Natalie advised.

That she could do. Dutch courage was always helpful when you never had any of your own. After raising her glass, she clinked it to her sisters', took a sip and prayed that the nerves dancing in her stomach would settle from a polka to a slow waltz.

"Dad's letter won't be as bad as you think it's going to be. Isn't that right, Rory?"

"Absolutely," Rory mumbled around a stuffed mushroom. "I felt much better about everything after I read mine."

Sierra thought of the men in her sisters' lives. "Chance and Hunter must be annoyed that I stole you away tonight."

Natalie snorted. "Fat chance. They're having some kind of a men's night out. I think gambling is involved."

"And beer," Rory said, reaching for a mozzarella stick. "They were quite happy to see the last of us."

"You guys really hit the jackpot, didn't you?" Sierra asked.

"Oh, yeah," Natalie said with a smile.

"Definitely," Rory said.

One look at the expressions on her sisters' faces confirmed her belief that she was doing the right thing. They'd not only found men and love, but they'd also had wonderful adventures. She'd settle for the man. That much she was pretty sure she could do. And she didn't even mind if the relationship was temporary. Whatever her father said in his message, she wasn't going to let it dissuade her. She'd just look at her sisters.

Better still, she'd let herself remember that kiss.

She let go of the inhaler, then drew the letter out of her bag and set it on the table in front of her. There was her name, written in her father's hand. She wasn't aware that she'd clenched her hands into fists until Natalie covered one of them. "He loved us. We know now that he regretted the promise he made to mother to stay away."

Rory took Sierra's other hand. "It's like when you get called to the principal's office. The anticipation is always worse than the reality."

Sierra had never been called to the principal's office in her life. Since she'd always caused her family so much trouble with her illnesses, she'd concentrated on being perfect in everything else. It was the least she could do.

Sierra resisted the urge to use her inhaler. Her breath was short, but not nearly as much as it had been when that stranger had kissed her.

Pushing the thought away, she focused on the letter. She could do this. She really could. From the envelope, she pulled out a single folded sheet of paper and opened it up.

Dearest Sierra, my beautiful dreamer,
Even when you were little, your imagination and
your curiosity amazed me. And you were so smart,

that sometimes you scared your mother and me. My biggest regret is that I didn't have more time to spend with you.

You of all my daughters have the power to make all your dreams come true. Don't be afraid to dream big. And always remember that life is better than any dream. It's a better adventure than anything you can find in a book or a movie. Trust in yourself and take the risk of believing that, Sierra.

Love,
Harry

When she realized that she was chewing on her bottom lip, Sierra made herself stop. Finally, she said, "I didn't think he knew me that well."

"Of course, he did," Rory insisted, her characteristic impatience clear in her voice.

Sierra shook her head. "He was always going off with the two of you, and I had to stay home because I was sick."

"What about all the time he spent with you when you were in the hospital?" Natalie asked. "Whenever he could, he'd stay the night. We were always jealous. I think Mom was too."

For the first time since she'd taken the letter out of her purse, Sierra glanced up and met her sisters' gazes. "I guess I don't remember." But she'd had dreams of someone holding her hand. Had that really been Harry?

Sierra turned to Natalie. "I mostly remember that he taught you to crack safes." She shifted her gaze to Rory. "And he took you horseback-riding."

"But he read books to you," Natalie said. "Rory and I used to sit outside your bedroom door and listen. He never read books to us."

"I do remember some of that," Sierra said with a sudden smile. "Once he read me 'Goldilocks and the Three Bears,' and he told me Mom would probably have a fit because Goldilocks was a housebreaker and a very bad role model."

"That sounds like him," Natalie said.

"Aren't you going to look at the photos?" Rory asked.

"Oh. I forgot." There had been pictures in her sisters' letters, too. Sierra slipped hers from the envelope and spread them out on the table. One had been snapped when she'd given the valedictory address at her high-school graduation. Another was one of her poring over books at her college library. Both were typically Sierra, the studious bookworm, she thought.

Then the third one caught her attention. She was sitting on a park bench in Rock Creek Park watching the joggers and in-line skaters whip by. It had been one of those perfect spring days that were so plentiful in DC. She'd been a freshman in college, and she'd been so envious of the skaters.

"There you go," Rory said, pointing to the picture. "He knew you all right. Look at the expression on your face."

"What expression?" Sierra asked, studying the picture more closely.

"The one that you always had when Rory and I got to do something and you couldn't." Natalie tapped a finger on the photo. "You're wishing you could be skating, too."

She'd tried to satisfy her wishes by daydreaming, Sierra recalled. She still did.

"This picture is another way he's telling you that if you believe in yourself, you can do anything you want," Rory said.

Sierra swallowed to ease the lump that had formed in her throat. Had Harry really believed that?

"So, tell us." Rory reached for another shrimp. "What is it that you really want?"

That man in the bar.

The thought slid so easily into her mind that, for a moment, Sierra couldn't speak. Panic bubbled up. She couldn't want *him*. He was so out of her league. Besides, she had a perfectly logical five-step plan, and she couldn't see that man fitting into any kind of plan.

"That's got to be a tough one for you," Natalie commented. "Your life's just about perfect. You've accomplished everything you've set out to do."

Sierra glanced down at her father's words and then back up at her sisters again. Then she took a deep breath. "I want to initiate a sexual relationship with a man."

"Oh." Her sisters spoke in unison, then exchanged a quick glance.

"You and Bradley Winthrop are getting serious then?" Natalie asked.

"No." Sierra frowned. "Bradley and I are just friends." She tilted her head in thought. "We go to dinner and the opera together, and we visit interesting exhibits at the Smithsonian. Our relationship is stimulating on an intellectual level, but it's strictly platonic."

"Then you've met someone new?" Rory asked.

Sierra thought of the man in the bar. "No. I haven't selected the man yet. But I'm ready for a relationship that will be physically stimulating. So I'm going to find a lover."

"What can we do to help?" Natalie said.

Sierra blinked and stared. She'd expected a negative reaction—especially from her oldest sister. "Nothing." She took another sip of her martini. "I have a plan, and you're not going to talk me out of it."

"Why would we do that?" Rory asked.

Once again, Sierra stared at her sisters. "Because I...because you..." She drew in a deep breath. "I was so sure that you'd try and talk me out of it."

"Yeah, well, Natalie and I have already discussed the issue. And we decided that we couldn't very well do one thing and lecture you to do another. You were the one who encouraged me to go after Chance."

"And you were right there cheering me on after I met Hunter." Rory took her hand.

"In fact, if you hadn't brought it up, we were going to suggest that you become more socially active and get out and meet someone," Natalie admitted.

"Following Harry's advice has been very good for us, so if you've decided to take a lover, we'd hardly be the ones to give you any grief," Rory added.

Even as relief flowed through her, Sierra felt nerves once more begin to jump in her stomach. They weren't going to argue. She felt as though she'd geared up for a battle and the enemy had turned tail and run before she'd had a chance to fire off the first shot.

"You mentioned a plan," Natalie said. "I'd like to hear more about that."

"Me, too," Rory said. "We might have some suggestions."

Sierra nearly smiled as she reached into her bag for her note card. "That's more like it. For a minute I thought that perhaps my sisters had been replaced by aliens."

Natalie's brows shot up. "We just want the chance to offer advice. Isn't that what sisters are for?"

"Yes," Sierra said as she sorted through the contents of her bag.

"How many steps?" Natalie asked. "With Chance, I only needed about three."

"Ha!" Rory pointed a pepper strip at Natalie. "I win. I only needed one step with Hunter."

Sierra could feel her day planner, her inhaler, the pills, and the pack of note cards. Frowning, she opened the mouth of the bag wider. The single blue note card listing the steps wasn't there. Had she dropped it in the bar? If she went back to look for it, she might run into that stranger again.

Pushing the thought and the temptation firmly out of her mind, she cleared her throat and focused her attention on her sisters. "As part of my research on my new book, I've been studying the sexual practices of urban dwellers."

"City people?" Rory asked.

Sierra nodded and then took another sip of her martini. "Rad and George have been kind enough to allow me to do some of my research right here on Wednesdays when they reserve this dining room for speed dating."

"Speed dating?" Natalie asked.

"You know," Rory said, "it's kind of like musical chairs. Remember the episode they did on *Sex and the City* with Miranda. She talked to each date for about ten minutes to see if something clicked."

"Whoa." Natalie's frown deepened as she studied Sierra. "You're going to choose a lover during a ten-minute conversation?"

"No. The speed date is step one," Sierra explained. "Step two is to analyze the data I collect and then select a lover."

"Time out," Rory said. "A speed date is just a prelude to a real date. How can you possibly gather enough data to select a man as a lover?"

"By using the time efficiently. I see no reason to bother with casual conversation. After I tell them that I'm looking for a lover, I'm going to ask each man a few questions. Their answers will provide me with a profile of just what kind of lover they will make."

Rory and Natalie exchanged a glance, then looked at Sierra.

Sierra began to chew on her bottom lip again. These were her sisters all right. She'd lost count of the times that Natalie and Rory had looked at her in just this way when she was growing up, as if she were the alien. "You don't think it will work?"

"No." Her sisters spoke in unison, and then Natalie said, "That's not it. We think it might work too well—especially if you tell them right up front that you're looking for a lover."

"I don't see why I should hide my intentions."

Natalie shook her head. "There are times when a little subtlety is…advisable."

"You don't know what kind of men come here. They could take advantage of you," Rory added.

"But I do know what kind of men come here. I've been studying them for three months now. My research assistant and I have taken copious notes and written up several case histories."

"As a psychologist, you know that people lie," Rory said. "They can easily pretend to be something they're not."

Sierra frowned.

"Right. We all wear disguises," Natalie added.

"During that speed-dating episode on *Sex and the City*, even Miranda lied," Rory said. "Didn't she tell one guy that she was a flight attendant?"

Sierra set her clasped hands on the letter. "All right. Perhaps, I won't tell them straight out that I'm looking for a lover. But I'm going to ask them some questions."

"Such as?" Rory asked.

"They're very simple—kind of like a Rorschach test without the pictures. Things like what kind of musical instrument or breed of dog would you like to be, or what three things would you take to a deserted island with you?"

"And from that you'll learn…?" Rory asked.

Sierra could feel her cheeks redden. "The subject's answers will provide a profile of his sexual preferences as well as indicate his style of lovemaking."

"Really?" Rory asked.

"My research assistant, Zoë McNamara, and I have been testing it on volunteers. When we interview the test subjects, we've found that our profiles have been quite accurate."

Natalie tapped her fingers on the table. "What will you do with your results?"

"I'll take them home and run a match with my own profile. After that, I'll contact prospective lovers according to how well they match up with me."

For a moment, neither one of her sisters said a word.

"You don't think it will work?" Sierra finally asked.

Natalie drank some of her martini, then said, "I've no doubt that you'll probably get an accurate profile of the parties involved. But what you've described is a very…cerebral process. And taking a lover—well, it's a very physical thing. There has to be a certain…chemistry. I'm not sure you can predict that with a quiz."

Rory leaned forward. "I'm on the same page here as Nat. Did you ever give this quiz to Bradley?"

"Well, yes," Sierra replied.

"How well did his profile line up with yours?" Rory asked.

"Almost perfectly."

Rory turned her hands over, palms up. "There you go. A perfect match, but no chemistry. Your relationship has remained platonic. That's not a recipe for success in a love affair."

"The up side is she'll be right there at a table with them. She could shake their hands," Natalie pointed out.

"Right," Rory said.

Natalie turned to Sierra. "The important thing is not to over-think this whole thing. You have to learn to trust your feelings. If an electric shock goes up your arm and right down to your toes, then you might want to move that candidate to the top of your list—no matter what the quiz results tell you."

"Or if you look into his eyes and your knees turn to jelly, he's another prime candidate for a lover," Rory said. "The first time I met Hunter, it was his eyes. He looked at me as if he were the Terminator and I was his prey. I lost every thought in my head."

Sierra drew in a deep breath. "I don't usually have that kind of reaction to men." Except to the stranger she'd just kissed in the bar.

"Then it's high time you did," Natalie said.

"And under no circumstance should you take a lover unless you do," Rory added.

"One thing more," Natalie said. "Once you've found a candidate, I want the name so that I can run a check on him."

Rory shot Sierra a sympathetic glance. "That's what comes of having a sister who's a cop."

"And if your experiment works, Rory will press you for an interview so that she can write the whole thing up in *Vanity Fair*. That's what comes from having a sister who's a journalist."

For the first time since she'd pushed her way through the front door of the Blue Pepper, Sierra felt some of her apprehension ease. Oh, the nerves were still dancing in her stomach, but she was going to go through with her plan, and she felt much better that she was doing it with her sisters' approval. And Harry's. Raising her martini, she said, "To chemistry."

"To chemistry," her sisters repeated.

"And to Harry," Sierra added as she touched her glass to theirs.

3

THE BEATLES ratcheted up the rhythm on "Yellow Submarine" just as the first raindrops splattered against his windshield and the cars in front of him slowed to a crawl. Ryder slammed on the brakes and hit the button to put the top up on his car. Then, cutting into the far-left lane, he gained a dozen car lengths before those vehicles also came to a halt.

The skies opened up with a vengeance. As the minutes ticked away without even a trickle of movement in any lane, the Beatles ended their song, and the last hope Ryder had of getting to the Blue Pepper by five o'clock evaporated. Mark Anderson was going to have to wait.

He wasn't pleased because his intuition told him that Mark needed more than advice. But something had come up that had made time tight for Ryder today.

Jed Calhoun had called him late last night, and he could hardly refuse to do a favor for an old friend. Especially when that friend was in trouble. He and Jed had worked for the government in a special-operations unit, and the man had saved his life.

According to Jed, the last job he'd done for the government had gone wrong, and he'd become the scapegoat. Clearing Jed's name was just the kind of job that Ryder liked. So today he'd settled his old friend on the houseboat he kept on the Chesapeake. Jed's safety would be assured there until they handled the problem.

And if the trip to the houseboat had allowed him to get in a little fishing, well, a man had to recharge somehow.

He fiddled with the radio dial, switching to an all-day news station that offered traffic updates. But he spotted the medevac helicopter overhead before the announcement was made about the fifteen-car pile-up about a mile ahead.

Leaning back, Ryder willed his tension to disappear. His two years in the special operations unit he and Jed had served in had taught him the value of channeling frustration away. No way was he going to lecture himself that he wouldn't be in this situation if he'd stayed in the city.

For the time being, there was nothing he could do. An accident would take time to clear. The emergency vehicles would be slowed down because of the rush-hour traffic and the weather.

For five minutes, Ryder focused on relaxing both his mind and his body, something that his afternoon of fishing hadn't quite accomplished. Try as he might, he couldn't quite clear his mind of two problems. First of all, with every minute that ticked by, his intuition was telling him that Mark needed him. Spurred by his thoughts, he reached for his cell, punched in the number that Mark had given him and left yet another message on his voice mail. Mark hadn't been answering his cell since Ryder had taken his call the night before. Not a good sign.

That done, his mind drifted to his second problem—the other person who'd been haunting his thoughts—Dr. Sierra Gibbs.

How often had he thought of her in the past twenty-four hours? Too often. How much did he want to kiss her again?

Too much. How many times had he reached for his phone to call her? Too many.

Ryder shifted into a more comfortable position, tucking his hands behind his head. What exactly was it that had kept her in his thoughts for a night and most of the day? Not the fact that she was beautiful. Of course, he'd been attracted by that. He was a man. But his fascination with Dr. Sierra Gibbs went deeper. First of all, there was her response when he'd kissed her. She was so generous, holding nothing back. And there was the innocence he'd sensed beneath the passion. That had certainly pulled at him too.

Dr. Sierra Gibbs was a puzzle: nervous, passionate, innocent, honest. Those eyes couldn't lie. Maybe it was the honesty that drew him the most. And dammit, he'd always liked puzzles.

Most women, he could figure out. His mother, who'd left him for a man who'd promised money and didn't want a kid, had been easy to peg. And his aunt, who'd taken him in and loved him unconditionally until she'd died, he'd come to understand too, and he still mourned the loss.

And then there'd been the women he'd dated—well, he'd had an understanding with them. Any relationship he'd ever had with a woman had been simple and uncomplicated and based on mutual pleasure. Mostly, they'd parted as friends. And when he'd had regrets, they'd been temporary.

But none of those women had ever touched him the way that brief meeting with Sierra Gibbs had.

As ridiculous as the idea was, he couldn't rid his mind of the suspicion that the woman was actually thinking of taking a lover based on that to-do list. Perhaps she already had. The thought of that had been gnawing at him all day. He didn't like the idea one bit. If she was going to take a lover…

With a sigh, Ryder reached for his phone again. In his experience, the best way to solve a problem was to face it head on. Maybe his life was due for a bit of complication. He punched in the number that he'd memorized from her card the night before.

SURVEYING THE MESS on her usually neat desk, Sierra was chewing on her bottom lip when the phone rang. "Yes?"

"Dr. Gibbs?"

"Yes." She recognized the voice immediately. She'd been thinking about him all day. Daydreaming about him. A part of her had been wishing that he'd call. Another part of her, the old Sierra, had been hoping that he wouldn't. She'd gotten over the first two hurdles of her plan—opening the letter and telling her sisters—but now that she was faced with implementing it, the old fears and insecurities had resurfaced. She was back to feeling like Jane Eyre again. "It's you, isn't it? You're the man I met in the Blue Pepper last night."

"To be a bit more precise, this is the man you *kissed* in the Blue Pepper last night. Is it raining there yet?"

"No." She could hear the grin in his voice, and picturing it made her remember his mouth. When her knees weakened, she sank into her chair. How could he have this effect on her?

"I didn't expect you to call. What do you want?"

"For starters, I want to kiss you again."

Sierra's breath caught in her throat as the little thrill moved through her. She swallowed as a burst of panic followed in its wake. "I…think the kiss was a mistake." As soon as the words were out she bit her bottom lip. Oh, yeah. Timid little Jane was back all right.

"That's an interesting theory, Doc. We can test it the next time we kiss."

"That's not going to—" Sierra cut herself off. The last thing she wanted to do was to issue a challenge. He'd already told her the danger in doing that. She'd spent a long, sleepless night and most of the day thinking about this man and his effect on her. The pile of folders in front her testified to how little work she'd accomplished, and she'd just come from explaining to her research assistant that she was behind.

She had a pretty good idea that the memory of that kiss was the reason she was backsliding. She'd already decided that this man was not the type she'd be able to follow a five-step plan with. Last night they'd nearly jumped to step five after one kiss! And she'd convinced herself that she needed her plan. It was her security blanket.

"You were about to say?" he prompted.

"Something I'm sure I'd regret."

He laughed and the sound had her lips curving. She could picture him in her mind quite easily. Right now, there was an engaging gleam of laughter in his eyes and a smile curving his mouth.

That mouth. She tried to erase the image from her mind, but a whirlwind of sensations was already whipping through her. This—this was what she was afraid of. But there was a part of her that had been dreaming of this and more…

"Fess up, Doc. You were about to say that we weren't going to kiss again. And I had my counterargument all ready."

"Your counterargument?"

"Be prepared is my motto. Picked it up in the Boy Scouts. You want to hear it?"

Amused in spite of herself, Sierra said, "I'm not sure."

"Be a shame to waste it. I geared it to suit my audience.

You being a scientist, I figure you're going to be curious about whether or not what we both felt last night was some kind of fluke—a one-time flash in the pan—or whether it might happen again. And again. From a scientific viewpoint, the only way to find out would be to run the experiment again, right?"

Sierra's smile widened. "Nicely done. But it seems to me if I answer your question, I'm issuing an invitation."

"Yep. That's the way I see it too. How about it?"

"I don't think so." She bit back a sigh of regret.

"I didn't take you for a coward, Doc."

His comment hit the bull's eye and had Sierra straightening her shoulders. "I'm not."

"Then how about meeting me for a drink at the Blue Pepper later this evening?"

Panic and regret warred inside her as she took a deep breath. "I can't. I have plans. In fact, I'm on the way to the Blue Pepper to meet someone now."

"Your sisters?" he asked.

"No." She paused, frowning. "How did you know I have sisters?"

"I was curious so I asked the bartender about the women you were in such a rush to join last night. Look, how about if I offer you an incentive to meet with me? I've got something—a blue card that fell out of your bag last night."

Sierra felt the heat rise in her cheeks.

"Looks like a to-do list."

"I…it's…" What must he think? She placed a hand against her heart to keep it from hammering right out of her chest as the steps she'd written down scrolled through her mind. *Speed date, analyze data, select a lover, select the proper sex techniques…* She could pretty much guess what he might be thinking.

"I figured you might want it back."

"No." She drew in a deep breath and let it out. "It's noth-ing. You can just throw it away."

"Sure thing. So…if you're not meeting your sisters, I assume you've got a date tonight?"

"Yes." Relief streamed through her. He wasn't going to press her about the list.

"You've already selected a lover then?"

"No," she said as a knock sounded at the door and Zoë McNamara, her research assistant, peeked in.

"I was hoping I would catch you," Zoë said.

"Can you hold for a minute?" Sierra said into the phone.

"I'm not going anywhere," he said.

"I didn't mean to interrupt," her assistant said.

"You haven't." As she gestured her into the office, Si-erra studied the small brunette in front of her. In terms of looks, she and Zoë were polar opposites. Her assistant was a short, slender woman with brown hair that she wore pulled back into a braid. But Sierra could see herself in Zoë's total dedication to her studies and to the project they were working on. Zoë wore reading glasses with large dark-framed lenses that made her look like a total, aca-demic nerd—exactly what Sierra had been for the last eight years.

She was determined to change that.

"What is it, Zoë?"

"I came for the reports you wanted me to look over."

"I haven't gotten to them yet," Sierra said. They were somewhere in the pile of work on her desk.

Zoë reached into one of the pockets in her baggy sweater. "You left this on my desk."

Sierra stared down at the blue note card that contained the questions she needed for her speed dates. How could she have possibly left it on Zoë's desk? If she'd gone to the Blue Pepper without them, the evening would have been a complete waste.

"Thank you." Sierra reached for the cards.

Zoë hesitated, then cleared her throat. "Is anything wrong? I mean…you never forget things. And I've never known you to fall behind on your work."

"Maybe I've been working too hard," Sierra said. But she was pretty sure that the reason for her distraction was right now on the other end of her cell phone. The thought made her frown.

"Well, then…" Stuffing her hands in her pockets, Zoë backed toward the door and then turned and scurried through it.

Sierra sighed. Looking at Zoë was too much like looking into a mirror, and she was tired of the image.

As she lifted the phone to her ear, she took a quick glance at her watch. "Hi. Look, I have to go. I'm late. And I hate to be late." She grabbed her canvas bag and slipped the blue note card into it.

"You'd better take your umbrella. I'd say it's going to start to rain in DC within the next twenty minutes or so."

As if to confirm his prediction, a roll of thunder sounded. Sierra glanced out the window and saw the sky was growing steadily darker. Where had she put her umbrella? Not in her bottom drawer where it should be. Not on her bookshelves. Turning, in a complete circle, she spotted it leaning in the corner next to the door. Tucking her cell phone under her ear, she scooped the umbrella up and stuffed it under her arm.

"So who's the 'sort of' date with?"

"I don't know." After stepping into the hallway, she set the canvas bag and umbrella down so she could lock her door. "It's sort of a blind date."

"Why in hell does a woman who looks like you have to go on a blind date?"

There was such astonishment in his voice that Sierra stopped at the head of the stairs. "Thank you. I think that's a compliment."

"You don't have to thank me for speaking the truth. But blind dates can be dangerous. What do you know about this guy?"

Sierra smiled as she reached the first landing. "You sound like my sister Natalie. She's a cop. And it isn't just one guy I'm going to meet tonight. I'm going on a sort of group blind date. Have you ever heard of speed dating?"

"No."

Sierra stepped out of the Whitman Building and cut across the quad in the direction of P Street. "It's kind of like musical chairs. I'm going to meet and talk with a series of men. I get ten minutes with each one. Then someone blows a whistle and we each move on."

"So you've got ten minutes to make your impression?"

"Yes." Sierra gave the sky a wary glance.

"Sounds like you gotta judge a lot of books by their covers."

"True. But this process eliminates much of the pressure of a regular blind date."

"And you haven't had to spend a whole evening with a dud as you might on a blind date."

"Something like that."

"Do you do this a lot?"

"This is my first time. I've observed the ritual as part of my research on a book I'm writing, and I've come up with a few questions to utilize the time efficiently. But I'm a little nervous."

"Why don't you practice on me?"

"What?" Sierra nearly stumbled as she turned onto P Street.

"You know. Give the questions a dry run. I'm stuck in a traffic jam that shows no sign of clearing, and I've got an alarm on my watch. Let me just set the time for ten minutes. There. No, wait. What kind of music do you like?"

Sierra couldn't prevent a laugh. "What does that have to do with—?"

"I'm not there in person, so I want to set the mood. Just name your favorite kind of music."

"You're serious."

"The seconds are ticking away. We only have nine and a half minutes left."

"Okay. Okay. I like Bach." This was ridiculous. When an oncoming pedestrian bumped her elbow, Sierra moved to the edge of the sidewalk, out of the stream of traffic.

"That's it? Bach? I have to come up with Bach on a car radio?"

"No." She grinned. "I also like Sinatra, Count Basie, the Beatles, the Beach—"

"Stop right there. The Beatles I can handle. They were having a retrospective on one of these stations. Hold on."

Thunder rumbled overhead again, and Sierra edged closer to the wall of a building. It occurred to her that she was having a ridiculous conversation with a stranger she'd kissed in a bar, and she was enjoying it. The sound of "I Wanna Hold Your Hand" thrummed in her ear.

"Can you hear it?"

Sierra very nearly giggled. "Yes."

"Okay. I'm resetting my watch for the full ten minutes."

Sierra glanced at her own watch. If she gave him the full amount of time, she ran the risk of being late.

"What do we do first?" he asked.

Sierra drew in a deep breath as she pulled out the blue card she'd written her notes on. "We introduce ourselves and shake hands. I'm Sierra Gibbs, and you're…?"

"Ryder Kane."

"Oh."

"You don't like my name."

"No. That's not it at all. I just remembered that I didn't even know your name until now. But I do like it. It…suits you."

"Thanks. I think."

"You don't have to thank me for speaking the truth."

His laugh began deep in his throat and blended into the building crescendo that the Beatles were providing in the background. "Touché. I like you, Dr. Gibbs."

"I like you, too. I don't understand it." To her surprise, Sierra found herself relaxing and leaning against the wall. She didn't understand that either. She hardly ever relaxed around men. The first raindrops fell, and a few stores down, a young woman gathered up the pieces of colored chalk her little girl had used to make a drawing on the sidewalk.

"No doubt, it's my charm," Ryder said.

Sierra giggled. "No doubt." The raindrops began to fall harder, and she backed into the recessed doorway of a shop entrance where the owner had already put up a closed sign. "We don't even know each other."

"Well, that's the purpose of a speed date, right? So do you like movies?"

"Love them."

"What's your favorite movie?"

"I'm supposed to be asking the questions," Sierra said.

"Humor me. I'm curious."

"*Casablanca.*"

"That's my favorite too. What's number two on your list?"

"*Raiders of the Lost Ark*—the whole trilogy."

"Good choice," Ryder said. "George Lucas is a great filmmaker. He made my top ten. And you can't beat those films for rip-roaring adventure. What's in your number-three slot?"

"Hitchcock. *Psycho, Rear Window, North by Northwest, To Catch a Thief.*"

"That's amazing. They're all number two on my list. Now for the big question. Why do you love to watch movies?"

Sierra bit back a sigh. "That's easy. I love movies because they allow me to do all the things that I can't do in real life. How about you?"

"I like them because they end happily. That's something that you can't always get in real life either."

"True. I'm a fan of happy endings too."

"Seems we have something in common, Doc. What about books?"

"Is it my turn to ask questions yet?" Sierra asked dryly.

Ryder chuckled. "Sure. Go ahead."

Sierra glanced down at her blue card. "If you were a musical instrument, which would you choose to be—a guitar, a keyboard or drums?"

"That's easy. Depending on my mood, I'd be all three."

A little arrow of heat shot through Sierra even as she turned over the card. According to her notes, a man who favored a guitar was not only very good with his fingers, but very attentive to details. A master at foreplay. The man who preferred a keyboard would also be clever with his hands and very skilled at improvising. He'd provide a lot of fun in bed. The drummer would be more demanding.

And he'd provide earthy, down-and-dirty sex. As her knees went weak, Sierra leaned against the wall of the building. Was it possible for a man to embody all three styles of love-making?

"Earth to Sierra," Ryder said. "How'd I do on that one?"

"Fi—" Sierra cleared her throat and tried again. "Fine. You did just fine."

"So, tell me—what did you learn from that question?"

"Learn?" Thunder rumbled overhead and Sierra backed further into the shop entranceway.

"C'mon, Doc. This is some kind of psychological test, right? I say guitar and you slip me into a neat little category."

Sierra blinked. Ryder Kane's easy, laid-back manner hid a very sharp mind. "Sort of. Is that why you said you could be all three? Because you don't like to be categorized?"

"Nope. I said all three because it's the truth. Now it's my turn. Which one of those instruments would you be?"

"You're not supposed to ask that yet. I have more questions."

"Aw, c'mon. Bend the rules, Doc. I'm curious. Would you be a guitar, a keyboard or a set of drums? Wait. Give me a minute. Let's see if I can guess."

Sierra glanced up from the note card and saw that the rain was pouring down in earnest now. Pedestrians were huddled beneath umbrellas and hurrying to their destinations, and traffic on the street had slowed. She really should go. Her plan had been to arrive at the Blue Pepper early enough to review her notes and run through her introduction in her head. But the urgency she usually felt about arriving early had washed away as easily as the traces of chalk on the sidewalk nearby.

"You're definitely not drums," he said.

"No." Sierra nearly smiled at the idea. According to her notes, "drums" were aggressive, loved fast, hard sex and could last all night. She had no problem imagining Ryder Kane being all of those things. Doing all of those things. To her. The images tumbling into her mind sent rays of electricity right to her core.

"I'm betting on the guitar over the keyboard," he finally said. "But it's a close call. Am I right?"

Sierra tried to gather her scattered thoughts.

"Are you still there, Doc?"

Sierra moistened lips that had gone as dry as her throat. "The truth is…." Pausing, she cleared her throat. "I have trouble imagining myself as any one of the three. Of course, I'm aware of what each instrument represents."

"So it's hard to give an unbiased answer."

"Exactly." Sierra found herself relaxing a bit. It occurred to her that she'd never felt this comfortable talking to a man before. On the street, rain was pouring down in sheets. Pedestrian traffic had cleared, and her position in the recessed entryway made her feel as if she were alone with Ryder.

"What are the three instruments an indication of?"

"They're supposed to suggest what your style is as a lover."

"Ah. Well, the only true way to discover what style a person has as a lover is to experience it. And even then, the person's style might change depending on the two people involved and the particular moment."

There was a pause while neither of them said anything, and the Beatles sang merrily about loving me, do.

"I've given a lot of thought to what particular style I'd like to use with you, Doc. You interested?"

More images flashed through Sierra's head—each one

of them some variation of Ryder Kane, his naked limbs
tangled with hers.

"I'll take that as a yes. First, I'd want to kiss you again.
You have the most amazing mouth, and I bet there are fla-
vors that I haven't yet discovered."

Sierra pressed fingers to her lips.

"Then I'd want to touch you—all over—for a very long
time. Your hair first. I wanted to run my hands through it
the moment it came loose."

An image formed in her mind of Ryder doing just that.

"Then there's a spot right in the hollow of your throat
where your skin is so delicate that I can see your pulse push
against the skin. Touch it for me, Sierra."

She already had. The frantic beat of it against her fingers sent ribbons of heat radiating through her entire body.

"And then I'd want to run my fingers over the skin right
above your breasts and slowly around and beneath them.
Do you like to have your breasts touched, Sierra?"

"I…you…" Words were eluding her, blocked out by the
images in her mind and the sensations streaming through
her. But her answer seemed to satisfy him, because he
went on. And on. And she went on imagining what it would
feel like if he traced little patterns between her breasts and
on her stomach.

She pressed her hand to her waist. Her body was on fire
one second and icy the next. Then he was tracing patterns
on the back of her knee, on the inside of her thigh.

She sighed as explosions of pleasure shot across her
nerve endings. Her eyes closed. Her bones began to soften.
In some far corner of her mind, she knew where she was
and that an occasional person still passed by with an umbrella tipped against the pouring rain. But she was trapped
by Ryder's words in an alternate reality.

"And then, I'd have to touch you inside. I wouldn't be able to help myself. I'd have to slip my fingers inside you."

It was a good thing that she was leaning against the door of the store because she felt dizzy. And the fire burning in her center had become so intense it was a wonder she didn't melt.

"I've been fantasizing about what your eyes will look like when I make you climax."

She was fantasizing, too, and Sierra felt herself slipping. In another few seconds, she would be sitting on the street. She struggled to get a grip.

"Imagine that my fingers are inside of you right now, Sierra. Can you feel them?"

She could imagine it all right, and the sensations that sprang from the image were so real that she couldn't suppress a moan.

"I'm going to start moving them slowly—in and out. Can you feel that?"

She felt such heat—huge waves of it—and every muscle in her body was tightening, reaching for that promise of pleasure…. In an effort to remain standing, she pressed her legs tightly together.

"Would you like me to go deeper?"

"Yes." She could almost feel the pressure of his fingers—right where the tension was coiled tightest at the center of her body. She wanted—no, she needed—to be touched right there, at that farthest point.

"I'm going deeper, Sierra."

His voice was so low, and in response to the words, every muscle in her body strained toward the climax, which built and built until the release shot through her in one, long widening wave of pleasure that went on and on.

Reality trickled back in bits and pieces. Her breath was

coming in short gasps, and she was still standing, thanks
to the solid door at her back. She felt…weak, but…won-
derful.

A car honked on the street. Another answered, and then
a third. Sierra opened her eyes to see a man roll down the
window of his car and wave a fist in the air at the vehicle
in front of him. "You idiot!"

The man in the car blocking the intersection opened his
window and made a rude gesture.

As the discussion on the street increased in volume, Sierra became very much aware of her surroundings. She
was standing in the doorway of a shop in the middle of
Georgetown and she'd just…

"Sierra?"

She'd just…he'd just… Some of the heat in her body
flooded her cheeks. "You…I…we just had phone sex."

"Just trying to make the most efficient use of my ten
minutes. How'd I do?"

Phone sex. She'd never in her life done anything quite
that…wild before. And it certainly hadn't been in her five-
step plan. But then she'd known that this man would be
hard to follow a plan with. And there was a part of her that
had enjoyed every minute of it.

She wanted to laugh. "You're…" She paused to search
for the right word.

Just then, she heard an alarm sound.

"Our time's up. As a speed date, how would you rate
me, Doc? And remember that I have a very fragile ego."

"Right. I'll bet it's about as fragile as a steel-rein-
forced door."

Ryder laughed. "Good one. If you were here, you could
see me pulling the imaginary arrow out of my heart."

As the picture formed in her mind, she smiled—until

she glanced down at the blue card she'd dropped. Stooping to snatch it up, she said, "I really do have to go."

"Remember me during those speed dates."

That wouldn't be a problem, Sierra thought. She had a feeling that phone sex was going to be a tough act to follow. She raised her umbrella and stepped out into the rain.

"Wait. I have a favor to ask you."

"What?"

"I'm supposed to meet a friend at the Blue Pepper at 5:00, and I'm going to be late. He's a tall blond, in his early thirties, good-looking in a rich-boy, prep-school kind of way. His name is Mark Anderson. George, the bartender, knows him. Could you keep an eye out for him and tell him I'm delayed and I want him to wait for me?"

"Sure. I'll tell George to send him to my table."

"Thanks. It was very nice speed dating you, Dr. Gibbs."

"I…enjoyed it, too." Sierra quickened her pace when the Blue Pepper came into view.

"One more thing."

"What?"

"Just so you know, this was my first attempt at phone sex. Normally, I like my sex up close and very hands-on. And I have this feeling, kind of like a theory, that you and I are going to have some very good sex."

Sierra barely kept herself from stumbling right into the glass door of the Blue Pepper. Impossible or not, she had the same feeling. And as a theory, she was very much afraid that she wanted to put his theory to the test.

THE RAIN had just let up as he reached the Vietnam Memorial. He'd chosen this spot for his meeting because he'd been sure that it would be fairly private. And he'd been right. Only a few tourists were standing in front of the wall, hardy souls who didn't mind the thunderstorm that had just passed over the DC area.

He moved quickly to one particular section of the wall and scanned the names until he found the one he was look-ing for.

Brian James McElroy, the source of all of his prob-lems. A wave of anger moved through him. He had to clench his hands into fists and take several deep breaths to control it. Brian McElroy was dead. He hadn't been an MIA. He'd died when his platoon had been almost wiped out thirty-five years ago.

He was dead and he should have stayed dead. He would have if it weren't for that reporter. Now two men were threatening everything he'd worked for—his dreams, his fu-ture. And the future of the country. He had to put a stop to it.

Another burst of anger surged through him, and he wished for the brandy that he kept in the bottom drawer of his office. A sip of that would have settled him.

Out of the corner of his eye, he saw the man approach-ing and he turned abruptly away from the wall to intercept him and steer him away from the Memorial.

"Have you eliminated the problem yet?" he asked the man when he was sure that they were totally alone.

"We searched his apartment, but there was nothing in his computer about the name you were interested in."

He kept his curses silent and asked instead, "He's prob-ably carrying the file with him. You should have had him by now."

The three beats of silence spoke volumes. He found himself clamping down on both anger and impatience. The matter had to be handled quickly, and incompetence was something he had a great deal of trouble tolerating.

"He's been moving around," the man said. "I'll have him tonight. The calls on his cell have been monitored. He's due at the—"

"No names."

"He's due at this bistro in Georgetown for a meeting at 5:00."

"He's meeting with someone?"

"Yes."

"Who?"

"We weren't able to pick that up. He hung up before—"

"Spare me the excuses." He waited, breathing in and out until the fresh bout of fury ebbed. He had to keep his mind clear. Stopping short on the path, he considered for a moment. "You'll have to pick up whomever he's meeting with also."

"Now wait. The deal we made was that I would deliver the journalist. The B…bistro is a popular place. How am I supposed to snatch two people?"

"Deals change. Hire some extra help. If the story leaks to anyone…"

He nodded reluctantly. "All right. I'll handle it."

"I'll expect a successful report by midnight."

"Here?"

He shook his head. "The parking garage near the mall on 7th Street. Top level."

"What should I do with this extra person?"

Leaning closer to his companion, he pitched his voice very low. "The same thing you're going to do with the journalist. Erase the problem."

4

"IF I WERE a body of water, what kind would I be?" he repeated.

"Yes. Ocean, lake or river?" Sierra struggled against a yawn as she studied the man across the table from her. He'd introduced himself as Richard Parker, and if she'd had to choose one word to describe him it would be *cautious*. He was the polar opposite of Ryder Kane.

In the silence that stretched between them at the table, Sierra could hear the band starting to play on the patio. The tune had a rhythmic Latin beat. Not a Beatles song. She bit back a sigh. No matter how hard she tried to stay focused, her mind kept returning to the phone conversation she'd had with Ryder. She couldn't get him out of her mind.

Rad blew two sharp notes on his whistle, signaling that five minutes had elapsed, and Sierra returned her attention to the man sitting in front of her. Richard Parker had used four of those minutes deciding whether he was a guitar or a keyboard. In the end, he hadn't been able to decide—which meant that he was a perfect match for her in terms of a musical instrument. She'd wavered between the guitar and the keyboard also.

"Hmmm." Richard frowned as he laced his fingers together in front of him. "This is a trick question, right?"

"There's no right or wrong answer."

"That depends on what you hope to gain by asking it. Tell me again what the purpose of this little quiz is."

"To see whether or not our sexual styles mesh."

"Right. I'm going to need a little time for this one."

Surprise. Surprise. Tamping down on the urge to tap her fingers on the table, Sierra nodded. "Go ahead. Take all the time you need."

Richard had identified himself as an attorney at a law firm with four stuffy names in its title. She figured that was why he needed time to analyze and think every question through. Not that she could fault him for taking his time. In fact, she sympathized with him. When she'd given herself the little quiz, she'd thought and rethought her answers for nearly half an hour. Caution was something she and Richard Parker had in common.

Neither one of them would ever have Ryder Kane's impulsive nature. Richard was not a man who would grab a woman and kiss her senseless in a bar before he'd even been introduced to her. She studied his serious expression. This was a man who would never make her giggle.

Focus, she scolded herself. Richard Parker was the best-looking of the seven men she'd speed dated so far—if you liked fair-haired men with smooth palms and bronzed skin that came from a tanning salon. Up until yesterday, Sierra would have thought that slender, blond men were her cup of tea. But somehow her taste had switched to dark-haired men with callused fingers.

Richard Parker and Ryder Kane were different in other ways too. She could picture Richard quite easily in a courtroom where his careful, meticulous manner would impress a jury. He was smooth, sophisticated-looking, and she didn't doubt that he could order the perfect bottle of wine to go with a meal. And Richard would perform each activity with that serious expression on his face.

On the other hand, Ryder Kane was a man she could picture in a multitude of settings—in a boardroom or a dark alley, in the city or the country, on the deck of a ship or behind the wheel of a very sleek, fast sports car. Sometimes he would have that glint of humor in his eyes. Other times, he would have a hint of danger. And ever since their phone conversation, she'd been picturing his face above hers and imagining what it might feel like to have their bodies pressed together, moving in tandem. Each time the image filled her mind, a sharp arrow of pleasure shot through her.

"Sierra?"

She blinked and brought her wandering mind back to the man sitting in front of her. Richard Parker, she reminded herself. The cautious attorney. "Yes?"

"I seem to recall that there's erotic symbolism associated with water."

Sierra felt color rise in her cheeks. "Yes."

"Can you elaborate on that or would that be against the rules?"

Sierra's fingers tightened on the blue note card. Ryder would never have asked such a polite question. He would probably have just given an accurate guess as to what the three bodies of water symbolized. And she imagined his answer to the question would be all three. The thought made her smile.

Richard frowned. "What's so funny?"

"Nothing." Sierra cleared her throat. "But I can't elaborate. That would be against the rules."

Richard nodded. "Then I'm going to go with the lake. I think that's my safest choice."

Exactly, Sierra thought. The lake had been her choice too. There wasn't a doubt in her mind that making love with Richard Jensen would be safe and thoroughly predictable. She would find none of the danger and mystery that the ocean suggested, and certainly none of the speed and adventure, the headlong rush to pleasure that a "river" might offer.

And that Ryder Kane might provide.

Even without finishing the quiz, she was certain that the man sitting across from her would fit her profile perfectly just as Bradley Winthrop had. But she was also suddenly quite certain that she didn't want to be a lake anymore. Nor did she want to have an affair with a man who would offer her the safe, the predictable and the dull.

Had a chance meeting and a speed date with Ryder Kane spoiled any chance she had of finding a lover?

Unless it was him?

A flood of feelings washed through her—panic, excitement, anticipation. Was she actually thinking of asking a man like Ryder Kane to be her lover?

No. The whole idea was ridiculous. She wasn't his type. He wouldn't agree.

Rad blew three sharp blasts on his whistle—a two-minute warning. Ruthlessly, Sierra pushed Ryder out of her mind and put all of her efforts into focusing on Richard Parker. She smiled. "We're not going to have time to finish the quiz."

"Did I do well enough that we could finish it the next time we meet?"

Sierra drew in a deep breath. "No. There's no need to finish it. You did just fine."

He frowned slightly. "But you aren't going to agree to meet with me again, are you?"

"No, I'm not going to meet with you again," she said.

He nodded, the same sober expression on his face. "There's nothing I can do to change your mind?"

Tell me you're going to kiss me and make my lips vibrate when you do. But Richard Parker would do neither of those things. So she shook her head. "No."

As she watched him rise and walk away, she realized she might as well be watching herself. With the exception of her academic work, she'd gone through life always taking no for an answer.

Ryder would never take no for an answer. They were so different—worlds apart. Was that why she was so attracted to him?

She was about to get up when a man sat down in the chair opposite hers.

"Are you Sierra Gibbs?" His voice was breathless, his face tense.

"Yes." She held out her hand. Rad hadn't blown the whistle yet, and she'd thought Richard was her last date. "And you're…?"

He gripped her hand hard. "Mark Anderson. The bartender said that you had a message for me."

"Oh. Yes." She'd completely forgotten the favor that Ryder had asked of her. "From Ryder Kane. He got caught in traffic on the beltway. He wants you to wait."

"How long?" Mark's gaze shifted to the bar, and he suddenly stiffened.

Sierra realized in that instant that it was fear fueling his tension. She could feel it in the hand still clenching hers and see it in his eyes. "I'm not sure."

"I can't wait. I was followed. I thought I'd lost them. But they're here, and if they see me talking to Ryder, they'll be after him, too."

Sierra reached into her bag. "Let me call the police. My sister is—"

"No. I can't talk to the police. Not yet. Too many people will be affected if what I've discovered leaks out. That's why I called Ryder. He's a straight thinker, and I can trust him." His gaze darted again to the bar as he leaned closer. "I need your help."

"What can I do?"

"I'm going to leave something on the chair. Promise me you'll see that Kane gets it. He'll know what to do."

"Of course, but—" Sierra let the sentence trail off when Mark rose and dashed toward the stairs. Rising, she stepped around the table and saw that he'd left a large book on the chair. While she stuffed it into her canvas bag, she kept her eyes on the entrance to the restaurant until she finally spotted Mark pushing his way through to the street.

He'll be all right, she told herself. This was Georgetown after all.

A second later, she saw another man leave the restaurant and turn purposefully in the same direction Mark had taken. Coincidence?

She had to make sure. That was the only clear thought in her mind as she hurried toward the stairs.

To HIS RELIEF, Ryder squeezed his car into the mini-sized parking space on the first try. He reached into the glove compartment, pulled out his gun, and tucked it into the back of his waistband. The same intuition that told him Mark Anderson was in trouble was telling him that he might need to be armed. Levering himself out of the car, he indulged in a quick stretch, then locked up and headed toward the corner.

He was a mere two and a half blocks away from the

Blue Pepper, so perhaps his luck was changing. *Frustrating* was the one word that had summed up his trip into DC. Even after the traffic had finally cleared, it had taken him nearly an hour to break free of the logjam that the pile-up had caused.

And thanks to his conversation with Dr. Sierra Gibbs, the wait had been damned uncomfortable. He was looking forward to seeing her again. This was the first time he'd ignored his intuition where a woman was concerned. But hell, he thrived on danger in his professional life. Wasn't that why he did favors for a fee and carried a gun? Perhaps it was time that he took a risk in his personal life too.

After reaching the corner, Ryder turned right. Now that the rain had stopped, people were spilling out of restaurants and bars to fill the outside tables. He moved toward the edge of the sidewalk and picked up his pace. His interest in Sierra Gibbs was only one reason why he was hurrying. Deep in his gut, he had a very bad feeling about Mark Anderson. As he approached the Blue Pepper, he caught the strains of music coming from the bistro—something with a Latin beat. The type of music playing the night he'd met Sierra.

He was remembering his first glimpse of her when he saw the man push through the doors of the Blue Pepper and run up the street. And instant later recognition flashed through him. Mark Anderson—and he looked as though he was fleeing for his life.

Ryder broke into a run. A block away, tires squealed as a dark-colored van turned the corner Mark was headed for, and two men leaped out. Both were built like linebackers. Another man was closing in on Mark from behind.

Dodging his way around a pair of lovers holding hands, Ryder pulled out all the stops. He was almost directly across the street from the Blue Pepper when two things happened at once. Sierra burst through the door and started running toward the corner, and one of the muscle-bound guys dragged Mark Anderson into the van.

"Sierra!" Ryder shouted the word, but he was sure the music drowned out the sound.

One of the men turned toward Sierra just as another tough-looking character burst out of the restaurant and started up the street in her direction.

She was nearly to the van. Fear streaked through him as he dashed between two parked cars and then barely missed an oncoming car. Tires screeched and horns blared. Ryder vaulted over the hood of a sporty convertible parked at the curb and sprinted toward the corner.

Seconds mattered and the gap was widening. Even if he took out the man who was following her, she was no match for the thug still waiting for her at the van.

Ryder'd never been a great believer in ESP, but he willed Sierra to turn. She did. But the men were too close. He was still too far away.

He wasn't going to make it in time.

"WAIT," Sierra shouted. "You can't—" She stopped short the moment the heavyset man turned toward her. He was bald and built like a tank. And his pal had just shoved Mark Anderson into the van.

"I want to see Mr. Anderson," she said.

He held out his hand and motioned her forward.

Staying right where she was, she tried to see inside the van. "Mr. Anderson?"

There was no answer. Not a good sign. The heavyset man took a step toward her.

She took a step back.

A screech of tires and the blast of a horn had her glancing over her shoulder. Fear trembled in her throat when she saw the other man walking toward her. She swallowed hard. They'd boxed her in.

Her mind emptied. There was no time to weigh options or calculate odds. She whirled away from the van, but it was too late. A hard tug on her jacket slowed her momentum. Then when the fabric ripped, she shot forward like a stone released from a slingshot.

"I've got her."

The other man had adjusted his path to intercept her. She was headed straight toward him. For one second, fear became so bright that it nearly blinded her. Buildings blocked her on one side, parked cars on the other. Both men were getting closer. Acting on pure instinct, she used the only weapon she had and swung her canvas bag with all her might into the oncoming man's face.

He howled with pain and stumbled. She dodged to his right and raced past him.

Another man was racing towards her. An instant later, he grabbed her and she felt the breath leave her body as they hit the cement.

THE SECOND his arms clamped around her, Ryder swiveled his body so that he took the impact when they hit the sidewalk. Then he rolled with her into the shelter of a glass-fronted store entrance.

A bullet cracked the display window behind them.

He held on to her tightly for a second. "Sierra, are you all right?" He was pretty sure he'd tackled her in time, but it had been close.

"Yes. Ryder, it's you. Thank God."

Shifting slightly on top of her, he pulled his gun out of

his waistband. When he tried to lever himself away, her arms grabbed him like a vice.

"Don't get up. They're shooting at us."

"I noticed. You stay put." As he pulled free, he glanced around. It was just as he feared. The display windows that angled from the sidewalk to the door of the shop were not going to provide much cover. Crouching, he moved to the edge of the entranceway, then risked a quick look through the window. The man Sierra had clocked with her bag was still holding his face, and blood was streaming through his fingers. The other good news was pedestrians and sightseers had ducked into doorways or stores. The bad news was the man with the gun was only ten yards away.

A bullet cracked the glass right over Ryder's head. He drew in a deep breath, dove out of the doorway, and rolled. Prone, he aimed and fired three times.

The shooter's gun hit the sidewalk first. The man followed. After springing to his feet, Ryder kicked the gun out of the man's reach as he sprinted toward the corner. The van was half a block away, and he could only make out three letters on the license plate. GBH.

Dammit, he wanted to give chase. They'd taken Mark Anderson, and they'd damn near snatched Sierra Gibbs. There'd been that one endless moment when he'd been sure they would. He wanted to get his hands on them.

He scanned the street for some kind of vehicle—a bike or a motorcycle. Luck wasn't with him. Swearing under his breath, he checked out the parked cars, but he was out of luck there too. They were all of the upscale variety that would require precious seconds to break into and hot-wire. It was only in movies that private investigators or cops were able to conveniently commandeer cars and give chase. Real life wasn't like that.

He was turning to check on Sierra when he spotted a leather case lying next to the curb. Stooping, he picked it up. The initials M.A. were embossed on the cover, and inside was a Palm Pilot. He slipped it inside his pocket and turned.

What he saw had his fear, fury and frustration vanishing in one wave of surprise. Sierra Gibbs was leaning over the body of the man he'd shot as if she tended to wounded men every day. He hurried toward her.

"He's still breathing," she said as he reached her. She'd rolled her jacket up and was using it as a pressure bandage on the man's side. "I've called 911."

Her voice was steady, and when she glanced up at him, he saw that her expression was calm, and she appeared to know what she was doing. This woman was a sharp right turn from the nervous woman he'd first spotted through the window of the Blue Pepper. The contrast fascinated him. "You amaze me, Doc. I never pictured you as the Florence Nightingale type."

"When I was growing up, my sisters always took more risks than I did. The least I could do was to learn how to deal with the results of their adventures, so I took a first aid course. You got him in the shoulder too, but I don't think it's serious."

He placed his hands over hers and helped her increase the pressure. "I like your style, Doc."

A siren sounded in the distance, and people began to step out of the doorways they'd ducked into. Sierra didn't take her eyes off his. "I'm not sure what to think about yours. They kidnapped your friend, you carry a gun and you shot this man."

"That about sums it up."

"Who are you, Ryder Kane?"

Out of the corner of his eye, he saw the squad car pull to the curb. "That's easy, Doc. I'm the man who just saved your pretty little butt."

And I'm in danger of becoming stuck on you. Ryder was pretty sure he hadn't said that out loud. Still, it gave him pause. There was never any predicting when one of his flashes of intuition would strike, but this one stunned him. He'd sensed that she'd be different for him. But he certainly didn't intend to get stuck on her. That wasn't his style.

As an ambulance pulled in behind the squad car, Ryder gathered his thoughts. "It's my turn for a question, Doc. Just who are you that this man you're nursing would want to shoot you?"

5

RYDER DIDN'T LIKE police stations. They were smelly and noisy, and once the cops learned he did private investigative work and ran a high-tech security firm, most of them didn't particularly like him. However, the dapper-looking detective who'd been interrogating him for the past hour and a half was not most policemen.

For starters, Matt Ramsey was very well dressed—designer suit, gold watch—and he'd walked into the room with two mugs of coffee. Good coffee. Ryder's guess was that it had been French-pressed. He'd also brought in a file folder and a book, and so far, he hadn't mentioned either one.

The tall, soft-spoken Ramsey reminded Ryder a bit of Peter Falk's seemingly bumbling detective in the old *Columbo* series. Of course, Ramsey dressed better, and he didn't appear bumbling at all. But both detectives sought in their own way to disarm their suspects, and what Ramsey shared in spades with the fictional Columbo was thoroughness and a razor-sharp mind.

That was one reason why Ryder had allowed the detective to take him through his story three times. Another reason was because he could see Sierra in a similar room on the other side of the squad room. There was a woman with her, and Ryder recognized her as one of the two Sierra had joined at the Blue Pepper the night before. The cop sister, he surmised. As long as Sierra was within view and was safe, he could afford to indulge his curiosity. And he was curious about the file and the book that were sitting on the table next to Ramsey's now-empty coffee mug.

"And you have no idea why Mark Anderson wanted to talk to you?" Ramsey asked.

"You've asked me that question three times."

Ramsey smiled and shrugged. "Sometimes the third time is the charm."

Ryder leaned forward, his patience suddenly stretched thin. "If you aren't going to arrest me, I'd like to leave. My story isn't going to change, and you've had plenty of opportunity to check it against the other eye witness's story."

Ramsey met his eyes. "You're referring to Dr. Sierra Gibbs?"

"I am."

"How well do you know her?"

"Is she the reason I'm getting the star treatment?"

For a moment, Ryder thought he saw something in Ramsey's eyes. Respect?

But all Ramsey said was, "Star treatment?"

Ryder waved a hand. "Decent coffee and a detective who doesn't look as if he's slept in his suit."

This time it was a flash of humor that appeared in Ramsey's eyes, and for the first time since he'd come into the room, the detective smiled. "Okay, I guess I'm busted."

"Who are you and why are we wasting time when we should be trying to find out who snatched Mark Anderson and who shot at Dr. Gibbs?"

"In answer to your first question, I work on a special task force that handles high-profile cases in the Capitol District. And you rate what you refer to as the 'star treatment' partly because it's Mark Anderson who's been kid-napped and partly because my partner is Detective Natalie Gibbs, Dr. Gibbs's sister."

"So…you and your partner have a personal interest in this case."

Ramsey nodded and tapped the manila file folder he'd brought into the room. "Personal enough that we ran a background check on you. You want to know what we found out?"

Ryder leaned back in his chair. "Sure."

"Not a hell of a lot. Most of the files we brought up when we ran your name are classified. Working in DC, I've run into that kind of thing before. You were trained in the marines, and then drafted into Special Forces, and you've done some secret work for the government. That has me suspecting black ops."

Ryder said nothing, but his respect for Ramsey went up another notch. There weren't many men who'd have dug up as much.

"There's a gap between the time you left the service of your country and opened your security business here in DC. I don't suppose you'd like to fill me in on that part of your life?"

"Nope."

"I didn't think so. Then there's the fact that in your current line of work, you've crossed paths with several of my colleagues and they give you mixed reviews. All in all, you have the reputation of being damn good but a bit of a rogue," Ramsey finished.

Ryder shrugged. "I'll plead guilty to both of those."

Ramsey's eyes remained steady on his. "How about answering my earlier question? How well do you know Dr. Gibbs?"

Not as well as I'm going to know her, Ryder thought. What he said aloud was, "I told you I ran into her for the first time last evening at the Blue Pepper. I talked with her briefly on the phone today and asked her to give a message to Mark Anderson because I was going to be late for the meeting I'd scheduled with him."

"Two conversations total?"

"That's correct."

"You asked a woman you'd only just met to deliver a message that put her life on the line."

"If I'd known—" Ryder cut himself off and clamped down on the anger he was feeling. What Ramsey had said was nothing less than the truth. He'd put Sierra in the path of that bullet. "I'm fully aware that what I asked Dr. Gibbs to do nearly cost her life. I was there. If she hadn't clocked one of them in the face with her bag, they'd have shoved her into that van with Anderson. Having failed that, plan B was to shoot her." He rose. "If we're though here, I'd like to start finding out what the hell Anderson is involved in. Have you talked to the man I shot?"

Ramsey shook his head. "I have men at the hospital. He's still in surgery. The prognosis isn't good."

"What about the partial license plate I gave you?"

"We're working on compiling a list of vans with those three letters." He shrugged. "Problem is you weren't able to tell what state it was from."

"In other words, so far you've got squat."

"We know from Dr. Gibbs that Anderson spotted someone in the bar and she saw a man follow him out. And we've got the book Anderson left behind. His instructions were to give it to you. You'd know what to do."

Ryder examined the book that Ramsey pushed across the table. It was the size of a textbook and the title was *Viet-*

nam: The Unsung Heroes. He noticed that a page was marked and discovered that the bookmark was one of his cards. Favors for a Fee. Ryder skimmed the page, which seemed to be about Vice President John Gracie's platoon in Vietnam.

"Mean anything?" Ramsey asked.

Ryder shook his head. "All he told me was that he had something he wanted my perspective on. He didn't mention Vietnam or the vice president, and I'm certainly no expert on either one. But he did mention something hot and political. I suppose the VP would certainly qualify as hot and political. As I mentioned, the connection was lousy. Anderson's editor at the *Post* will know what stories he was working on."

Ramsey nodded. "He says that Anderson was working on the vice president's upcoming visit to Korea and the administration's push to bring them to a nuclear arms agreement. In his spare time, he's working on a book on the vice presidency. That could be why he bookmarked the chapter on Gracie's service in Vietnam. According to his boss, Anderson is a fan of Gracie."

Ryder shrugged. "So are a lot of people. He's a war hero, and as politicians go, he seems to be one of the good guys."

Ramsey nodded. "I sent two of my men over to Anderson's apartment. The place was trashed, and his computer—if he kept one there—is missing. As soon as we're done here, Detective Gibbs and I will be going over to the *Post* to look through Anderson's office."

"I'll go with you to the *Post*."

"No. I think I have another job for you." Ramsey tapped the manila folder in front of him. "You also have the reputation of being a straight-shooter. You better be telling me everything you know."

Ryder thought of the Palm Pilot that was in his jacket pocket. If he turned it over, there was no telling when he'd see it again, and he was sure that Mark had left it for him. He leaned forward. "If I had any more, if I had even a hunch what this was all about, I wouldn't be here letting you grill me. Tonight Sierra got put on somebody's hit list. I intend to get the bastards."

Ramsey nodded. "We're on the same page with that. But there's the little matter of protecting Dr. Gibbs while we do that."

"I'll take care of that part," Ryder said.

"Okay." Ramsey gave him a brief nod. "I won't lie to you. That's the answer I wanted. The District doesn't have the resources to assign someone to her twenty-four/seven. But now I'll ask the question that my partner's going to want to know the answer to. Is there anything personal going on between the two of you?"

"I told you that I met her at the Blue Pepper for the first time last night, and today I talked to her on the phone."

Ramsey studied him. "A personal relationship could get in the way of protecting her."

Ryder leaned forward. "I won't let it. She wouldn't have been shot at tonight if I hadn't asked her to deliver that damn message. I know that and you know that. I'll keep her safe. You have my word on that."

Ramsey leaned back in his chair. "I don't suppose there's any chance of persuading you to let my department handle the matter of finding out who kidnapped Anderson."

Ryder's answering smile was grim. "Not a chance in hell."

SIERRA WATCHED Natalie pace the length of the interview room for the fifth time. Pacing was the way her sister had always worked off steam.

"You're angry with me," Sierra finally said.

"No." Natalie turned and started down the length of the room again. "I'm angry that someone took a shot at you. And I'm furious with Ryder Kane. He's the one who dragged you into this mess. If he was in the room right now, I'd—"

"He saved my life."

"Yeah. Well, it was the least he could do since he put you in that bullet's path in the first place."

Sierra said nothing for a minute. Out of habit, she reached into her bag and closed her fingers around her inhaler. Just in case. She had to think of a way to tell Natalie what she'd decided, and her sister was not going to take it well.

She wanted to have a sexual relationship with Ryder Kane. Just saying that silently to herself made her tighten her grip on her inhaler. She wasn't even sure when she'd reached her decision. It might have been during that long boring speed date with Richard Parker. But she had a suspicion that a part of her had decided during that first kiss.

She took a quick sideways glance through the glass and saw that he was still seated across from Detective Matt Ramsey. His sexual profile was eons away from hers. And perhaps that was part of his attraction. Still, it scared her a bit.

Nerves fluttered in her stomach. But she didn't seem to need her inhaler. She wasn't at all sure she could figure out a way to let Ryder know what she'd decided. And she was pretty sure a step-by-step plan would be pretty useless. Those had always been her security blankets in the past.

Maybe it was time she got rid of the plans. Maybe this new person she was beginning to discover inside her wouldn't need them. Curiosity, fear and excitement bubbled up. She felt as if she was going to walk a tightrope without a net.

Glancing up, she saw that Natalie was still pacing.

"Anger won't solve anything," she said. "It will only cloud your thinking."

Natalie drew in a deep breath and let it out on a sigh. "Thank you, Dr. Gibbs." But her gaze went to the glass wall, and Sierra knew that she was looking bullets at Ryder. "What do you know about him?" Natalie asked.

"A lot and nothing." How was she going to explain to Natalie what she wasn't sure of herself?

Natalie turned back to her, a question in her eyes.

"On some level, I feel this connection to him, as if I've known him for a long time. It's hard to explain. I know we like the same movies, but I have no idea what he does for a living or anything else about him except that he saved my life by shooting a man down on the street tonight. No matter how much I try to analyze it, I can't figure out why I should feel this sense of kinship. Unless it's the chemistry."

Natalie's eyes narrowed. "Chemistry? Time out. Just when did you discover that you and this man you've only met once have chemistry?"

"When I ran into him at the Blue Pepper last night, he kissed me and I kissed him back."

Natalie stared at her. "You kissed a man you'd never met before?"

"I know it wasn't part of my plan. Step one was a speed date. And I kissed him before we even had the speed date. I kissed him before I even knew his name. I've never done anything like that in my life."

"I thought you said that Ryder Kane wasn't at the Blue Pepper tonight."

"He wasn't."

Natalie frowned. "Then when did this speed date take place?"

"We had a speed date over the phone. Just before he asked me to deliver the message to Mark Anderson."

Natalie shook her head as if to clear it. "Let's go back to the kiss and the chemistry."

It seemed to Sierra that that's what she'd been doing ever since Ryder Kane had kissed her. Clasping her hands together in front of her she said, "The kiss just happened. And it was…amazing. I've never felt that way before in my life." And she very much wanted to feel that way again. She met her sister's eyes. "It doesn't make any sense, and it doesn't fit with the steps I laid out in my plan, but I think he's the one I want to have a sexual relationship with. It'll probably just be a fling, but—"

"Shit," Natalie said.

Sierra's stomach sank. "I know I'm not his type. And I'm not sure that he'll be interested. I—"

"Shut up for a minute," Natalie said. "I need some time to get my mind around this."

Sierra chewed on her bottom lip. Now that she'd put her thoughts into words, the nerves dancing in her stomach had gone from a waltz to a polka.

"Okay." Running a hand through her hair, Natalie drew a chair around the table, sat down next to Sierra and took her hands. "First off, let's get one thing clear. You don't have enough confidence in yourself. Don't say he might not be interested. Ryder Kane or any other man would jump at the chance if you told him you wanted to have sex with him. I'm just worried that Ryder's not the right kind of man for you."

"You said to go for chemistry."

Natalie sighed. "Yes, I did, but in this case...I've read his file. He owns some business called Favors for a Fee but he's also done some secret work for the government. Matt suspects black ops. That could mean assassinations, that kind of thing."

A little shiver moved through Sierra. "I know he has a violent side. I saw him shoot someone."

"And that doesn't scare you?"

"Yes. He scares me. The way I feel about him scares me. But it doesn't seem to matter." She leaned toward her sister. "We had phone sex, and it was the most exciting thing."

"Phone sex?"

"I reached orgasm. So I think it qualifies as phone sex. At least that's the general consensus in the data that I've gathered. Would you agree?"

"You've gathered data on phone sex?"

Sierra nodded. "There's a consistent pattern of phone sex and cyber sex in the dating practices of single people." Pausing, she studied her sister. The old familiar expression was back on Natalie's face, the one that always made her feel as though she was visiting from another planet. "You don't approve of my having phone sex."

Natalie frowned. "Stop putting words in my mouth. You can have any kind of sex you want. And I'm doing my best not to hover over you like a big sister. I'm just worried. You're a bit inexperienced when it comes to the opposite sex." She sighed. "I've just never pictured you with a man like Ryder."

"Me either." But since he'd kissed her, she couldn't seem to imagine herself with anyone else. "He makes me feel so...different. I think that I could let loose with Ryder Kane."

Natalie sighed. "That's the way that Chance made me feel."

"But you and Chance had a lot in common. Ryder and I don't." She sighed. "It's not like I'm looking for my soul mate. I just want to have a really memorable fling. Besides," Sierra played her trump card, "Harry said to dream big."

Natalie's cell phone rang. "Detective Gibbs." Then she mouthed the words, "It's Matt," to Sierra.

A moment later, Natalie jumped up and began to pace again. "I don't like it." There was another pause while Natalie listened to what Matt was saying. "Yes, I can see… Right. I'll tell her." Natalie was still frowning when she pocketed her cell.

"Bad news?"

"Mixed. Matt has just made a deal with Mr. Kane, and Kane Management is going to provide you with a bodyguard until this mess is cleared up."

"A bodyguard?" Sierra asked.

"The bad news is it seems that Kane intends to handle the job personally—twenty-four/seven."

Sierra felt a little thrill run along her nerve endings.

"Unless you object."

Sierra met her sister's eyes steadily. "No, I don't object."

"And you're sure you want to have an affair with him?"

"You're not going to talk me out of it."

"I can see that. You were always the stubborn one."

Sierra blinked. "I always thought of myself as the pushover."

"Wrong. You're stubborn, smart and sexy. Remember that." Natalie crossed to her, then reached for Sierra's hands and squeezed them. "I just want the best for you, sweetie. And if I tried to talk you out of doing this, I'd not only be wasting my breath, I'd be giving you advice that I didn't follow when I went after Chance. It's just that there's a good possibility that whoever kidnapped Mark Anderson will come after you again."

As a little thrill of excitement shot through her, Sierra drew in a breath and let it out. "I didn't think…I didn't hope for this. But he's doing it again, isn't he?"

"What do you mean?"

"First you read Harry's letter and you have this amazing adventure and fall in love with Chance. Then Rory opens her letter, and she has this marvelous adventure with Hunter. Now it looks I'm in the same boat."

Natalie's eyes narrowed. "You can't think Harry has his hand in this."

"Not directly, but when you went after Chance and Rory went after that interview with Hunter, you each did the kind of thing that Harry would have done. Of course, I figured that both of you inherited more of Harry's genes than I ever did. And I didn't expect to get the same advice he gave the two of you. But it looks like I'm going to have an adventure too."

Natalie studied her sister for a moment. "You should not be looking so damned happy and excited about the fact that someone might try to kill you again."

Sierra couldn't prevent the laugh. She should be scared to death. And she should be using her inhaler. But she hadn't—not once since she'd left the Blue Pepper. In fact she hadn't had to use it since she'd kissed Ryder Kane. "Ryder saved my life once. I think I can depend on him to do it again. There's something about him. I've been trying to analyze it, and I think it's competence. I think he's the most competent man I've ever met."

Natalie's eyes narrowed again. "You're trying to make me feel better about this."

"How am I doing?"

This time Natalie couldn't prevent a short laugh. "Your usual commendable job." Then her expression sobered. "I won't stop worrying about your safety, but if this Ryder Kane's the one you want to have a sexual relationship with, you go for it." She paused, and then continued. "And I am going to give you some advice. Harry was right. It seems to me that if you have one problem, Sierra, it's that your dreams are never big enough. You want the adventure, you want the sex. Just don't be afraid to go for everything."

Sierra swallowed hard and smiled, thinking, *If you dream too big, you always get hurt.* "Any suggestions about what I should do first? I don't want to scare him away."

Natalie smiled. "You can't. Until we get the guys who tried to shoot you, Ryder Kane will be sticking to you like glue."

WHEN THE CAR pulled up next to his on the top level of the parking garage, he leaned forward and spoke to his driver. "I'll be back shortly."

After alighting from his car, he walked to the cement half wall that offered a good view of the Washington Monument. When the other man joined him, he kept his eyes on the view. "Tell me you have the journalist."

"The journalist is no longer a problem."

"And his notes?"

"He didn't have anything on him."

The flash of fury was so consuming that for a moment he felt he'd choke on it. He concentrated on breathing until the constriction in his throat eased. Then he relaxed his clenched hands. When he finally spoke, his voice was mild. "He had a file with notes in it at the meeting. Until we have it, we're still in danger."

"There was nothing on his computer at the *Post* and nothing in his desk relating to the names you gave me."

"What about the person the journalist met?"

"It's being handled. There were complications at the scene. One of my men was shot."

Pushing down his anger once again, he made himself breathe—in and out. He couldn't let himself lose control. The stakes were too high. And anger never solved anything. Fine men had lost elections when they were perceived to have uncontrollable tempers. But his voice was tight and harsh-sounding when he finally said, "Tell me he's dead."

There were two beats of silence. "He's in surgery. I've got someone at the hospital monitoring his progress."

This time, he found it even harder to relax his fists. "He can't be allowed to talk to the police. Nothing can be traced back to me or my office."

"Understood."

"And the other person, the one the journalist met at the bistro?"

"I've got men following her."

"Her? Do you know who she is?"

"Dr. Sierra Gibbs. She's in the psychology and sociology departments at Georgetown. The bartender pointed out her table to him. He didn't stay long. But he left a book with her."

For the first time since he'd left his limousine, he began to breathe more easily. "She must have his notes. He must have passed them to her in the book."

He didn't turn to face the man, and he managed to keep his voice mild and pitched low. "You know what you have to do."

"I have three men following her."

"Good. Don't bungle it this time. And once you have what I want, you'll have to dispose of her. Make it look like an accident."

6

As HE CLIMBED the stairs to the front porch of Sierra's apartment in Georgetown, Ryder extended his hand for the key and she dug it out of her purse. They hadn't exchanged more than a few words in the squad car that had delivered them to his car, and since her apartment was only three blocks from where he'd parked, they'd walked. There was a great deal he wanted to say, but first he wanted her safely inside her apartment. Then he wanted to lay down some ground rules. However much he might want Sierra Gibbs, his first priority had to be to keep her safe.

Striding across the wide front porch, Ryder discovered the house had two front doors.

"Which one?" he asked.

"The one on the right."

"The left one leads where?"

"To the lower flat. My neighbor's in California for the week."

"Tell me about your place. Is there another locked door at the top of the stairs or is this it?"

"There's another door. You can use the same key."

Ryder nodded, admiring the fact that she was all business. Truth told, his admiration for Dr. Sierra Gibbs increased with each new thing he noticed about her. Beneath that fragile appearance, he was beginning to think there was one tough cookie. The contrasts in her continued to fascinate him.

"Okay, Doc, here's the deal. We're going to do our best not to make any noise as we climb the stairs. No more conversation. Once we reach the top, you're going to stay put until I search the apartment. If you hear anything, any sound at all, you're going to run like hell. Understood?"

She nodded. "You think someone is here?"

There was something in her voice, but he could have sworn that it was excitement rather than fear. "That's what I'm going to find out. Once I'm sure that the place is secure, we're going to talk. You ready?"

At her nod, he turned and, like shadows they climbed to the second floor. The stairway was narrow, the slanted ceiling overhead low as in many of the old homes in Georgetown. The night-light in the outlet at the top of the stairs illuminated a small landing. When they reached it, Ryder turned and motioned for her to stay. Then he unsheathed his gun. With his free hand, he unlocked the door and opened it slowly. He listened for any sound, any movement. There was nothing.

After feeling along the wall, he flipped the light switch, then went in low, fanning his gun in a wide arc. The room was narrow, long and empty. At the far end, a counter and stools separated the living area from a galley kitchen that was spotless. He crossed to it, checked behind the counter, and then turned to study the room again.

There was a couch, a small TV, a few tables. But what caught his eyes was the large-screen plasma TV on one wall and the bookcase beneath filled with tapes and DVDs. Moving closer, he noted some of the titles: *Casablanca* was there along with the *Raiders of the Lost Ark* trilogy, and the Hitchcock thrillers she'd mentioned. But there was also a *Thin Man* collection and all the Dirty Harry movies. So she was a Clint Eastwood fan. And she had a complete collection of the James Bond movies as well as the DVDs of four seasons of Buffy the Vampire Slayer. He tried to fit together the puzzle piece of her taste in action-adventure thrillers with the tightly wound woman he'd first glimpsed through the window of the Blue Pepper. Was she hooked on adventure movies because she had so little of it in her own life? Finally, he shook his head. He didn't understand her fully. Not yet.

Then he noted that the movies were organized by genre and arranged alphabetically. That fitted with the woman he was coming to know. She was organized. His own collection at his apartment was mainly organized by whatever he'd watched recently.

Moving to the couch, he took in the way the magazines were stacked, their edges perfectly aligned with the edges of the glass-topped coffee table. A small wastebasket at the side of the couch held several candy wrappers. His lips curved in a smile. So the doc was a bit of a junk-food addict.

His gaze swept the room again. Aside from the movie collection and the candy wrappers, the room had about as much personality as a motel room.

The first door he opened led to a bathroom. The window was locked, the shower stall empty. But Sierra's scent enveloped him. The lemony fragrance was stronger near the jars and bottles that formed a straight line on a glass shelf.

The next door led to a bedroom. Once again, he went in low and swept the room with his gun. No one. While he methodically checked the closet and the locks on the windows, his mind catalogued other details. The bed was black wrought iron and covered with satin and lace. Numerous pillows were stacked against the headboard and resting against them was a stuffed red fox with a goofy grin on its face. Somehow the mix of the feminine and the unexpected fit Sierra Gibbs to a T.

One wall was filled with photos, family, he guessed as he scanned them briefly. And then there was the watermelon-colored chaise lounge beneath the window. On it was an opened book titled *The History of Sex*. The doc was full of surprises. He could easily picture her lying there in something filmy and soft, that tiny line forming on her brow as she read.

He could picture her just as easily lying on that lounge doing something much more pleasurable than reading about sex. An image filled his mind of lying there with her, of having those long legs tangled with his. He tried to push it out of his mind, but it lingered. Just how long was he going to be able to wait to touch her again? Phone sex was a poor substitute for the real thing.

She was right outside on the landing. He could go to her now. Swearing softly, he strode from the bedroom. He couldn't afford to think about that. Right now his job was to keep her safe.

Crossing the living room in three quick strides, he opened a final door. Even as he skimmed his gun over the interior of the room, he blinked in surprise. The walls were red, and a print of bright red poppies took up nearly one wall.

Though there were indications of order, the decor could best be described as bordering on chaos. And her scent—that blend of citrus and summer—was everywhere. Neat piles of folders were stacked everywhere—on the floors, on bookshelves and even on the two chairs. Only the desk was free of them, but its surface was covered with papers. Moving closer, he could see that the drawings on the papers were of figures in various sexual positions. Interesting and unusual sexual positions.

This time he didn't fight off the fantasies that took shape in his mind. He could imagine taking her in each one of those positions. Right here in this room. On the desk. On the floor.

Common sense told him that he would have to be patient. Above and beyond the danger that she was in, there was an innocence about her that told him he would have to go slowly.

He wondered how long he could get common sense to prevail.

RYDER KANE moved like a predatory cat. She hadn't heard one noise since he'd left her on the landing. Once she'd caught a glimpse of him moving past the crack he'd left in the door.

As the seconds ticked by, the reality of her situation began to sink in. At the police station, she'd still been riding high on adrenaline. But Ryder's caution was getting to her. Someone had tried to shoot her, and they just might try it again. Of course, danger was the downside of having a marvelous and exciting adventure. Still, she wasn't really afraid, and she hadn't needed her inhaler once. She'd given that some thought on the ride from the police station. Perhaps it was only the old Sierra who depended on her inhaler.

But the new person she was discovering within herself might still need it when she made her proposition to him. She'd been tongue-tied on the ride from the station. He'd been silent too. Had he started thinking about her as merely a job?

No, she wasn't going to think that way. That was the old Sierra, and she didn't want to be that woman anymore.

She recalled what he'd said in that phone conversation. If he was having second thoughts about having real sex with her, she'd just have to change his mind. The right approach would be key. The problem would be to keep her focus. She hadn't been able to during the ride from the police station to his car. A plan would help. But she hadn't been able to come up with even a first step, not while she was sitting so close to him.

The fact that she wasn't able to think clearly when he was close might prove to be a problem. She drew in a deep breath and let it out. She'd deal with it.

A car drove by on the street below. A few houses up the street it slowed, the engine idling as Mrs. Hagerty's little shih tzu started to bark.

She pulled a note card out of her canvas bag and wrote 1 on the top line. She tapped a pencil against her chin. The key question was, what approach would work best with a man like Ryder Kane? Sierra had a hunch that he'd be swayed more by action than by words. Yes, a practiced seduction would be the best plan, and that wasn't one of her strengths. Or at least it hadn't been. But she was different with Ryder. And she did know intellectually what went into seducing a man. She had scads of research—narratives, magazine articles—and there were so many ideas she wanted to try out. Step one would be to—

The creak of a floorboard interrupted her thoughts. Sierra strained to listen. She was almost positive that the noise hadn't come from inside the apartment. And she hadn't moved.

She heard it again. This time she could definitely pinpoint its location. The porch. At two in the morning, there shouldn't be anyone on her front porch. Her neighbor seldom had visitors even when she was in town. And she wasn't.

There was another noise—a quiet, tinny sound of metal against metal.

Someone was definitely on the front porch and that person wasn't ringing the doorbell. Acting on instinct, she stuffed the note card back in her bag, then leaned down and pulled the night-light out of the outlet. Quietly, she let herself into her apartment and locked and bolted the door. Ryder strode from her office as she turned.

"Someone's trying to get in the front door," she said.

Ryder didn't even blink. "I didn't see a back way out. There isn't one?"

"No."

Taking her arm, he urged her toward the bedroom. As she watched him raise the window and deal with the screen, the nerves in her stomach transformed into an icy ball of fear. She knew what he was going to do. Directly below the window, the roof sloped sharply, and there was a twenty-foot drop to the side of the house.

Ryder had swung one leg over the sill when he turned to her. "Tell me you're not afraid of heights."

She drew in a breath and let it out. "I'm not afraid of heights."

"You're lying through your teeth, Doc. But we can't stay here. I don't know how many there are or what kind of fire power they have. Some battles, you just have to retreat from and fight again the next day."

Sierra moistened her lips. "Right."

He climbed out onto the roof, and with one hand gripping the sill, he extended the other one to her.

"If you could just lay it out in steps for me, I think I can do it."

"Steps?"

She nodded, knowing that he was going to give her the you-must-be-an-alien look.

Instead, he said, "Step one, give me your hand."

She put her hand in his and swung one leg over the window ledge. The moment her foot touched the roof, a shingle broke free and they both listened as it slid off the edge and hit the ground below. Sierra tried very hard to suppress the image of herself doing the same and instead concentrated on breathing in and out.

"I don't think the step-by-step thing is going to work," Ryder said, gripping her hand tightly. "In cases like this when I'm being chased by men with guns, I operate pretty much on instinct and intuition. So let's try this."

The steady sound of his voice was soothing her.

"Have you ever played Follow the Leader?"

"No."

"It's a simple game," he said easily. "You just do exactly what I do. First you're going to sit down on the roof just like I'm doing."

Gripping his hand tightly, Sierra drew her other leg over the ledge and sat down beside him.

"Good job. Now we're going to just inch down the slope on our butts. Got it?"

She didn't say a word. But with his help, she managed to make it down the incline until her feet were propped against the gutter.

"Now, I'm going to go first." He released her hand, then twisted onto his stomach and lowered his feet over the side. "Watch and do exactly what I do." Balancing his weight on his forearms, he began to inch his body backwards. "The trick is to get as far off the roof as you can before you drop. That way it's a shorter fall. You've got to appreciate the logic of that, Doc."

"This isn't logical." Sierra could barely recognize her own voice, it was so tight with fear. "I'm not going to be able to jump."

"Okay, forget logic. Just push everything else out of your mind and think of this. Those bastards kidnapped Mark Anderson and shot at you. Are you going to let them win?"

A second later he disappeared over the side of the roof.

Wood splintered as her apartment door crashed open. Fear lodged once again in her throat and iced her veins. But this time it pushed her into action. Twisting onto her stomach, she concentrated on doing exactly what Ryder had done, letting gravity pull her backward. A second later, she was hanging by her hands from the gutter.

"Trust me, Doc. I'll catch you."

His voice was only a hoarse whisper, but it was enough. Closing her eyes, she said a quick, silent prayer and dropped. Arms clamped around her and they both fell on the grass. An instant later, Ryder was on his feet, pulling her with him.

"Is there an alley?"

"That way." She pointed with her free hand.

The first bullet ricocheted off the drain pipe of the garage as they tore through the gate. They ran then, but not to the end of the alley as she'd expected. Instead, Ryder pulled her into a yard about three doors down from her house. They raced across the grass and around the side of the house. She was struggling to suck in air when he dragged her behind one of the large, thick bushes that bordered the front of the house. Before she could blink, he pushed her down, and then sat in front of her so that his body pressed hers into the brick wall of the house.

It was only then that she fully realized she was out of breath. Automatically, she thought of her inhaler. Maybe she needed it after all, but her bag was trapped against the wall. When she tried to wiggle it free, Ryder turned his head and spoke in a low voice. "We have to be perfectly still."

"Why? What are we doing here?"

"Hiding in the bushes."

"I got that. But I thought that the plan was to run away and live to fight another day."

"Still is. But I want to see what they're doing. From what I can see they've left one man stationed at the front of your place. There's no sign of the ones who broke through the door. They're either searching the apartment or they've come after us."

She could see that his lips were moving, but his words had become no more than a buzz in her ears. The sensations that came from being near him had sneaked up on her. She'd gradually become aware of the hardness of his body and the torrid, liquid heat that was flowing from him to her. The feelings were so vivid. She could feel the press of each one of his fingers on her shoulder. His scent was just as she'd remembered it, and she felt the warmth of his breath on her lips each time he drew in air and expelled it. Desire was winding tight inside of her.

"We won't have to wait much longer," he whispered.

Suddenly, she didn't want to wait. It seemed she'd been waiting all of her life.

"I want to kiss you."

"Sierra…"

"I have to kiss you." She was shocked when the words

slipped out of her mouth. But it was nothing less than the truth. There was such an ache building inside of her, sharp and compelling. "I can't wait." She didn't care where they were or who was after them; she simply had to feel that mouth pressed against hers again. Tightening her grip on his shoulder, she tried to draw him closer.

"We can't make any noise," he warned.

Sierra wasn't sure if Ryder closed the distance between them or she did. All she was aware of was the brush of his lips against hers. This wasn't the hard pressure she'd experienced before. His mouth was so gentle, so teasing. The ache inside her grew stronger.

"We shouldn't be doing this," he whispered, and she could feel his breath move into her. And all the while his mouth continued to move softly over hers, as if he couldn't stop himself. The possibility thrilled her, but it wasn't enough, not nearly. She shifted just a little to ease the awkwardness of their positions.

"Shhh."

This time, she raised her hand to his cheek, and she was the one who closed the distance. At last. The fit of his lips to hers was just as perfect as she'd remembered, his flavor just as unique. Beneath her hand, she felt the sharp line of his cheekbone, the strength of his jaw. *Yes,* she thought as the sensations she'd been imagining streamed through her. *Oh, yes.* If she had any doubts that this was the man she wanted, they streamed away.

SHE WAS DRIVING him crazy, he thought as he shifted his position slightly and took the kiss deeper. He had no business messing around with her when they hadn't made their escape yet. But he didn't seem to have control of himself where she was concerned. When she'd said she had to kiss him, he hadn't been able to refuse. And now, with the taste of her surrender streaming through him, he had even less choice.

He wanted his hands on her, but there was no way he could do that. Not here, not now. Even more, he wanted her hands on him. The feel of that soft palm against his cheek had him imagining those clever hands of hers all over him.

Pleasure turned sharp and twisted. He had to put a stop to this now before—

A rustle in the bushes nearby had him slipping a hand behind her neck as he drew away. He said nothing and willed her to do the same.

Seconds ticked by as neither of them moved. There was another rustle, and this time Ryder spotted the squirrel under the lowest branch of a nearby bush. For a moment, they merely looked at one another, and then the squirrel turned and raced away.

"A squirrel," he whispered as he once more turned to peer through the bushes. The next sound he heard wasn't a squirrel. It was footsteps, and they were close.

He gripped the hand that she'd left on his shoulder and turned his head slightly.

"Ever play Statues, doc?" he asked very softly.

"No," she whispered.

"Piece of cake. Just freeze until I tell you it's safe."

SIERRA WENT stock still and listened hard. At first she heard only the usual night-time noises—the chirp of insects, a dog barking some distance away. Then, closer, she heard the crunch of gravel. Every muscle in her body tightened as the sound grew louder. Whoever it was had followed the same route they had. Had he been close enough to see them duck into the bushes?

She held her breath, comforted somewhat when Ryder's hand tightened on hers. Through the bushes, she could just make out a beam of light as it played itself over the shrubs. There was one moment when it seemed to linger on the bush they were hiding behind, but then it moved on. She didn't let out the breath she was holding until she heard the sound of footsteps on the sidewalk ten yards away. The moment the steps faded, Ryder squeezed her hand again and whispered, "The good news is that they're piling into the van."

"And the bad news?" Sierra asked.

"There's a lot of it. For starters, there are three of them. One of them just came down the front steps. So he stayed in the apartment most likely to search for something while the other one followed us."

"What were they searching for?" Sierra asked.

"Good question. Ramsey told me that they'd trashed Mark Anderson's apartment. Maybe they think he gave you something. The timing of their arrival makes me think they knew when you'd be coming back here. There's a good chance there's an informant down where your sister works."

"And?"

"If that doesn't worry you, it should."

"Everything worries me. I'll worry more if I think you're holding something back."

"If they have an informant on the police force, then chances are some very powerful people could be involved in this."

"So what's the next part of your plan?"

He turned then and kissed her hard. "Just in case I haven't mentioned it, you're all right, Doc."

"Thanks." The kiss hadn't been long this time, and it

had been kind of…friendly. But her lips were vibrating again.

"As for my plan—I don't have it all mapped out yet. The way I figure it, they're going to canvas the neighborhood for a while in the van, widening their area with each sweep. The final bad news is that between our position right now and my car, there's P Street—which is dead at this time of the night. We'll stick out like a sore thumb."

"Why don't we take my car?"

Ryder stared at her. "You have a car? I didn't see it when we ran past the garage."

"My neighbor pays extra to park there when she's in town. I use the street."

"You know, if you ever decide to give up the halls of academia, I could use someone like you at Kane Management." The sound of a car's motor had him turning toward the street again. Through the bushes, Sierra watched the dark-colored van make its way up the street.

When it turned the corner, Ryder pulled her up and drew her out of the bushes. "It's safe to make a run for it. Lead on, Dr. Gibbs."

When they reached the car, he took her keys and opened the passenger door. "Crouch on the floor and keep your head down."

She waited until he'd climbed behind the wheel and maneuvered the car out of the parking space. Then she said, "What's next?"

"We're getting the heck out of here."

7

SIERRA WOKE SLOWLY to the smell of coffee. Odd, she never smelled coffee when she woke up. Tasks in the kitchen weren't one of her priorities, so in the mornings she made do with instant. As she burrowed deeper into the pillow, trying to snatch that last few minutes of sleep before she had to face the day, something else struck her as odd. She could have sworn that the bed was swaying slightly—almost as if it were a cradle that was being rocked.

Then it came back to her in a flash. She was on Ryder's houseboat on the Chesapeake Bay. He'd explained where they were going before she'd fallen asleep in the car. Exhaustion had hit her hard, probably due to the adrenaline rushes she'd experienced earlier in the evening. She vaguely remembered Ryder carrying her to the cabin, tucking her beneath the covers, and telling her that they'd talk in the morning.

Sitting up, she surveyed the room. There was a masculine feel to it—pine furniture with Shaker lines, a quilt in a brown-and-gold pattern. A closet door stood slightly ajar and she saw men's clothes hanging neatly inside.

Through the window, she saw the sun shooting bright sparks off an expanse of water, and the scent of coffee was coming from a thermal pot that sat on the nightstand next to the bed. Groping for it, she poured herself a cup and took a sip in the hopes that caffeine would clear the cobwebs out of her brain.

She took another swallow of the coffee. The scent in the room—something intensely male—was Ryder's. She would have recognized it anywhere. So this must be his room.

Where was he?

And why hadn't he stayed with her last night? A little voice nagged.

He wanted her. Surely she couldn't have mistaken the signs. Hadn't he told her that he did? And when she'd kissed him while they were hiding in the bushes, it had been just as intense, just as arousing as the first kiss they'd shared. Merely thinking about the way he'd made her feel was enough to start clouding her mind all over again.

So why hadn't he stayed with her last night? Had he changed his mind?

She took another swallow of coffee and set the cup on the bedside table. If he had changed his mind, what was she going to do about it? The old Sierra would have accepted his decision and gone back to her research and her books and her movies.

But she wasn't that person anymore. She wasn't sure who she was. Not Jane Eyre certainly. She'd whapped a man in the face with her canvas bag and she'd jumped off a roof. Buffy would have been proud of her. And she hadn't had to use her inhaler once. She'd thought about it in the bushes, but she'd kissed Ryder instead.

The memories made her smile. Whoever she was, Sierra Gibbs was definitely off the sidelines. And she was involved in an exciting adventure with a man who made her want to forget the lists she'd always run her life by. The whole thing scared her—and that meant that the old Sierra wasn't entirely gone. But she was thrilled, too, and she wasn't about to turn back.

She drew in a deep breath. If Ryder Kane had changed his mind about wanting her and making love to her, she'd just have to figure out a way to make him change it back.

Tossing the quilt off herself, she noted that she was still dressed. Her shoes were tucked neatly by the end of the bed, and right next to them was her canvas bag.

A glance at her watch told her that it was ten o'clock. Relief streamed through her. She hadn't slept that long. All she had to do was find Ryder and have that talk.

After fortifying herself with another swallow of coffee, she grabbed her canvas bag and fished in its depths for her comb as she made her way to the bathroom. But it wasn't her comb that her fingers closed around. It was a key.

She pulled it out and cupped it in the palm of her hand. It wasn't hers. She'd given her keys to Ryder. And this one had a plastic grip and a number stamped on it that suggested it belonged to a storage locker.

Her heart skipped a beat, and then kicked into high gear. Did it belong to Mark Anderson? Could it have fallen out of the book he'd left with her?

After hurrying into the bathroom, she did her best to make herself presentable. Then she headed to the door, opened it, and climbed up a short flight of stairs. She had to find Ryder.

She spotted them immediately—Ryder and another man. The stranger was wearing cut-off shorts and T-shirt, and he had a fishing pole in his hands. His blond hair was long enough that he'd gathered it into a short ponytail at the nape of his neck, and though he looked very laid back in his attire, he projected the same aura of competence that Sierra had sensed from the very beginning with Ryder. Neither of the men noticed her as she quietly climbed the rest of the stairs to the deck.

Ryder was wearing black jeans and a black T-shirt and he was carrying a leather briefcase.

"Hopefully, I'll be back this evening," Ryder said. "I don't expect any trouble. No one followed us here, and there's no record anywhere that I own this houseboat."

"What do I do if trouble shows up?" the stranger asked.

Ryder's smile was grim. "Eliminate it."

"What about the woman?"

"Keep her here."

"And if she objects?"

"She's reasonable."

"She's a woman. Sometimes they're not reasonable."

"You're a Shakespeare nut. Think *Taming of the Shrew.* This one's like the sweet sister, Bianca. Plus, she has a very logical mind. Someone tried to kill her last night. Just explain to her that this is the safest place for her until I figure out what's going on."

Ryder was leaving her. The hurt arrowed through her, carrying echoes of past experiences. Everyone in her life had left her. Her sisters, every time they went off with Harry. And Harry had left her too. Twice.

Now Ryder was about to do the same thing. Riding on top of the ache came anger. She'd jumped off a roof for him, she'd hidden behind bushes, they'd used *her* car to escape, and now he was going to leave her with a complete stranger on a houseboat? The idea made her so…so furious that she couldn't think.

She raced up the stairs and strode across the deck. "You are not leaving me on this boat."

SHIT. Ryder thought the word, but he didn't say it out loud. When he'd taken the coffee into the bedroom, she hadn't stirred, and he'd planned to sneak away before she woke up. And before he was tempted to wake her up.

"She sure doesn't come across like Bianca."

"Thanks, pal," Ryder muttered under his breath. He didn't appreciate the humor he heard in his old friend's voice. Nor did he appreciate the fiery light in Sierra's eyes as she stormed across the deck.

"You *were* going to leave me here, weren't you?"

Ryder had handled his share of angry women before. Willing his muscles to relax, he managed a smile. "Sleep well?"

"I slept fine. And wherever you're going, I'm going with you."

Reason, Ryder reminded himself. And logic. That was the way to go. But it was hard to keep his mind on either one when she stood there only about a foot away with her eyes burning like fine sapphires and that long golden hair blowing in the wind. He wanted to touch her, taste her. Every time he saw her, he wanted her more.

The tug-of-war between what he should do to keep her safe and what he wanted to do had kept him awake most of the night. But Ramsey had been right. Becoming her lover right now wasn't the best idea. So he'd come up with a plan. Under most circumstances, plans weren't his forte. Usually, he depended on spur-of-the-moment decisions. But on the drive to his houseboat, he'd decided that for her safety, he'd try to keep his hands off her until the threat to her safety had been eliminated. To do that, he needed some distance.

It had been hard enough to walk out of the bedroom

without waking her. Taking her. How in hell was he supposed to walk away when she looked like some warrior goddess ready to do battle?

Sierra took a step closer and poked a finger into his chest. "Don't even think of talking me out of it."

Jed rubbed his chin. "Could be I've got to brush up on my Shakespeare, but if it's the play I'm thinking of she reminds me more of Kate."

Sierra whirled on him, fisting her hands on her hips. "We haven't even been introduced and you're calling me a shrew?"

Jed managed to keep his expression sober as he raised his free hand, palm out. "Jed Calhoun, ma'am. Ryder and I worked together in the service. He's doing me a favor by letting me stay here. And I…think I'll just go fishing and let the two of you work this out."

"I could use a little moral support here," Ryder muttered.

Jed gave Ryder's shoulder an encouraging pat. "Sorry about that. I try to stay out of domestic squabbles." He included Sierra in his smile. "But you can go ahead and take your time settling things. I intend to walk up the shore a bit and find me a spot where I can fish the entire day away. I won't be back until sundown."

"Hey," Ryder said as Jed walked down the short gangplank, "you were supposed to play bodyguard here."

"I don't need him as my bodyguard," Sierra said. "I've got you."

Jed grinned at Ryder from the shore. "She's definitely not Bianca. If you need some help, give me a ring. I've got my cell."

Ignoring Jed, Sierra tapped her foot and glared at Ryder. "Well?"

He cleared his throat and tried to focus. But the lecture he'd given himself during the night, the plan he'd mapped out, seemed far less operational when she was standing close enough that he could smell her, close enough that he could recall each and every nuance of her taste. "Look, I can understand why you might be a little annoyed. But my priority is to—"

She cut him off by poking a finger into his chest again. "*Annoyed?* Annoyed isn't the half of it. I jumped off a roof because you asked me to. I thought…I hoped that I'd earned just a little bit of your respect."

"You have." Ryder frowned. "This doesn't have anything to do with how much I respect you. I made your sister a promise that I would keep you safe."

"Well, that figures." The wind had whipped her hair into her face and when she shoved it back, he saw the mist of tears in her eyes. He reached out to her then, but she took a quick step back.

"In one breath, Natalie tells me that I should reach out and grab what I want, and in the next she's asking you to make me a boat prisoner until the whole thing has been wrapped up."

"She didn't. I—"

Sierra actually pushed him with the flat of her hand this time. "And don't tell me this doesn't have to do with respect."

Whirling away, she strode to the other side of the deck, then turned to face him. "You described me as Bianca, the sweet biddable younger sister. That's what I've been all my life." She started toward him. "I thought you were different, that you understood. But you're just like everyone else. My sisters, my father—they were so good at grabbing life, but they left me behind because they wanted to keep me safe. They couldn't trust me to keep up."

"Whoa, now wait just a moment." He snagged her by the shoulders when she reached him. "I trust you."

"Not enough. Or you'd take me with you."

He gave her a little shake. "This isn't about you. It's about me. I don't trust myself. I—" How was he going to explain it to her when he was still trying to understand it himself? "I'm not going to be able to be near you and keep my hands off of you. When you kissed me in those bushes last night, I couldn't stop you. I couldn't stop myself. I can't seem to resist you."

Her eyes widened. It wasn't merely surprise he saw. There was heat too. And that damn pulse at the base of her throat was hammering again. The combination was shredding his control.

Sierra moistened her lips. "What if I told you that you didn't have to? I want your hands on me."

Logic. Ryder dug deep to find some. "That would be a mistake."

"Then you didn't mean what you said in our phone conversation?"

"Yes. Yes, I did." He was hip-deep in quicksand now and sinking fast. It wasn't helping at all that the details of what he'd said to her on the phone were pouring into his mind just as they had during the long night he'd spent sleeping on the deck. Just looking at her was making his hands itch and his mouth water.

"Look, Doc, I want to do all those things I talked about and more. If the circumstances were different, I'd do them right now. We wouldn't even make it to the bedroom."

Ryder watched the pulse skip at her throat, felt his own heart kick up its rhythm in response.

So much for using logic and reason. Every word he spoke only served to arouse them both. And it wasn't helping one bit that he was touching her.

Dropping his hands from her arms, he took a careful step back, closed his fingers around the railing behind him and gripped it hard.

"I wouldn't object to that scenario." She stepped toward him and put her hands on his chest. "I was going to try and seduce you, but I didn't have time to list the steps, and I'm not very good at seduction."

He grabbed her wrists and broke the contact. "Doc, you're a natural when it comes to seduction."

He swallowed once. He'd just have to lay it on the line for her.

"If we give into what we're feeling, it could interfere with my ability to protect you. Let me give you a 'for instance.' Last night when I left you standing on the landing, I was supposed to be checking your apartment for intruders. But I got distracted the moment I stepped into your office. One glance told me that there was no one there, but I didn't give you the all clear or come back and get you. Instead, I left you standing there on the landing, unprotected, while those thugs were jimmying the door. And do you know what I was doing? I was looking at those diagrams on your desk and fantasizing about taking you in every single one of those positions. Right there in your office. On your desk. Disgusting, huh?"

SIERRA TOOK one careful breath, hoping it would do something to cool the heat that had just flared through her body.

"You see the problem, Doc?"

Had he hoped she'd be shocked? Well, she was. But she was shocked at her own response, not at him. She'd never wanted anything or anyone as much as she wanted him. It terrified her. It energized her.

If she just had some time to plan…but she didn't. Taking another breath, she said the first thing that came into her mind. "Some of those positions look pretty tricky. But you'd know how to manage all of them?"

His eyes narrowed. "You're not disgusted."

She shook her head. "I want to try those positions with you."

"You're something else, Doc."

She recognized the look he was giving her. It was a variation of you-must-be-from-another-planet look. A mixture of panic and desperation sprinted through her. "Forget I said that. I'm not good at this. If I don't have a list to follow, I just blurt things out." He opened his mouth, but she raised a hand. "No. Let me finish."

Oh, how she needed a pencil and a note card. But even as she tried to organize her thoughts into a list, it came to her in a flash. If she was going to convince him, she had to tailor her argument to suit him. And he was a businessman. "Okay. You asked me for a favor yesterday—two, in fact. And I delivered on both. I let you speed date me over the phone, and I gave your message to Mark Anderson. So I'm making you a business proposition. I want two favors in return."

"A quid pro quo?" he asked.

"Exactly. Number one, I want to have a sexual relationship with you, and number two, I want to help you find Mark Anderson."

In the silence that followed, the nerves in her stomach began to dance again.

"How about a compromise?" Ryder finally said.

"What?"

"We'll make love, but you'll stay here on the boat with Jed until I figure this out."

"No. I want to help you find Mark," she repeated. "You weren't there. You didn't see the look in his eyes when he asked me for help. Besides, the thugs who kidnapped him tried to shoot me and they came after me again last night. I'm not just going to sit here and wait for you to take care of everything. I've spent my life sitting on the sidelines, watching and dreaming. I'm twenty-six and the only adventures I've ever had are the ones I've experienced vicariously in movies and books. This is my chance to change that. Can you understand that?"

The problem was that he could understand it too well. Wasn't it his own love of adventure that had prompted him to create Favors for a Fee? "Sierra—"

She raised a hand. "Let me finish. If it's the distraction that worries you, I have a solution for that. It's something I do all the time when I'm trying to juggle projects. It's just a matter of compartmentalizing our activities. During the day, we can investigate why those people kidnapped Mark Anderson and why they tried to kill me. But that leaves our nights free to…."

"Try those positions?"

He was getting good at blurting things out himself, Ryder decided. He vowed that later he'd try to analyze just what it was that had destroyed his thin layer of resolve. Right now, he had to concentrate on not caving anymore.

Sierra was blinking at him. "Yes. I mean…if you'd be interested in doing that. And there are other things from my research that I'm very curious about."

"The diagrams are part of your sex research?"

"Yes. But I can't help but wonder if all of those positions are possible."

He took her hand and raised it to his lips. There were so many women inside of her. The nervous Nellie he'd first glimpsed at the Blue Pepper. The cool, focused scientist who could talk so calmly about plans and compartmentalizing and sex research. The passionate woman who'd poked him in the chest a few moments ago and who came alive in his arms when he kissed her. And the innocent seductress who was standing in front of him right now. He wanted all of them. "Those positions are right up my alley, Doc. I'm good with diagrams."

"And you'll let me help you find out why Mark Anderson was kidnapped and who tried to shoot me?"

"One favor at a time, Doc." He ran a finger over the pulse at her throat. "Your skin is very delicate here."

Her breath hitched, and her eyes grew smoky for a second before they cleared and focused. "Two heads are better than one. Besides I already found—"

"How about this for step one?" He brushed his lips along the line of her jaw.

She placed two hands against his chest. "You're trying to distract me."

"You've already distracted me. Turnabout's fair play."

"Please." She increased the pressure against his chest. "This is important to me. I was angry before, but what I said was true. I've spent my whole life being left behind. Plus, I think I can help."

Ryder sighed. Today seemed to be his day for going against his better judgment. "Okay. Okay. We'll work together. I'll take you with me."

"Good. Well, then we should get started."

"Right." There were some ground rules to be laid down. Later. Right now, he wanted a real taste of her.

Lowering his mouth, he took what he'd been craving

since he'd kissed her in the bushes. Her mouth was just as soft, just as warm as he'd remembered. Her flavor streamed into him, as surprising as it had been the first time. One look at the doc and a man expected sweet, and it was there. But there was a tartness beneath and as he took the kiss deeper, he discovered something darker and richer, like the kind of chocolate that was sold only in the most exclusive shops.

He drew back a little to see that her eyes were open and on his.

"I thought…I can't think while you're kissing me."

"That means I'm doing it right."

"But…shouldn't we be doing something?"

He brushed his mouth against hers, and then trailed a line of kisses to her throat. "We are."

"I thought…"

He nipped her ear. "You think too much, Doc."

Her breath caught when he dipped his tongue into her ear.

"Shouldn't we…?"

"Compartmentalize?" He drew her closer, felt her body fit against his. "That's exactly what I'm doing." When he gripped her hips, she scooted up and wrapped her legs around him. "You've got a logical mind, Doc. And if I recall correctly, the sexual relationship was the first favor on your list?"

"Yes."

"Then let's check it off."

8

ONCE INSIDE his bedroom, he kicked the door shut and turned to press her against it. Then he drew back and let her slide down him until her feet were on the floor. "Last chance, Doc. If you want to change your mind, say the word now."

The offer was so sweet and if she had any sense she'd take him up on it, but there was heat and that hint of leashed violence in his eyes. Both pulled at her. "I'm not going to change my mind."

"Good." He began to unfasten the buttons on her shirt. Just the barest brush of his fingers on her bare skin when he shoved her shirt down her arms made her tremble.

He stopped and studied her for a moment. "You're not afraid?"

She shook her head. "Just a little nervous."

"Why?"

"I don't want to disappoint you."

His lips curved a bit as he lowered his eyes to what he'd uncovered. "You're not disappointing me. I already like the view." Very slowly, he drew his finger along the lace of her bra. "You keep surprising me, Sierra. And women don't, as a rule. I like that you're all practical on the outside, and then there's this little lacy fantasy beneath."

He traced one finger down her breast, and then circled her nipple until she trembled again.

"I like it when you do that."

"You do?" She searched his face.

"You certainly didn't disappointment me during our phone conversation either."

"I didn't?" She searched his face. It was hard to concentrate when the movement of his fingers down her stomach left a trail of fire.

"Just listening to the way your breath hitched when I told you how I wanted to touch you inside made me so hard I nearly came. That's never happened to me before."

"Me, too. I mean…" She was so aware of when his hands stopped moving and simply rested at her waist. She felt the heat and pressure of each one of his fingers on her skin. He was standing close, but she wanted him closer so that hard lean body would be pressed against her. She could anticipate that instant whirlwind reaction, and she wanted it with a desperation that was new to her.

"I was thinking—probably your influence, Doc." Leaning down, he brushed his lips over hers. "But since we both found the phone sex pleasurable, how about if I begin by touching you just the way I told you I was going to?" He drew one finger down the front of her slacks to the V between her legs.

Sierra's breath hitched.

"I figured we could run a little experiment and test my theory to see if real sex is better than phone sex. What do you think of that?"

She wasn't thinking. How could she when heat was coursing through her? He was barely touching her, but her insides were melting. And if she was recalling her chemistry studies correctly, it would only be a matter of time until she evaporated.

He slipped two fingers between her legs and pressed up hard.

Sensation—huge waves of it—shot through her. As he withdrew his fingers, her body arched trying to maintain the contact for as long as possible.

"Ryder."

The breathless way she said his name started a drumbeat in Ryder's head that tore at his control. He heard her surrender in the sound, saw it in those fathomless blue eyes. He'd barely touched her, and she was his. The power of that simple realization sang through him.

If he kissed her now, there would be that instant fire. He felt it searing his nerve endings. He could have her right now, right against the wall where they stood. He was skilled enough and she was ready. The sex would be hot and hard. Wonderful.

And wrong for her. Ryder gave his head a little shake to rid it of the images that had tumbled in. He'd seen that vulnerable look in her eyes—that fear that she'd fail. So he'd go slowly with her this first time. He might not be good at planning, but he would do his best to stick to this one.

Ryder drew in a deep breath and felt it turn to steam in his lungs. To keep his hands as well as his mind occupied, he unsnapped her slacks and then pushed them to the floor. When he caught a glimpse of the white lace thong, his own breath hitched.

"Doc, you're killing me here," he murmured as he ran a finger along the thin band of lace that curved beneath her navel. "I feel like it's my birthday, and I just opened the best present ever."

"You can thank my sister Rory for them," she said.

"I will indeed." It took some effort, but he managed to

draw both his hand and his gaze away from the bit of nothing that was covering her. "I'm not good at plans, but I had
one when we came in here."

Once more he fought off the impulse to grab her, to lift
her so that she could wrap those long legs around him
again and he could take her right where they stood.

Her eyes, the deep-blue color of a calm sea at twilight,
were steady on his. Raising his hands, he touched only her
hair, threading his fingers through it the way he'd been
wanting to.

"I think in our phone conversation I started here." He
kept his eyes on hers as he traced one finger down her
throat. "Your skin is so delicate here. I can feel your pulse
pushing against my finger," he said, echoing the words
he'd used during the phone call.

She could feel it, too. Her whole body was reaching out
to him, yearning. She trembled as he brushed his fingers
over the lace that covered the tops of her breasts. Little explosions of pleasure shot along her nerve endings. Then
he was circling his thumbs ever so lightly over her nipples. She felt them harden, straining for a closer, firmer
contact.

"Is this as good as you imagined when we were talking
on the phone?" he asked.

She had to gather her thoughts and struggled to form
the word. "Better."

"Good."

Then he began the whole process over again with his
mouth. Shudders moved through her as he used his tongue
on the pulse at her throat. His mouth was hot and so soft.
The sudden scrape of his teeth along her collarbone had
her gasping his name.

"This wasn't part of the original scenario," Ryder murmured as he moved his mouth lower. The warmth of his breath on her skin sent spears of heat right to her center.

"Sometimes there's value in going with the flow. Wouldn't you say?"

Yes. She would have said it if she could have. But her breath backed up in her throat as he slid his tongue beneath the lace that rode along the tops of her breasts. She knew she was still standing, her feet on the floor, her back against the wall, but Sierra would have sworn she was floating, suspended somewhere above the floor, as he continued to sample her as if she were a delicacy he'd been craving.

At long last, he shoved the lace aside and took the tip of one breast into his mouth.

She shuddered and arched her body.

Even as he turned his attention to her other breast, his hand moved lower to trace the lace ribbon of the thong where it disappeared between her legs.

"Ryder." She wasn't sure if she moaned or said the word.

"You fascinate me, Dr. Gibbs."

Sierra sighed, seduced by the words as much as his touch.

He retraced the ribbon of the thong again and again.

"Please." This time she heard the breathless sound of the word.

"Do you want me to touch you inside?"

"Yes."

He pushed lace aside, parted her and felt her close around his finger as he entered. She was so hot, so wet, and even tighter than he'd imagined. Struggling against the need to rush, Ryder withdrew his finger.

"No," she protested.

"Shhh," he murmured as he slid two fingers into her,

then curved them and began to explore. When he thought he had the right spot, he began to rub.

She arched against him. "Ryder, I…can't…"

"Yes, you can." Keeping the pressure steady, he increased the pace. "Let loose, Doc. C'mon. Come for me."

She cried his name as her whole body stiffened. He watched as the climax moved through her and finally peaked. Then he caught her against him when her body went weak.

Once again two competing needs spiked inside him. He wanted to drag her to the floor and pound himself into her. But he also wanted to give her more. He wanted to give them both more. Holding her close, he sank with her to the floor. Then he positioned himself between her legs and began to use his mouth on her. Her dark, rich flavor filled him, drugged him, and sapped his control. When her body bowed as she tried to reach for her next climax, he clamped his hands on her thighs and drew back.

She gasped his name, and he knew that her quick, agile mind was thinking only of him. Feeling intensely powerful, he leaned forward and began to taste her again.

SHE COULDN'T THINK. The sensations were so sharp, the world he'd shot her into so airless. She'd never known her response could be this intense, this nuanced. She'd thought that there couldn't be any more, that she was sated, but with his teeth and tongue and lips he was tempting her to reach for more.

But it was just beyond her grasp. Each time she came close, he withdrew until the possibility passed.

"Please." She wanted him to stop. She wanted him to go on.

"Just a little longer," he murmured.

He continued to hold her right there on the edge where the promise of pleasure fueled an almost intolerable greed.

She wanted, no she needed more. But that clever, wicked mouth only teased and promised.

"Soon," he taunted. But at the last moment, he pressed his hands hard against her thighs and once more withdrew his mouth. A moment later, he left her entirely. The shock of it, the loss tore through her.

"Do you want me inside you, Sierra?"

"Yes." Opening her eyes, she saw that he'd risen to his knees. He'd shoved his jeans down and was sheathing himself in a condom. Strength poured through her, and she got to her knees.

"Come," he murmured as he reached for her.

Grabbing hold of his shoulders, she positioned herself so that she was straddling him. Together, they lifted her hips so that he was just pressing against her entrance. His fingers gripped her hard, but she used gravity to lower herself onto him.

He drew in a sharp breath. "I don't want to hurt you."

She sank a bit lower. "You will if you don't hurry."

His laugh was short, harsh. "I'm afraid I'll be in too much of a hurry. I want to take this slow and easy."

This time it was her turn to take a sharp breath as she lowered herself even farther. "Fast...I want fast."

Ryder felt his choices and his control slipping as she wiggled until he was filling her to the hilt. Then he began to move.

A moment later, she was moving with him, matching his thrusts, and crying out his name. He watched her ride out the climax, holding his own back. He wanted to capture this image of her in his mind. When he felt her go limp, he held her close. But it seemed only seconds passed

before she began to move again, gripping his hips and pis-
toning herself on him.

He could have sworn that he heard something inside
himself snap. Then he was moving too, driving himself
deeper and deeper into her until he knew nothing but a dark
explosion of pleasure.

THE ROOM was quiet except for the sound of breathing and
the soft lap of the water against the side of the boat. Those
details were the first sign to Sierra that her mind was beginning to clear. She and Ryder were lying on the floor,
tucked together like spoons. Sunlight was pouring through
the window behind them. She could feel the warmth of it
on her shoulder and legs, but it couldn't compete with the
heat radiating from the hard length of Ryder's body,
pressed against her backside. His arms were wrapped se-
curely around her, and she'd never felt better in her life.

If it hadn't meant moving, she would have searched for
her bag and dug out a note card so that she could list what
she'd done and what she'd felt. And what Ryder had done
to her. She never wanted to forget a second of it. But she
didn't want to move either. She could have lain just like
this for hours. Perhaps she already had?

The thought had other details flooding into her mind—
Mark Anderson's disappearance, the shooting, the escape
from her apartment. And the key.

"Are you all right?" Ryder levered himself up and
turned her so that he could see her face.

"Yes. I'm fine. I just—"

He moved his hands to her shoulders. "You're all tense.
Was I too rough with you?"

"No. You were…amazing. I—" She hesitated when
the thought occurred to her that perhaps the experience

hadn't been as amazing to him. "Was it…I mean…did you enjoy it?"

He smiled slowly before he leaned down and brushed his lips over hers. "Do you want me to give you a grade, Doc? Maybe rate you on a scale of one to ten?"

She stiffened until his lips pressed more firmly against hers. He took the kiss deeper, and she felt her muscles melt and her bones begin to soften. No one had ever made her feel this way with a kiss.

When he finally raised his head, he waited until she met his eyes and said, "I enjoyed it so much that I can't wait to try another position." He sighed. "But I think it's time to put your compartmentalizing plan into use and get to that second favor you asked for."

A cell phone rang, and Ryder reached for his jeans. After extracting it, he raised it to his ear. "Ryder here."

Sierra studied him in the ensuing silence. Whatever the news was, it didn't look good. Glancing at her, he mouthed, "Matt Ramsey."

Then he said into the phone, "Keep it out of the papers. And I'll post a guard at his door twenty-four/seven. Yeah. I'll keep you posted."

"What?" she asked the moment he closed his cell.

"A jogger found Mark Anderson lying in the woods off one of the bicycle paths in Rock Creek Park. He's alive, but barely. Ramsey's going to keep it out of the papers. He'll call me as soon as they know more."

As he began to gather up his scattered clothes, Sierra rose and went to the dresser to rummage through her canvas bag. "I just remembered. I have something that I didn't give the police. I just found it this morning. It must have dropped out of the book Mark handed me."

Ryder took the key from her outstretched palm and

studied it. "Number 123. Looks like it belongs to one of those lockers where you put in money and then take out the key."

"The question is which locker?"

"Yeah."

"And what's in the locker that Mark would give you the key?" Sierra asked.

"Something that he didn't want the thugs following him to get their hands on. Which means even though they snatched him, they're still looking for something. That would explain why they trashed his apartment and erased files on his office computer. And why they searched your place last night. They don't have what they want yet."

"It has to be the story he's working on. They obviously don't want anyone to know about it."

Ryder tossed the key into the air and caught it in his palm. "When he called to cancel our first meeting at the Blue Pepper, I caught the words *hot* and *political*."

"I'm betting he kept notes. I always take notes when I do research."

"If that's what's in the locker, we have to find them before our competitors do. And we have to work fast because he may have told them where the locker is."

"But they don't have the key," Sierra pointed out. "He wanted you to have the key."

"And he also left me something that might help us figure out where the locker is."

"What?"

He fished the Palm Pilot out of his jeans pocket. "Just a little something that I didn't hand over to the police either. Mark managed to drop this before they shoved him into that van. It's got his appointment schedule in it."

"Do you have any idea where the locker is?"

"Not yet. I skimmed through his schedule last night and took some notes. I'm willing to bet it's somewhere between the newspaper office and the Capitol. Or it's close to the Blue Pepper. He probably had to stash whatever it is in a hurry. We'll try to figure it out over breakfast." Taking her shoulders, he gave her a little push toward the shower. "A smart lady I know said that two heads are better than one for that kind of stuff."

When he followed her into the shower and turned the spray on, she said, "I've never showered with a man before."

"Want me to leave?"

She moved toward him and placed a hand on his chest. "I'm thinking that two heads might be better than one when it comes to showering too."

"I think we're on the same page there, Doc. But we wouldn't want to jump to conclusions without testing the theory." Drawing her with him, he stepped into the spray. Then he leaned down and said. "I just thought of a new position we ought to test out, too."

She laughed as he lifted her and pressed her against the shower wall.

9

RYDER LOVED PUZZLES, and the woman seated across from him dipping a French fry delicately in ketchup was the most intriguing one he'd run into in his whole life. She'd barely said a word on the drive to the shopping mall on the outskirts of DC. He'd spent most of the time on his cell phone arranging to have his men cover Mark Anderson's hospital room and collecting reports from the assignments he'd given them.

Most women would have peppered him with questions each time he'd finished a call. Instead, Sierra had found a classical music station on the car radio to help her think. Though she'd leaned back and closed her eyes, he had almost heard that first-class brain of hers clicking along at warp speed. In between his phone calls, he'd found the silence that stretched between them... companionable.

Although he'd never worked with a partner in his life, and certainly not one he was supposed to be protecting, he was beginning to feel at ease with her. Why? That, he was going to figure out. Just as he was going to figure her out.

Right now she was chewing on her bottom lip and frowning down at a street map of DC she'd picked up at a mall kiosk. At noon, the food court was busy. Above the noise of conversations and a thoroughly disgruntled baby at a nearby table came the sound of canned music. He was pretty sure that Sierra had isolated herself from all of it.

From what she'd said and what he'd observed, she'd led a pretty isolated life so far. And now because he'd agreed to do two favors for her, he was put in the position of drawing her out of the cocoon she'd wrapped herself in and setting her free. The prospect of that intrigued him. It also scared the hell out of him because something told him that Sierra wasn't the only one who would change during the process.

She'd spread the street map out on one side of the food in front of her, and a blue note card sat on the other side. She'd left the canvas bag in the car, but she'd brought one of the note cards with her. Every so often, she would take a bite of her cheeseburger or reach for a French fry. Then she'd jot another note down on her card.

She'd explained when she picked up the map that she was going to go over Mark's appointment schedule and then trace the possible routes he'd taken the day he was snatched.

"Any ideas yet about where we're going to find the lock that the key fits?" he asked.

She set down her half-eaten cheeseburger and picked up the Palm Pilot he'd given her, which shared Mark's schedule for the day he'd been shoved into the van. "For 10:00 a.m. it says the Esquire Health and Fitness Club."

"I did some checking. The Esquire is a club that caters to political bigwigs—members of the Senate and House, ambassadors from other countries, visiting dignitaries. Mark isn't a member."

"He could have been an invited guest."

"That's what I'm thinking."

"At three, he had a meeting with someone at Le Print-emps," Sierra said.

"That's an exclusive hotel that prides itself on offering privacy to guests."

Sierra nodded. "I've been there. My sister Rory's fiancé is thinking of buying it because they met for the first time there in the lobby. I wonder who Mark met."

"Yeah. We're going to check it out."

"And at five, he wrote down the Blue Pepper. That was his meeting with you." She turned the map around so that he could read it. "I've marked the possible routes between those places. What's your best guess for the location of the locker?"

"Union Station." Ryder tapped a finger on the map. "It's right there almost on a direct line between the Esquire Club and Le Printemps."

"I thought of that, but if he knew he was being followed that last day, a stop at Union Station might raise suspicions. I'm wondering what kind of lockers they have at the Esquire."

"Good thinking, Doc. We'll make that our first stop."

When she glanced up at him, there was a gleam of excitement in her eyes. "We could go there right now."

Ryder shook his head. "Not yet. First we're going to finish our lunch. Then we're going to do a little shopping."

Her eyes widened. "Shopping?"

"If we're right and Mark stashed his notes in a locker, then someone wants them just as much as we do. Chances are good that they'll be watching the spots he visited that last day. I don't want anyone recognizing you when we pay these places a visit. So we're going to change your appearance. I've packed some things for myself in my duffel bag, but you're going to need a complete wardrobe change. You up for that, Doc?"

She took a deep breath before she spoke. "Yes. Yes, I

think I am." Pausing, she lifted a French fry halfway to her mouth, and then set it down. "I was just thinking that investigative work was a lot like the kind of research I do. But I've never had to wear a disguise before."

He took her hand and gave it a squeeze. "You'll do fine." Ryder's intuition was telling him that he might be the one who might not do so well. He couldn't help thinking of the complications Henry Higgins had run into when he'd transformed Eliza Doolittle. To ease her nerves and perhaps his own, he searched for a change of topic.

He shoved his box of French fries toward her and waited until she'd taken one.

"You fascinate me, Doc."

"Why?" She glanced up at him.

The surprise in her eyes and the almost instant coloring of her cheeks told him that she wasn't used to getting compliments from men. He'd have to fix that. "Why do you fascinate me? 'Let me count the ways.' For starters, most women I know don't eat fast food—at least not in public."

Sierra glanced down at the wrappers on the table as she shrugged. "It's quicker than getting something delivered—and very convenient. Sometimes when I get involved in a project, I forget to eat."

"Same here. What's your favorite fast food?"

"French fries. For delivery, it's pizza. But for takeout, I like chili. The Blue Pepper has a fabulous recipe."

Ryder nodded again. "It's excellent, but I know someone who makes it even better. You'll have to try it. Another thing that I'm curious about is those note cards. Why blue?"

Her smile was wry. "A remnant from my childhood, I suppose. My father was color-blind, and blue was about the only color he could see. He always said it was his favorite, so I used to surround myself with blue things. I suppose in the hope that he would notice me."

"I don't know how he could have missed you." He glanced at the straw-colored linen jacket and slacks she was wearing. "I notice that you don't wear a lot of color these days."

She shrugged. "My strategy didn't work. He left us all when my sisters and I were ten."

"And you compensated by burying yourself in school-work?"

Her chin lifted. "I discovered I was good at it. I wasn't adventurous like Natalie and I was never brave enough to dash into life head-on the way Rory did. The academic life seemed to suit me."

And you don't wear blue or strong colors of any kind anymore, he thought.

"What about you? How did you end up in the security business?"

He smiled. "I discovered I was good at it."

Her lips curved. "Touché." She set down her pen and took off her glasses. "How did you discover you were so good at security work?"

How indeed? It had been a long time since Ryder had allowed himself to think about his early life on the streets of Baltimore. Maybe she had a right to know the truth about him before things went any further between them.

Meeting her eyes, he said, "I misspent most of my youth breaking the law, outwitting cops and security guards, and I was good at that. My experience gave me first-hand knowledge of how the criminal mind works."

For a moment, she didn't say anything. He searched those clear blue eyes, but he didn't see any trace of shock or fear or disgust. He should have seen all three.

"Why?"

It wasn't the reaction he'd expected. "Doesn't my checkered past worry you at all?"

"Why should it? My father was an international jewel thief who wouldn't give up his career to share a life with his family." She paused and then said, "And you're avoiding my question. Why did you decide on a life of crime?"

He regarded her steadily. "Partly for the sheer fun of it."

She nodded. "You remind me of my father. That's the part of his profession he couldn't give up. The risk factor. My sister Natalie says she can understand that craving for adventure, but I never could. I was always too afraid."

He reached for one of her hands and brought it to his lips. "Perhaps I can change that."

"I think you already have," she said in a dry tone that he was coming to enjoy. He scraped his teeth on her knuckle and watched her eyes darken this time to the deep-blue color of the ocean on a cloudy day.

"You're still avoiding my question. You decided on a life of crime partly for the fun of it and partly for what else?"

He might have tried a lie. He was certainly skilled at telling them. But there was something about those eyes that compelled the truth. "My mother left town when I was twelve, and my aunt became my legal guardian. A couple of years later, she became ill and needed surgery. Then her sick leave ran out, and her boss terminated her because the cost of insurance for his employees was going to skyrocket."

"Isn't that illegal?" she asked tightening her grip on his hand.

"Sure. A lot of things are illegal. That doesn't mean that people can't get away with doing them."

"So you decided to even the score by doing some illegal things yourself—and getting away with them."

It wasn't criticism he saw in her eyes, but understanding. It had a warmth spreading through him that he hadn't felt in a very long time. "My aunt got her operation."

"And you never got caught?" she asked.

He shook his head. "I couldn't afford to. She wouldn't have approved of my strategy. If she'd learned about it, it would have killed her. As it was, she died anyway from complications after surgery."

"I'm so sorry." Sierra turned her hand and linked her fingers with his.

Ryder said nothing. He was too shocked. He'd never told anyone about how his aunt had died, but the words had slipped out so easily.

Then Sierra said, "Nat said that you might have done some black ops work for the government."

Ryder's mouth very nearly dropped open at her matter-of-fact tone. Maybe she could understand why he'd ventured into a life of crime when his aunt had taken ill. After all, she was a psychologist, and she had a kind heart. But if she knew about the work he'd done for the government, he couldn't for the life of him figure why she was sitting across from him right now.

He leaned forward. "Do you have any idea what black ops are?" he asked.

"Just what I've picked up from movies and books."

"That's fantasy stuff. I've killed people, Doc."

Her eyes remained steady on his. There'd been a trace of fear when he'd told her that he was going to change her appearance, but he couldn't see even a flicker of it now. What kind of a woman was he dealing with?

"You shouldn't be here with me, Doc. Your father's career aside, we come from very different worlds."

"I know." Her eyes never wavered from his. "But from

the first time we met, I felt this connection. It doesn't seem to matter that we're different. I feel that I know you. Can you understand that?"

He nodded. He shouldn't be able to understand it, but wasn't he feeling the same way?

She continued, "I could never have asked you the two quid pro quo favors, or done what we've done together if I hadn't felt this connection with you," she said.

He turned her hand over and pressed his lips against her palm. Even as he watched her eyes darken again, he lectured himself. He should never have agreed to do those favors. Hell, he never should have asked her for any favors in the first place. But he didn't withdraw his hand from hers. "We could be skating on pretty thin ice here, Doc. You have any second thoughts, you let me know."

"I don't have any second thoughts. Do you?"

He smiled at her. "No room for them. I'm too busy thinking of what position we could try next."

When the blush stained her cheeks, he lifted his milkshake and tapped it lightly against hers. "Let's drink to that feeling of connection. For as long as it lasts."

As soon as Ryder said the words, Sierra felt a sliver of pain pierce her heart. Nevertheless, she was grateful that he'd said what she already knew to be true. Whatever was between them was temporary. She'd better remember that. They did come from different worlds, and on top of that, he was too much like her father to want to spend an extended amount of time with someone as ordinary as she was. She could accept that, the same way she'd come to accept what Harry had done. If there was one lesson she'd learned from life it was that, with the exception of her sisters, she was better off not depending on anyone, because you always faced disappointment if you did.

But that didn't mean that she couldn't enjoy the time she had with Ryder. Especially when what he was offering her was so much more than she'd ever hoped for. Lifting her milkshake, she took a sip, and then said, "Are you done with your fries?"

"I'm willing to share."

While she dunked one in ketchup, he turned the blue note card around. "You've got a real knack for making lists."

"It helps me to think."

"I've always admired people who can plan and organize."

"I've always admired people who don't have to."

"Different worlds again, Doc. Dodging cops on the streets of Baltimore taught me to rely on instinct and intuition. Plans are okay to a point, but in my experience, even the most well-laid ones have to be changed. Take my plan for handling you. It vanished the moment you asked for two favors."

Glancing back down at the note card, he read it out loud. "Number one, book on the unsung heroes of Vietnam—section that mentions Vice President John Gracie. Number two, Vice President Gracie's upcoming trip to Korea. Number three, book on the vice presidency."

"There's an obvious, recurring theme here," Sierra said. "Repetitions and patterns are very significant in the research I do."

"You think the vice president is involved in this?" Ryder asked.

"I think we have to consider it. Mark's words to you were *hot* and *political.* You're convinced that whoever is behind Mark's attempted murder is someone with a lot of power."

"The vice president has that all right. He also has a huge following, and there's never been a breath of scandal around him. His personal life could be a poster for the all-American family. When his wife died five years ago, they'd been happily married for over thirty years. Shortly after that, his son, Jack, became both his chief of staff and his campaign manager. There's even a rumor that there's another political family dynasty in the making."

"I think we should pay him a visit," Sierra said.

Ryder grinned at her. "Me, too, but getting an appointment with the vice president is tricky business. Your sister and Ramsey might have to be the ones to do that—unless we can find Mark's notes. There might be something there that we can use as leverage."

"I also looked at Mark's schedule for the previous day, the day he cancelled his appointment with you. He wanted your perspective on something, this story he was working on, but he cancelled. I was wondering why."

"The connection was bad, but I caught the word *delayed*. Maybe he met with someone else. Are you finished with that cheeseburger?"

She pushed it toward him, then used the stylus on the Palm Pilot. A moment later, she frowned. "His schedule for the previous two days is blank. If he had to clear his schedule for two days, maybe he went on a trip."

Rising, he gripped her by the shoulders and drew her up for a quick kiss. "Good work, Doc. Come to think of it, maybe *delayed* had to do with a plane or a train." He reached for his phone and punched in numbers. "I'll have one of my men check into it."

Sierra sat back down in her chair. Her lips were vibrating again. Was she ever going to get used to his kisses? While Ryder gave orders to someone on his cell phone, she tried to gather her thoughts. By the time he finished his call, she was focused again.

"Let's get started," she said.

He began to pile the wrappers from their food on a tray. "Step one is your makeover."

SIERRA STARED at the image in the mirror and tried not to gape. *Makeover* was much too weak a word for what had been done to her. She didn't recognize herself. This must have been what Eliza Doolittle had felt like when Henry Higgins had finished with her. But at least for Eliza the change had occurred gradually. For one panicked moment, she looked around for her canvas bag, and then she remembered that they'd left it in the car.

"You all right?" Ryder asked from somewhere behind her.

She nodded and was surprised to see the woman in the mirror nod too. Together they drew in a deep breath and let it out.

Sierra could see Ryder's image in the mirror, and Julius, the hairdresser, was there too. His anxious face was hovering to her left. Melinda, the personal shopper that Ryder had hired to assemble some outfits for her, was to her right. But Sierra couldn't take her eyes off the stranger staring back at her.

She felt Ryder's hand on her shoulder. He pitched his voice low this time so that only she could hear. "You're sure you're all right?"

"I feel like I've been swept up in a reality TV nightmare," she said dryly. "That's not me in the mirror."

Ryder kept his voice low. "It's just a part of you."

Sierra wasn't so sure. She'd certainly never envisioned herself looking quite like this. The long hair was gone. That had been the first shock. The woman staring back at her had fringed bangs and layers of blond hair framing her face and curving in below her chin. Lifting her hands, she pulled the hair back and took in a relieved breath when she discovered that she could still fasten it into a ponytail if she wanted to. Now the face in the mirror seemed a bit more familiar, and she took comfort in that.

"Let's get her out from under that robe so we can see the total effect."

It was the personal shopper talking. Melinda was a petite brunette who weighed less than one hundred pounds and looked as though she'd just stepped out of the pages of a fashion magazine. Seconds later, Sierra found herself standing in front of a three-way full-length mirror. Oh, no. This definitely wasn't her at all. A lacey little shell stopped well short of her waist. So did the faded, hip-hugging jeans. Instead of a belt, Melinda had threaded a gauzy white scarf through the belt loops, assuring her that doing so was the current trend in Hollywood.

Sierra raised a hand to her chest. Once again, the woman in the mirror imitated the movement. Her hand sported a French manicure, and so did her toes. She glanced down to see them peeking out of high-heeled red sandals.

Oh yes, she'd definitely been swept up in a reality TV nightmare. Sierra reminded herself to breathe as a kaleidoscope of MTV-like video images streamed rapidly through her mind. The entire makeover had taken less than two hours—thanks to the fact that Ryder had either bullied or bribed people into making it happen.

The personal shopper had made her model at least ten

outfits for Ryder until he'd settled on three. The "jean ensemble" she was wearing, a pale-blue silk business suit that made her feel like an Alfred Hitchcock heroine, and a red slip dress that left more of her bare than it covered. In addition to that, Ryder had picked up a baseball cap, sunglasses, a jean jacket, a purse and heaven knew what else. The duffel he'd stuffed everything into seemed bottomless.

Two hours. That wasn't much time to engineer a total transformation unless, of course, you were some kind of a fairy godmother. And yet Ryder had accomplished it. No wonder he'd led the Baltimore cops on a merry chase. She shifted her gaze to his image in the mirror for a moment. He was standing only a few feet away, and he looked worried. About her.

What she saw in his eyes stiffened her spine immediately. All her life people had worried about her. First her parents, then her sisters. Wasn't that part of what she wanted to change?

She glanced back at the stranger in the mirror. Hadn't Ryder just told her that the woman in the mirror was a part of her? Whoever she was, she looked like someone who wouldn't be tempted to hide away in an office doing research. This woman looked like someone who lived life to the fullest. She also looked like someone who wouldn't be satisfied just doing research on sex. Sierra knew for a fact that she was never going to be satisfied with that again either. So they did have something in common.

The woman looking back at her wasn't Wonder Woman. But she wasn't Jane Eyre either. In fact, she looked a lot like the woman Sierra Gibbs would like to be. The question was—did she have the courage to really walk in this woman's shoes?

Yes. Yes. Yes. She drew in one last deep breath and let it out. Then, straightening her shoulders, she turned to face Ryder. "You're right. She is a part of me."

"You like, then?" Julius asked, clasping his hands together in delight.

"Yes, I like. I like very much."

Ryder took her hand. "I like very much also."

Then she spoke in an undertone only he could hear. "Can we please leave now?"

He threw back his head and laughed as he placed sunglasses on her nose and drew her out of the room. "My thought exactly."

10

SIERRA HAD almost mastered walking in the three-inch sandals by the time they pushed through the glass doors of the mall. The muggy heat slammed into her, almost stopping her in her tracks. But Ryder pulled her forward. They'd parked close, but thanks to the denim jacket and baseball cap Ryder had insisted she wear, she could feel sweat running down her back by the time they reached it.

While she waited for Ryder to unlock the door, she noticed the van. She might not have given it a second glance if it hadn't been blocking the path of a car pulling out of a space one lane over. The woman driving the car had to lean on her horn several times to get the driver to move.

She closed her hand around Ryder's wrist. "The next lane over, the dark van. Tell me I'm being paranoid."

"Shit!" Ryder exclaimed as a large man climbed out.

Sierra recognized him as the man who'd been beckoning her toward that same van last night. Icy fear filled her veins.

"You got good eyes, Doc," Ryder said, as he linked his fingers with hers. "Let's go."

Hand in hand, they raced back toward the mall entrance. Just before they reached the curb, something smacked into the asphalt to her right and propelled a small rock into her leg.

The big guy was shooting at them. Sierra's heart shot to her throat and plummeted to her stomach. As Ryder pulled the first door open, she caught the large man's reflection in the glass, and another man had joined him. By the time they made their way through the second door, their pursuers were entering the first door.

As they broke into a run, Ryder glanced at her, and she could see he was grinning. "Ready to have some fun?"

Fun? Before she could think of an adequate reply, he squeezed her hand. "Remember that scene in *North by Northwest,* right near the end? Cary Grant and Eva Marie Saint have just snatched the statue with the microfilm away from James Mason and they're racing through the woods."

Sierra drew in a deep breath. "I remember that they ended up hanging by their fingernails from Mount Rushmore."

Ryder laughed as they careened around a fountain. "Well, I hope it won't come to that. Just relax and follow my lead, Doc."

Relax? As they dodged an unsuspecting shopper, Sierra reminded herself to breathe. "You're not wearing three-inch heels."

"Thank heavens."

Indeed, Sierra thought. She didn't dare look down as they tore past one shop after another. Her feet seemed to be on auto pilot, and she certainly didn't want to interfere with whatever they were doing.

"Hang a right, Doc."

She did and nearly crashed into an astonished woman laden with bags. At the last moment, Ryder released her hand and she veered around the woman, then joined hands again with him. They were eating up ground, but based on the disgruntled noises and shouts behind them, their pursuers were close.

She could hear her own breath whistling and her ankles were registering major complaints when they reached the next corner. A column of glass-walled elevators blocked their path and on either side of them escalators rose slowly toward the upper two levels of the mall.

Just then one of the elevators opened its doors, and people flowed out.

"This way." Turning on a dime, Ryder pulled her toward it, angling his way along the edge of the crowd. They squeezed into the elevator just as the doors began to slide shut.

Sierra caught a glimpse of the two large men trying to fight their way towards them. They weren't going to make it in time, and they didn't look like happy campers. Her relief was short-lived. As the elevator inched its way up to the second level, she peered through the glass and saw their pursuers start to push their way up one of the escalators.

"They're gaining on us," she said.

"Give me your hat and the sunglasses, and take your jacket off."

Turning, she saw he had the duffel open and he was already pulling on a white T-shirt with Orioles scrawled across the front. When she handed him her baseball cap and sunglasses, he put them on, the hat backwards, and then stuffed her denim jacket into the duffel.

"Sorry." He grinned at her as he ran his fingers through her hair to muss it a bit. "We don't have time to change your shoes."

They'd been shot at and two men built like trucks were chasing them. Her heart was beating like a metronome on speed, and Ryder looked like a man who was having the time of his life. "I don't understand you," she said.

"It takes time. I'm an acquired taste."

When the elevator stopped, he locked his hand on hers and said, "They'll be looking for a woman in a baseball cap and a man in a black T-shirt. So we'll just stroll out of here, and then run on my signal. Got it?"

Praying that her ankles would survive, she nodded as the doors slid open. She caught sight of one heavyset man scanning the throng of people pouring out of the elevator, but she kept her gaze straight ahead to where three rows of shops fanned out like the spokes of a wheel. Ryder chose the one to their right, and the moment they turned the corner, he said, "Run."

They did. Later the images and sensations would come back to her—feet pounding on polished marble floors, skidding and recovering as her muscles strained and her ankles screamed. She'd also recall the wide eyes of oncoming shoppers as they parted to let them through. She'd almost gotten used to the burning sensation in her lungs when Ryder hung a right into a narrow hall. He picked up the pace then, dragging her past a bank of phone booths, an ATM machine, restrooms, until he reached a door with no label on it.

Sierra dragged in air while he tried the door with no success. As he rummaged in the duffel, he shot her that wicked grin again. "Having fun yet?"

He didn't wait for an answer. Not that she could have given him one. Speech was a ways off yet. In the meantime, Ryder dropped to his knees and inserted a thin piece of metal into the lock. "Watch my back, Doc."

She turned. They were at the far end of a corridor, but the lighting was good. Anyone passing by would be able to see them quite clearly. Five seconds and then ten ticked by. She didn't catch so much as a glimpse of the two large men. Had they given them the slip? Her heartbeat wasn't racing quite as fast. And she suddenly realized that it wasn't fear, but a strange sense of exhilaration that had filled her. Could it possibly mean that she *was* having fun?

"Bingo," Ryder murmured as the door clicked open. Then he rose and pulled her into a small, dark room and closed the door. Before she could even think, he grabbed her and planted his mouth on hers in a long, consuming kiss. In that instant, she wanted nothing more than him.

It was just that simple. Just that terrifying.

She was trembling when he broke off the kiss and said, "You were great. Fabulous. You're a natural."

His words of praise sent a mix of feelings tumbling through her: doubt, hope, astonishment. When he pulled her close for a hard hug, she let herself simply cling to him. A natural? He had to be kidding. She'd never in her life even imagined herself dodging bullets and escaping from bad guys. That was something Natalie was good at. Or Rory. But not Sierra.

And yet she had. Since she'd met Ryder Kane, she'd done a lot of things she'd never imagined herself doing. When he drew back, she tried to study his features in the dim light from the red exit sign above the door. He wasn't grinning now, and his eyes looked very dark.

"You all right?" he asked as he tucked a strand of hair behind her ear. "You need your inhaler or anything?"

She shook her head. "No, I don't." The more she thought about it, the more she became convinced that she hadn't really needed it for a long time except as a crutch.

"Good," he said with a short nod.

A few seconds passed, and neither one of them moved. Gradually, Sierra's body began to register that it was still pressing lightly against his. And the heat began to build at each and every contact point.

She cleared her throat. "What are we doing in here?"

"Buying ourselves a little time. There's a possibility that those goons will give up and go back and wait by your car."

"But you don't think so."

"No. One of them may go back to wait at the car, but I'm betting the other two will prowl the mall for a while. They know the general location of where we disappeared. Whoever is behind this is dead serious, and I suspect that person has both powerful connections and deep pockets. There's only one way they could have located us here at the mall. They must have been able to put a tap on Ramsey's phone."

"And they pinpointed the location of your cell phone?"

He smiled. "Yeah. The technology is expensive, but it's out there."

"How much time are we buying?" Sierra asked.

"Enough for me to come up with a plan."

"You don't have one?"

"I'm sure that intuition will kick in at any moment." With a finger he played with her earring. "You know, sometimes it helps if I get involved with something else that takes my mind off the problem for a while."

"Really."

Ryder laughed softly. "That dry tone of yours really gets to me, Doc. What I was thinking of was to put favor number two on the back burner for a while and work on favor number one."

"You want to compartmentalize."

"Exactly."

"In a locked utility closet in a mall?" The idea amused and thrilled her at the same time.

He raised her hand and kissed her fingers. "I'm good at improvising."

She'd never before thought that she was. But the intimacy of the situation and what he was suggesting had images tumbling into her mind. And the teasing way he was seducing her was somehow even more erotic than if he'd just kissed her. She took a quick look around the cramped space, and then met his gaze. "We might have to invent a new position."

Ryder grinned at her. "I'm your man. But before we do, I've got a little fantasy that's been running through my mind ever since you stepped out of that dressing room in those jeans. Are you game?"

She nodded.

He set his duffel down on one of the counters. "Okay, back away as far as you can."

As she did, Ryder moved until his back was against the door. The room was lined with counters and shelves, making the space they stood in about three by three. "Now, take that scarf off."

Sierra blinked at him as she moved her hand to the knot at her waistband. "This scarf?"

"Yeah." From the moment she'd stepped out of the dressing room Ryder had thought she'd looked like a present a man might risk anything to open. "Take it off."

She did. Slowly, pulling it free from her belt loops inch by inch, holding his gaze all the while. When it was all the way out, she draped it around her neck. "Step two?"

"The jeans."

When she unsnapped them, the noise was loud in the room, and as she began to slide the zipper down, he was sure he heard the sound of each piece of metal unlinking.

"It's exciting to watch you," she said.

"Ditto."

When she slid the jeans down her legs, he swallowed hard. "You're not wearing any panties."

"The pair I was wearing showed above the waistline of the jeans, so…" She stepped out of the jeans.

He unfastened his own and freed himself. Then he found the condom, slipping it on as he moved toward her. "I'm going to have to skip a few steps here." In one smooth move, he closed his hands around her hips and lifted her against the wall. "I think we're going to have to repeat a position too. I can't seem to help myself."

"Not a problem," Sierra said, wrapping her legs around him and doing everything she could to urge him closer.

"Don't wiggle." He lifted her, found her and thrust in.

"Ryder."

The thready sound of her voice as she said his name pulled at his control. He could feel the strain on every muscle as he held himself still.

She was the first to move, but he gripped her waist hard when he heard the approaching footsteps. "Shhh."

When it took only that one warning whisper to still her, he was again impressed by this woman.

"What?" The word was barely a breath in his ear.

"Footsteps," he whispered as the sound grew closer.

Neither of them breathed as the steps slowed to a stop on the other side of the door. Holding her against the wall, he withdrew and lowered her carefully to the floor.

Meeting her eyes, he mouthed, "Stay." Then moving silently, he reached for the duffel, pulled out his gun, and turned, keeping her behind him as he adjusted his jeans. He'd bolted the door from the inside, but he couldn't be sure that a key wouldn't release it. On the other hand, a person with a key wasn't likely to be one of the two thugs they'd been running from. Either way, if someone came through that door, they were not going to see Sierra.

The knob turned slowly. Then the door clicked against the jam.

The bolt held.

Again the knob turned, and the bolt held. Five seconds stretched into ten before the footsteps sounded once more and gradually faded away.

Ryder slipped his gun back into the duffel. Behind him Sierra said nothing. What could she say? he thought. The gun was a concrete illustration of what he used to do for a living, and a reminder of how different their worlds were. A definite mood breaker. But when he turned, it wasn't shock or disgust he saw in her eyes. Even in the dim light, it was clear to him that she was sitting on the floor, silently laughing.

Laughing. Kneeling down, he used a finger to tilt up her chin so he could see her eyes. "Doc, I am never going to figure you out. What the hell is so funny?"

She clamped a hand over her mouth as she tried to swallow the laugh, but she couldn't. He saw the tears come to her eyes before she managed to gather control. Finally, she said, "I think that gives new meaning to the phrase, coitus interruptus."

Shaking his head, he joined in her laughter, sitting down on the floor next to her and pulling her close. When their amusement finally subsided, she laid her head in the hollow between his shoulder and his neck, and for a moment, as the silence stretched between them, he felt a warmth move through him.

Then she removed the white scarf from around her neck and said, "Now where were we before we were so rudely interrupted?"

"I was in the middle of a lust attack."

"Ah, yes. I have an idea…about this scarf. I came across it in my research for my book…" Leaning forward, she whispered her step-by-step plan in his ear.

Ryder cleared his throat. "It's an interesting idea, and you're very persuasive, but step three has me a bit worried."

STEP THREE had her a bit worried, too. But she'd done the interview herself. She'd taken very careful notes, and she was very curious about just how it would work. It was the way he'd looked at the scarf when she'd been taking it off that had given her the idea. And she'd felt the way his hands had tightened on her as she'd described what she wanted to do. When in the world would she ever have another chance to try it out?

She smiled at him before she brushed her lips lightly against his. "Just follow my lead."

He grinned at her. "Touché, Doc."

"Now step one is very simple. All you have to do is take your jeans off."

Sierra thought her heart might just pound out of her chest as she watched him rise and do just that. Step two was trickier. But she could do it. When he stepped out of his briefs, her throat went dry and she couldn't stop herself from reaching out a hand to touch him.

"If you do that, we're never going to get to step two."

"Okay, but then I'll want a rain check," she said. Then gathering her focus, she glanced up at him. "The position is a little tricky."

"My specialty." He knelt down again. "Just turn around."

"First, I have to tie the scarf." She carefully looped it

over the base of his penis. Then she gently tied it. "Is that okay?"

"You're doing fine, Doc. You want to put the condom on?"

The tightness in his voice had her glancing up, and the heat in his eyes was enough to sear her nerve endings. She moistened her lips. "I can do that."

"Fine." He handed it to her.

It took her a few seconds, the quick hitch of his breath making her fumble. When she was satisfied, she couldn't resist running her fingers down the length of him.

He groaned. "You're running out of time, Doc. If you still want to try this scarf thing, you'd better turn around."

As she turned, she lifted one leg over the scarf so that she was straddling it. Once she was on her knees facing away from him, she said, "Not I'm supposed to pull the ends of the scarf taut. The tension is supposed to increase your pleasure. I'm going to do it now. Ready?"

"Go ahead."

She gently pulled the ends of the scarf until it was taut between her legs.

He groaned, and she immediately dropped the scarf. "Are you all right? Did I do it wrong?"

"You did it just fine, Doc. Damn near perfect."

"I'll do it again then. Just let me find—"

When she leaned over, he gripped her hips and drew her back. For a brief moment, she could feel the hard length of him between her legs, pressing, seeking.

"I—"

"It's time for step four." His mouth moved along her shoulder, sending little tremors through her. "Just relax."

"I'm trying, but I…ohhh."

He slid a finger into her and slowly withdrew it. The

pleasure was so sharp, so piercing that she lost both her breath and her concentration.

"Lean forward and prop your hands against the wall."

She would have done anything he asked. "Please."

She felt him enter her then, not all the way.

"I'm going to take you now, Doc. I can't wait any longer."

Then he was stretching her, filling her. The pressure and the angle of his penetration was so different. Slowly, he withdrew and then pushed into her again. "If you want me to stop…"

"No." Reaching back, she tried to get a grip on his hip. "Don't stop."

"Then hang on. It's going to be a hard ride."

Bracing her arms against the wall, Sierra rode with him. His thrusts were long and hard, and she met each one with greed, clenching her muscles around him to keep him inside for as long as she could. But it wasn't quite enough. "Faster," she urged.

Just when she thought she couldn't stand it anymore, he increased the pace. At the same time, he moved one hand from her hip to just the right spot between her legs. When he sank his teeth into her shoulder, the climax ripped through her. Before she let it sweep her up, she said, "Come with me, Ryder. Come with me."

Even as the world spun away, she felt him tighten his hold on her and thrust one last time.

"NICE SCARF TRICK," Ryder said when he could. He was sitting on the floor, and Sierra was on his lap, her head resting again in the crook of his shoulder. And he had no desire to move.

"I have more," Sierra told him.

"Good to know," Ryder said. "We probably shouldn't try them out here though."

"No. Of course not." She lifted her head and started to rise. "We have Mark Anderson to think of."

He gripped her hand and met her eyes. "We're going to solve this thing, Doc."

She nodded.

"And we're going to use that scarf again." He grinned at her. "I have some ideas of my own. In the meantime, intuition has struck." He took her hand and helped her rise. "Here's my escape plan. Step one, we change clothes."

Sierra put on the blue silk suit he tossed her along with pearl earrings, and she breathed a sigh of relief when he handed her a pair of sling-backs with two-inch heels.

"Wear the sunglasses again."

When she turned to glance at him, she blinked and stared. He was wearing linen pants with an unstructured navy jacket. The shirt was silk, open at the collar, and he had a gold and diamond ring on his pinky. But the most significant change in his appearance was the wig. It was blond and meticulously styled.

"If I passed you on the street, I wouldn't recognize you."

"That's the whole idea. The man who tried the door may or may not have been one of those goons who chased us. But we're going to proceed on the theory that they're out there still looking for us. They'll have someone at your car in case we try to use it."

"So what is step two?" Sierra asked.

He grinned at her. "We use a pay phone to call a taxi, and then we're going into DC. Our first stop is the Esquire Health and Fitness Club."

11

WHO WAS the real Sierra Gibbs?

Sierra pondered the question as she stood in the lobby of one of DC's posh chain hotels. Their exit from the shopping mall had been without incident, thanks to Ryder. But when their taxi had pulled up at the Esquire Health and Fitness Club, they hadn't gone in. Instead, Ryder had steered her across the street and into the crowded lobby of the hotel, saying, "I have some phone calls to make. I want to arrange a meeting this evening with your sister and Ramsey, and I don't dare use my cell."

Now she stood a few feet from where Ryder was making his calls, and she was studying her image in the glass wall of the lobby gift shop. The image was different than the one she'd seen in the dressing room. Then she'd looked like Britney Spears. In the blue suit, she looked sophisticated and sexy—a Hitchcock heroine. She kind of liked the look. Ryder would say that the woman staring back at her was a part of her, too, and she was almost coming to believe that.

What part of her would she see when she wore the red dress? she wondered.

The other question that she was occupying herself with while she waited for Ryder to finish his calls was—who was Ryder Kane?

Narrowing her eyes, Sierra turned and studied the suave-looking man standing just a few feet away and talking on the phone. She'd told him the truth in the utility closet. If she hadn't known who he was, she might never have recognized him. With his sunglasses, neatly arranged blond wig and designer clothes, he was a far cry from the man she'd first met in the Blue Pepper. This man was ultra smooth, a classy dresser, and he looked as if he frequented both a gym and a salon. A metrosexual. It occurred to Sierra that he would fit right in with the movers and shakers in the nation's Capitol.

Ryder Kane wouldn't ever fit into that crowd. Unless he wanted to.

She continued to study him as he dropped another quarter into the pay phone. Everything about the disguise he was wearing shouted class and money. Everything about the Ryder Kane who'd first kissed her in the Blue Pepper shouted danger and excitement.

She couldn't imagine the man currently in front of her pulling a gun, but Ryder looked perfectly natural when he held one. There was a dark, ruthless streak in him. But there was a rock-solid kindness too. Ryder Kane was a man who did favors for his friends. She thought of Mark Anderson and Jed Calhoun. And those friends turned to Ryder when they needed help.

There were so many facets to him. She wondered if she would ever get to know them all.

There wasn't a doubt in her mind that the man with the designer clothes and worldly airs who hung up the phone and turned toward her was someone who was much closer to her world. He'd probably come close to matching her sexual profile. But there wasn't a doubt in her mind that she preferred the real Ryder Kane to this smooth sophisticate.

What did that say about Sierra Gibbs? She'd always thought of herself as rational and sensible. But a rational, sensible woman would never have made love with a man in a utility closet.

"Ready?" Ryder asked as he took her arm.

"For what?"

He shot her a grin. "More fun."

Her brows shot up. "Tell me it won't involve running away from those two thugs who chased us through the mall."

"No. I think we've taken care of them for the moment. Your sister and Detective Ramsey are leaving for that shopping mall as we speak. If our friends are still there, they will be picked up for questioning and charged in the kidnapping of Mark Anderson."

"How is Mark?"

Ryder's grin faded. "No change. He's in a coma, but his parents are there, talking to him. The doctors say that there's hope. The guy who shot at you is in intensive care. Your sister and Ramsey have a man stationed outside his room so that he can be questioned as soon as he regains consciousness. According to Ramsey, Mark's editor can't confirm that he was out of town on Monday or Tuesday. One of my men is still checking plane, bus and train passenger lists."

They were nearly at the revolving doors leading to the street when she remembered to ask, "So what's your plan when we get to the Esquire Club?"

"We're going to test your theory that Mark left something for me in a locker there."

"I know that." She pulled him out of the stream of traffic. "Details might be nice."

He drew a finger along her jawline. "There's that haughty, sarcastic tone again. You know there's something very provocative about it—like you're issuing a challenge."

"You haven't answered my question."

He shrugged. "I can't. I won't know how to play it until I actually get in there."

"I'm not good at improvising."

His eyes darkened. "You did pretty well in that utility closet."

She had. They had. Sierra felt heat stream through her body. For a moment, all she was aware of was Ryder. He was close, their only point of contact his hand on her arm, but she felt the pull. And she was almost sure he was going to kiss her.

At the last moment, he pulled back and then drew her toward the revolving doors. "You're a very distracting woman, Doc."

When they stepped out onto the street, the humidity enveloped them again. As they paused to wait for the traffic to clear, he said, "You know, with those sunglasses and the stylish suit, you've got a kind of prima-donna thing going. I think we can play with that."

"Play with that? What is that supposed to mean?" she asked as they crossed the street.

"First time I saw you, I thought of Audrey Hepburn. Remember her in *Charade?*"

"Yeah, and what I remember most is that Cary Grant lied his head off in that movie."

"Yeah." He chuckled. "Great flick."

They reached the other side of the street. "You're not helping me much here."

"When Jack Nicholson played the Joker in the first Batman movie, he said he let the costume do the work. I think that's the way to go here."

Exasperated, Sierra took a calming breath and thought of her inhaler. But she clamped down on the urge. She was done with that.

"Here we go," Ryder said they as approached the glass doors of the Esquire Health and Fitness Club.

Even as a mix of panic and anticipation streamed through her, an idea popped into her mind in a flash. "Did you ever see the movie *The Pelican Brief?*"

"Sure. Denzel Washington and Julia Roberts—two of the most beautiful people in Hollywood in a John Grisham thriller. Hell of a way to kill a couple of hours."

"Remember the scene when they visited the sanitarium to question that young law student?"

"Sure."

"You distract the manager, and I'll look for the note-book." The moment the words were out, Sierra couldn't believe she'd said them. She didn't have a plan. She didn't even have a first step in mind.

Ryder looked at her as he pushed through the doors of the club. "You sure you want to do this?"

He was giving her a way out. But the trust she saw in his eyes did a lot to help her combat the panic bubbling up in her stomach. Drawing in a deep breath, she nodded.

He squeezed her hand. "Pick up the cues I give you and run with them."

Cues? As Ryder drew her toward the reception desk, she struggled against the second thoughts flooding her mind. Everyone was staring at her, from the fresh-faced young man behind the health-drink bar to the muscle-bound man behind the reception desk.

"See. The prima-donna thing is working already," Ryder said in a tone that only she could hear. Then he drew her forward.

"I'm Richard Moore, the manager. May I help you?" A well-turned out man in impeccably neat clothes had joined Mr. Muscle behind the reception desk. He could have passed for a proper British butler.

"I believe I have an appointment to discuss a membership in the club," Ryder said.

Sierra blinked. He was speaking with a French accent. Would he expect her to do the same? Even as she reminded herself to breathe, Richard said, "What time was your appointment?"

Ryder glanced at his watch. "Three o'clock. We're a few minutes late. I hope that's not a problem."

"No." He was scanning a leather-bound book with a faint frown. "The problem is that I have no record of your appointment." He leaned forward a little and pitched his voice low. "And this is a men's club. We do not allow women."

Ryder turned and spoke in French to her, and she had no idea what he'd said. She'd studied Russian and Spanish in school. This time her panic must have shown on her face because he took her hands and squeezed them. Before she could even decide what to do, he turned back to Richard. "My fiancée doesn't speak English. I don't want to turn her out on the street alone. If you could please make an exception. She can sit over at the health bar while we talk."

Richard's frown was deepening. "I suppose we could do that, but that still leaves one problem. I have no record of an appointment at three, Mister…?"

"Ranier. Charles Ranier. Senator Hayworth's secretary called and made the appointment."

Richard was beginning to look nervous as he scanned a message pad. "We have no record of the call."

Ryder turned to her again and spoke in rapid French.

With adrenaline zipping through her, Sierra found herself putting a hand on his arm, praying that she wouldn't blow his little charade.

"But I can easily check with the senator."

Ryder's smile was sad as he turned back to Antoine. "I'd rather you didn't. His secretary is getting on in age. Over breakfast Donny was saying that he was afraid he'd have to let her go. I don't want to be the one to worry him even more or to push him to that decision. Please, I want your word that you won't disturb the senator."

"Very well."

Ryder glanced at his watch. "We're relocating here to DC at the embassy. I wanted to get this settled before the move. Donny insisted that I join. Perhaps on my next visit we could talk?"

"The senator is a very special member," Richard said. "Why don't we step into my office and I can go over the membership benefits?"

"Merci," Ryder said. Then he took Sierra's arm and drew her toward the health bar.

"How did you know to drop Senator Hayworth's name?" she said under her breath.

"His picture is in the foyer. He's on the board. I told you something would occur to me." After ordering her a bottled water, he pressed the key into her hand and spoke so only she could hear. "While I keep Richard occupied, see what you can find out."

Sierra felt another rush of adrenaline and fear as she watched Ryder walk away and join Richard in his private office. What in the world was she going to do? And why in the world had she thought she could do this? Mr. Muscle and Mr. Boy-next-door were both looking at her. And she could hardly sweet-talk either of them into giving her a tour when she wasn't supposed to be able to speak English.

But Ryder seemed to trust her to think of something. Her only other choice would be to be a coward and sit on a stool until he came out of the office.

That was not an option. She'd jumped off a roof, and she'd outrun some men who were trying to shoot her. She was not going back to sitting on the sidelines and watching life go by.

Taking a deep breath, she surveyed her surroundings. Beyond the health bar was a wall of windows that looked down into the actual gym. The men working out were mainly in their mid-fifties to late seventies, and each seemed to be in the company of a younger man wearing a T-shirt with the letters EHC on the back. The music flowing through the speakers was Chopin if she wasn't mistaken. Very dignified.

Ryder had said that Mark Anderson wasn't a member. Whose guest had he been?

Tucked between the entrance to the gym and the bar, she could see an open archway with a flight of stairs leading downward. To the locker rooms? A white-T-shirted man came up the steps and exited through a door to the gym proper.

She waited until Mr. Muscle was occupied with a member, and the young man behind the bar picked up the phone. Then she eased off her stool and slipped through the archway.

Her heart was racing by the time she reached the foot of the stairs. It was a locker room all right. The scent of chlorine was strong in the air and she could hear the faint sound of water splashing as she turned and walked past the first few rows. There were padlocks on the locker doors. And then she saw the discreet sign on the final row that read Guests. Rounding the corner, she saw keys sticking out of several lockers. And there it was, number 123.

When she heard the sound of footsteps, Sierra dropped the key, and while she bent to retrieve it, the steps grew closer. Taking a deep breath, she quickly inserted the key and pulled the door open. There it was—a spiral stenographer's notebook. Too big for the purse that Ryder had given her. She certainly couldn't just carry it out with her.

The footsteps paused. Grabbing the notebook, she stuffed it into the front of her skirt and pulled her suit jacket down over it before she turned.

The man stood only a few feet away wearing nothing but a towel. He was large, and the expression on his face was anything but happy. "If you're a thief, you've picked the wrong place."

12

SIERRA DREW IN a deep breath and prayed for inspiration. What would Ryder do in this situation? What would Julia Roberts do? She quickly decided that pretending not to speak English was not an option. "I'm not a thief."

"I just saw you take something out of that locker, and you're not a member or a guest because they don't allow women here. That spells thief to me." He inserted a key in a locker and pulled out a cell phone.

"Please," she said. "Don't call anyone. I can explain." She hoped. Thinking on her feet had never been her strength.

He paused, cell phone in hand. "You can explain to the club manager."

"No, I can't." In her mind, she tried to recall exactly what Julia Roberts had done in *The Pelican Brief*. For starters, she'd lied through her teeth. Sierra drew in a deep breath and plunged ahead. "Please don't call him. I convinced the young man at the desk to let me run down here, and I don't want him to get in trouble."

The man paused to study her.

Her heart was pounding so hard that he had to hear it. And she was very much afraid that she was flushing the way she did whenever she lied.

"Even if I believe that, it doesn't explain why you're here."

"My boss was a guest here a few days ago, and he sent me to get something he left in his locker. He gave me the key." Smiling, she held out her palm with the key in it. "You can see that I didn't break in."

The man frowned. "Why didn't he come himself?"

"He's Mark Anderson of *The Washington Post.* You may have seen him here."

"Sure. He's a frequent guest. I saw him here on Wednesday. He plays a mean game of racket ball. Jack Gracie didn't look happy when the game was over."

Sierra felt her heart take a fast little leap at the mention of the vice president's son's name. "It must have been the excitement of winning that made him forget to check his locker carefully. He left some notes here. He couldn't come himself to get them." That much was true. She pulled the notebook out and showed it to him. "Please. It's a new job for me, and I assured him I could do this." She waited for a moment, and plan B came into her head. If he punched numbers into that phone, she was just going to make a run for it.

He set the cell phone back in his locker. "I guess you're telling the truth. But you'd better get out of here. If Richard gets wind of this, Larry at the desk will be fired."

"Thanks." She gave the man a three-fingered wave as she backed her way down the aisle. Once she reached the end, she raced for the stairs. Halfway up, just when she was ready to breathe a sigh of relief, she spotted Mr. Muscle on his way down.

"What do you think you're doing? Women aren't allowed down there."

She shrugged, fluttered her hands and said, "La toilette?" Then she prayed that his French was as bad as hers. When he reached her, he took her arm and drew her up the stairs with him. Her tension eased when Ryder hurried across the lobby to her, speaking French all the way. He took her hands, squeezed them and then as he turned back to Richard, he kept his arm around her.

"My apologies," he said. "She didn't understand that she shouldn't wander about. I hope no harm was done."

"Don't worry about it," Richard assured them with a wave of his hand. His voice and his manner had warmed considerably since he'd ushered Ryder into his office. "I'll be looking forward to hearing from you when you get settled. And in the meantime, I'll watch for your check."

The two men shook hands, and then Ryder was practically shoving her through the front doors.

"We need a taxi," he said to the doorman, and then he steered her a few feet away.

"Well?" he said in a low voice.

"I got it. A notebook."

"I knew you could do it," he said.

"I still don't believe I lied like that. A man caught me closing the locker. I told him that I was Mark Anderson's secretary and that he'd sent me to get his notebook. He believed me." She pressed a hand against her heart.

"The first lie is always the hardest. After that they just seem to flow."

"And that's not all. Guess who Mark played racket ball with? Jack Gracie," she added before he could answer.

"Good work. You're a natural, Doc." Then he grabbed her by the shoulders and kissed her.

Just that press of his mouth against hers brought back everything: need, delight, along with the memory of everything they'd shared, everything they might share. She poured herself into the kiss and what had begun as friendly and congratulatory changed.

This kiss was different from the other ones they'd shared. His hands were so gentle when he moved them to frame her face. And his mouth was softer as if he were kissing her for the first time. Very slowly, he moved her until her back was against the building. It wasn't heat she experienced this time, but a warmth that moved through her slowly. She felt that she was coming home.

Her hands gripped his shoulders. On some level she was aware that they were standing on a busy street. She heard some chuckles and a whistle from passersby. But her world was narrowing slowly like a spotlight on a stage until all she knew was this man and this moment. He held her trapped against the wall and she didn't want to go anywhere.

IT HAD BEEN on impulse that he'd kissed her. Just like the first time. Only, what Ryder was experiencing wasn't anything like the first time. That time she'd exploded in his arms. As the sweetness and the power moved through him, Ryder's intentions changed. He didn't want to let her go. That truth, simple and terrifying, stunned him. Still, he held on. One more moment, he promised himself.

He knew that he was standing on a sidewalk, but he could have sworn that the solid concrete beneath his feet was shifting. *You,* he thought. *You're the one.* He recognized the same sensations that he'd felt when he'd first really looked at her in the Blue Pepper. Slapping one hand against the building for balance, he drew back.

Ryder studied her then and saw a question in her eyes. He was almost sure it echoed the one that was forming in his mind. He wanted to say something, but he wasn't sure what would come out of his mouth. One thing he was sure of was that he wasn't steady. He certainly wasn't in control. And he wanted to kiss her again. He needed to—

A car backfiring on the street had him stiffening and turning, his hand slipping automatically beneath his jacket to settle on his gun. Fear and anger moved through him as he scanned the street. The traffic was sluggish, and a few pedestrians shot him a curious glance. The doorman in front of the health club had his back to them, his hand out, signaling for a taxi.

Ryder eased his hand away from his gun. They'd been lucky. And he knew better than most that luck could run out. He was being careless. Clamping down on what he was feeling he turned back to Sierra and said, "I'm sorry for that."

"Oh," she said and dropped her eyes.

He gripped her chin and waited until she was looking at her. Then he spoke in a voice that only she could hear. "Not about the kiss. In fact, I want a rain check on that. But it's the wrong time and the wrong place, Doc. I'm not doing my job. Dammit, I wasn't doing it at the mall either."

She studied him through those sober blue eyes. "I think you did an exceptional job at the mall. Two men shot at us and you got us out of there."

"But you were the one who spotted them. Not me."

"Sir, I have your taxi," the doorman said. "Where to?"

"Le Printemps," Ryder said.

He waited until the taxi drew away from the curb before he continued, "I'm going to call Jed Calhoun as soon as we reach Le Printemps. He'll take you back to the houseboat until I can figure out who's behind this."

For a moment there was silence in the taxi except for the muffled noise of the traffic and the bursts of static from the driver's radio. Then Sierra opened her purse.

Was she looking for a tissue? Panic streamed through him. Lord, he hoped she wasn't going to cry. "Look, it's for the best. You did a great job in there, but you're distracting me. I'm not the man to protect you."

When she continued to search through her purse, he said, "Do you need your inhaler?"

"I don't need the inhaler. I'm never going to need it again. I need something to write on. I think more clearly when I write things down."

It wasn't until she turned to face him that he caught his first glimpse of the fury in her eyes, and it nearly singed his skin.

"Well, then I'll just have to improvise." She poked a finger into his chest. "First, do you make a habit of reneging on your favors?"

"No, I—"

She poked him again. "Don't interrupt while I'm improvising. Number one, we agreed that you would do me two favors, right?"

"Yes, but—"

"Let me finish. Number two, I'm satisfied with everything that you've done so far. Have you been satisfied with what I've done?"

"Doc, I—" He wasn't satisfied with how their conversation was going.

"You said I did a good job in there. Did you mean it?"

Ryder had a distinct feeling that he was being led down a garden path. "I meant it."

"And in the mall? How did I do there?"

"Great. If this were a movie, I'd give it two thumbs up. But it isn't. And I promised your sister and Matt Ramsey that I'd protect you."

She clicked her purse shut. "I'm not going back to the boat with your friend. You agreed to grant me two favors, and I'm collecting on them. We'll just go back to my original suggestion and compartmentalize. No more utility closets. For as long as we need to, we'll just focus on finding out who is trying to get rid of Mark Anderson."

"And you," Ryder pointed out.

"You, too," she said. "They found us at the mall by tracing your cell. And they shot at you too. So why don't we concentrate on figuring out what Mark was working on that would motivate someone to kill him and us? If I go back to the boat, I won't be thinking about the case at all. I'll be worried about you. Since time is a factor, I think my talents would be better utilized if we continued to work together on this."

Shit, he thought to himself. She had a point. If he sent her with Jed, would he be able to stop worrying about her? No one should be able to trace the location of his houseboat—but what if someone had?

Even as he made his decision, he wondered if he was being influenced by his desire simply to have her with him.

"Okay," he finally said. "We'll go with your compartmentalization plan."

She lifted her jacket and pulled out the notebook. "We'd better start with this."

HIS HAND was shaking when he hung up the phone. But the fury that he'd been struggling to control all day finally began to ease. He had to put the inefficiency he'd been forced to tolerate out of his mind. The important thing was that the quarry had been spotted and would be intercepted soon.

And that would finally be the end of it.

A glance at his watch told him that he had a half hour until his meeting with Senator Hayworth. His temper had to be completely under control by then. The majority leader had an uncanny knack for sensing any kind of weakness or trouble. And if he did, the rumors would start. Hayworth's early support was essential. Once he was on board, others would follow. By the time the senator walked in the door, he had to be calm. Confident. The upcoming negotiations were crucial.

Rising, he crossed to a cabinet and poured a snifter of the brandy he kept for his most influential guests. He allowed himself one swallow, savoring the taste and the warmth that spread through him. Then he returned to his desk and glanced down at the photos of the two people who'd been eluding him for the past twenty-four hours. Fury bubbled up again, and he took another sip of brandy.

He'd come too far and worked too long to have the truth revealed at this point. And what really mattered—a record that had been built in public service over the past thirty-five years or one incident that had occurred so long ago? Even the reporter had seen his point, and he'd agreed to hold off on the story.

But that could hardly have been left to chance. One person knowing the truth was one too many. If it leaked out, everything would be over. That was why the other two had to be eliminated also.

He glanced once more at the two photos in front of him. The psychologist should have been snatched with the reporter. She was a pretty little thing in a mousy sort of way. Even before he'd compiled the file on her, he'd known that she would have to be taken out of the picture. And his instincts had been right. She was brilliant. If Anderson had managed to give her even a hint of what he'd uncovered, she would put it together.

His gaze shifted to the other photo. The information

he'd gathered on Ryder Kane was much more disturbing. The man was not only smart, he was dangerous.

He wasn't even aware that the glass in his hand had broken until he felt the stinging sensation. Glancing down, he saw the pieces of glass in his palm, and the blood mixing with the brandy. Swearing, he dropped the shards in a waste basket, then drew out his handkerchief and carefully wiped and wrapped the small slice the glass had made.

Rage surged up again, and he fought to shove it down. He wasn't quite in control. But he would be. He poured himself another brandy, and this time he took a long swallow.

Turning, he gazed out the window of the office at the view. In the distance, he could just make out the gleaming black granite of the Vietnam Memorial. The jungle of Vietnam, that was where it had all started, and the secret had been kept for thirty-five years.

He swallowed the last of his brandy, and then glanced once more at his watch. In half an hour, an hour at the most, Ryder Kane and Sierra Gibbs would no longer be threatening his future. He took deep calming breaths as he walked to his desk and sat down. He let his gaze sweep the office, taking in the rich gleam of dark woods and the upholstered chairs that he'd insisted on when he'd come here. There was power here. But it wasn't absolute power. That could still be his. It *would* be his.

13

THE TAXI was still inching its way through traffic when Ryder handed the notebook back to Sierra. "See what you can make of it."

While she read it, he took a quick look around, noting the cars both behind and in the lane next to them. It took him a moment to spot a dark-blue sedan that had been with them since they'd left the Esquire. Coincidence? Could be, but he was leaving nothing to chance anymore.

When he glanced back at Sierra, she was digging into her purse.

"I need something to write with," she said.

Ryder reached deep into the duffel. Once he handed her the pen, she began to make a list on a sheet she'd torn out of Mark Anderson's notebook. His notations were cryptic and at times hard to decipher. They were mostly about a man Ryder had never heard of—one Brian James McElroy. The man had been born in 1945 in Kansas City, Missouri, graduated from a local high school, attended college where he'd played baseball before he'd gone to fight in Vietnam.

That was when the information had gotten sparse. According to Mark's notes, McElroy hadn't come home from the war. In parentheses, there was the word left, followed by a question mark. There were numbers too. Ryder had thought they might refer to the division that McElroy had served in. At face value, he couldn't see much there that would get Mark Anderson kidnapped and nearly killed, and he was interested in discovering what Sierra would see.

She had three items on her list, he noted before he glanced once more at the cars surrounding them. The blue sedan he'd noticed earlier was now three cars back.

"There's not much here," Sierra said. "When I found out that Mark had played racket ball with the vice president's son, I thought we'd find something in these notes that would give us some idea of what's going on."

"What do you have on your list?"

"Just random notes. I'm trying to make some connections, but I haven't really thought it through yet."

"Two heads are better than one," he said and was pleased when her lips curved. She didn't smile nearly enough.

"Number one is a question. Did McElroy die in Vietnam or was he an MIA?"

"Good point," Ryder said. "I can put someone on that."

"He's from Missouri." She glanced up at him then. "You're going to think this is a stretch. But so was Harry Truman, and he was a vice president."

"You're thinking of the book Mark's writing on the vice presidency. I thought about it too." He saw the hint of excitement in her eyes.

"Vice president Gracie is from Missouri too," she said. "It's probably a coincidence."

"Could be." But he'd felt that little rush he'd seen in her eyes when that same thought had occurred to him. "Maybe you're connecting more dots than you think. We keep coming back to Vice President Gracie. I wonder if he and McElroy served in the same unit in Vietnam."

He glanced out the back window of the taxi, then leaning forward, he said to the driver, "Change of plan. I want you to drop us off at Union Station." When he met Sierra's questioning glance, he said, "A blue sedan has been following us ever since we left the Esquire."

"What's the plan?" she asked.

"We're going to lead them on a merry chase," he said with a grin.

"TELL ME you're all right."

Sierra heard the concern in her sister Natalie's voice and said, "I'm better than all right. I'm having…fun."

The merry chase had involved losing themselves in the crowd at Union Station, changing into new outfits and taking a new taxi to a hotel a few blocks from Le Printemps so that they could use the pay phones. Ryder figured that someone might be watching Le Printemps so they might not have time to make any calls there.

"I've had the updates from Matt," Natalie said. "Getting shot at is not fun."

"Well, not that part maybe. But we just lost the two men who followed us into Union Station. And you'd be surprised, Nat. I'm really getting good at this disguise thing. Nowhere near as good as you are, of course."

Sierra was now wearing the red sundress, the high-heeled sandals, and she'd tied the white scarf around her hair in a sort of turban. The result was that she looked a lot like one of the femme fatales that appeared in every film noir ever made. Each time she caught her image in one of the glass-fronted shops that lined the lobby, she felt wonderfully wicked. And she couldn't help wondering if that woman was a part of her too.

One thing was certain. She'd come a long way from the

Sierra Gibbs who could barely scrape up the courage to open her father's letter two days ago.

"I'd feel better if you'd let Ryder Kane tuck you away in a safe place until this is over," Natalie said.

"I won't do that." She'd come out of the safe world she'd been hiding in, and she didn't think she'd ever want to go back. "I found Mark's notebook. We think his notes are connected to the story he was working on."

Natalie sighed. "That's what Ryder told Matt. If that man doesn't take good care of you—"

"He is. He does."

"I intend to see for myself later today. Your bodyguard has set up a powwow at his place tonight at seven. I'm bringing Chance, and Rory and Hunter will want to tag along, too."

Ryder tapped her on the shoulder, signaling her that it was time to hang up.

"I've got to go, Nat. We have to keep the calls under two minutes so that they can't be traced. But I want you to know that I'm following Dad's advice, and I think I inherited more from him than any of us thought."

"That's what I'm afraid of," Natalie was saying as Sierra hung up the phone.

"I've GOT one more call to make," Ryder said, studying her.

"Me, too," Sierra said. "I want to check in with my research assistant. She'll be worried that I didn't show up for our meeting this morning."

"Watch the time." Ryder kept his gaze on her as she turned back to the pay phone. He'd barely been able to take his eyes off her since she'd stepped out of the ladies' room at Union Station wearing that white scarf in her hair. He doubted she'd done it intentionally, but every time he looked at it, he was finding it more and more difficult to compartmentalize.

And he had to if he wanted to keep her safe. According to Matt Ramsey, the DC police hadn't made any more progress than he and Sierra had, and Mark Anderson was still in a coma.

It was going to take some time to figure out what role Brian James McElroy was playing in everything. And his intuition was telling him that they were running out of time. Living and working in DC, he'd become familiar with the way that political power brokers operated. If McElroy had something that would tarnish the record of someone like John Gracie, there might be other people who had a stake in preventing that from happening.

They were running a risk going to Le Printemps, but it was the quickest way to find out who Mark had met with on Wednesday afternoon. And that information just might allow them to connect all the dots.

Ryder scanned the lobby again before he inserted a quarter in the phone and punched in a number. There'd been no sign of the blue sedan on the trip from Union Station to this hotel. He was as certain as he could be that they were safe for the moment.

The phone on the other end rang three times before Jed Calhoun picked up. "Yeah?"

"I need two favors."

"Two? I'm just collecting on the last one you owed me."

Ryder grinned. "Just think of it this way. I'll be in your debt again—big-time."

"I don't like the sound of this. What do I have to do?"

"First, I want you to find everything you can on a Brian James McElroy born in Kansas City in 1945." He filled Jed in on all of the other information they'd found in Mark's notebook.

"Okay. That should be easy enough."

And it would be, too. Jed was the best man he knew when it came to hacking into computer systems and getting information that was supposedly secured. It was one of his many talents.

"Well? I'm waiting for the other shoe to drop," Jed said.

"You've got connections at the Pentagon. I want you to contact them and get me anything you can on McElroy. He either died or went missing in Vietnam, maybe in 1970."

There was a beat of silence on the other end of the line, and Ryder held his breath. It was a big favor he'd just asked, and it wouldn't have lessened his regard for Jed if he'd refused. For the last three years, the man who'd been known as Jed Calhoun had disappeared off the face of the earth, and contacting anyone at the Pentagon threatened the anonymity he'd worked so hard to establish.

"You got it," Jed said.

"You're sure?"

"Yeah. I came back here with the intention to clear my name. I'll have to get in touch with these people sooner or later. When do you need the information?"

"Yesterday."

Jed laughed. "Should have known. How do I contact you?"

Ryder told him about the meeting he'd arranged with Matt Ramsey and Natalie Gibbs at his apartment that evening. "One other thing."

"The favors are piling up."

"Just keep track of the tab. I may need you to take Dr. Gibbs off my hands." He summarized their morning's adventures.

"You weren't kidding when you said you'd owe me big-time, Pal. That woman is no Bianca."

"No, she's definitely not," Ryder said as he scanned the lobby again. The younger sister in Shakespeare's play had been predictable, and Sierra Gibbs was anything but. That damn white scarf she was wearing was driving him nuts.

And if he looked at her, he was going to get ideas that he'd be better off not having.

"Zoë?"

"Where are you?" Zoë asked. "We had a meeting scheduled for ten-thirty this morning. When you didn't show up and didn't call, I was nearly frantic."

Sierra could picture her research assistant quite clearly in her mind. Zoë would be sitting at her desk, a worried frown puckering her brow.

"I'm sorry. I just got…distracted." Sierra felt a flush stain her cheeks. Very distracted. If she remembered correctly, at ten-thirty that morning, she and Ryder were trying out a very interesting sexual position.

"Are you in trouble? Should I call your sister?"

"No. My sister Natalie knows where I am. There's nothing to worry about." At least not right now, she added to herself.

"You never miss a meeting."

"I don't have time to explain everything. You can call Nat and find out where we're meeting later today. I want you to join us and I'll fill you in then. In the meantime, I need your help on a research problem. I want you to find out everything you can on a Brian James McElroy—born in 1945 in Kansas City."

There was a beat of silence, and then Zoë said, "That's it! I should have thought of it sooner. Your speed date was a success and you want me to check him out for you. But…"

Sierra could picture the frown returning to Zoë's forehead.

"Nineteen forty-five? He's a little old for you, isn't he?"

"He's not a man I speed dated. This McElroy either died in Vietnam or went missing around 1970. I need everything you can find on him, and it's a matter of life and death. I figure you must still have contacts in the CIA. I need the kind of stuff that no one else will be able to find."

There was another pause on the other end of the line. Instinctively, Sierra knew that she was asking a big favor. Zoë never referred to her former job in the intelligence community, nor why she'd left it.

"Okay. And I suppose you'll need this ASAP?"

Sierra let out the breath she'd been holding. "By our meeting this evening, if you can do it."

"I'll get right on it."

"I'm also interested in any connection you can find between this McElroy and the vice president."

This time there was no hesitation when she asked. "What are you involved in?"

"I'll fill you in when we meet." She'd just hung up the phone and had turned to tell Ryder what she'd done, when it rang.

"Pick it up." Ryder was standing not three feet away, facing her, and he had the receiver of the pay phone at his ear.

The phone rang again.

When she picked it up, he said, "Hi, Doc."

"You're calling me on the phone." The absurdity of it made her giggle. "Why?"

"I want a favor."

Her amusement faded and her throat dried when she saw the heat in his eyes.

"Do you remember our last phone conversation?"

Just the mention of it had the memories and the sensations flooding back.

She moistened her lips. "But we had a plan."

"I'm improvising. I want to make you come again."

Her breath hitched. "Here? You can't."

"You know I can. It's just a matter of how. I have three ways in mind. And they all involve that scarf. Would you like to hear them?"

Her insides were melting. She glanced around the lobby, where a number of people were milling about: a young mother pushed one child in a stroller and held another with her hand. A tall man in a gray suit pulled a suitcase on rollers. Two teenagers laden with packages rushed past. No one was paying them any heed. "Ryder…"

His voice was soft as he continued. "Picture this. First, I'm going to undress you—somewhere near a bed. I haven't made love to you on a bed yet. And then I'm going to take that scarf off your head."

Even as thrills shot through her, she said, "Are you thinking of bondage? I've never done that."

His mouth curved. "Then we'll have to try it. But I'm not thinking of tying you up. I have something else in mind." His voice lowered. "I thought I might tie some knots in the scarf. Three or four. Next, I'll ask you to widen your stance just a little. Do it, Sierra."

She moved her feet apart as he asked.

"Now I'm slipping the scarf between your legs and pulling it taut until you're dampening it. Can you feel it pressing against you, Sierra?"

She could.

"Do you want to know what I'm going to do next?"

"Yes." She barely recognized the breathy sound of her own voice. He was all she was aware of now. The noises in the lobby had faded so that she felt as if she were trapped in a little bubble with only Ryder. His eyes were hot and dark as they gazed at her. His hand gripped the phone so tightly that his knuckles had turned white. But in her mind, it wasn't the phone he held in that hand. It was the scarf.

"I'm pulling it taut, then releasing it. Pulling it taut and then releasing it. How does it feel, Sierra?"

Biting back a moan, she closed her eyes. She was going to figure out how he could do this to her. Someday. But it was difficult to think with the pressure and the heat building inside her. His voice was all she could hear now.

"I'm dropping one end of the scarf."

No. She barely kept herself from crying out the protest. She wanted the delicious torture to go on.

"Now I'm pulling the other end slowly. Very slowly. Can you feel the friction of the first knot as it moves past your clit?"

She could.

"The second knot is larger. It's not pulling through so smoothly. I'm tugging on it right now. Can you feel it?"

She could feel the pressure building and building.

"It seems to be caught. One more tug."

Sierra moved her legs together. The orgasm began exactly where he'd made her imagine the pressure and it built slowly, moving deeper and deeper.

"That's it. Come for me, Sierra."

The murmur of his words in her ear drove her higher and higher to an airless peak where pleasure buffeted her again and again.

"That's it. Don't worry. I've got you."

She was aware that strong arms had clamped around her, and then she was falling.

RYDER WASN'T SURE how long he held her pressed against him. What he was growing more and more sure of was that she felt just right in his arms. On one level, he was keeping his eyes on their surroundings, doing his job. But on another level, he was wondering what he was going to do about Sierra Gibbs.

She'd gotten to him. And it wasn't just that she was the most responsive woman he'd ever been with. What he was feeling went way beyond the great sex. When he was making love to her, watching the pleasure he could evoke move through her, she was his. And he wanted her to be his. Maybe even permanently.

Permanent and *commitment* were never words he'd associated with his previous relationships. He'd learned not to depend on anyone or anything that morning when he'd woken up in the small apartment and found himself alone. All his mother had left was a note telling him to call his aunt.

But he wanted something more than temporary with Sierra. This was new territory—and he was going to have to give it some thought.

When she stirred in his arms, his grip tightened automatically.

"Wow," she said as she raised her head to look at him. "When you promise a favor, you really deliver."

Ryder's eyes narrowed even as his heart contracted. The favor. Was it possible that she saw what was happening between them as simply part of the damn favors he'd agreed to do for her? A part of him wanted to set her straight. But how could he when he hadn't quite figured it out for himself yet?

The smile she shot him was wicked, and there was a mischievous gleam in her eye that he'd never seen before. "Maybe it's time I did you a favor."

Before he could say a word, she'd slipped her hand into his and was drawing him toward the registration desk. Whatever she was up to, he should put a stop to it. They still had to get in and out of Le Printemps before they met with Natalie and Matt Ramsey at seven.

"Follow my lead," she murmured when the young reception clerk signaled her forward.

Ryder barely kept his mouth from dropping open when she began speaking in Russian.

When the young man glanced at him helplessly, Ryder said, "She always lapses into Russian when she's excited."

"So sorry." Sierra fluttered her hands and drew in a deep breath. "You have a reservation for Gibbs."

The man whose name tag read David punched numbers into his computer. When he glanced at Ryder again, his smile was tentative and apologetic. "I'm sorry. There's no reservation for Gibbs."

Sierra lapsed into Russian again. Ryder could pretty much follow what she was saying. They were here in DC to celebrate their first anniversary. It was to be a surprise for her husband. Her hands waved in his direction. And the travel agent had promised her that everything was in order.

David glanced at Ryder again.

Ryder placed a hand on Sierra's shoulder. "English please, dear. He can't understand Russian."

This time Sierra explained everything in accented English. Admiration shot through him when tears thickened her voice.

David busily punched the keys of his computer again.

"We do happen to have a suite that's available—if that would be all right."

Sierra beamed a smile at him and spoke more Russian.

"I think that's a yes," Ryder said. A few seconds later, he had the plastic key cards in his hand, and a bell man was hurrying over to take his duffel.

After waving him away, Ryder took Sierra's arm and drew her toward the bank of elevators that filled a narrow hall off the main lobby. "You speak Russian."

She grinned at him. "Did I surprise you? I wanted to."

"Doc, you never cease to surprise me. But why use Russian at all? I'll bet you could have just asked for a room and gotten it."

She shot him the dry look he'd come to love. "I'm following the lead of someone who's a lot more inventive than that."

Even as he laughed, he experienced the same clutch around his heart that he'd felt before. Because he was beginning to think that she was the perfect woman for him.

But he couldn't think of that now. Not until they figured out what was going on. But lust was safe enough, and he wanted Sierra Gibbs with a desperation that increased each time he had her.

The elevator was crowded, so they didn't speak until they stepped out onto their floor. He reached for her, but she took a quick step back, raising her hands, palms out. "This is my favor so I call the shots."

He held out the key card. "After you, Doc."

He remained near the door while she inspected the suite. The only way he'd be able to go along with her rule was to keep his distance. The suite was large with a sunken living room and a baby grand piano tucked away in the corner by the windows. Sierra paid no attention to the view as she moved purposefully to the bedroom door and peered in.

He could almost hear the wheels turning her head as she mentally listed her steps for seducing him. How hard would he have to work to distract her from them? he wondered.

"You mentioned a bed. There's a first-class one here," she said as she glanced back over her shoulder.

"No rush." He moved toward her. "I was thinking of the grand piano."

"Really?" She gave it a glance and then looked at him through narrowed eyes. "You're trying to distract me."

"I'll have to try harder."

She backed into the bedroom with one hand raised to ward him off. "Try all you want as long as you remember I'm calling the shots." When she backed into the side of the bed, she stopped and said, "I want you to take your clothes off."

"That'll work," he said dropping the duffel. Then he did what she asked very slowly while he watched the expressions that moved over her face. When he was wearing nothing but his briefs, he said, "Your turn, Doc."

She reached behind her for a second and then with nothing more than a wiggle to encourage it, the red sundress pooled at her feet. Ryder felt his mouth go dry. She was wearing nothing but a pair of lacey white panties and high-heeled red sandals. One foggy thought crossed his mind. If he'd known how easily that dress would come off, he wasn't sure he could have been coherent during those phone calls he'd just made in the lobby.

He took a step toward her, but she quickly moved out of reach.

"One request, Doc. Whatever else you've got on that list of yours, keep the shoes on."

She shot him a smile. "I can do that." Then she was moving toward the bathroom. When she reached the door, she turned back. "But I'm going to remove the scarf. It's part of step three."

"What's step two?"

"Lie down on the bed, and if you're a good boy, I'll let you know."

SIERRA WAITED only until he sat down on the edge of the bed before she disappeared into the bathroom. She was very much afraid that if she saw him laid out on the mattress, she might jump him. And she had a plan.

Or at least part of a plan. Steps one, two and three had been easy. But after that…she drew in a deep breath and let it out. She'd just have to let her instincts rule. After turning on the faucet, she ran the scarf under the water and then wrung it out a little. She only wanted it to drip when she squeezed it.

The research she'd completed on modern couples' use of sex toys had unearthed some innovative ideas that didn't require Internet shopping. Whipped cream, honey, chocolate, strings of beads and scarves were pretty common household items. The things that could be done with scarves had fascinated her the most. And Ryder's inventiveness had inspired her.

Turning, she walked back into the bedroom and very nearly dropped the scarf when she saw Ryder stretched full-length and totally naked on the bed.

Her mouth was dry, her heart pounding, and she had to swallow twice before she spoke. "You're trying to distract me again."

This time when he met her eyes, he wasn't smiling. Instead, the look he sent her was so hot that she was sure the nerve endings along her skin began to sizzle.

"How am I doing?" He turned on his side and raised himself on his elbow.

"Great." It took every bit of will power she had to walk, not run, to the bed. "Don't you want to know what steps two, three and four are?"

"What I want is to be inside you. Right now." He held out a hand. "Let me make love to you, Sierra."

"I have an idea." At least she thought she did. Most of what was in her head was draining away. "Maybe there's a compromise we can work out." She climbed up on the bed and pushed him back against the pillows. "Give me fifteen minutes, and then you can take over and do anything you want."

His eyes narrowed, but he didn't reach for her. They both knew that if he did, she wouldn't be able to resist. "Five minutes."

"Ten."

"I'm not sure I can keep my hands off of you for that long, Doc. How about we shoot for seven and a half?"

His words and the intensity of his look as he said them sent power shimmering through her. She nodded. "Deal. I'll just have to work a little faster than I'd planned." Although there wasn't much of a plan in her head. Step two...she paused to consider, then said, "I want you to clasp your hands over your head."

As he did what she asked, he said, "Are you going to tie me up with that scarf?"

Her brows shot up. "I have something else in mind."

"Should I be worried about step three again?"

"You tell me," she said as she moved over him until she was straddling him. The quick hitch of his breath as she did send her confidence soaring.

"You're not quite in the right spot, Doc."

"No. But I'll find it in about seven minutes."

Her idea in straddling his waist had been to kill two birds with one stone. Put herself in a position of power and get temptation out of sight. But she could feel the heat of his skin against her center and the promise of his erection against her backside.

Better not think about that yet.

"Step three, close your eyes."

When he did, she found it was just a little bit easier to concentrate without his intense gaze stirring up her senses.

"Step four," she said as she lifted the scarf and squeezed a single drop of water on a spot just below his throat. She felt his stomach muscles tighten beneath her, saw his knuckles whiten. Encouraged, she continued to squeeze droplets of water down his chest to a point at the apex of her thighs. It was then that she realized she didn't have a step five in her head. She'd have to improvise.

"Step five," she said as she inched backward and then leaned down to lick away the last drop of water that had dripped from the scarf.

The low deep moan he made vibrated through her, and bolstered once again, she continued to lick one drop at a time off his skin. "You taste wonderful," she murmured as she reached his throat. "Better than ice cream or chocolate or…" When he murmured her name, she felt it vibrate against her lips, and following an impulse, she used her teeth on him.

He arched against her, and as she retraced the path she'd just taken, she took a detour to his nipples. His taste was different there—richer. The next spot she lingered over was his stomach where his skin had grown more damp than it had been before, and so hot, she could feel the fire spread from her mouth to her center.

And then she went lower, and lower, using her lips and teeth and tongue until she was straddling his thighs. There was something else she was supposed to do with the scarf, but she couldn't think what it was. All she knew was that she had to taste him. Leaning over, she took him into her mouth and began to lose herself in him. Would she ever get enough of his flavor? Texture?

As HE WATCHED her through half-closed eyes, Ryder knew what it was like to be slowly driven crazy. Or perhaps it was a done deal, and she'd already pushed him over the edge. He certainly felt as if his limbs, indeed, his whole body were encased in a straitjacket.

And he wasn't even sure when the paralysis had crept in. The weakness had begun when she'd started to enumerate those slow, methodical steps—leaning over him with that serious frown as if he were some subject she was determined to study thoroughly. Then he'd lost track of everything but that wonderful, clever mouth of hers as it had moved over him. How could it be so soft and so demanding at the same time?

And now he couldn't move. All he could do was watch her take him into her mouth, release him, and then take him in again. Each time the heat grew fiercer, each time the pleasure grew sharper. He'd never before turned over this much control to a woman. He'd never before known what it was like to be trapped between twin desires. He wanted to end the torture. He wanted it to go on. And on.

Just as he thought he couldn't stand it any longer, she released him to move up his body—until she was almost where he wanted her to be.

"The condom," he said in a voice he barely recognized as his own. "On the nightstand."

She reached for it, tore the package open, and began to sheath him in it. The soft pressure of her fingers as she accomplished the task nearly did him in.

She lowered herself onto him just a little. He arched, but she evaded his thrust by moving upward and then she leaned down to whisper against his lips, "Step number six. You can come in. I want you inside of me, Ryder. Now."

Ryder felt like a racehorse shooting out of the gate. Then she was beneath him on the bed, and he thrust into her with one hard stroke. She was so tight, so hot, so incredibly ready for him. Giving himself a moment, he lay perfectly still. But even as he dragged in a breath, his body began to move, withdrawing and plunging into her again and again.

He couldn't seem to get deep enough. And each time he withdrew, she seemed to clutch more tightly around him as if she would never let him go.

He didn't want her to. In some vague corner of his mind, he knew that he was losing parts of himself that he'd never get back. But he simply didn't care. All that mattered was Sierra. He lifted his head enough to see that her eyes were open and on his. He increased the pace, felt her match him. Perfectly.

His voice was raw and barely audible when he managed to say, "Step number seven. Come with me, Sierra."

And she did, moving faster and faster as he drove them both higher. He felt her clutch him even more tightly when her convulsions began.

His own climax hit him, slamming into him with such force that his vision grayed. All he could see was her; all he could call was her name as he shattered.

14

USING THE SLEEVE of her terry-cloth robe, Sierra wiped steam off the full-length mirror in the bathroom and studied her reflection. She definitely wasn't the woman she'd been three days ago before Ryder Kane had kissed her. But she wasn't Britney Spears or Eliza Doolittle or a Hitchcock heroine either.

Just who was she? The question had the nerves tangling in her stomach. Had she changed so much that she didn't really know herself anymore?

She raised one hand and ran her fingers over her lips. The transformation had all started with a kiss. Of course, she'd known from an early age that kisses had a tremendous power. In the stories her father had read to her as a child, kisses had the power to turn a frog into a prince, to wake up Sleeping Beauty, and to bring Snow White back to life.

One thing she was determined to make sure of. She was not going to turn into that old Sierra Gibbs ever again once the favors Ryder was doing her were completed. Despite the band of pain tightening around her heart, she continued to study herself for one long moment. She liked the new Sierra better.

As for the dents in her heart, well, she'd deal with them. She'd suffered losses before, she'd lost both of her parents, and she knew better than most that nothing in life was permanent. Ryder was a man who did favors for people and he craved adventure. Just like Harry, he'd feel the need to move on. She'd better be prepared for that.

But she would never regret asking him for those two favors. The whole adventure had been worth it to learn that she was more Harry's daughter than she'd ever believed herself to be. As for Ryder—well, the risks she'd taken with him had been worth everything.

There were so many facets to the man, so much to admire. There was the lover whose face she saw above hers, so intent on giving her pleasure. Then there was the warrior, the man who'd drawn his gun, rolled into the street and shot the man who was trying to kill them. And there was the kid who loved to watch classic movies and race through a mall like a crazy person.

And she was going to lose them all.

But she'd survive. She'd just have to map out a plan. Turning, she moved to the door. Some kind of twelve-step recovery program would be good. There had to be one she could develop.

But the moment she stepped into the bedroom of the suite and saw him on the bed smiling at her, a new rush of feelings streamed through her. He was fully dressed in jeans and a black T-shirt, his back propped against the headboard and his legs crossed. And it felt so right to see him there sitting on a bed they'd just made love on.

The way her heart was taking a slow tumble had her realizing it was much more than lust or friendship that she felt for this man. And perhaps it wasn't just a kiss that had transformed her.

She opened her mouth, not sure of what she was going to say when he gestured at the mattress and spoke. "I didn't know what kind of candy you liked best so I brought a selection."

"A selection?" Her gaze fell on the candy bars spread out next to him. She counted eight.

"That's all they had in the machine, so I got one of each. What's your favorite?"

She moved closer and studied the array. "What is this?"

"A little brain-food picnic. After all, we've got to be relatively safe here. And before we leave, I thought it might be a good idea to review what we've got so far and bounce some theories back and forth. Besides, we haven't eaten since noon. What do you say, Doc?"

A mix of relief and disappointment moved through her. They weren't going to talk about anything personal. They were going to talk about the case. It was better that way. She wasn't ready. She...

Compartmentalize, she told herself as she reached for a plain chocolate bar.

"A purist," he said, patting a space on the mattress. "I'm not surprised."

Her chin lifted as she joined him, sitting cross-legged next to him as she unwrapped the candy. "Actually, I prefer chocolate-covered caramels. The expensive kind made by a chocolatier."

He tore the paper off a bar that boasted peanuts and then said around a mouthful, "Probably aren't any additives in that fancy stuff. My own personal opinion is that it's the unpronounceable chemicals that help me think more clearly."

Closing her eyes, Sierra swallowed the mouthful of chocolate she'd let melt on her tongue and sighed. "Additives or not, chocolate is definitely brain food."

Ryder reached for his second bar. "The best. As soon

as endorphins start flooding your system, your brain cells start perking up. Of course, soft drinks work, too—especially the kind with extra caffeine and real sugar. Take your pick."

Sierra eyed the four cans sitting on the bedside table and selected a diet cola.

Ryder sighed. "I figured you'd skip the extra sugar. Now, I'll have to think harder."

Sierra popped the last bite of chocolate into her mouth and said around it, "I can hold my own. How did you know I'd love this?"

"I'm a genius at following clues. You had a burger and fries at the mall, and I checked out your kitchen. You don't cook. Your favorite kind of chili is something you have to pick up or eat at a restaurant. But the biggest clue was the candy wrappers in your waste basket. It follows that you're a junk food addict." He spread his hands and shrugged. "Who'd have thought we have so much in common?"

Sierra took a long swallow of diet cola. They really didn't have much more than a love of junk food and classic movies in common. She'd do well to remember that.

RYDER POPPED the tab on a caffeine-and-sugar laden soft drink and took a long swallow. She shouldn't look so sexy in a unisex terry-cloth robe. And he should be able to ignore how she affected him and focus on the puzzle they had to solve.

He'd bought the candy and the colas as much to keep his hands busy as to help them think about the case.

"How did you ever get into black ops?"

Ryder nearly dropped the can of soda. Of all the questions in the world, that was one he hadn't expected. She was looking at him as if she'd just asked him why he preferred nuts in his candy bars. "Why do you want to know?"

"Because I want to know more about you."

"Okay. I can understand that." He leaned back against the headboard. "It's a short, boring story. After my aunt died, things were getting pretty hot for me on the street, and I decided that a stint in the marines would be a nice sabbatical."

"A sabbatical?" Sierra raised her brows. "I'm surprised they haven't thought of putting that on a recruitment poster."

"Not manly enough."

"And...?" she prompted.

"The first time we did target practice, I was transferred to a Special Forces unit."

"You were a good shot," she said.

"Yeah. And I did a tour of duty in Rwanda. We didn't have the right kind of leadership or equipment. A lot of lives were lost because of those inefficiencies. But I believed in what we were doing there. Can you understand that?"

She nodded. "Ethnic cleansing is horrible."

"When I was recruited for more covert operations, the job was presented to me as a more efficient way to handle problems that the regular armed forces couldn't. I was good at killing, and I saw it as an opportunity to make a difference. That kid I used to be in Baltimore never thought of making a difference for anyone but himself or his aunt." He met her eyes steadily. "I believed that I could make a difference. That was the way I thought back then. I regret it now, but I can't take it back."

Her gaze didn't waver from his as she took his hand and linked her fingers with his. "Why should you? You were just a kid. You made the best decision that you could."

"Yes, but that doesn't change what I did. I killed people."

"All you can do in life is make the best decision that you can at the time. It's something that I've realized recently about my father. When he left us, he thought he was doing what was best for my sisters and me. I think that's all you can ask of people. Realizing that has helped me to forgive him."

She offered him the last half of her candy bar.

As he took the bite she was offering, a warmth blossomed inside him. He hadn't expected her to understand. Since he wasn't sure he understood it himself, he'd seldom allowed himself to reflect much on that part of his life.

"And look what you're doing now. You operate a business where you do favors for people. And you make a difference for them," she said.

"You know, Doc, it's a damned shame you aren't a psychiatrist, complete with a couch. It's a real waste of talent."

He leaned over and kissed her softly on the mouth, and the warmth spread, easing something inside him that he hadn't been aware of.

When he drew back, he saw a question in her eyes that he was sure reflected the one in his. But he wasn't sure how to answer.

Finally, she asked, "What made you get out?"

His smile was wry. "You might say I grew up and realized that everything's not black and white. In fact, we live in a pretty gray world. I couldn't justify what I was doing anymore, so when my tour was up, I said good-bye."

"And now you work for yourself, and you're the only one deciding what's black and what's white."

"Exactly." He reached over to take her chin. "I would only kill someone in self-defense now—or in defense of a client. Favors for a Fee is not some sort of hit-man service."

"I never thought it was."

There was a fierceness in her tone that had the tension in him easing once again. "My turn, Doc. Why sex research?"

The heat immediately flooded her cheeks. "The answer to that is short and boring too. I was curious."

"Give me the longer version."

She began to fold the now-empty candy wrapper she was still holding. "I was hired by two departments at Georgetown: Psychology and Sociology. I funded the original studies with a grant I applied for through the sociology department. But then I got the book contract, and the psychology department urged me to widen the scope of my work to include personality profiles. So far my research assistant, Zoë McNamara, and I have contacted and interviewed hundreds of people. We're concentrating on single people who live in cities."

"So it's a sort of modern-day Kinsey Report?"

"Nothing quite that revolutionary. A lot of people are doing sex research nowadays. The bottom line is that I applied for the original grant because I was curious. There was a lot I didn't know about modern-day sexual practices. I hadn't had much experience learning them firsthand. It was just one more way that I decided to live life vicariously."

"Like living your life through movies and books," Ryder said.

"Yes." She met his eyes steadily. "I'm not going to go back to being that person. I have you to thank for that."

"My pleasure, Doc." He grinned at her. "Either it's quite a study you've done, or you're just a natural."

She squeezed his hand. "I want you to know that I don't think that I could have done any of what we've done with anyone else. I can't thank you enough for the favor."

His eyes narrowed. The favor. Again he wondered if she thought what had happened between them was all because he was doing her a damn favor. Annoyance boiled up, and he wasn't sure what he would have said if the phone hadn't interrupted him.

"Yeah," he said into the receiver.

"Don't kill the messenger," Jed said.

"Hang on." Ryder answered the question in Sierra's eyes by saying, "It's Jed. While you were in the shower, I called him to let him know he could contact me here for a while." Then he said to Jed, "What have you got?"

"I located the high school in Kansas City where your Brian James McElroy went, and guess who graduated with him?"

Ryder thought for a minute. "I'm going to take a wild guess."

"Go for it."

"Vice President John Gracie."

Sierra's eyes flew to meet his at the same instant that Jed swore in his ear. "Shit. I had to dig deep for that. If you already knew, why didn't you tell me?"

"I didn't know. I told you it was a wild guess."

"Yeah. You and your intuition. Something tells me that you're going to guess the answer to my second question too. Guess where Anderson was during the two days before he disappeared?"

"Kansas City?"

"Bingo," Jed said. "He contacted some of the people I talked to."

"You got anything yet on McElroy's service in Vietnam?"

"Working on it."

"See if there's any connection between him and Gracie there."

"Don't tell me your intuition is failing you on that one."

Ryder laughed. "Keep digging. I wouldn't have made the guess if you hadn't asked the question."

"Tell me," Sierra said when he hung up the phone.

"Vice President John Gracie went to high school with Brian James McElroy. Jed's pissed that I guessed, but you're the one who pointed out they're both from the same state. And Mark Anderson was in Kansas City on Monday and Tuesday. Let's see what else you can come up with." He reached onto the bedside table for a hotel notepad and pen and handed them to her. "Go ahead. Make a list."

He watched while she did, numbering the items neatly. His anger from a few minutes before had drained away. As well it should have. The problem wasn't hers. It was his. He hadn't sorted out his own feelings, and until he did he'd better keep both of their minds on the case.

She was frowning now and tapping the pen on the pad as she thought. Her hair was falling over her cheek, and he had to resist the urge to tuck it behind her ear.

"Okay, I'm ready," she said as she tucked it back herself. "Number one, Mark Anderson has a story. One that has him worried, so he calls you to get your perspective."

"But he misses that appointment because his flight back from Kansas is delayed," Ryder added.

"Number two, Mark's working on a book about the vice-presidency. Number three, John Gracie is the current vice president and there's a lot of buzz about his upcoming campaign for the presidency in 2008."

"Word is, he's going to announce right after the first of the year," Ryder commented.

"Number four, the book Mark Anderson gave me to pass on to you was about *Vietnam: The Unsung Heroes,* and he marked it on a page that mentions John Gracie."

"Jed is checking to see if McElroy and Gracie served together in Vietnam."

She glanced up then and said, "I'd like to look at that book Mark gave me."

"Ramsey is bringing it to our meeting. What else have you got?"

She glanced at her notes. "Number five is Mark's appointments on the day he disappeared. First to the Esquire Club where he left his notes on Brian James McElroy. And where he played racket ball with John Gracie's son, Jack."

"According to Ramsey, Jack has been his dad's chief of staff and campaign manager for five years—ever since Mrs. Gracie died." Running a hand through his hair, Ryder rose from the bed and began to pace. "Something must have happened to alert Mark that he was in danger. So he stashed his notebook in a locker, knowing he could get it later."

"Or so he could send you to get it."

"If someone was following him that day, they would know his schedule even without having his Palm Pilot. So they could have had someone waiting at the club to see if we showed up. That would explain how the tail picked us up."

"Mark's second stop was Le Printemps." She glanced up from her notes. "My sister Rory met the current man in her life there. She took Nat and me on a tour to show us exactly what happened."

Ryder paused in his pacing to stare at her. "You know the layout."

"Sure. Hunter Marks is thinking of buying the hotel as an engagement present for her."

"You're amazing, Doc." He grabbed her hand and

pulled her off the bed. "C'mon. We're going to Le Printemps, and you're going to find out the name of the person Mark met with at four o'clock on Wednesday."

She blinked. "You think I can do that?"

"I'm beginning to think you can do anything you set your mind to."

Sierra narrowed her eyes as Ryder dug into his duffel.

"What do you think?" He pulled out the hip-hugging jeans. "Britney Spears or the suit for the Princess Diana look?"

"Britney wouldn't stay at Le Printemps. They cater to celebrities who want to remain anonymous. She doesn't."

"The blue suit then."

"And what are you going to do while I find out who Mark Anderson met with?"

He grabbed her by the shoulders and gave her a quick, hard kiss. "We have to go with the assumption that somebody is keeping a close watch on the places that Mark visited the day he was snatched. So I'm going to be watching your back."

15

RYDER TRUSTED her to get the information. That was the thought that drove Sierra as she walked into the dimly lit bar of Le Printemps. The doorman had recognized her from the tour Rory had given her, and her explanation that she wanted her fiancé to see the place too had gotten them into the lobby.

Fiancé. She was surprised at the ease with which the word had slid off her tongue. But she hadn't missed the way Ryder's hand had tightened for an instant on her arm.

The wave of confidence she was feeling as she entered the bar faded the moment she saw the bartender. He was not the same man that Rory and Hunter had introduced her to. The one who'd mixed martinis for them that day had been young and eager, just out of college with a hotel management degree. She recalled that Hunter had been impressed with him.

The man who walked toward her as she slid onto a stool was older, and he had a sour expression on his face. His name tag read Gilbert, and he was built like a bouncer.

What in the world was she going to do now?

RYDER CHOSE a seat in the lobby that offered a view of both the front and side entrances and the bar. He'd taken a risk coming here, and then he'd doubled it by bringing Sierra with him. On one level, his justification was simple. He was beginning to think that finding out who Mark Anderson had met in the bar was essential, and they needed the information fast.

Assigning one of his operatives to the job would have taken too much time. And if he'd handled it himself, his attention would have been divided. The most crucial job for him to handle right now was to watch both their backs until they found out the answer to the crucial question: Why did someone want Mark Anderson and Sierra Gibbs dead?

Once they knew that, they would be close to figuring out who was after them. Already, Ryder was beginning to think that he wasn't going to like the answer to either question.

As he watched Sierra pause halfway to the bar, his lips curved in a smile. That hesitation was a sure sign that whatever plan she'd gone in there with was shot to hell. That was why, by and large, he hated plans. A moment later, she straightened her shoulders in that characteristic way she had and picked up her pace. Ryder's smile widened. She thought of herself as a coward, but he'd yet to see her back down once she started something. She also thought she needed to map everything out, but her mind was as agile and inventive as any he'd come across. He wished he could be a fly on the wall so that he could experience firsthand what kind of a story she'd spin for that bartender.

He swept his gaze across the lobby again, noting the elderly gentleman reading a paper and a very well-dressed couple being escorted in by the doorman. The man at the reception desk was speaking in rapid Italian to an elderly gentleman in a pin-striped suit. There was no sign of the muscle-bound trio from the mall, but he was sure that whoever came after them next would be harder to spot.

At least that was the way he would have played it. He shifted his gaze back to Sierra. He could have told Jed to come and get Sierra. If she'd been an ordinary client, he would have. But she'd wanted so much to break out of the shell that she'd encapsulated herself in. And he'd wanted her out of it, too. Because he wanted her free to be with him. Was it as simple and uncomplicated as that?

He glanced around the lobby again. Five minutes. If she wasn't out of the bar in five minutes, he'd go in and give her a hand.

"WHAT CAN I get you?" Gilbert asked as he placed a cocktail napkin in front of Sierra.

She smiled. "A martini straight up with an olive." At least she knew what kind of drink to order.

While he mixed it, she racked her brain for a plan. She'd have settled for just the first step.

Gilbert set the drink in front of her. "Your room number?"

She took a quick sip of the martini. "Actually, I don't have a room here." She extracted a bill from her purse and set it on the bar. "I'm...meeting someone."

He frowned. "The name and room number of the person you're meeting then?"

Sierra knew a minute of pure panic. What was she going to say? Glancing over her shoulder, she saw Ryder sitting in the lobby where he could see her. All she would have to do was signal him, and he'd walk right in, ad-libbing glibly, and rescue her.

But he trusted her to handle it by herself. Straightening her shoulders, she turned back to the bartender and tried another smile. Beyond him, she could see herself in the mirrored wall. The sunglasses gave her an air of mystery and suggested that she was some sort of celebrity. And the blue suit still had that Hitchcock heroine thing going— cool, blond, sexy and gutsy. A spy. Eve Marie Saint playing a double agent in *North by Northwest*.

The least she could do was to give it a shot.

"I'm meeting Mark Anderson."

"Mark Anderson. One moment." Moving a discreet distance away, Gilbert picked up a phone and punched in numbers. When he turned back to her, his frown was even deeper. "We don't have anyone by that name staying here, and we restrict the use of the bar to registered guests. We especially discourage unaccompanied women from hanging out here, if you get my meaning."

Sierra blinked at him and stared as the implication began to sink in. He couldn't possibly think she was some kind of call girl. She shifted her gaze to her image in the mirror. Could he?

The idea struck her as so ridiculous that she laughed and the nerves that had been tightening inside her suddenly eased.

"It's not what you think. I mean, I'm not what you think." Did he actually think she was Julia Roberts in *Pretty Woman,* waiting for Richard Gere to sneak her into his room? Stalling, she looked into her purse while she tried to think up an identity. Not a movie star. He might be too familiar with them. But it had to be someone close to celebrity status.

"Just who are you then, Miss?"

It was the lipstick and compact that Ryder's personal shopper had tucked into her purse that inspired her. Taking a deep breath, she said, "I'm Bailey Tannenbaum, vice president of Tannenbaum Cosmetics." Then she held her breath. Bailey and her sister were not only the heirs to the Tannenbaum Cosmetic fortune, but Bailey, a tall leggy blonde, had recently made the covers of the tabloids when some nude pictures of her had been released on the Internet.

Recognition dawned slowly on Gilbert's face.

Stifling a sigh of relief, she continued, "Since you're a man, you might not be familiar with our cosmetics. But we're big on the West Coast, and Mark Anderson wanted to interview me about my role in the business." Her heart was beating so loudly that she was sure Gilbert would hear it.

"I'm staying at the Four Seasons," she continued, "but too many people recognize me there and there's no hope of privacy. Mark recommended this place, and I'm impressed. In fact, I'm going to mention it to my sister and my mother. We'll be making several promotional trips here over the next year."

"Mark Anderson, you say?"

Sierra nodded. "He's a reporter with *The Washington Post*—tall, sandy-blond hair. He said he met someone for an interview here on Wednesday at four. You may have seen him?"

Gilbert's brow cleared for the first time since she'd confessed that she wasn't a guest. "Oh yes, I believe I did. There was a blond young man who had a drink with Vice President Gracie. The VP comes in here occasionally to meet with people. The Secret Service approves of our rules. And I'm sure that the management would want to provide you with the same privacy and security. What time did you say Mr. Anderson was going to meet you here?"

Trying to remain calm, Sierra glanced at her watch.

"Five o'clock." Then she frowned. "He's half an hour late. I expected him to be waiting for me." Glancing up, she said, "I think I'll give him a little jingle from one of the pay phones in the lobby."

RYDER WAS just about to go after her when she slipped off the bar stool and started toward him. Not a minute too soon, he thought. There were two men at the main entrance who'd been talking to the doorman for several minutes, and he didn't like the looks of them. Most of the pedestrians battling the DC heat wave were tourists wearing shorts, or the occasional businessman carrying his suit coat instead of wearing it.

These men had their jackets on, and while they weren't having the luck that Sierra'd had with the doorman, he didn't trust that they wouldn't eventually succeed.

He caught movement out of the corner of his eye and saw that the bell captain had stepped from behind his counter to talk to a similarly attired man who'd just entered through the side doors. How many more were there? he wondered.

"I did it," Sierra said when she reached him.

"Hold that thought, Doc. We have to get out of here fast." He grabbed her hand and steered her behind a row of potted palms. "Don't look back, and keep your pace steady. They've got both entrances to the lobby covered. I have to believe that they spotted us going in, so we've got to change what we look like again."

"The ladies' lounge is straight ahead."

"One of them is already in the lobby, so we'll take the stairs."

When they reached the third floor, he looked into the hall and spotted what he was looking for—a chambermaid's cart in front of a room door. After knocking on the half-open door, he slid his arm around Sierra's waist and stepped into the room.

The maid was in the bathroom, and Ryder beamed her his best smile. "Could you finish with that later? My wife isn't used to the DC heat. She has to lie down for a while."

Taking her cue, Sierra moved to the bed and stretched out. Two minutes later, they were alone in the room, and she sat up to find that Ryder was already pulling clothes out of the duffel.

"Very smooth. You've done that before, haven't you?" she asked.

"A few times." He tossed her jeans, a T-shirt and the jean jacket. "You're getting to be pretty smooth at this yourself."

His praise sent a ripple of pleasure through her. "I told the bartender I was Bailey Tannenbaum."

"The rich Bailey Tannenbaum whose nude video is available on the Internet?"

She nodded happily as she stripped out of her suit. "And he believed me."

"Can't say I blame him," Ryder said as he watched her wiggle into the jeans.

"From what I saw in the tabloid headlines, that video is X-rated. I can't imagine myself in one of those," she said.

Ryder sure as hell could. But it wasn't a sex video he was thinking of as he watched her pull the T-shirt over her head.

In his experience, major flashes of intuition were never predictable, and it was a hell of a time for this one to hit him. He couldn't afford to be incapacitated, yet his knees had gone weak, and he was certain his heart had skipped a beat.

Sun was pouring through the opened drapes and dust motes were swirling. Ironically, the clock radio was playing a Beatles' song. On some level, his mind was recording all the details, and they would come back to him later. Right now, he was sure of only one thing.

He'd fallen in love with Sierra Gibbs.

He wanted to shout it to the world. He wanted to grab her and tell her.

It wasn't something he'd been looking for. It hadn't been something he'd even wanted. He'd been cruising along in his own lane, happy with the life he'd created.

And he quite simply didn't want to be in that lane alone anymore. The thought terrified him, and he was pretty damn sure if he blurted it out right now, it would terrify her too.

He needed to mull this over. And for the first time in his life, he realized that he needed a plan. Very deliberately, he turned back to the duffel and dug out the outfit he was going to wear. Plan A involved getting Sierra to safety ASAP. Step one of that plan would be to get out of the hotel. Plan B—telling her that his whole world had changed—would have to wait.

"I certainly never thought I could tell one lie after another," Sierra was saying. "My heart was beating so fast I thought it would pop right out of my chest. I'm sure I could never pass a lie detector test."

Glancing into the mirror, Ryder adjusted his cap, and put the finishing touches to his disguise. When he turned back, Sierra was staring at him.

"You're a cop."

"Temporarily." Reaching back into the duffel, he tossed her a wig and a baseball cap. "They're looking for a blond and a tall dark-haired man. And if the man behind this has the kind of resources I believe he does, the men outside have up-to-date photos of both of us. So you're going to be a redhead." Turning her around, he snapped cuffs on her wrists. "And I'm taking you into the station."

"What did I do?" Sierra asked as he urged her toward the door.

"I'll figure that out if someone asks. I hope no one will. People don't often question cops."

At the door she paused. "Wait. I got so caught up in how I'd tricked that bartender into telling me that I forgot the most important thing. The man Mark Anderson met in the bar was Vice President Gracie."

"I figured," he said. "It all seems to circle back to him."

"Do you really think he could be behind all this?"

"That's the million-dollar question, but my guess is that Brian James McElroy is the key to solving this whole puzzle."

16

"OKAY," Rory said as she made a selection from a cheese tray. "What's Ryder like?"

"I…he's…" Sierra shot a glance to where Ryder was seated with the other men in the kitchen of his apartment. How in the world was she supposed to describe a man like Ryder Kane? "Smart. And sweet," she finished lamely.

"Forget the broad generalizations," Rory said. "We want details."

"Don't let yourself be pressured by the investigative reporter. Take your time," Natalie said. "But we do want details."

That was the problem. She'd been so bombarded by new information about Ryder since he'd ushered her into the apartment he lived in above the offices of Kane Management that she hadn't had time to sort through them.

First of all, she'd thought that Favors for a Fee was his only business, but it turned out that he also ran a very high-tech security business that serviced both corporate and government clients. And then there was his apartment.

The best word to describe the place Ryder called home was *plush*. And he seemed to have a butler of sorts—a man named Jensen. He'd given her a quick tour before Natalie and Rory had arrived with their respective significant others in tow. Chance Mitchell and Hunter Marks had hit it off with Ryder from the get-go and were presently seated around the kitchen counter, drinking beer while they waited for Jed Calhoun and Zoë to arrive. Matt Ramsey had remained at Mark Anderson's bedside since the reporter was showing signs of coming out of the coma.

"Hunter really likes Ryder. And he's usually very reserved with strangers," Rory said. "You really ought to try this brie. It's wonderful."

"Chance likes him too," Natalie said as she spread cheese on a cracker.

"He's got a sort of a butler," Sierra blurted out. Not that Ryder had introduced the tall broad-shouldered Jensen as his butler. No. He'd introduced Jensen as an old friend and business colleague. Then he'd added, "Jensen takes care of this place for me."

"You have something against butlers?" Rory asked.

Sierra shook her head. She was pretty sure that Jensen wasn't to blame for her sudden attack of nerves. But she still wasn't sure what was.

"Jensen is more than a butler, I'd wager," Natalie said.

Sierra agreed. The tall, broad-shouldered man looked more like a bodyguard. At first glance there was a toughness about him that was formidable, but when he smiled, all of his features softened, and his eyes crinkled at the corners.

A sudden thought occurred to her. Was he yet another man that Ryder was doing a favor for? But he certainly performed a butler's duties. First, he'd ushered her into a room where she could freshen up; second, he'd served drinks as her sisters and the men had arrived, and right now he was cooking a pot of chili in the kitchen.

Chili. Ryder had asked Jensen to make the chili and he'd guaranteed that she'd prefer it to her favorite takeout version from the Blue Pepper. And then there was the Beatles music that was seeping softly into the room from some kind of invisible sound system. And the collection of movies that were stacked in a helter-skelter fashion beneath the large-screen TV. All of those details had her chest tightening. But there was more.

"There's a Degas hanging in a room off the foyer," she said. "I think it's an original."

"A Degas?" Rory jumped up from her seat. "I've got to see it."

Sierra thought she'd be able to organize her thoughts and pinpoint the cause of her nerves when Natalie rose and followed Rory out of the living area. But the reprieve was short-lived. Jensen was crossing to her with a wine bottle in his hand.

"May I refill your glass?" he asked.

"Thank you." As he poured, she drew in a deep breath. In any study, the more details one had, the easier the analysis became. "Have you known Ryder long?"

"We go back a ways," Jensen said. "I served with him on several operations when we worked for the government. He saved my life on the last one. My leg got messed up pretty good so I had to retire. When Ryder left government work and went into the security business, he looked me up and offered me a job."

"As a butler?"

He smiled and his eyes twinkled. "Not exactly. He asked me to live here and take care of the place for him. He likes to keep a place in town for convenience. But he spends as much time as he can on that houseboat. My main job here is to oversee the office and do the odd job now and again when he's involved in doing favors. He's a good man."

"There's a Degas hanging in the room off the foyer."
The moment she'd blurted that out, she could have bitten
her tongue.

Jensen winked at her. "There's a Monet on the wall in
his bedroom. I helped him select it myself."

Ryder was rich. Sierra reached for her glass of wine and
took a swallow as Jensen walked away. Why did that have
the nerves dancing in her stomach?

"I Wanna Hold Your Hand" began playing softly, and
Ryder turned just then to send her one long, searing look.
Everything else emptied out of her mind, and what filled
it was a sudden flash of insight.

It wasn't the Degas or the Monet or that Ryder was rich
that was bothering her. It was that she'd felt at home from
the moment Ryder had ushered her into the apartment—
just as she'd felt oddly at home on his houseboat. And
she'd felt at home in the bushes, in a utility closet, in hotel
rooms, in taxis. Wherever Ryder was, she felt as though
she belonged.

That had been the connection she'd felt the first time
she'd looked into his eyes at the Blue Pepper. Sierra took in
a shaky breath and let it out. She didn't need a degree in psychology to know that she'd fallen in love with Ryder Kane.
The question was—what was she going to do about it?

"THEY'RE QUITE a trio, aren't they?"

Ryder dragged his eyes away from Sierra and turned his
attention back to Chance and Hunter. Chance was the one
who'd asked the question. Of the two men, he was the most
outgoing, and he was engaged to Natalie, the cop. Hunter
was much more reserved, and he was engaged to the most
effervescent of the sisters, Rory.

"Yes," he said simply. The truth was he hadn't taken

time to study the three sisters together. He'd been so focused on Sierra and how his campaign was working. He'd formulated his own little list while he'd been changing. Odd thing was, he'd pictured it in his mind on one of Sierra's blue note cards.

Step one, he was going to give her some romance. There hadn't been much of that in their relationship so far. He might have to wait until they apprehended a killer before he told her how he felt, but in the meantime, he could play Beatles music and feed her chili.

"You know, of course, that Natalie will kill you if you hurt Sierra."

"Yeah." Ryder sent Chance a rueful smile. "I got that during my first meeting with her."

"She's a tough lady," Chance said.

"Rory's small, but she's tough too," Hunter said.

"When it comes to toughness, I'll place my money on Sierra."

The two men studied him for a minute, and then they exchanged a brief knowing look before raising their glasses in a toast. "Welcome to the club."

"Passed the test, did I?" Ryder asked as he set down his glass after the toast.

Chance grinned at him. "Yeah. It's clear you're hooked. And we know exactly how you feel."

"Have you told her yet?" Hunter asked.

Ryder shook his head. "I won't until we eliminate the threat."

"Good plan," Chance murmured as Natalie and Rory reentered the room with a tall man and a mousy-looking bit of a woman in tow. Once they'd all gathered in the living area on the two oversized couches that faced each other, Sierra introduced Jed and Zoë.

So the mouse was Zoë McNamara, Sierra's research assistant. Ryder noted that she was all business as she sat down on the edge of the couch next to Sierra and placed her manila folder on the coffee table in front of her. Chance and Hunter chose seats directly across from Natalie and Rory. Ryder slid into the spot opposite Sierra, leaving Jed a seat across from Zoë.

"Jensen's going to serve the chili, so we can eat and work at the same time. I have a theory about food stimulating creative thinking," Ryder said.

"Have you ever conducted a study on that?" asked Zoë.

"No," Ryder replied. It occurred to him that except for two things—she was short and had brown hair—Zoë reminded him very much of the Sierra he'd first spotted through the glass windows at the Blue Pepper.

Not anymore, he thought. When he shifted his gaze to Sierra, he saw that she was looking at Zoë, too. Was she thinking the same thing?

"Ryder's theory about food is more intuitive than logical," Sierra said.

Jed snorted, muttering something about intuition as he pulled a notebook out of his pocket. While Jensen set wide-rimmed mugs of chili in front of them, Ryder said, "To bring you up to date, I'll start off by sharing what we have so far."

AS RYDER SUMMARIZED what they'd discovered, Sierra sampled the chili. It was mouth-searingly hot. Perfect. As she took a second bite, she listed in her head the salient points Ryder was making. Mark Anderson calls Ryder and asks to meet with him at the Blue Pepper at five o'clock. He has something *hot* and *political* that he needs Ryder's perspective on. At five-thirty, he calls to postpone. The cell-phone connection fades in and out, but the word *delayed* comes through, and he seems worried his phone is tapped. On Wednesday, before his rescheduled appointment with Ryder, he plays a game of racket ball with the vice president's son and stashes his notes on Brian James McElroy in his locker at the Esquire Club. Later he meets one on one with Vice President Gracie at Le Printemps. When Mark arrives at the Blue Pepper, he tells Sierra he's being followed and he leaves a book, *Vietnam: the Unsung Heroes.* The book is marked with one of Ryder's business cards on a page that mentions John Gracie, and also tucked inside is a key to a locker at the Esquire Health and Fitness Club. Mark tells Sierra that Ryder will know what to do.

"Have I left anything out, Sierra?" Ryder asked.

"No." She pictured the list in her mind. Everything was on it.

"I brought the book," Natalie said. "And I checked into it. One of my sources says that the book is being promoted by a powerful conservative group that's supporting Gracie's run for the presidency in 2008."

"This whole thing has somehow got to go back to John Gracie," Ryder said. "His name is popping up everywhere. We need to know what he's got in his past that would motivate murder."

"You seriously think the vice president is behind this?" Chance asked.

"Politics is a dirty business at best," Ryder said. "Gracie may not be personally involved, but he's got the kind of name recognition and reputation that could attract people with power, people who might have a vested interest in getting him elected."

"Why don't I start the ball rolling?" Jed pulled a notebook out of his pocket. "It's public knowledge that John Gracie was a stellar athlete and valedictorian of his class at Jefferson High School in Kansas City. He came from middle-class parents. He was shipped out to Nam in 1968, right after graduating from Yale Law School. While he was there, he won a medal of honor for saving the life of his captain and several fellow officers during an air raid. Shortly after that, his parents were killed in a plane crash. Lots of coverage of that in the local papers. War Hero Suffers Loss at Home. His tour of duty ended when he was seriously injured in an attack that wiped out the rest of his platoon." Jed paused to flip a page of his notebook over.

"He spent a year at Walter Reed and underwent several plastic surgery procedures before he went back to Kansas City," Zoë said. "He also worked there in rehab getting used to his fake leg."

Jed sent her a surprised look. "Are you sure about the plastic surgery? None of my sources at the Pentagon had that piece of information."

"There was nothing about that in the recent article that appeared in *Vanity Fair*," Rory said. "Though everyone knows about the missing leg. Gracie won two elections as governor of Missouri, based on his popularity as a war hero. He married while he was in office and had one son, Jack. After that he went on to campaign for U.S. Senator."

Zoë shrugged. "I have some contacts at the CIA. One of them knew about the plastic surgery."

"Did either of you dig up any hint of scandal?" Ryder asked.

"No." Zoë and Jed spoke in unison, and then met each other's eyes across the table.

"Not on Gracie," Zoë said, opening her folder. "Brian James McElroy is a slightly different matter."

"His academic career is less distinguished," Jed said. "He got through college on a baseball scholarship and he was a much better pitcher than a student. But he managed to string out his educational deferment until 1968."

"I tracked down a teacher who actually had both of them in a class," Zoë said. "She remembered that although the two men came from different backgrounds, they were rivals of a sort. She remembers McElroy as one of those brilliant students who seldom chose to apply himself to class work, but when it came to the athletic field, he often bested Gracie. McElroy was shipped out at the same time as Gracie and served in Gracie's unit," Zoë added.

"No medal of honor for McElroy," Jed said. "In Vietnam, he ran a profitable black-market business. And there was a rumor that he tried deserting, but when he was caught, he claimed he'd been taken prisoner by the Cong. My source at the Pentagon said that he had a reputation for being able to talk his way out of anything."

"Evidently, his luck ran out," Zoë said. "My source at the CIA said that he would have been facing a court martial if he hadn't been killed."

Jed gave a low whistle. "I didn't get that. Just who do you know at the CIA? Or are you so good that you can hack into their files?"

Zoë's chin lifted. "I used to work there."

For two beats everyone at the table stared at Zoë. Sierra knew that her work at the CIA was a sore spot with Zoë. She never talked about it. She shifted her gaze to Jed Calhoun. The man must really be rubbing Zoë the wrong way to make her blurt it out like that.

"Obviously, you've both got excellent sources," Ryder said, "but the fact remains, we still don't know why McElroy poses a threat to Gracie." He swept the table with his gaze. "Any ideas?"

"There's something that we're missing," Sierra said. "I need something to write on."

"I need to pace," Natalie said, rising.

"Brain food," Rory said, taking a bite of her chili. Sierra glanced up in surprise when Ryder shoved one of her blue note cards across the table. He was being so sweet to her. First the music, then the chili and now he was providing her with blue note cards. She recalled Rory's stories about ex-boyfriends who'd always given her a "dumping" gift. Was Ryder being nice because he was close to finishing the favors?

Even as her heart sank, she pushed the worry out of her mind. She had to concentrate on the case. Quickly, she listed all of the things that Ryder had mentioned in his summary.

"Sierra's right. We're missing something," Ryder said.

The room grew silent for a few minutes. Natalie was pacing, Rory was eating, and Ryder was staring at the ceiling, thinking. Chance and Hunter were both frowning thoughtfully. Jed and Zoë were eyeing each other warily.

Finally Ryder said, "This is a brainstorming session. No idea is too silly. Just lay it out there."

Sierra had no idea how the idea popped into her head. It didn't follow from anything on her list. "What if Brian McElroy is still alive?"

Everyone turned to stare at her.

"He's a con man of sorts, and he's facing a court martial. He's tried to desert once. What if he survived the attack? Everyone else is either dead or badly wounded. So he sees his opportunity and takes it. He switches dog tags with someone else and slips away. It would be the perfect opportunity to disappear."

Hunter nodded. "She raises a good point. I know something about disappearing and creating a new life. With the kind of black-market contacts McElroy had, he could easily have gotten a new identity. And he would also have had the money from his black-market dealings."

"Why resurface now?" asked Natalie. "And why would it threaten Gracie…unless…"

"He's got something on Gracie that we haven't dug up yet," Ryder finished.

"Blackmail," Chance said. "Gracie's building a coalition of powerful people to back him for the presidency. Ryder's right. They might be willing to pay a lot to silence a man like McElroy."

"Then even if McElroy did survive Vietnam, there's a good chance he's already been silenced permanently," Sierra said.

Once again, everyone turned to stare at her.

"I was just thinking. They tried to kill Mark, and then me—just because he talked briefly with me at the Blue Pepper. There's a good chance that Brian McElroy has already been eliminated."

"You may be right," Ryder said. "All the more reason why we have to find out what Mark knew. And fast." Turning to Natalie, he said, "You've got contacts through that special unit you work in. Can you call in any favors and get us a meeting with Vice President Gracie?"

"It would help if I had some leverage," Natalie said.

"Tell him that Sierra Gibbs wants to meet with him to discuss the notebook that Mark Anderson gave her at the Blue Pepper on Wednesday night," Sierra said.

For the second time in as many minutes, everyone turned to stare at her.

"You can't be serious," Natalie said. "He could very well be the man who's trying to kill you."

Sierra lifted her chin. "You wanted leverage. If he's behind this, he'll agree to see me when he hears I have the notebook."

"It's too dangerous," Natalie said. Then she looked at Ryder. "Tell her it's too dangerous."

"Hear me out. We'll meet in a public place," Sierra pointed out. "And I'll be meeting with the Vice President of the United States. If we're right and all of this is about protecting John Gracie, then I think I'll be pretty safe with him. Whoever is trying to kill me won't do it anywhere near him. And meeting with him can't be any more dangerous than what's happening now. Ryder and I won't be safe until we get to the bottom of this, and we'd better do that before they get to us."

There was a beat of silence in the room.

"Her idea just might work," Ryder said. "And she won't be alone. We'll negotiate the time and the place so we'll be able to cover her, and she'll wear a wire. This could be our one chance to end this."

Natalie was frowning. "I don't like it, but I'll make some phone calls."

Ryder turned to Zoë and Jed. "I've got some state-of-the-art equipment downstairs in the office. Jensen will take you down, and I want the two of you to see if you can find what it is that Anderson discovered to make him suspicious. There's some detail that we've overlooked."

As they left, he turned back to the group still seated on the couches. "Now let's brainstorm how we're going to pull this off."

HE REPLACED the phone, and leaned back in his chair. So they wanted a meeting, did they? Well, they would have it. But he'd named the time and the place.

And he'd take care of Dr. Sierra Gibbs once and for all.

Reaching into his desk drawer, he pulled out brandy and poured himself a glass. He wouldn't leave this to his hired help. They'd bungled it so far. This job he'd handle himself.

Tomorrow night his problems would be over.

17

"YOU'RE SURE you know what to do?" Ryder asked as he pulled up in front of the tall federal-style house. Gracie had insisted that the meeting take place at a party he was attending at the home of Millie Langford, one of Washington's premier party-givers. Lots of meetings took place at Millie's parties. Deals were made, coalitions formed, compromises negotiated. The good news was that Kane Management had handled Millie Langford's security for three years now, and Ryder knew the place inside and out. The bad news was, he knew there were too many exits.

"As soon as the VP arrives, you'll be escorted by one of the Secret Service men to a study," Ryder said. "They'll probably choose the room after he gets here, so you'll have to let me know."

Sierra nodded.

Ryder waved the parking valet away. Then he got out of the car and circled to open her door. "As soon as I know where you are, I'll be close by."

They'd been over the plan dozens of times, but he was reluctant to let her go. More than anything he wanted to put Sierra back in his car and drive her away. If he could have thought of a better plan, he would have done just that. But so far, his intuition had failed to provide one.

What he said was, "You're wired. Jed and I will be

within calling distance as soon as we know which room you're in. You let me know anytime you want to get out."

She nodded again, then squared her shoulders and walked up the front steps of Millie Langford's Georgetown home. Ryder pushed down an impulse to go after her. They needed to put an end to this as quickly as possible. Mark Anderson had come out of his coma, but he hadn't recovered his memory. The doctors said he needed time and rest. And Sierra's plan was as safe as they could make it. He and Jed and Jensen had looked at it from every angle. Natalie Gibbs and Matt Ramsey had given it their approval.

The problem with plans was that something could always go wrong.

SIERRA IGNORED her tumbling stomach and concentrated on just placing one foot in front of the other as she stepped through the front door of Millie Langford's house. She could do this. Ryder had faith in her.

A man who looked like every Secret Service agent she'd ever seen in the movies asked her to follow him the moment she'd given her name to another man checking invitations at the door.

Information swirled through her mind as they walked down a hallway. Zoë and Jed had thoroughly briefed her on Brian McElroy and John Gracie. Ryder had chosen her clothes and briefed her on the layout of the house. And Natalie had filled her in on the legendary parties that Millie Langford threw where all the beautiful and powerful people in Washington wanted to be seen.

Sierra caught glimpses of the lights and the glitter through the open doorways that led into the solarium. It was a world that she'd only ever seen in movies. Mozart blended with the buzz of conversation and the clink of glasses. There were tables laden with food. White-coated waiters circulated through the crowd carrying trays of champagne.

"In here, miss," the man said as he opened a door at the end of the hall.

The room she stepped into was small and dim. The walls were lined with books, and a green-shaded reading lamp sitting on an antique desk offered the only light.

"The room's at the end of the hallway to the left as you enter the house," she murmured into the microphone. It was state of the art, and it wasn't taped to her chest like the ones in movies. Instead, Ryder had merely tucked it into her bra. "The room faces the street, so it doesn't have a balcony."

"GOOD WORK," Ryder murmured into her ear. *Bummer* was what he said to himself.

"It's not one of the rooms you were counting on."

"No matter," Ryder assured her. "I know exactly where you are." Giving up on finding a parking spot anywhere near the Langford house, he pulled his car in next to a hydrant and jumped out.

Already things weren't going in an ideal way. The vice president hadn't even arrived and Sierra had already been escorted to a room, one that was tricky to get to without being spotted. The Secret Service men accompanying the VP wouldn't take kindly to anyone loitering about.

Jed was stationed on the long terrace that ran along the back of the house. Ryder spoke to him. "Jed, have you got her location?"

There was no answer.

"Jed? Can you hear me?"

Silence.

"Shit," Ryder muttered as he cut through an alley that would take him to the back of the Langford house. He'd been right. Even the best-laid plans could go haywire.

SIERRA JUMPED when a man stepped out of the shadows. He was tall and neatly turned out in a tuxedo. But she couldn't see his face clearly.

"Good evening."

The voice sounded like the vice president's, but even with the limited lighting, she could see that this man was younger.

"You're not John Gracie."

He moved toward her then, and she caught the glint of light on the small gun he held in his hand. She froze. Before she could even think of moving, he had her arm in a vice-like grip and the gun pressed into her side. Then he leaned close and spoke directly into her ear, his voice barely audible. "Not another word. Take the mike off and put it on the desk."

She hesitated.

"I'll shoot you here before your Mr. Kane can rescue you. Then I'll shoot him."

The matter-of-fact way he spoke had fear streaming through her, and her hand shook as she did what he asked. Then she walked with him toward the door he'd entered from.

"THE VICE PRESIDENT has just arrived."

It was Zoë's voice in his ear. And it was neither the news nor the voice Ryder wanted to hear. Sierra hadn't said anything in the time that it had taken him to get to the back of the house. Her last words hadn't been good.

"You're not John Gracie."

Who in the hell had met her in that room?

Party guests had spilled out of the solarium and into the gardens. As long as he was in their sight, he didn't run. Panicking the guests was not going to help them. He found Jed just getting to his feet behind a potted tree. Then he spoke to Zoë and Natalie who were in a van a block away.

"Bad news. They knocked Jed out for a bit, and someone has Sierra."

"Copy," Zoë said.

Then he heard Natalie's voice. "What can we do?"

"You watch the front entrance and send a couple of my men to the back just in case I'm wrong. But I have a hunch where he's taken her."

"Intuition?" Jed asked as he followed Ryder through the terrace doors.

"It's more of an educated guess. If I wanted to get her out of here, without anyone being the wiser, it's the route I'd take."

"Intuition," Jed said, resignation in his tone.

"Pray I'm right."

TALK, Sierra told herself as the man prodded her through a gate and down a narrow lane. He'd urged her down a flight of stairs to a cement-floored room that had probably once held carriages. Then they'd exited the house through a small door that opened into a narrow alley. Ryder would know about the exit, she reminded herself.

In the meantime, she had to do something to thaw the paralyzing cold that had settled over her. She had to think. Ryder would come as soon as he could. As they passed beneath a streetlight, she suddenly realized who he must be.

"You're John Gracie's son. Jack, right?"

"Right."

She searched her memory for what she knew about Jack Gracie. For years, he'd served as his father's chief of staff and campaign manager. But he had always kept out of the spotlight.

They were walking too fast, so she pulled up short. "Your father agreed to speak with me. I spoke with him this morning."

"Wrong. You spoke with me. Our voices are almost identical over the phone. A lot of people mix us up. I was very happy when you called. This little rendezvous will end the trouble you've been giving me."

His voice was calm and reasonable, a chilling contrast to the leashed violence she sensed as he jerked her forward. He was walking even faster now.

This time to slow him down, she stumbled and fell to her knees.

"Get up." He pulled her arm, and Sierra cried out.

"My knee." She might have faked the fall but the scrape was real.

"The car is only a short distance away."

"Give me a minute," she said. "Why are you doing this? Why can't I just talk to your father?"

"Because you'll upset him. My job is to make sure he doesn't get upset by people who are out to ruin his reputation."

He pulled her to her feet, but as he dragged her forward, she limped to slow him down. "How could I possibly ruin his reputation? It's stellar. What does Brian McElroy know about him? What did Mark Anderson know?"

He stopped and turned toward her. "You know about Brian McElroy then?"

"Yes. I read the notes that Mark Anderson made on him. I know all about Brian McElroy."

His grip on her arm had her wincing, but it was the anger flashing into his eyes that told her she wasn't dealing with a rational person. Fear sliced through her.

"Don't look away," he said.

She couldn't have taken her eyes off of him if she'd tried. That would be like turning your back on an approaching predator.

His smile sent an icy shiver through her. "You know nothing. But from what I've read about you, you're smart. I can't take the risk that you'll figure it out the way that reporter did."

As he pulled her forward, Sierra stumbled again. This time she hadn't faked it. She wished badly she could make a run for it. But even if she could pull free of him, he'd shoot her down. She didn't doubt that for a minute.

"If you stumble again, I'll shoot you right here. You've caused me no end of trouble. You and Mr. Kane."

For the length of time it took them to walk out of the narrow lane, Sierra said nothing. But she knew that she had to. She had to keep Jack Gracie talking. She had to give Ryder time. That's what a Hitchcock heroine would do.

And this was her chance to find out why Jack Gracie wanted to kill her.

"If you're going to shoot me, at least tell me why. There's no one at the Pentagon or the CIA who has anything bad to say about John Gracie's war record."

"Of course not. There isn't anything to find. John Gracie's war record is beyond reproach."

"Then why…?" Sierra let her question trail off as the answer came to her in a flash. Was this what Ryder felt when his intuition kicked in? It was all so simple really. The details swirled through her mind—a platoon in Vietnam where the only survivor had lost a leg and had to have plastic surgery. She'd almost had it when she'd suggested that Brian McElroy hadn't died in Vietnam, but merely assumed a new identity. But that wasn't the whole of it. What if Brian McElroy had survived and stolen the identity of John Gracie? McElroy was facing a court martial, and this was his way out. What if, with the help of plastic surgery, he'd actually turned himself into John Gracie? He was brilliant; he'd gone to school with Gracie and knew him well.

There was only one way to test her theory. Stopping short, she dug in her heels. "The real John Gracie died in Vietnam, didn't he? Your father is Brian James McElroy."

He twisted her arm behind her back and urged her forward.

"I knew you'd figure it out. But the knowledge will die with you."

The pain seared through her arm and helped her to shake off the cold fear. "How long have you known about this?"

His laugh was mirthless and chilling. "I learned when that reporter called me last Sunday. I didn't know what he was talking about at first. He'd done an interview with my father for that book he was writing. And he was excited because he'd found something interesting, something he couldn't explain. He thought he was talking to my father and he wanted to meet. It seems that in all the research he'd done, he'd discovered that John Gracie—the real John Gracie—had been right handed. But he'd noticed that my father was a lefty. A lefty. Can you imagine that? He was flying out to Kansas City to do a little more research, and he'd be back on Tuesday. He wanted to meet with my father when he got back."

They'd reached another gate. He released her and said, "Open it."

While she purposefully fumbled with the latch, she said, "What did you do?"

"I confronted my father and he told me the truth. For thirty-five years, he's been living a lie. And he'd never told me."

Though she couldn't see his face, she could hear the fury in his voice and feel it when he wrenched her arm and shoved her through the gate.

"Everything—everything we've worked for was at stake."

Ryder. He had to be close. If she could just keep him talking a few more minutes...

"You played racket ball with Mark on Wednesday morning, but it was your father who met with Mark Anderson on Wednesday afternoon."

"Yes. Somehow he arranged that meeting without letting me know. And Anderson spooked him. My father told him that he really was Brian McElroy. We could have denied it. After all these years and all this work, my father was actually thinking of not running for the presidency. I couldn't allow that. So I took care of it."

"You tried to kill Mark Anderson because your father was threatening to take his name out of the presidential race?"

"We were going to be the next dynasty—like the Adamses, Kennedys and the Bushes. I had people and corporations lining up to back us. And he told me it couldn't happen. That the truth would have to come out now. I couldn't allow that. I convinced him that I could handle it, and I can." He gave her a push. "C'mon. The car's just around the corner."

Where was Ryder?

"YOU SEE THEM?" Ryder asked.

"Yeah," Jed said.

Two thugs were in a dark-colored sedan parked near the end of the street, and if his hunch was right, Sierra and her captor would appear around the corner at any moment.

"I'll take the one on the passenger side," Ryder said.

They had to work quickly. The man who'd taken Sierra had hurried her out of the house through the old carriage room, just as he'd thought. Jed had gone through the small door just in time to see them exit through the gate at the far end of the narrow alley. In an effort to head them off, he and Jed had taken an alternative route and cut through a nearby yard.

Crouching low, he and Jed moved forward, past a new Beetle, a Porsche and a Mini Cooper. They opened the sedan's doors at the same instant. Jed's man grunted and Ryder's moaned as they hit the cement. They dragged the men back two cars and Jed got behind the wheel. Ryder barely had time to conceal himself behind some shrubs when he saw the man and Sierra turn the corner. As the man pushed her past a streetlight, he caught sight of the gun at the same time he recognized Jack Gracie.

It wasn't a perfect plan. If Gracie noticed there was only one man in the car before he got close enough for Jed to make his move...

Ryder saw the moment that Gracie figured it out. In one smooth movement, the man wrapped his arm around Sierra's neck and held her in front of him like a shield.

Ryder stepped out of the bushes. "Let her go, Gracie."

"Yes," Sierra said in a calm voice. "Let me go. Mr. Kane and I aren't the only ones who know. My sister works for the DC police, and she knows. And so far you haven't killed anyone. Mark Anderson's come out of the coma. The doctors say he'll be fine."

The careful, soothing way she was talking to Gracie signaled to Ryder the unstable state of mind the man was in. He held his gun steady and waited for his chance.

"I don't think Mark Anderson wanted to print that story. I think he admired the work your father has done. It's not too late."

"It is. I tell you it is. I'll kill you all if I have to," Gracie hissed.

Jed slid out of the car and aimed his gun at Gracie too.

"He's mine," Ryder said and watched with some satisfaction as Gracie swung the gun in his direction. Jed would take him out, but before either of them had a chance, Sierra lunged for his gun arm.

Then Ryder was only aware of a series of bright images. The flash of gunfire, the movement of Gracie's arm as he struck Sierra to the ground. Ryder launched himself at the man. There was another burst of gunfire. He felt the impact as it slammed into his shoulder, but he forced Gracie to the ground.

They rolled twice before Ryder managed to get on top. Gracie grabbed his throat, but Ryder delivered a blow to the man's jaw. A lethal arrow of pain shot up his arm. Ryder's vision grayed for a moment, but he managed to lean forward and press his other forearm into Jack Gracie's neck, cutting off his air. The man went still beneath him.

"I've got him," Jed said as grabbed Gracie's wrists and slipped cuffs on them.

"Sierra?" Ryder could see her now. She was on her knees a few feet away. He felt another sharp stab of pain when he levered himself off Gracie, and when he reached for her, one of his arms wouldn't lift.

"You're hit," Sierra said. "Your shoulder. He shot you in the shoulder."

For a moment the world was foggy again, and all Ryder could see was Sierra's face. "You're all right."

"I'm fine. You're not. You're bleeding."

It was getting darker, harder to see. "You got him, Jed?"

"*You* got him. He's cuffed and down for the count, and I'm calling in the troops."

Ryder felt Sierra's arms go around him and then his world faded to black.

18

"If this is a family meeting, you don't have to drag me along," Zoë said.

Sierra turned to her as they reached the door of the Blue Pepper. "My sister Natalie called the gathering to celebrate the closing of the Gracie case. You were a lot of help to us, and I want you to be there."

Sierra stopped short when she spotted Ryder's red convertible turning the corner, but her heart sank when she saw only Jed and Jensen were in it. There was no sign of Ryder.

She put a hand on Zoë's arm. "Let's wait for them."

They might have news of Ryder. There'd been no sign of him since he'd checked himself out of the hospital two days ago. She'd held his hand while they'd patched up his bullet wound, and she'd slept in the chair by his bed.

In the morning she'd still been holding his hand when Natalie and Matt Ramsey had stopped by to report on what they'd learned from the vice president and Jack Gracie. Brian McElroy had indeed stolen John Gracie's identity. When the bomb had destroyed the other members of his platoon, McElroy had known that his face and legs had been damaged, and that Gracie was dead. It was while he'd been lying there, waiting for someone to find him that the plan had been born, and he'd switched dog tags with Gracie. Then with the help of plastic surgery, he'd actually looked like Gracie, too.

Initially, his purpose had been to escape court martial. But during the time he'd spent in rehabilitation, McElroy claimed he'd become a changed man and thought he could make up for his life so far by stepping into John Gracie's shoes. He'd already known a lot about the man. Once he was released from the rehab centre, he'd gone back to Kansas City and moved into Gracie's family home. And he'd studied. Eventually he'd become the role he'd decided to play—John Gracie, returning war hero.

According to McElroy, his son Jack, though brilliant, had always been a bit unstable. From the time he was a child, he had been prone to flashes of uncontrollable temper. After his mother's death, the attacks had become more frequent. McElroy had tried to keep an eye on Jack by putting him in charge of running his office. For the most part, Jack would do an exceptional job. He was an astute politician and well-liked in Washington circles. But on the occasions when things didn't go his way, his temper could be a problem.

That had been one of the reasons that McElroy had been having second thoughts about running for the presidency even before Mark Anderson had come around asking questions about his relationship with Brian McElroy. When he'd met with Anderson at Le Printemps, McElroy had admitted the truth to Anderson. In light of John Gracie's record, Anderson had offered to keep the secret. But McElroy had asked for some time to think it over. Although he'd admitted telling his son about his confession, he claimed that he'd had no idea about Jack's dreams of a presidential dynasty and no knowledge of his plans to kill Mark Anderson.

When Natalie and Matt had left the hospital, Ryder had sent Sierra home to get some rest. The next day, he'd checked himself out of the hospital and disappeared.

There'd been *some* good news in the past two days. Mark Anderson had made a full recovery, and Brian McElroy had offered him an exclusive interview in which he would confess the story of his thirty-five-year impersonation of John Gracie. It was Rory's opinion that even though Brian McElroy wouldn't ever be president, he was going to become a rich man once he decided what book contract to sign. In the meantime, Jack Gracie was being evaluated to see whether or not he was fit for trial.

But none of that news had come from Ryder Kane.

She'd spent two days without him. That had given her two long days and nights to ponder the question that currently overrode all others in her life.

What was she going to do about Ryder Kane?

And she not only had her answer, but she had a plan.

What she didn't have was Ryder Kane.

As the two men crossed the street, Sierra glanced sideways at her reflection in the glass door of the Blue Pepper. The woman she saw was no longer a stranger to her. In the short, brightly colored skirt and white strapless top, she was the new Sierra Gibbs. And thanks to Harry, she was dreaming big.

"Good evening, Sierra."

Sierra smiled as Jed reached her.

"What are you doing here?" Zoë asked.

Jed looked down as if he were just seeing Zoë for the first time. "Oh, it's you. I was invited."

"So was I."

His brows shot up. "That's not a problem for me. Is it a problem for you?"

Zoë's frown deepened. "Of course not."

"Then after you." Jed gestured with his hand and then followed Zoë through the doors of the Blue Pepper.

Jensen chuckled as he paused by her side.

"What is it with the two of them?" Sierra asked.

Jensen's eyes twinkled. "I'd say they're attracted to one another, and neither is too thrilled about it."

"Jed and Zoë? They're so different."

"Sometimes it's more interesting that way," Jensen said.

Of course, Jed and Zoë weren't any more different than she and Ryder were. And yet she and Ryder had found common ground. A lot of common ground. As soon as she found him, she was going to point that out to him. "Do you know where Ryder is, Jensen?" she asked.

"I do, but I'm sworn to secrecy," he said as he held the door open for her.

"I thought he would be here tonight."

Jensen smiled. "I can say this much. You're a smart woman."

So he *was* going to be here. As a mix of panic and anticipation raced through her, Sierra passed through the glass doors of the restaurant. She was about to take the biggest risk she'd ever taken.

Once inside the Blue Pepper, Sierra blinked, blinded for a moment by the darkness after the bright sunlight on the street. She nearly bumped right into Rad.

He grabbed her hands and held her at arm's length. "Look at you. Rory and Natalie told me you'd changed...but I never expected. The shoes, the clothes. And the hair! Ooooooh my! That's a fabulous cut!"

It took her a moment to grasp the fact that the Blue Pepper was empty. And dark. That was why she couldn't see very well. Even Zoë, Jed and Jensen had disappeared into the dimness.

"Where is everyone?" she asked.

"This way," Rad said as he turned and led her up the short flight of stairs into the bar.

As she drew closer, she could see candles flickering at intervals along the bar. And the TV was on.

"What's going on?" she asked Rad. "Where is everybody?"

"They're on the patio, but a gentleman asked me to give you this." It was then that Rad handed her the card. When she glanced down, she could hardly make out the four words. Grant me a favor?

"Where is he?" she asked Rad.

"He'll join you in a few moments."

A favor. Is that all he was interested in?

Walking forward, her heart shot to her throat when she saw the candy bars and canned soft drinks lined up on the bar. She drew in a deep breath and willed her nerves to settle. But her mind kept returning to the favor. A little flame of anger began to burn inside her. After drawing in another deep breath, she climbed up on a stool.

Without even looking back at Rad, she said evenly, "Tell him I'm waiting."

AFTER GLANCING at his watch, Ryder stepped out of the shop and crossed the street to the Blue Pepper. Rad would have had time to escort her to the bar. If she'd agreed to see him. If she hadn't...well, he'd cut off her escape.

Plans had their merit, but you still had to be able to improvise if things went wrong. And this particular plan had begun to take on a life of its own, like the plant that ate Boston.

Two heads were better than one. He'd come to believe that, as long as it was Sierra he was dealing with. But when he'd consulted her two sisters about tonight, it hadn't been long before they'd consulted Chance and Hunter. Shortly after that, Jed, Zoë and even Jensen had offered input, and somehow George and Rad had gotten into the act.

Pausing at the door of the Blue Pepper, Ryder pulled out the blue note card on which he'd written all the steps and made an attempt to review them. As he skimmed down the list, he couldn't help but wonder how in the hell Sierra did this. How was he supposed to remember all the steps he'd written down?

Most importantly, how was he supposed to deal with the woman who'd just walked into the Blue Pepper? If she hadn't arrived with Zoë, he might not have recognized her.

That realization had started the panic coursing through his veins. He certainly hadn't recognized the outfit. The skirt had been short and slashed with color. The white top had been strapless, and she'd looked as if she'd been poured into it.

Who had she gone shopping with?

This was definitely not the same woman he'd seen pacing in front of the Blue Pepper. He wasn't at all sure it was the same woman who'd held his hand all night at the hospital two days ago. Oh, he knew she'd changed. But the fear that gripped him now was that she'd continued to change during the days that he'd left her alone.

Who was she now?

He sure as hell wasn't going to find out by studying a damn note card. Stuffing it back in his pocket, he pulled open the door of the Blue Pepper and strode up the stairs to the bar.

He stopped short the moment he saw her, sitting on the stool. Meeting her in the bar had been Natalie's and Rory's idea. This was where they'd first met and kissed.

The music that was now being piped into the room—

"I Wanna Hold Your Hand"—had been his own idea and he'd phoned Rad that afternoon to add the candy bars and soda. But she wasn't eating the candy, and she hadn't even turned to look at him.

"Sierra?"

She turned then, but he had to move closer to see her face. The heat and fury in her eyes nearly had him stepping back.

She poked a finger into his chest. "You owe me an explanation."

Some of his tension immediately eased. This Sierra he recognized. "I wanted to see you alone for a few minutes before we join the others."

She poked him again. "That's not what I'm talking about. I want you to explain why you disappeared."

"I had to," he said.

"Really."

The familiar dry tone had his heart taking a tumble.

She fisted her hands on her hips. "You really are like Harry, aren't you? You think you can walk into my life, make me crazy about you and then walk out of it again? And this." She picked up the card from the bar and waved it in his face. "You think you can just waltz back into my life and ask for a favor?"

"Yes. Yes, I do." He grabbed her by the shoulders and kissed her. Once he did, and once she returned the kiss, he felt bolstered to continue. Dragging himself back from her, he said, "It's the last one I'll ask of you."

She drew in a deep breath. "You didn't call."

"I wanted you to have time. To think. We were on a roller-coaster ride together. I thought you needed some distance."

"You're the one who needed some distance."

He dropped his hands from her shoulders and ran one through his hair. "Yes. Maybe I did. I wasn't careful enough with you. I nearly got you killed."

"You're the one who got shot."

He grasped her shoulders again. "Look, I wanted us both to have a little time. I've always gone with my instincts, trusted my intuition, but you're a planner. I didn't want to rush you. And maybe I didn't want to rush myself. This is too important." He gave her a little shake. "You're too important."

After dropping his hands again, he pulled the crumpled blue note card out of his pocket and slammed it on the bar. "I even made a damn list."

She picked it up and while she read it, he held his breath.

Five, ten and then twenty seconds ticked by. The only sound that filled the bar was the Beatles song once more building to a crescendo while he waited for her to get to the last step. The one that said, Get Married.

It was going on a minute when she lifted her head and met his eyes. Hers were filled with laughter.

He frowned as her giggle bubbled up and escaped. "What's so damn funny?"

"There are twenty-five steps."

"Hell, don't you think I know that? I talked to your sisters, and they talked to Chance and Hunter. Then Jed and Zoë and even Jensen got involved in the act. Rad and George put their two cents' worth in. And the whole thing is a bust. I'm never ever going to make another one of those damn lists."

"Ryder, I—"

"No." He held up one hand to silence her, while he dug in his back pocket with the other one. "I should have gone with my instincts."

SIERRA FELT the silk tighten and when she glanced down she saw that Ryder had secured her wrist to his with a white scarf. Her heart swelled. But when she glanced up at him, she said, "That's the favor? Does it have to do with those bondage games we meant to try?"

He frowned. "That's not what this is about. I'm tying you up so that you will know that I'm not walking away." He drew in a deep breath. "Ever. And you're not going to walk away from me either. Got that?"

She smiled at him. "Yes."

"Did you mean what you just said—that I made you crazy about me?"

The smile held steady. "Yes."

"Okay." He drew in a deep breath. "Then I'm just going to cut to step twenty-five. It's the only one that matters." He drew her off the stool and dropped to one knee.

She dropped to her knees in front of him. "This is where it started."

"Yes." He took her hand. "I love you. Will you marry me, Sierra Gibbs?"

For a moment, she said nothing. Because she was thinking of Harry's advice: *Always remember that life is better than any dream. It's a better adventure than anything you can find in a book or a movie.*

Harry was so right.

Laughing, she lifted her hands and framed his face. "If I say yes, can we finally play those bondage games?"

He was chuckling too as he lowered his mouth to hers. In the background, he could hear cheers, whistles and applause. And beneath all that, the Beatles sang on. He spoke in a voice only she could hear. "Sure thing. In every position."

Epilogue

"THREE MARTINIS straight up with an olive." George placed the glasses on the three napkins he'd set on the bar. "And congratulations times three."

"Thanks, George," Sierra said.

"And thanks again for throwing us this engagement party," Natalie said. "It was sweet of you to invite my partner and Tracker McBride and the Wainwrights too."

George winked at them. "Two out of the three of you got engaged right here in this restaurant. That's good for business."

Sierra swept her gaze around the bar of the Blue Pepper. The men, including Ryder, Chance and Hunter, had gathered at the far end of the bar to watch the end of an Orioles game. The discussion seemed to be centered on whether or not the current batter should have been called out at first base. Jensen and Jed were voting yes, but they were outnumbered.

Natalie's friends, Sophie and Mac Wainwright, were seated with Zoë at a nearby table. The salsa band was tuning up on the patio, and shortly, Rad would show them to their table.

That was why she'd asked her sisters to join her at the bar for a moment. She took Harry's letter out of her pocket and set it on the bar. "Did you bring yours?"

·Natalie pulled hers out of her blazer jacket, and Rory dug hers out of her purse. When the letters were lined up in a neat row, Sierra said, "If he hadn't sent them, we wouldn't be here tonight celebrating."

"We owe him for that," Natalie said, picking up her glass.

"Here, here," Rory said as she raised hers.

"We owe him a lot," Sierra said. "His advice not only led me to Ryder. It changed me for the better."

"He did that for all three of us," Natalie said.

"But I was thinking that the advice he gave us in those letters goes beyond that," Sierra said.

"Meaning?" Natalie asked.

"An engagement is scary enough, but it's only the beginning," Sierra said. "It's the next part that's really scary."

"Yeah, the marriage part," Rory said. "Happily ever after is a tall order."

"True," Natalie said. "And Harry blew that part."

"I think that Harry sent the letters to help us with the happily-ever-after part, too. I think we're supposed to keep following his advice. He doesn't want us to repeat his mistake."

Natalie looked at Rory. "She definitely is the smartest one."

Rory raised both hands, palms out. "You won't get any argument from me."

They reached for their drinks. "To Harry," they said in unison and clinked glasses.

As the band on the patio started to play, Chance broke away from the group at the end of the bar and held out his hand to Natalie.

"If we're going to celebrate our engagement in a proper way, I think we should get on the dance floor."

Natalie smiled at him as she slid from her stool. "Just as long as you have another proposition for me."

"Let's hope I never run out," Chance said as he led her away.

Hunter was next and he held out his hand to Rory. "Feeling daring? You know I'm not the dancer that Chance is, but if you're willing…"

With a laugh, Rory slid from her stool. "Don't worry, I'll lead."

When Ryder came over, he sat on the stool next to Sierra's, and Sierra felt the same sense of kinship that she felt whenever he was near.

"We've never danced together," she said.

"No." He smiled ruefully at her. "There're a lot of things we haven't done together yet." He leaned closer and spoke softly, "Any chance I could talk you into getting out of here? I had in mind trying one of those positions on the desk in your office. We still haven't gotten around to fulfilling that particular fantasy of mine."

When he straightened she said dryly, "I take it you don't dance."

He ran a finger down her nose. "You see right through me, Doc. I don't dance well at all."

"Neither do I. In college I was always pretty much a wallflower. Natalie and Rory tried to teach me, but it wasn't the same."

Ryder studied her for a moment. "You want to dance."

She nodded. "It can't be that hard. Remember *The King and I* with Yul Brynner and Deborah Kerr?"

"The waltz." Ryder grinned at her. "I'm going to make mistakes just like he did."

She met his gaze steadily. "Me, too. And not just in the dance."

"Yeah. We'll both make some." He leaned down and brushed his lips softly against hers. "But you're the world's greatest planner, and I'm pretty good at improvising. If we put our two heads together, we should do all right." He held out his hand. "Care to risk it, Doc?"

"Yes." Sierra took his hand. With Ryder, she was willing to risk it all.

Good Night, Gracie

KRISTIN GABRIEL

Dear Reader,

One of my favourite quotes is "A dream is just a dream. A goal is a dream with a plan and a deadline." (Harvey Mackay) We all have dreams, and my heroine, Gracie Dawson, is no different. But it's not until she turns her dream of seducing her best friend into a goal – with a plan and a deadline – that her life suddenly takes a turn in a new and exciting direction.

I'd love to hear what you think about *Good Night, Gracie*. Please write to me at PO Box 5162, Grand Island, NE 68802-5162, USA.

Happy reading – and may all *your* dreams come true!

Kristin Gabriel

To all the wonderful authors of Mills & Boon® Sensual – thanks for the memories.

Prologue

"IT'S OVER."

The words she'd been dreading to hear rang in Gracie Dawson's ears. *It's over.* Her dreams of attending law school—of finally embarking on a life of her own—were over. Goliath had won again.

"I knew those biddies at the historical society would reject us." Cat Sheehan mixed drinks behind the mahogany bar while Cat's sister Laine sat shell-shocked on a bar stool between Gracie and waitress Tess Applegate.

As usual, the bar was empty of customers. Temptation was owned by the Sheehan sisters and housed in the same old brick building as Between the Covers, the bookstore Gracie had inherited from her aunt. Recent road construction had caused business to dwindle at both establishments, but that didn't make accepting their loss any easier.

This time Goliath had come in the form of city hall, with plans to demolish the building in order to widen the street. Appealing to the Kendall Historical Society to have the building declared a landmark had been their last hope.

Temptation was like a second home to Gracie and these women like a second family. She'd let them down. Just as she'd let down her aunt Fran, unable to challenge the insurance company that had refused to cover all the medical expenses incurred during her decade-long fight against kidney disease. They'd gone to lawyers for help, but none of them had been willing to take on the sprawling legal department of a huge corporation.

That made them gutless wonders in Gracie's estimation. She'd heard too many stories of people like her aunt at the mercy of bureaucrats and pencil-pushers. Gracie was ready to do some pushing herself—or shoving, as the case may be. But she needed a law degree first and that took time and money. Both would be in short supply now that she'd be forced to relocate the bookstore.

But she believed in loyalty—and keeping promises. Before her aunt had died, she'd told Gracie that as long as Between the Covers existed, a part of her would live, too. Gracie had vowed to keep her legacy alive.

She owed Aunt Fran that much.

Anger flared inside of her at the unfairness of it all. Her aunt had died eleven months ago, worn-out from the struggle of battling both the disease and the bill collectors whom she just managed to satisfy. She'd left everything to Gracie. The house. The bookstore. Her prized collection of Harlequin romance novels. Though she'd never married, Fran Dawson had been a romantic at heart.

Gracie had come to live with her in Kendall, Texas, when she was fifteen years old, after her parents had answered a call to become missionaries. Adjusting to life in Kendall had been difficult at first, made even more so by the tight cliques at her new high school. Losing herself in all those romance books had helped ease the transition.

So had Gilbert Holloway, the high school's resident computer geek, who had become her best friend. They'd spent most of their free time together watching vintage comedy shows on television and making big plans to attend the same college somewhere on the East Coast after graduation.

Then her aunt had been diagnosed with kidney disease and Gracie's plans had drastically changed. Chronically ill, Fran had depended on her for care and to help run Between the Covers. Gracie had never told anyone how much she'd missed going off to college like the rest of her classmates.

Just like she'd never told anyone how much she hated the bookstore.

Except for Gilbert.

He'd left for Boston after graduation and never looked back. For the past ten years, they'd corresponded almost daily by e-mail, his messages like a lifeline to her as her aunt's condition had worsened. He let her whine and rant and worry without judging her. Gilbert was the only man who understood her. The only man who knew how much her dreams meant to her.

Perhaps that's why she had so much trouble meeting men in Texas. Even while taking night classes over the past ten years to obtain her bachelor's degree, dates had been few and far between. None of the men she met ever lived up to Gilbert.

Maybe he was just safe. A man she could dream about without ever having to follow through. And dream she did, though Gilbert would never know about those fantasies. That was the *one* thing about her life that she didn't share with him.

Though she'd done plenty of looking, Gracie had never found a local version of Gilbert. She hadn't seen him in over a decade, but he was still the example she measured other men by.

Not that she'd done a lot of measuring lately. Running the bookstore didn't leave much time for a social life. This latest news meant putting everything in her life on hold indefinitely.

So be it. She wasn't about to surrender to the Goliaths of this world. Gracie Dawson would find a way to survive. She always did.

Laine visibly deflated beside her, making Gracie realize she'd only been thinking about herself. Temptation had been in the Sheehan family for over twenty years, handed down to the sisters by their mother, Brenda. Cat ran the bar while Laine worked full-time as a magazine photographer. They loved Temptation as much as she hated the bookstore.

"The city wants a new road, so we're out," Cat said, breaching the silence. She looked over at Gracie. "Did you really think we'd change anything tonight?"

Despite knowing it was a long shot, Gracie had

counted on it. Which was ridiculous, since nothing in her life ever turned out as she planned. At twenty-eight, she was certainly old enough to know that by now. It was time to start coping with reality.

"Where am I going to store all those books if I can't find a new place in thirty days?" she wondered aloud.

Nobody had any answers for her. Gracie knew she'd have to use every cent of her savings to make this move once she found a new location. A place that would undoubtedly charge higher rent for the bookstore than she was paying now. Add to that the advertising dollars needed to retain their old customers, as well as garnering new ones, and the task seemed overwhelming.

"How will I find another job as good as this one?" Tess asked. She'd hired on as a waitress a year ago, forming a fast friendship with Gracie, Cat and Laine.

Gracie wished she could offer Tess a position at the bookstore, but she'd be lucky to retain her assistant manager, Trina Powers, once they moved the store. Her budget had already been sliced and diced to the bare bones.

Laine looked up at her sister. "How are we going to explain this to Mom?"

Tess reached over and patted her hand. "Brenda will understand. She'll be pissed but she'll deal with it."

Angry tears gleamed in Laine's eyes. "I just can't believe it."

Cat pushed a cosmopolitan toward each of them. "Had faith in the system, Lainey dear?"

"Yes, I did," Laine replied, crushing the letter in

her hand. "This isn't right. How can they just take away everything we've worked for?"

"Because they can." Gracie took a sip of her drink, knowing this news had them all reeling—even Cat. She was just better at hiding it than the rest of them. They were at the mercy of the people in charge, powerless to change anything now.

She hated that feeling. That's why becoming a lawyer had been her dream for so long. She wanted to make a difference in peoples' lives.

Gracie watched Laine get up and turn away, making her wish she could have done something to make this situation turn out differently. It had been her idea to approach the Kendall Historical Society, hoping her exhaustive research into the history of the old building would sway them enough to name it a landmark. She'd handed it all over to Laine to make the presentation, but Gracie obviously hadn't given her enough ammunition.

Gracie slipped off the barstool and walked over to Laine, then put her arm around her shoulder. "This isn't your fault."

A bitter smile flickered on Laine's mouth. "Sure it is. If I'd talked to the right person, made the right argument…"

"It wouldn't have mattered. The city would still be steamrolling over our businesses."

"Maybe."

Gracie knew all too well how futile it was to imagine what might have been. You had to face life head-on and find a way to survive.

Her parents hadn't made it, succumbing to a jungle fever only six months after moving to South America. Neither had Aunt Fran. Gracie had survived through a lot of loss. But she was tired of just surviving. Tired of existing in limbo.

Now she wanted to live—*really* live.

"What are you going to do now?" Laine asked her.

"Find someplace cheap to lease for Between the Covers." Gracie looked around the bar at the oak paneling on the walls and the unique architectural detail on the high ceiling that matched that of the bookstore. "Whatever I find, it will never live up to this place."

"I've got money from my new job, if you need anything—"

"I'll be fine." Gracie knew she'd be able to handle the expenses by using her savings for law school. She'd been accepted at the University of Texas for the upcoming fall semester, but now that would never happen.

Maybe it was time to find a new dream.

Laine was watching Gracie, a mix of worry and self-recrimination in her eyes.

"You shouldn't take so much on yourself," Gracie told her, searching for some way to comfort her. "There's nothing more you can do here. Why don't you go away for a few days? Take some time for yourself."

Laine shook her head. "I can't. I just turned in my first assignment. I don't want it to be my last. Not to mention Aunt Jen is making me crazy. Those wild-fires in California are threatening…" her voice trailed off, then she looked up at Gracie. "June 30, right?"

"That's D-day apparently. Less than a month away."

Gracie's mind whirled with everything that needed to be done in that time. But she simply couldn't deal with it at the moment. Maybe she should take her own advice and get away from the bookstore for a few days. Her ten-year high school reunion was coming up this weekend in Kendall. That would be a perfect excuse to make a temporary escape from her responsibilities.

And a perfect excuse to fulfill the one dream she'd never dared to pursue.

1

ZACH MADDOX SAT illuminated in the blue glow of the computer screen. He'd been there for hours, cross-coding files and making another security sweep of the hard drive. At least, that was the excuse he was using to stay on the job. The reality was that he'd been waiting to hear from Gracie. He knew this was the day the decision was due from the Kendall Historical Society. He hoped her silence meant that she was out celebrating.

Yawning, he stretched his arms over his head, trying to ease the stiffness in his shoulders. He'd spent more time in this chair the past few months than he had in his own bed. Despite his efforts, they weren't any closer to discovering where Gilbert Holloway was hiding. The man had disappeared three months ago.

Holloway, a key witness in a conspiracy case involving credit card theft, had demanded police protection in return for his testimony. Closing his eyes, Zach wondered for the thousandth time why he'd let his partner stay alone with Holloway that night. The rookie had been determined to prove himself, but

Zach should have followed his instincts and pulled the duty himself.

That mistake had gotten Ray shot and cost him the use of his legs.

Some thug had broken in shortly before dawn, apparently to scare Holloway into silence. Ray had fallen asleep on the living room sofa. When he'd heard a window break, he'd panicked and pulled his gun before taking cover.

According to Ray's story, the thug had wrestled him for it while Gilbert escaped out the back door. The gun went off, wounding Ray and scaring the thug away. Zach still remembered coming in that morning to find his partner unconscious on the floor in a pool of blood.

The kid had taken a bullet in the back and it had been touch-and-go for a while. Long enough for Zach to feel out of control, a sensation he always did his best to avoid. So he turned his attention to something he could control—bringing the shooter in. He was certain Holloway could identify him—now he just had to find the guy.

Footprints in the dew-laden grass had led them to a neighbor's garage, where Holloway had apparently hot-wired a Jeep Cherokee before taking off to parts unknown. Three days later the Jeep had been found abandoned on a back road in southern Ohio, but there was no sign of Gilbert Holloway anywhere.

His best guess was that their star witness had staged a disappearing act for his own safety, not trusting the police to protect him anymore. Zach supposed he couldn't really blame the guy—though he thought Holloway was a bit of a wimp. One of those computer jockeys who lived, ate, and slept in front of a keyboard and monitor.

Like Zach was doing now.

At least he had a good reason. All of their leads had turned out to be dead ends. The only hope of finding Holloway now was connecting with one of his friends in cyberspace. Someone who might drop a clue as to where the man would hide.

It wasn't much to go on, but Zach didn't have any alternatives.

A ding resounded from the computer, signaling an incoming e-mail. Zach sat up straight in the chair, his pulse picking up speed.

Gracie.

His reaction had nothing to do with the case and everything to do with the woman on the other side of that e-mail. A friend of Holloway's from high school, the two of them had corresponded daily for the past ten years. After Holloway had disappeared, Zach had taken up the slack, pretending to be Gilbert. At first, he'd hoped to catch a break in the case, thinking Gracie Dawson might reveal something useful. After all, it seemed she knew the guy better than anybody.

But he soon discovered she knew nothing of Gilbert's foray into the criminal world. Zach should have stopped corresponding with her when he realized she couldn't help him locate Gilbert, but something kept drawing him to her e-mails. Something he couldn't quite pinpoint. Her witty, irreverent style? The way she made him laugh? Or maybe the loneliness he glimpsed between the lines. The same loneliness that engulfed him when he stopped working long enough to notice it.

He soon found himself caught up in the details of her life and in the woman herself. Zach knew how much she'd loved her aunt. How much she hated working at the bookstore. How long she'd dreamed of going to law school so she could become a plaintiff's attorney and fight all the injustices in the world.

A noble ambition. One that made him admire her all the more. Zach had tracked down an old high school yearbook in Gilbert's house to find her picture. He knew people changed over ten years, but she'd still have those same wide blue eyes. That same enticing smile.

He knew it was crazy to lust after a woman he'd never even met—one who lived over a thousand miles away. But maybe that's why she appealed to him.

Zach wasn't looking for a close relationship with a woman. He had seen too many fellow officers leave a wife and family behind to risk inflicting that kind of heartache on anyone. That's why he kept his relationships short-term, preferring to devote himself to his work. Everybody had to make choices in life.

Zach chose to go it alone.

He reached for the mouse, clicking on the e-mail. The subject line read *Plan B*. That wasn't a good sign.

Hi Gilbert,
I guess I'm not cut out to chase ambulances. Besides, who wants to graduate from law school when they're thirty-four years old? If you haven't guessed by now, the Kendall Historical Society turned down our application. So that means I'll have to find a new place for Between the Covers in the next twenty days and work there for approximately the next twenty years to pay off all the bills.
But no more whining. I promise.
Did you get your invitation to our high school reunion? Are you coming? It's been ten years since we've seen each other. That's much too long. I miss you, Gil, and I really need to see you.
Please say you'll be there.
Love, Gracie.

Zach read her e-mail again, feeling the pain behind her words. Giving up law school was killing her, no matter how she tried to brush it aside. Just last month she'd sent him an e-mail telling about her acceptance at the University of Texas. Her excitement had jumped off the computer screen.

Now she was in pain, though he knew she'd never reveal it to anyone else. Zach just wished there was some way to make her feel better. The same helplessness that had come over him in the hospital gnawed at him now.

Please say you'll be there.

Zach was so tempted. But how could he fly off to Texas when he had a job to do? Besides, she wanted to see Gilbert Holloway, not him. She didn't even know Zach existed.

He hit the reply button, then poised his fingers over the keyboard, hating the thought of causing her more disappointment. For a moment, he considered putting off a reply until tomorrow, but he didn't think he should give himself that time to mull over his response. His strong desire to see Gracie might overcome his better judgment.

Staring at the blank screen, he searched for the perfect words to let her down easy. At least she could commiserate with Cat, Laine, Tess and Trina. He'd read enough stories about them in her e-mails to make him feel as if he knew them all personally.

But Gracie was the one he saw when he closed his eyes at night. The one he made love to in his dreams.

"Just do it," Zach muttered to himself, hating any kind of procrastination. He believed in taking action, no matter what the consequences. That philosophy had saved his life on more than one occasion.

But as he started to type Gracie's name, a pop sounded from the computer and the screen went black, leaving him in total darkness. He rose from the chair and flipped up the light switch on the wall. Nothing. The electricity was off. What he didn't know yet was the reason why. A simple power failure or something more sinister?

Pulling his gun from his shoulder holster, Zach moved into the hallway. He didn't have a flashlight on him, but he knew the house well enough to navigate his way through the darkness and into the living room. Once there, light from the street lamps shone through the large picture window, illuminating his path. He could see the shadow of the bloodstain on the carpet where Ray had fallen—a daily reminder of how much was at stake in this investigation.

He cocked the gun, then moved into the kitchen. Two voices, both male, emanated from the garage. Zach stopped when he heard a door open into the house and leaned back against a cupboard.

"Yeah, it sucks, but at least we get overtime," said one of the men.

"Does overtime include the last four hours we spent at the bar watching the Red Sox?" asked the other.

"Hey, I'll earn a lot more than that if the Sox can win that thing. I've got a couple hundred bucks on 'em."

Zach holstered his gun. He recognized the voices and knew he wasn't in any danger. They belonged to the department's technicians, Shawn Foy and Jason Billings. Now he just had to find out what the hell they were doing here.

As the two men rounded the corner, the beam of a flashlight landed directly on Zach. They both jumped in surprise when they saw him.

"Damn," Shawn exclaimed. "You scared the crap out of me, Maddox."

"The lights were all off," Jason said. "We thought the house was empty."

"You were wrong." Zach held one hand in front

of his face to shadow it from the beam. "Turn that thing another direction before you blind me. Did you two shut off the electricity?"

"Sure did," Shawn replied. "We've got orders from Brannigan to close up the house and pack up all the equipment—including the computer."

Thomas Brannigan was Zach's commanding officer and in charge of the Holloway case. A veteran detective, he worked strictly by the book, which had caused more than a few skirmishes between the two of them. But he'd never done anything behind Zach's back before.

"Do you always work in the dark?" Zach asked, looking between the two of them.

Jason scowled. "It's not my fault. Shawn here thinks I'll turn on the ball game and leave him to do all the work."

"I don't think it, I know it," Shawn quipped. "That game was going into the fourteenth inning when I finally dragged him out of the bar. It's not worth losing my job over."

But Zach, once a rabid Red Sox fan, hadn't cared much about baseball over the past three months. All he cared about right now was solving this case. "Brannigan didn't say anything to me about moving the operation."

"We're not moving it," Jason said. "We're shutting it down."

Zach stared at him. "Like hell."

Shawn moved past him. "Sorry, Maddox, but we've got our orders. If you don't like it, you'll just have to talk to the boss. The sooner we get out of here, the sooner I can get back to the game."

Zach followed them into the small office and watched them unplug all the cables from the computer. He couldn't believe this was happening. Adding to his irritation was the fact that he hadn't gotten a chance to reply to Gracie's e-mail.

Certain there had to be a misunderstanding, Zach left the house and drove to Brannigan's home. The trip from Holloway's home on the south side of Boston took almost an hour. It was only when Brannigan answered his door wearing a robe and a scowl did Zach consider that he should have called first.

"Why the hell are you banging on my door at this time of night?" Thomas growled. "It sure as hell better be an emergency. My wife and kids are trying to sleep."

"We need to talk."

"Now?"

"It won't take long."

Brannigan's scowl deepened, but he opened the door wider and waved Zach inside. "Make it quick."

Zach crossed the threshold, almost tripping over a stuffed teddy bear in the foyer. Brannigan had four kids under the age of ten, a fact that was evident everywhere Zach looked. The toys littering the floor. The family pictures covering the wall. The cookie crumbs on the coffee table.

A sharp contrast to Zach's place, which barely had any furniture. Just a sofa, a bed, and a thirteen-inch television set. Not that he minded the Spartan environment, since he didn't spend much time there anyway.

"Well, get to it." Thomas tossed a Barbie doll off the sofa cushion before taking a seat.

"I heard a rumor that you're shutting down the Holloway case."

"It's no rumor," Thomas replied. "You know as well as I do that this case has reached a dead end. We can't afford to waste any more time on it."

Waste time? Zach was certain he couldn't be hearing him right. "So we just forget about it? Forget that Ray will never walk again? Forget that the scum who shot him is still out there somewhere?"

Brannigan's face hardened. "I'll never forget what happened to Ray. But you've been pushing the boundaries with this case ever since Ray got shot. I've given you some leeway, because he was your partner, but enough is enough. There are other cases to solve—other perps who need to be apprehended."

Zach rifled a hand through his hair, grappling for a way to change Brannigan's mind. His boss was a stubborn Irishman, but even he had to know this was a big mistake.

"You look like hell," Thomas said, scowling at him. "When was the last time you shaved?"

"Why the hell does it matter? I've been busy."

"You've been obsessed," his boss countered. "I tried to call you at home tonight to give you the news about the investigation, but I had to leave a message on your machine. You were sitting in front of that damn computer at the Holloway house again, weren't you?"

"That's my job," Zach reminded him.

"Don't give me that crap," Thomas spit out. "You're not on duty twenty-four hours a day. You've lost weight and look like you haven't slept in a week."

"Maybe if you worried as much about this investigation as you do about my appearance, we'd have found Gilbert Holloway by now."

Thomas slowly rose to his feet. "I've about had it with your attitude, Maddox. Don't push me."

But Zach didn't back off. "Hell, somebody's got to do it if we're ever going to find the bastard who shot Ray."

Thomas stared at him, a muscle twitching in his jaw. "I think it's time you took a vacation."

"I don't need a damn vacation. I just need to work this case."

"That's not going to happen. You're off the case and off the force for the next thirty days. Effective immediately."

His words were like a sucker punch to the gut. "You're suspending me?"

"Call it a mandatory vacation," Brannigan replied. "There's more to life than the job, Zach. You're going to burn out at this rate. You need to find yourself a beach somewhere in the Caribbean and start hunting for women instead of criminals."

He recognized that obstinate glint in Brannigan's green eyes. The man wasn't going to change his mind. Zach had gone too far this time.

"Now go home," Thomas ordered, ushering him

to the door, "and get some sleep. I don't want to see you for at least a month."

Before he could say another word, Zach found himself standing outside, the door slammed in his face. He'd blown it. Standing on the front porch, he replayed their conversation over in his mind, wondering if there was something else he could have said to convince Brannigan to change his mind.

It was too late now. He was off the case. But he had no desire to play beach bum for the next four weeks. There was only one place he wanted to go—one person he wanted to see. And the reasons why he should stay away didn't seem to matter anymore.

"Gracie Dawson, here I come."

2

THE NIGHT OF HER HIGH SCHOOL reunion, Gracie stepped into Between the Covers wearing her borrowed black dress and matching stilettos, feeling a little like Cinderella. Only she didn't intend to run away from her Prince Charming at midnight. Just the opposite, in fact.

She'd spent hours preparing for this night, grateful the reunion was in Kendall so she didn't have to factor in travel time. Yet, there was something pathetic about the fact that she hadn't left this place for the past ten years. Most of her classmates would be coming in from long distances.

"How do I look?" she asked her assistant store manager, turning in a slow circle.

"Sensational." Trina Powers walked out from behind the counter, the prosthesis on her left leg visible beneath her denim miniskirt. A motorcycle accident eight years ago had led to an amputation just above Trina's knee. Some days she used a wheelchair, but most of the time she wore the prosthesis, ignoring the stares of the customers and challenging anyone who tried to pity her.

Despite her disability, nothing ever stopped the thirty-two-year-old from performing her duties at the bookstore—or voicing her opinion.

"That's a Let's-Have-Sex outfit if I ever saw one," Trina said with a smile.

Gracie looked down at the slinky halter dress she had on loan from Tess. The four-inch heels belonged to Cat, who never seemed to have any trouble attracting men. "That's good because I'm definitely aiming for provocative."

"I know what we should do," Trina replied. "Let's ask the expert. Hemingway's around here somewhere."

Paul Toscano, an aspiring writer whom Trina had nicknamed Hemingway, was a daily fixture at the bookstore. Every morning he arrived with his laptop and a sack lunch, then settled into his favorite nook to work on his book-in-progress until closing time.

"Hey, Ernest," Trina bellowed, "come out here. We need your opinion on something."

Paul emerged from between the bookcases, pushing his wire-rimmed glasses up on his nose. His shirt and jeans fit loosely on his slight build and his auburn hair and beard were in need of a trim. His soulful brown eyes fixed on Trina and Gracie could see a blush form beneath his whiskers.

"You called?" he asked Trina.

"Gracie has a hot date tonight," Trina began, "and we need someone with a Y chromosome to tell us if this outfit she's wearing will trip his trigger."

His blush deepened as he turned his gaze to Gracie. "It's very nice."

Gracie wasn't going for nice. She wanted Gilbert's eyes to pop when he saw her. She wanted him to drag her up to his hotel room at the Claremont and ravish her. On second thought, *she'd* do the ravishing. After reading all those romances in her aunt's collection, she was ready to bring some of those erotic scenes to life.

"Nice?" Trina echoed, staring at Paul. "You're a writer. A wordsmith. Is that really the best you can do? How about sexy? Stunning? Irresistible?"

"Maybe I should take you with me to the reunion," Gracie said to her, "in case Gilbert needs some prodding."

"He won't," Paul said. "You look lovely."

Gracie wished she could be as confident. Gilbert hadn't responded to her e-mail, which wasn't like him. So she'd made a call to the reunion coordinator, who'd confirmed that he'd be there.

She took a deep breath, wondering what it would be like to see him again after all these years. Though there had been some gaps in his communications to her the past couple of years, he'd recently started e-mailing her more than ever.

Their exchanges seemed more personal somehow, with a sexual undercurrent that intrigued her, made her feel closer to him than ever. Maybe because they were both nearing thirty and still single. Whatever the reason, it was long past time to discover if their friendship could lead to something more.

"I looked Gilbert up in an old yearbook," Trina said, pulling one off the shelf. Between the Covers had every yearbook from Kendall High School dating back to 1934. "He's not exactly what I expected."

Gracie looked over Trina's shoulder as she paged to the senior picture section of the yearbook.

"There he is," Trina said, her finger tapping on his photo.

A stout teenage boy with shaggy dark hair, chipmunk cheeks and Coke-bottle bottom glasses that magnified his brown eyes stared back at Gracie. He wore a frayed denim jacket and a sullen expression, neither of which made him appear very appealing.

"Gilbert was never photogenic," Gracie said in his defense. "And he told me he lost a bunch of weight five years ago and had Lasik surgery, so the glasses are gone. Besides, I've gone out with plenty of guys who looked great on the outside but were jerks on the inside. At least I know Gilbert isn't a jerk."

"You're absolutely right." Trina closed the yearbook. "Besides, who am I to judge? It's not like I have a Gilbert or any other man knocking down my door."

Paul cleared his throat and started to say something, but before he could get the words out, Trina abruptly changed the subject.

"I found a couple of possibilities in the real estate section today." She moved to the counter and swiped the newspaper off the green marble top. "Not the best locations, but we obviously don't have time to be picky."

Gracie looked at the two items circle in red ink, guilt welling up inside of her. She hadn't given enough attention to their impending eviction, leaving all the work to Trina as she'd worked on the presentation to the historical society. That would change after this weekend. Then she'd make finding a new home for Between the Covers her first priority.

But right now all she could think about was Gilbert.

She wondered if he really had changed much physically since high school. Not that it mattered. He made her feel special and that was more important than a handsome face or a buff body. Still, a few doubts lingered in her seduction plan. What if the sparks simply weren't there? A wild weekend of hot sex wasn't worth ruining their friendship.

Was it?

The fact that she could even ponder such a question was proof that her long sex drought had taken its toll. Between running the bookstore and taking care of her sick aunt, Gracie hadn't been able to find much time for a social life.

"Here," Trina said, digging into her purse. "You'd better take these."

Gracie looked up from the newspaper to see Trina pull out a handful of colorful condom packages. Paul made a strangled noise in his throat at the sight of them.

"What?" Trina challenged, looking up at him. "You think a gimp can't get lucky?"

"You're not a…I never said…" Paul sputtered.

"Thanks," Gracie interjected, taking the condoms from her.

Why couldn't Trina see that the guy was totally in love with her? Or maybe she did see and just chose to ignore it. Paul wasn't exactly Mr. Exciting.

"Now go out and have fun," Trina said, propelling her toward the door. "And don't worry about the store. I can handle everything here."

"I'll help her," Paul said, then added quickly, "not that she needs it."

Trina laughed and Gracie was surprised by the pinprick of envy inside of her. She'd never had a man look at her the way Paul looked at Trina. The closest she'd come was in high school when Gilbert had asked her to the senior prom. She'd suggested they go out for pizza and bowling instead, fearing he'd only made the offer because she'd whined so much about not having a date. Now, ten years later, she was about to invite him to sleep with her.

She hoped it was an invitation he couldn't refuse.

ZACH STOOD IN THE BALLROOM of the Claremont Hotel wondering how he ever thought he could pull this off. The class of 1995 milled around him, their excited chatter punctuated by occasional shouts of recognition and giddy laughter.

He'd skipped his own high school reunion last year, where he no doubt would have felt as alien as he did now. Those days were a blur to him, mixed with unhappy memories of his father's abandonment when he was thirteen years old.

After he'd been made the man-of-the-house by default, Zach had given up sports and other school activities so he could go to work and help his mother keep their household afloat.

More than once, Zach had fallen asleep in class, exhausted from working double shifts at his job at the all-night delicatessen.

That was where he'd first considered a career in law enforcement, since it was a prime spot for the cruising patrolmen to take their breaks. He'd listened to their stories as he worked, enthralled by the excitement of it all. Compared to slicing salami and shredding lettuce, it had seemed like a dream job.

Now he knew that excitement came at a price. Like almost losing your partner. Or leaving a case unsolved. That still bothered him and he found himself scowling at the blond woman approaching him.

"Well, hey there," she said with a slight Southern drawl, "you don't look like you're having a very good time. Maybe I can fix that."

He pushed thoughts of the case out of his mind, forcing his face to relax into a smile. "I'm sure you can," his gaze dropped to the name tag on her ample chest, "Sandra."

She laughed. "You don't remember me, do you? Nobody's recognized me yet. I used to be a brunette back in high school. And a bit of a tomboy. Now, don't tell me your name. Let me guess."

He wondered how long it would take before she gave up, but he didn't mind waiting. Gracie hadn't shown up yet, so he had nothing better to do.

Sandra tilted her head to one side, looking him up and down. "You're Gilbert Holloway, aren't you?"

Zach blinked in surprise. He and Holloway were close to the same height and both had dark hair and eyes, but nobody would ever mistake them for twins. "How did you know?"

"Because I'm the official reunion greeter and the only two men who haven't picked up their name tags yet are Gilbert Holloway and Mitch Putnam." She laughed again. "But even with that Boston accent, I know you're not Mitch."

"Of course not," he agreed, wondering how she made the distinction. But he didn't want to blow his cover by asking. He was certain Gracie would realize he wasn't Gilbert as soon as she saw him. He just hoped she'd give him a chance to explain before revealing him as a fraud to everyone in the room.

Zach realized now that he'd been crazy to come here. Gracie wanted to see Gilbert, not him. She didn't even know him. Or realize that she'd been communicating with a complete stranger these past few months, telling him all her desires, spilling all her deepest secrets.

Making him fall in love with her.

Zach shook that unsettling thought from his head as soon as it appeared. He wasn't in love with her, just intrigued, maybe even infatuated. But that's as far as it went. That's as far as he'd allow it to go.

Despite his second thoughts, he'd come too far to back out now. Once he met Gracie and satisfied his curiosity, he could put her behind him. It might not be easy, but he'd done it before. All he wanted now was this one weekend with her. One weekend to fulfill the fantasies he'd had about her since her very first e-mail had touched something inside his soul.

Sandra peeled back the adhesive on Gilbert's name tag, then slapped it on his chest. "Can you believe how much everybody's changed? I wouldn't have recognized Stacie Winston if I'd passed her on the street and we started kindergarten together."

"A lot can happen in ten years," Zach replied, feeling more confident about pulling off this charade. Sandra didn't hesitate in accepting him as Gilbert Holloway.

Of course, he'd picked up on a few of the guy's mannerisms and speech patterns while acting as his bodyguard. Zach knew all Gilbert's favorite foods and little idiosyncrasies. And he'd read his journal, as well as all the e-mails exchanged between Gilbert and Gracie for the past decade, which were saved in a special file on Holloway's computer.

In some ways, he knew Gilbert better than he knew himself.

"I still can't believe it's been ten years since we graduated." Sandra leaned closer and lowered her voice. "Did you know Andy Winkleman's been married three times already? And Kendra Nebbles has four kids from four different men. I guess her parents shouldn't have forbidden her from taking that sex education class."

He knew all their names, having memorized them from the yearbook during his flight to Texas. Zach had treated this like any other undercover assignment, covering all his bases before he went into action. Only this assignment was personal and there was no set strategy—other than meeting Gracie.

He checked his watch, hoping he didn't have to wait much longer. "Do you know if Gracie Dawson's arrived yet?"

"Not yet." Sandra gave him a sly smile. "So tell me, were you two really just friends back in high school or was there more going on?"

That was a question Zach couldn't answer, so he hedged a little. "We've always been close."

She laughed. "And you've always been so secretive. I never could get any juicy tidbits out of you."

"I guess I'm just not a juicy kind of guy."

"Maybe not back in high school," she replied, her gaze roaming voraciously over his body. "But you have definitely improved with age."

Zach sensed it was time to move on, but before he could make an excuse to end their conversation, Sandra sidled closer to him.

"Can you believe it?" she asked in a hushed whisper, her gaze fixed across the room. "I think that's Allison Webb. Right over there, next to the punch bowl. Imagine her just showing up here like she graduated with all the rest of us! That certainly takes some nerve. Especially since I didn't even send her an invitation."

Zach followed her gaze and saw a tall blonde scoping out the room. "Did she drop out or something?"

Sandra looked up at him with a snort of disbelief. "How could you forget? It was the talk of the school for months. Allison just disappeared in the middle of our senior year. No warning. No explanation. Some people said she got pregnant. Others claimed she got busted for drugs and thrown in jail. But nobody ever knew for sure."

Now it clicked. In the back of the yearbook had been a mock-up of a wanted poster with Allison's picture on it and text underneath that read:

The senior class of Kendall High is offering a reward of one dollar for any information about AWOL classmate Allison Webb. She was last seen in the computer lab, wearing a pink sweater and white denim jeans.

"Well, it looks like the mystery will be solved tonight," Zach said. "All we have to do is ask her where she went and why."

Sandra smiled as she swept her arm in Allison's direction. "Be my guest, Mr. Holloway. I'll be waiting to soak up all your *juicy* tidbits."

Zach walked across the room, driven more by a desire to escape Sandra than any curiosity about Allison. As he approached her, she caught sight of his name tag, her eyes widening in surprise.

"Gilbert Holloway?" she said, looking him up and down.

"That's right," he replied. "How are you, Allison?"

"You know how I am." She moved closer to him and whispered, "The question is, what are you doing here?"

"Catching up with old friends," he replied, caught off guard by her reaction.

"Are you nuts?" she hissed. "This isn't the time to be playing games. There's too much at stake."

His instincts as a cop kicked into high gear at her words. It looked like there was more to the mystery of Allison than anyone here had imagined. There was something going on between her and Gilbert. Not a physical relationship, obviously, since she didn't realize he was an imposter—which left another incriminating possibility.

"I guess I like to live dangerously."

"I know why you're here," she accused, her gaze narrowing on him. "You want to see goody-two-shoes Gracie."

The jealousy in her tone was unmistakable. But he still couldn't be sure about her connection to Gilbert. He needed to draw her out and make her reveal something that would lead him in the right direction. "What makes you say that?"

"Maybe the fact that you're compromising the entire plan by showing up here tonight. Why did you insist that I make contact with Walker Mullen if you were planning to be here?"

Walker Mullen? The name didn't sound familiar. Just how many alumni from the class of '95 were involved in this case?

"In case you're interested, he bought my story about the stalker and is making the plans for us to travel incognito. I'm supposed to pick up the airline tickets at his agency on Monday."

So Walker Mullen was a local travel agent—and a dupe. That answered one question but still didn't get him any closer to finding Gilbert.

"Now you're taking a chance of blowing everything. And for what?" She rolled her eyes. "A chance to moon over Gracie Dawson?"

Zach wished he knew what she was talking about. He was floundering here and had no idea how to dig for more information without revealing himself.

"Let me buy you a drink," he offered, noting the empty glass in her hand. He could smell the alcohol on her breath and hoped a little more would help her loosen her tongue.

She shook her head. "I'm leaving now. Besides, I prefer to keep a clear head. It's safer that way. And I suggest you do the same—especially around Gracie. If she gets in the way…"

"What?" he prodded, his skin prickling at her tone.

"Just follow the plan and Gracie won't get hurt," Allison replied. "I know where she lives, so if anything goes wrong—and I mean, anything, then she'll be the one who pays. Got it?"

Before he could reply to her not-so-veiled threat, Allison turned on her heel and walked away. Zach started to follow her when another woman came into his view. The woman he'd flown over a thousand miles to meet. The woman he'd only seen before this moment in a yearbook and in his dreams.

Gracie.

3

GRACIE STOOD in the crowded ballroom at the Clare-mont Hotel, her gaze skimming over the faces of her old classmates. Some were familiar to her, some she barely recognized anymore. A few of them cast glances her way, but most were engaged in conversation, gathered in small clusters at tables or standing around the bar.

The one classmate she didn't see was Gilbert. Her heart sank when she realized all her preparation—the dress, the shoes, the romance books, just might have been for nothing. It looked like Gilbert was a no-show. Maybe her e-mail had sounded too desperate, too needy. She'd scared the man off. That was probably the reason he'd never bothered to reply to her.

Gracie walked over to the punch bowl, telling herself not to obsess about it. She could still have a good time tonight and reacquaint herself with all of her old classmates—although the thought of hearing all of their success stories depressed her even more.

"Gracie Dawson, is that really you?"

She turned around to see a buxom blonde barreling down on her. The woman held a name tag in one hand and a margarita in the other. Her face looked somewhat familiar, but Gracie couldn't place her.

"You don't know who I am, do you?" the woman said, laughing as she slapped the name tag onto Gracie's dress. "It's me, Sandra Atley. And here I thought geeky Gilbert would win the award for Most Changed Since High School."

"Geeky Gilbert?" she echoed, her heart skipping a beat. "Is he here?"

"Of course he's here," Sandra replied. "And wait until you see him. You won't believe your eyes." She grabbed Gracie by the elbow and pivoted her around. "He's right over…" Her voice trailed off and she frowned. "Well, he *was* right over there. I'm not sure where he is now."

Gracie smoothed down her dress and tried not to hyperventilate, aware that he could appear at any moment. "So how have you been, Sandra?"

"Fantastic," she replied. "I just got transferred to the Kendall State Bank from the main branch in Houston. It's great to be back home again. I'm still a teller, but I've got my eye on a management position. It's all about networking, you know, and I've already scored some great dirt on the current bank manager."

Gracie forced herself to maintain eye contact instead of looking around for Gilbert. *Let him come to me.*

"So what about you, Gracie?" Sandra asked. "Are you married? Any kids?"

"Oh, no," Gracie replied. "Not yet, anyway. The bookstore keeps me too busy."

Her smile softened with pity. "Are you still working there? It's such a sweet little place. I heard about your aunt passing away and meant to send you a card, but time got away from me. That's why I'm so excited to be moving back to Kendall. Everything in the big city is just rush, rush, rush!"

"So I've heard." Gracie didn't know what else to say, reminding her of how little she'd had in common with most of her classmates at Kendall High. She'd thought ten years might have changed that, but a quick perusal of the ballroom showed that many of the old cliques still remained, though the lines were a bit more blurred now.

She'd always been an outsider, along with Gilbert. Now she wanted to find him again and see if the bond they'd shared a decade ago was still there. A bond that had grown even stronger these past few months. He seemed more thoughtful in his e-mails now. Less cynical. Though he still had the ability to make her laugh.

She wouldn't be surprised if she was the one who had really changed, especially since Aunt Fran's death. After working through her grief, she'd become more driven than ever to pursue her dream to become a lawyer. Not that she'd ever succeed now—but Gilbert had always believed in her.

And that had made all the difference in the world.

"There's Honey Tate." Sandra pointed across the ballroom. "Rumor has it that she's marrying some senile oil tycoon from San Antonio. Remember how she was always flirting with all the male teachers in school? Looks like she was polishing her skills for the geriatric set."

"I don't recognize half the people here," Gracie said, still amazed at the changes in some of her classmates. She wondered if she looked as different to them as they did. Her hair was shorter than it had been in high school and she'd gained a few pounds. Though she'd skipped the boob job that had dramatically altered Sandra's appearance.

"Who is that over by the palm tree?" Gracie asked.

"Mitch Putnam," Sandra replied. "Isn't it a hoot? The guy's at least six inches taller than he was in high school. He must have gotten lifts or something."

"Maybe he just had a late growth spurt."

"It's certainly possible." Sandra adjusted her cleavage. "That's what happened to me." Then she dug her arm into Gracie's ribs. "Don't look now, but here he comes."

"Mitch?"

"No, Gilbert!"

Gracie's breath caught in her throat as she turned to see a man approaching them. But as soon as she saw him she realized it wasn't Gilbert. This man was too handsome. Too confident. Too…sexy.

Despite her disappointment, she couldn't take her eyes off him. She barely heard Sandra's whispered plea to put in a good word for her before she found herself standing alone with him.

"Hello, Gracie."

The way he said her name sent a shiver of awareness down her spine and she forced her gaze from his dark brown eyes to the name tag on his jacket.

Gilbert Holloway.

Her gaze flicked to his face again and she searched for some hint of familiarity. But without all that weight, and those glasses that had distorted his face, he looked like a stranger.

"I can't believe it's you," she breathed, still staring up at him.

"I can't believe how beautiful you look tonight."

His voice had changed, too, deeper now and more resonant. The boy she'd known had become a man in the past ten years. A sexy, virile, irresistible man.

"I don't know what to say," she sputtered, realizing she'd already blown her plan to be cool and alluring. She was gaping like an idiot and no doubt sounding like one, too.

"Then don't say anything. Dance with me?" he asked, holding out his hand.

She grasped it, relishing the way his broad fingers closed around hers. He led her onto the small dance floor, then pulled her into his arms.

Gracie was still in shock, but she managed to avoid stepping on his toes.

"We're finally together again," she said, "after all this time."

"Finally," he agreed, drew her even closer until her head rested against his shoulder. The old Gilbert had always smelled like pepperoni, due to his daily diet of frozen pizza. This new Gilbert carried the aroma of musk and man, an erotic combination that almost made her dizzy.

"When did you get here?" she asked, trying to regain her equilibrium. This was just Gilbert, after all. Her oldest and dearest friend. There was no reason for her heart to be tripping in her chest this way or for her knees to feel weak.

"My plane arrived in Dallas this morning and I drove a rental car from the airport."

"How was your flight?" Another stupid, mundane question, but she was still trying to wrap her mind around the fact that Gilbert was here, in her arms, and more incredible than she'd ever imagined.

"Fine. I slept most of the way."

She smiled up at him. "Slept? Does that mean you don't have anxiety attacks at thirty thousand feet anymore?"

He hesitated, then gave a short nod. "People change."

That was the understatement of the millennium. But Gracie wasn't going to question it, not when this reunion had turned out better than she'd ever imagined.

She swayed to the music, feeling like she was born to be in his arms. "Where did you learn to dance like this?"

A smile kicked up one corner of his mouth. "The Internet."

"No, really."

His smile widened. "It's the truth. I always wanted to learn how to dance, but never had the time. So I used a search engine to locate online dance lessons."

"Online dance lessons," she echoed, still skeptical. "Nobody learns to dance like this all by themselves."

"I might have honed my skills at a few clubs on the weekends."

His admission evoked a pang of envy at the thought of another woman in his arms. A ridiculous reaction, since they hadn't seen each other for ten years. The new-and-improved Gilbert had no doubt slept with countless women. He probably had to turn them away at his bedroom door.

But he wouldn't be turning Gracie away—not if she had anything to say about it. She even had a backup plan tucked away in her purse, in case he needed a little prodding in the right direction.

The thought of sleeping with him sent a shiver of uncertainty through her. Before, she'd envisioned the shy, gawky Gilbert from her high school days, a man who might be as inexperienced as she was be-tween the sheets. But something told her that he was as good a lover as he was a dancer. No doubt another skill that he'd perfected over the years, and not from any online lessons.

She hoped he wouldn't be disappointed—if they got that far. Maybe she needed to rethink this plan before she made a complete fool of herself.

The music ended, but Gilbert didn't release her from his embrace. "Shall we find a table and have a drink or keep dancing?"

As much as she'd enjoyed their dance, Gracie

needed a few moments alone to refocus. "A drink sounds good to me. Would you mind getting me a glass of champagne while I make a dash to the ladies' room?"

"Not at all," he replied. "Shall we meet at a table by the atrium?"

"See you there." Gracie watched him walk away, then took a deep breath as she went in search of a restroom. She found one in the lobby, enjoying the brief respite from the music and milling crowd to get her head together.

She walked inside the ornate restroom, the sinks and stalls on one side and a plush lounge area on the other. As she headed to a sink, she recognized two former cheerleaders from Kendall High, Carol Ann Blume and Mitzi Mobley. They sat on a suede sofa together talking, unaware or unconcerned of her presence.

Just like back in high school.

Gracie smiled to herself, remembering how much their behavior would have wounded her then. Now she had much bigger things to think about. The biggest at the moment being the man waiting for her in the ballroom. The man she planned to seduce tonight.

She pulled a paper towel from the dispenser, running it under cold water, then wringing it out before pressing it to her flushed face. As Gracie stood at the sink, part of their conversation caught her attention.

"Did you get a look at Gilbert Holloway?" Mitzi asked her companion.

"Oh, I know!" Carol Ann exclaimed. "Talk about a transformation."

"The guy went from geek to Greek god. Makes me wish I'd been nicer to him back in high school."

Carol Ann laughed as they got up and headed for the door. "Makes me wish I'd left my husband at home tonight!"

Gracie pulled the paper towel from her face, then touched up her makeup. As she applied her lipstick, she became more determined than ever. Gilbert might have changed on the outside, but he was still the same sweet guy on the inside.

So she didn't need to be intimidated by him. He was the guy who used to sing show tunes to her when she was feeling down. The same guy who had cried watching *Schindler's List*. Women like Sandra, Carol Ann and Mitzi would never appreciate his inner qualities.

Which meant she'd be crazy to miss this opportunity to take her friendship with Gilbert to the next level.

Refreshed and resolved, she walked out of the restroom and into the ballroom. She looked toward the atrium and saw Gilbert already seated at a table. Sandra stood on the other side of him, leaning just far enough in his direction to give Gilbert an R-rated view of her surgically bloated breasts.

"We were just talking about you," Sandra trilled as Gracie approached the table.

"Really?" She took a chair right next to Gilbert, then smiled up at Sandra. "You're such a dear. Thanks for keeping Gilbert company while I was gone. I can take over from here so you can go have some fun."

Disappointment flashed in Sandra's pale blue

eyes, but she hid it with a wide smile. "It was my pleasure. I'll see you two later."

"Bye," Gracie said, watching Sandra turn and head in the direction of another lone male. Then she reached for her champagne, suddenly aware that Gilbert might have been enjoying Sandra's little peep show. "I hope I wasn't interrupting anything."

"You're amazing," he said, turning to look at her. "You got rid of Sandra, but did it in such a polite way that she thanked you for it."

"That's called Southern manners. Also known as slopping sugar. Surely you haven't been away from Texas for so long that you don't remember how it works?"

He smiled. "I guess I just needed a refresher course. I'm a long way from home."

"Is Boston really so different from here?"

He met her gaze. "It's like another world."

When he looked at her like that, Gracie felt like they were the only two people in the ballroom. She found herself wishing she could read his mind. That she could know for certain this desire sizzling inside of her wasn't completely one-sided.

"By the way, I want to apologize for never responding to your last e-mail," he said. "I've been having some computer problems."

That made her feel better. "To tell you the truth, I wasn't sure you'd be here tonight."

"I should have called you," Gilbert admitted. "But I wanted it to be a surprise. I hope you don't mind."

"Not at all." Gracie drained her glass, sensing that

it was now or never. If she didn't make her move, she'd chicken out. But despite that she'd rehearsed this moment a hundred times in the last few days, Gracie couldn't make herself say the words. Coming face-to-face with Gilbert, a man she didn't even recognize anymore, was completely different than propositioning his picture in the yearbook.

So she settled for her backup plan.

"You're full of surprises lately," she said, setting the empty glass on the table. "I love the present you sent me."

He arched a dark brow. "Present?"

"Last week. The video." Gracie reached into her purse and pulled it out, almost spilling the condoms onto the floor. She hastily stuffed them back inside, hoping he hadn't noticed.

Gilbert didn't say anything, making her even more nervous.

"I brought it along in case the reunion got boring and we wanted to bail out and go watch it together," Gracie said, aware she was talking too fast. "You know, like old times?"

She wanted to sink into the floor. It sounded so lame. And transparent. They weren't in high school anymore. Gilbert spent his Saturday nights in clubs now, not watching old reruns on television.

His silence stretched into an eternity. Then he took the videotape out of her hands. "How about watching it right now? I think I have a VCR in my hotel room. I bet we can even order a pizza from room service."

"Pepperoni?" she said, relieved that he hadn't

rejected her offer. That's when Gracie realized just how much this night with Gilbert meant to her. She'd been alone for so long.

He grinned. "Is there any other kind?"

She looked around the crowded ballroom. "Would it look bad if we left this early?"

He tipped her chin up with one finger until her gaze met his. "I'm looking at the only person I came here to see."

Gracie's breath caught at the raw desire she saw in his brown eyes. So maybe the attraction wasn't one-sided, after all. That very real possibility both excited and terrified her at the same time.

"I suppose it will be fitting," she said, trying to lighten the moment, "since we skipped the graduation dance and watched old comedy shows on TV all night."

He smiled. "Then let's say good night, Gracie."

It was his signature line, the one that had always ended their telephone conversations in high school and his e-mail communications since then. For the first time since he'd appeared in the hotel ballroom, the man beside her seemed less like a stranger and more like the old friend she remembered.

Feeling more relaxed now, Gracie let him lead her out of the ballroom to the bank of elevators that would take them to his room. But she didn't plan to say good-night to Gilbert anytime soon.

If Gracie had anything to say about it, their night was just beginning.

4

ZACH HAD RESISTED his share of temptations on the job—like free merchandise offers from vendors seeking special treatment from the Boston P.D. and sexual propositions from women with kinky fantasies about a man in uniform. But none of them had even begun to compare to the temptation standing next to him now.

He slipped his key card into the hotel room door, his duty as a cop battling with his needs as a man. Gracie was everything he'd expected—and more. Not only was she a knockout, she was as genuine in person as she'd been in all of her e-mails—and so damn sexy he'd hardly been able to walk off the dance floor.

"After you," he said, holding the door open for her.

Zach inhaled the exotic aroma of her perfume as she walked past him, his gaze drawn to the enticing sway of her hips in that killer dress. He followed her inside, letting the door fall closed behind him.

He was in dangerous territory now.

Unfamiliar territory, too. He'd never lied to a

woman about his identity before. Now he found himself forced to continue to play the part of Gilbert Holloway. Deceiving everyone down in that ballroom had been innocent fun. But deceiving Gracie... Zach sucked in a deep breath, knowing he didn't have any other choice.

Especially now that the Holloway case had just been blown wide-open. The discovery of Allison Webb's connection to Gilbert, followed by Gracie's revelation that she'd received a gift from the guy last week made it impossible for Zach to reveal his identity. Not when he'd just been handed his first real lead in this case.

When Gracie had pulled that videotape out of her purse, it had been like a bomb had gone off in his head. The events of the past few months has swirled together in a chaotic whirlwind of memories. Ray unconscious and bleeding on the floor. Holloway's vanishing act. The long nights in front of the computer, searching for a break in this case.

Now, in the space of an hour, he'd had two clues land right in his lap. Zach tried to tell himself that the videotape might not mean anything, that it could be just an innocent gift from one friend to another. But his gut told him a different story. Holloway was on the run and wouldn't take the chance of making contact with Gracie unless it was important. Important enough to risk his life.

Judging by Allison's hostile reaction down in the ballroom, Gracie's life, or at least her safety, was also at risk. Zach's appearance as Gilbert at the reunion might have set something in motion that could prove dangerous to her. He was already responsible for one person getting hurt on this case. He damn well wasn't about to allow it to happen again. That gave him another reason to stay close to Gracie.

The king-size bed dominated the room and Zach's pulse picked up when Gracie sat down on it and crossed her legs. She probably had no idea how provocative she looked, with her stiletto heel dangling from one slender foot, how the shapely curves of her long legs sparked a primitive reaction inside of him.

At this moment, he wanted nothing more than to strip off her dress and pull her down on top of him to assuage the ache inside of him that had grown with each one of her e-mails over the past three months and each one of her smiles this evening.

But he couldn't take advantage of Gracie that way. Not when she thought he was Gilbert Holloway. So he corralled his lust, ignoring the heavy throb in his groin as he moved toward the bed.

"Shall we order the pizza first?" he asked.

"I'm not really hungry." She leaned back on the bed, her arms braced behind her. The angle highlighted the long curve of her neck and the creamy skin below. The slinky fabric of her dress molded against her breasts and outlined two perfect, pert nipples. "Are you?"

Zach stared, mesmerized. His willpower was quickly flagging and he couldn't remember the question. "What?"

A smile teased her pink lips, her tongue peeking out to moisten them. He almost groaned aloud, his hands curling into fists. Bringing her to his hotel room had been a bad idea. A very bad idea.

"I'm not really that hungry now," she repeated. "Are you?"

Hell, yes, he was hungry. Ravenous, in fact. He wanted to devour every inch of her, starting with her mouth and moving down her soft, supple body one delectable inch at a time.

When he reached her breasts, he'd take his sweet time, savoring each one. Then he'd move lower, tasting her. Driving her wild. Just like she was doing to him now.

"Gilbert?" she said, her brow crinkling at his long silence.

Zach collected himself. "Hungry? No, not really." Then he swept the videotape from the bed. "So why don't we skip the pizza and start the show."

"Sounds good to me," Gracie said. "Do you mind if I get more comfortable?"

If she got any more comfortable he was going to explode. He tried to ignore the incessant throbbing in his groin, telling himself this was his penance for lying to her. "Go right ahead."

She smiled, then kicked off her stilettos. They both hit the wall with a bang. "Those shoes were killing me."

He breathed a long sigh, both grateful and disappointed that her shoes were all she wanted to remove. Then she stood up and proved him wrong. Gracie lifted the hem of her dress to the top of one thigh, revealing a lacy black garter underneath.

His mouth went dry as she popped open the snaps, the sound reverberating inside of him. He watched her slide the silk stocking down her long leg. Her movements so slow and seductive that he could hear the rapid beat of his pulse inside his ears. Time stood still as she moved to the other leg, popping the snaps on that garter, then removing it along with the second stocking.

"There," she said, straightening to her full height. "That's much better."

Zach turned to the television set to insert the videotape into the VCR, grateful for a few moments to gather himself and figure out how to breathe again. He fiddled with the buttons for a while before finally pushing the play button.

"Here we go," he said, adjusting the volume with the remote control. Now he could focus his attention on this case instead of Gracie. All he had to do was keep his eyes on the television set.

Music from the introduction to the old Burns and Allen show filled the room. Taking a deep breath, he turned around to find Gracie propped on a pillow against the headboard.

She tossed him the other pillow, then patted the empty space beside her. "There's plenty of room here for the two of us. Certainly more room than that old love seat we used to share in your basement."

Jealousy, hot and swift, rose up inside of him at the thought of her cuddling with Holloway on a love seat. He knew they'd never been intimate, having read Gilbert's journal about all the missed opportu-

nities he'd had with Gracie. The guy had been seriously conflicted, lusting after his best friend but too
insecure about his weight and his masculinity to do
anything about it.

At the time, he'd felt a little sorry for the guy. Now
he could only be happy that Holloway hadn't acted
on his desires, a feat even more difficult than Zach
had imagined now that he found himself in a similar situation.

He took the pillow, but placed it on the foot of the
bed, then stretched out onto his stomach, his head
even with Gracie's bare feet. He tried to focus on the
show, looking for any clue that might lead him to Gilbert, but when the mattress shifted and Gracie joined
him at the foot of the bed, he knew he was lost.

He could smell the aroma of lilacs in her hair. Feel
the warmth of her body so close to his own. Hear the
soft laughter in her throat as she watched the show.
The minutes stretched into an eternity as he found
himself covertly watching her more than the videotape. Yet all too soon, the music flared and his gaze
flicked to the television to see the credits roll across
the screen.

Zach swallowed a sigh of relief. He'd made it. His
willpower had conquered his desire for her, though
it had been a close call. A *very* close call. He didn't
dare move off the bed and reveal the arousal that
would be all too apparent through his dress slacks.
Instead he turned to her, surprised how close she
was.

He sucked in a deep breath. If she didn't leave

in the next thirty seconds, his self-control was going to crumble. "I think it's time to say good night, Gracie."

She stared at him for a long moment. Then she leaned toward him and whispered, "Not yet."

He knew he'd lost the battle the moment her lips met his. He surrendered with a moan of anticipation that got lost in the sweet cavern of her mouth. It echoed deep within him as her sweet, sultry kiss filled the void that had ached inside of him for so long.

His conscience tugged at him to stop, but Zach couldn't pull back now. Not yet. Not when she tasted so good and leaned into him that way. Not when his hands on her breasts evoked those soft, needy whimpers in the back of her throat.

Somewhere in a corner of his lust-fogged brain, he knew that this wasn't right, that making love to Gracie while impersonating Gilbert wasn't fair to her. But when he broke the kiss to tell her, she pushed him back on the bed, then slid one hand down past his waist and placed it over the bulge in his slacks.

Zach groaned aloud, knowing he was lost now and didn't care if he ever found his way back. Her fingers moved over him, tentative and exploring. He closed his eyes, letting her set the pace and enjoying every second of it. She stroked the long length of him and he moaned aloud at the sensation. Then she replaced her hand with her mouth, working it up and down over the fabric of his slacks.

He almost lost control at the warm contact. Not ready for this real-life fantasy to be over, he pulled her up to him and kissed her with a need that almost scared him.

There had never been a woman like this before. No one who had driven him to this point of desperation. But Zach needed more than her body. He wanted part of her soul, a connection that would fill him completely.

She broke the kiss, then reached up to untie the knot at her nape, letting the bodice of the dress fall to her waist. No bra obscured his view as he gazed at her two luscious breasts, the nipples pink and pouting for his attention.

He just stared for a moment, watching her breasts rise up and down with her rapid breathing. Then her eyelids fluttered shut as he bent forward and flicked his tongue across one nipple, savoring the texture. She moaned deep in her throat, her body arching up to give him better access.

Like a banquet set before him, Zach laid her back on the bed, then settled in to enjoy the feast. She tasted even better than he'd imagined, her skin sweet and slightly salty as his tongue circled one nipple, then the other. They beaded under his mouth, and he saw her hands clench and unclench the bedcover as her body shuddered with need.

"Please," she murmured, leaving her wishes unspoken. But he knew instinctively what she wanted.

He wanted it, too.

Zach trailed kisses down her soft belly, slowly pushing her dress lower with his hands. She writhed on the bed, crying out when he reached the top of her black panties. He hovered there, drawing out the moment until she threaded her fingers in his hair and urged him to the essence of her.

Sliding his tongue over the hot, moist silk of her panties, Zach settled in for another feast. When she began to move against his mouth, he bracketed her hips with his hands, slowing her movements.

"Oh, please," she rasped, grabbing the headboard above her. "Don't stop."

He had no intention of stopping. But Zach had come too far and waited too long for this to end now. He wanted it to last all night. So he turned his head and dropped kisses on the tender skin of her inner thigh until her breathing slowed a bit. The combination of her cries and her scent soon drove him back to her panties again and he used his tongue to drive her wild once more.

"Wait," she gasped when she couldn't take it anymore, half sitting up on the bed.

He drew back, slipping the dress off her body in one fluid motion. She reached out for him, and pulled off his jacket, then his shirt and tossed them both to the floor.

He forced himself not to move when her hands settled on his belt and her fingers undid the buckle, brushing his arousal. Soon his belt was off, followed by his slacks and boxer shorts. He stood naked before her, his body taut and ready.

She wore only her panties, but left them on as she reclined on the bed once more and held her arms out toward him. This was the point of no return. But

Zach couldn't resist her invitation any more than he could stop breathing. He lay on top of her, his arousal sliding against the silk of her panties.

Gracie wrapped her arms around his neck, arching up against him. The friction of their bodies moving together almost undid him, but he held on long enough to become aware of the condom she'd placed in his hand. It was already unwrapped, making it a simple matter of rolling it onto his erection.

Or not so simple, he thought when she took over the task herself. What had always seemed like a chore now became one of the most erotic acts he'd ever experienced. Gracie used her hands and her tongue to bring him to the brink and back again.

Zach pulled her down on the bed, knowing he couldn't hold on much longer but determined to give her just as much pleasure as she was giving him. He slid her panties down to her ankles, leaving them there to prevent her from opening her legs for him too soon. She seemed to relish the silk bondage, her moans growing louder as his hands delved into the curls at the junction of her thighs.

He took his time, glad he still retained a thin thread of control that allowed him to explore her body. He watched her face when his fingers found the hot, moist center of her desire. She arched on the bed as he circled the tiny bud, her eyes closed and her lips parted. Zach wanted to watch her come to completion, but she refused to go alone.

After kicking off her panties, Gracie encircled his thighs with her legs, then drew him down on top of her. As his arousal penetrated the silken folds of her flesh, they both cried out, then moved in a primitive rhythm that neither one of them could control.

His climax came much too soon, washing over him at the same time that she screamed out a name. But not his name.

Gilbert.

He sunk on top of her, burying his face in the hollow of her neck as spasms racked both of their bodies. She clung to him, her arms and legs entwined around him until he didn't know where he ended and she began. It had been perfect.

Almost.

Gilbert. The name echoed in his ears and left a sour taste in his mouth. Afraid he was crushing her, Zach rolled to his side, taking her with him.

He was determined not to let that name ruin this moment. Zach was the one holding her. He was the one she leaned up to kiss now, a soft blush blossoming on her cheeks.

"It was definitely worth waiting ten years for you," Gracie said huskily, tears shimmering in her beautiful blue eyes. "I'll never forget this night."

Zach didn't know what to say. He certainly couldn't tell her the truth now. He could barely put two words together after what had just happened between them. It had been more than sex, more than lust. His reaction was something he'd never had with any woman before. Ever.

Worst of all, he'd barely put up a fight. Zach Maddox, who prided himself on his self-control, had wilted under her touch. But that didn't mean he regretted making love to her. On the contrary, he wanted it to happen again. And again.

But not until she knew the truth.

He wasn't sure how to tell her yet and now certainly wasn't the moment to do it. But Zach wasn't a man to run from a challenge. And he sure as hell wasn't going to run from Gracie Dawson.

She needed him to protect her, even if she didn't know it yet, at least until he found Gilbert and the rest of his partners in crime. Now he just had to figure out how to do that without complicating her life even further.

But thought was impossible with Gracie lying in his arms. His eyelids grew heavy and he felt more relaxed than he had in years. Zach told himself he'd figure it all out tomorrow, when he had time to make her understand.

She needed to know the truth about him so she could call out *his* name the next time they made love. And there would be a next time—Zach had no doubt about that.

Because he wasn't about to let Gracie go.

5

FOR THE FIRST TIME that Gracie could remember, the reality was better than the dream. She lay beside Gilbert the next morning, watching him as he slept.

The sun was just starting to slant between the part in the heavy blue drapes. The light glinted on the dark layer of whiskers covering his square jaw. She'd never noticed how thick and lush his eyelashes were before. Or that tiny scar just above his eyebrow.

Then again, she hadn't seen him in ten years. No doubt he had scars, both inside and out, that she didn't know anything about. She had scars, too, but at this moment they didn't seem to matter.

Gracie snuggled against his large, naked body, savoring the feel of his skin against her own. She closed her eyes as she remembered the delicious way he'd made love to her last night. More than anything, she wanted to repeat the experience.

But Gilbert was sleeping so deeply that she didn't want to disturb him. No doubt he was exhausted from his long flight from Boston—as well as the erotic trip they'd made together from friends to lovers last night.

It had been touch-and-go for a while. Gracie thought she'd had him when she'd stripped off her stockings, amazing even herself at her audacity. But he'd turned right around and started watching that videotape, seemingly oblivious to the fact that she'd been willing to strip off a lot more.

Fortunately that kiss had changed everything. She suppressed a shiver of delight, remembering all the places that he'd kissed her. Gilbert knew how to make love to a woman even better than he knew how to dance.

He was simply amazing.

But that wasn't the only word she could use to describe him. He was smart, sexy, funny. Her best friend. What more could a girl want?

That question caused her smile to fade. She did want more. But despite the incredible passion they'd shared, he hadn't said anything about staying past the weekend. This might just be a fling for him.

Hadn't she initially planned it that way herself?

She swallowed a sigh, realizing she'd never envisioned a night quite like the one they'd shared. The way he'd touched her. The way he'd held her. No man had ever made her feel so *cherished* before. That was the only word she could use to describe it.

And that's why she knew, deep down in her heart, that this couldn't just be another fling for him.

The melodic chirp of her cell phone made her sit up in bed. She glanced over at Gilbert, who was still fast asleep. Not wanting to wake him, she rose silently off the mattress and retrieved her purse off the chair. After digging inside, she plucked out her ringing cell phone, then carried it into the bathroom and closed the door.

She flipped open the phone, wondering who could possibly be calling her this early. "Hello?"

"Gracie, is that you?"

The deep voice sounded familiar, but she couldn't quite place it. "Yes, who is this?"

"It's Gilbert. I need your help."

"Try again." It was too early in the day for practical jokes. She leaned against the sink, the marble against her bare bottom a chilly reminder that she was naked. At the moment, she wanted nothing more than to climb back in bed with Gilbert and warm herself against his body.

"Gracie, what's wrong with you?"

"Nothing's wrong," she replied, losing her patience. "It's just that you're not Gilbert and it's too early to play games."

"Of course it's me," the man replied, an edge to his voice. "Gilbert Holloway, your best friend from high school."

His voice *did* sound eerily familiar, but she knew it was impossible. Time to call his bluff. "How can you be Gilbert when he's with me right now?"

"What?" The question was almost a shriek.

"You can't be Gilbert Holloway because he's here with me now. He's been with me all night."

"Oh, no." The man's groan carried over the line. "Oh, Gracie, I can't believe this is happening. Look, I'm Gilbert. I swear to you, I'm Gilbert."

She wondered if some of her old classmates had been up all night planning this prank. They'd probably seen her and Gilbert leave together and put two-and-two together. "I'm hanging up now."

"No! Wait. Please." The entreaty in his voice made her pause. This didn't sound like a joke. It sounded like a man desperate for her to believe him. *It sounded like Gilbert.*

She shook off that unsettling thought. This call had to be a joke. But how would any of her old classmates get her cell phone number? Gilbert had both her home number and her cell phone number, even though he'd always chosen to talk to her via e-mail. None of this made any sense.

"Who is this?" she demanded, hating that this man had ruined her morning. The guy on the line simply could not be Gilbert Holloway—he was in a bed just a few feet away from her.

Despite her words, she couldn't bring herself to hang up the phone. There was something about the caller—something about his voice—that kept her on the line.

"Look, I talked to someone who made it to the reunion," the caller said. "She told me there was a man there pretending to be me. I don't know what's going on, Gracie, but you have to believe me. I'm Gilbert."

"No," she breathed into the phone.

"I'm Gilbert Leopold Holloway," he said firmly. "I was named after my grandfather and lived in the same house where he was born at 1324 Mesquite

Road. That house was yellow with black shutters. You used to say it reminded you of a bumblebee."

An icy chill swept through Gracie that she couldn't blame on the cold marble. The voice sounded like Gilbert. And who else would know how she used to describe his old house? She passed it every day on her way to work. The new owner had repainted it years ago. Now it was white with pine-green shutters.

She closed her eyes, feeling a little dizzy. This couldn't be happening. The imposter story was ludicrous. Gilbert Holloway was right here with her. In bed. She opened her eyes, then peeked through the bathroom door just to see if he was the one playing the joke. But he was still asleep, no cell phone in sight. Besides, she reminded herself, he'd been asleep when it had rung.

She closed the bathroom door again, catching her reflection in the mirror. The color had drained from her face and her hair was a mess. Maybe this was a nightmare and she'd wake up soon. But the persistent crackle of the cell phone in her ear told her it was all too real.

"Where are you?" she asked him.

"I can't tell you. Not yet anyway."

"How do I know this is really Gilbert Holloway?" she insisted, still not wanting to believe it was true.

He hesitated for a moment, then said, "Do you remember when I asked you to the prom and you turned me down?"

"I didn't turn Gilbert down," she countered, not

ready to admit it was really him. "I just thought we'd have more fun away from all the hoopla."

"We went to that pizza parlor on Cummings Street. You started to order a pepperoni pizza, but I said we should live dangerously and order something else. Do you remember what it was?"

"Do you?" she challenged, hoping he'd be wrong.

"Canadian bacon and pineapple," he replied without missing a beat. "You loved it and I hated it. We had to pull over when I got sick on the way back to my house that night. Now do you believe me?"

Gracie sagged against the sink, barely resisting the impulse to hang up the phone and forget that this call had ever happened. But she couldn't go back now. She knew it was Gilbert on the line—which left her with another very important question.

"Then who is this man pretending to be you?" she choked out.

"I don't know," Gilbert replied, his voice frazzled. "There are a lot of people after me, Gracie. It could be any one of them. I'm in trouble. Big trouble."

Trouble didn't even begin to describe her situation. She'd slept with a stranger. Even worse, a liar. If the man would deceive her about his identity, even going as far as sleeping with her, what else would he do?

"Tell me what's going on, Gilbert?"

"I can't go into it now, Gracie. I don't have much time. But you need to get away from that man. I'll contact you again soon. Either later today or tomorrow. I need to get that tape back."

"Tape?" she echoed.

"The Burns and Allen tape I sent you a few days ago. Do you still have it?"

"Of course, I still have it. But I don't understand any of this."

"Look, I gotta go. Please, be careful. I'd hate myself if anything happened to you. Promise me, Gracie."

"I promise," she replied. "But—"

The phone went silent and she knew he wasn't on the line anymore. For a moment she just stood there, trying to absorb what had just happened.

Gilbert wasn't Gilbert.

The stranger in that bed had fooled her last night. Fooled everyone at the reunion. Gracie snapped the cell phone shut, furious with herself. She'd known it wasn't him the moment she'd seen him. But she'd let that name tag convince her, as well as her other classmates, who seemed to accept that he was Gilbert as readily as she had.

How could she have been so stupid?

How could she have slept with him?

A hot flush suffused her body when she thought of how eager she'd been to fall into his arms. So ready to believe that the handsome hunk in front of her was her geeky friend from high school. She'd been a much too willing victim of his deception.

Tears pricked her eyes when she thought of everything that had happened between them. He'd duped her so easily he must have laughed himself silly when she'd fallen asleep last night. But why would he make love to her?

That made no sense.

Unless he wanted the videotape, too. That possibility seemed like a certainty when she replayed their conversation from last night in her mind. They'd danced, talked. But he hadn't said a word about going up to his hotel room until she'd pulled the videotape out of her purse.

She remembered the strange way he'd acted when they'd first entered his room. Almost as if he was trying to avoid her. But she'd pushed ahead, blindsiding him with that kiss until he hadn't put up a fight anymore.

Humiliation washed over her. She'd made a complete fool of herself. Falling for the man's masquerade to the point of making love to him! That beautiful night—the night Gracie thought she'd remember the rest of her life—had been a complete sham.

All she wanted to do now was get as far away from him as possible. The only way this situation could get any worse was if she had to face him again.

Determined to disappear before that could happen, Gracie opened the bathroom door, wincing at the slight squeal of the hinges. The stranger still lay asleep in the bed, one arm stretched out over her pillow.

She swept up her clothes and hastily pulled them on, leaving half the buttons undone and her blouse untucked. Then she grabbed her purse and headed for the door. But as her hand touched the knob she remembered the videotape.

Swallowing a groan of frustration, she turned

around and headed back toward the television cabinet, keeping her gaze averted from the bed. She didn't want to look at the man again—didn't want to remember all the intimate things he'd done to her. All the things they'd done together.

She ejected the tape from the VCR, then stuffed it into her purse as she scrambled for the door. The creak of mattress springs sounded behind her, but she didn't hesitate as she bolted out of the door, letting it slam shut behind her.

Her dream of seducing Gilbert Holloway had turned into a nightmare. And something told her that nightmare was just the beginning.

ZACH AWOKE to the sound of a door slamming. He rubbed the sleep out of his eyes, then sat up, the sheet slipping down to his waist. For a moment, he couldn't place his surroundings. This wasn't his bed or his room.

Then he remembered his trip to Texas and the reunion. The Claremont Hotel and Gracie. It had been a night he'd never forget. He placed his hand on her side of the bed. The sheets were still warm from the heat of her body.

He was ready to warm them some more, remembering how she'd come apart in his arms last night. Hell, he'd barely held it together when he'd exploded inside of her. He wanted to do it again. Right now, in fact.

A good night's sleep had eased his guilt. There'd be plenty of time to reveal his identity. Better to do it slowly and earn her trust first. Then he could tell her the entire story, certain she'd understand the reasons he'd had to conceal so much from her.

"Gracie?" he called, assuming she was in the bathroom. He hoped she was still naked.

He swung his legs over the side of the bed and rose to his feet. He couldn't remember the last time he'd felt this relaxed. This…complete. Maybe Brannigan had been right about the vacation. But he knew it was more than the trip to Texas that had reinvigorated him.

It was Gracie.

He padded over the thick carpet to the bathroom, surprised to see the light on inside and the door standing half open. He pushed it open the rest of the way and stuck his head inside. No Gracie.

Perplexed, he turned around and scanned the hotel room. All her clothes were gone, along with her shoes and her purse. Zach walked to the hotel room door and opened it, peering out into the long hallway. But there was no sign of Gracie anywhere.

His gut told him something was seriously wrong. She didn't seem like the love 'em and leave 'em kind of girl. Not after what they'd shared last night.

In his mind, he went over every moment with her, trying to remember if he'd done something or said something to offend her.

But he was coming up blank. Unless…

Was it possible she'd figured out he wasn't Gilbert? Maybe sometime during the night Gracie had realized she'd made love to the wrong man. That thought made him feel sick inside. But he didn't know if it was true. There might be another reason she'd disappeared on him—like an emergency at the bookstore.

He walked over to the nightstand and pulled the telephone book from the drawer. After looking up the number for Between the Covers, he picked up the telephone receiver and dialed it, letting it ring ten times before he finally hung up.

Zach hated not knowing what was going on. Hated the sensation of being out of control of any situation. If something was wrong, then he wanted to help. Even if there was no dire reason for her sudden disappearance, he didn't want her running around Kendall alone—not after his conversation with Allison.

He took a deep breath and reined in his imagination. Now was not the time to panic. What he needed to do was shower and shave. Maybe a few minutes under a hot spray of water would clear his head. With any luck, Gracie had just gone out to get breakfast and would be waiting for him when he got out.

Bagels in bed sounded like the perfect way to start the day.

But when Zach stepped out of the bathroom twenty minutes later, the hotel room was still empty. He walked over to the bed and picked up her pillow, inhaling the scent of her perfume, which was still on the fabric. It hadn't been a dream. Gracie had been here with him last night, slept with him, made love with him.

So why had she run off without waking him?

Zach figured he had two choices. Forget about her or find out why she'd run out on him without even saying goodbye.

The choice was so easy to make it scared him.

6

ZACH DIDN'T START to panic until he turned his rental car onto the street where Gracie lived and saw a police cruiser sitting in front of it. Remembering Allison's veiled threat, he swerved to the curb, then jumped out of the car and ran up to the front porch.

If anything had happened to Gracie...

The battered front door stood open, hanging half off its hinges, and he could see the desolation inside. All her furniture was overturned in the living room, the ripped cushions spilling their white stuffing onto the beige carpet.

He stepped inside the house and glimpsed the broken dishes and pottery shards littering the kitchen linoleum. Books lay everywhere, the pages torn out and crumpled over the floor. Tiny shards of glass glittered in the rays of the morning sun that shone through a broken window.

A hurricane could have ripped through Kendall and caused less damage.

His years as a cop told Zach that this was more than a simple break-in. There was anger behind this crime. Maybe even hate.

His chest tightened as he scanned the room for blood, his mind flashing back to the day he'd found Ray bleeding on the floor at Holloway's house. The same sense of dread filled him now as he moved farther into the house, taking care not to disturb anything.

The sound of a gasp made him turn and he saw Gracie staring at him from the hallway. Her face paled and he could see her pulse jumping in her throat.

"What are you doing—?" she began.

Before she could get the words out, Zach crossed the short distance between them and swept her into his arms. "Thank God, you're all right."

Relief crashed through him, making it hard to breathe. He savored the feel of her in his arms, warm and soft and unharmed. If he'd had any doubt about his feelings for her before, he knew now that this was more than a long-distance infatuation. Last night had been his first clue. Today was his confirmation.

Gracie struggled in his embrace, her hands pushing hard against his chest. "Let go of me!"

He loosened his grasp, pulling away just far enough to take a quick inventory of her body and reassure himself she wasn't hurt.

"I said let me go!" she cried, twisting out from beneath his hands.

A cop emerged from another room and scowled at Zach, his hand reaching for his holster. "Back off. Now."

Zach released her immediately, aware that she

didn't share his warm, fuzzy feelings. Just the opposite, in fact. Anger blazed in her blue eyes, turning them almost sapphire. The high blush on her cheeks was almost the same color as the red tank top she wore.

Zach held up both hands to show the cop he didn't mean any harm. "It's okay. I'm a...friend."

"That's not true!" Gracie whirled around to face the cop. "This man pretended to be an old classmate of mine at my high school reunion last night. The truth is that I've never met him before. But he lied—about his name and his life. About everything."

The cop arched a brow in Zach's direction. "Is that so?"

"I can explain," Zach began, wishing he knew where to start. It was a long story and neither the cop nor Gracie looked like they were in the mood to hear it.

"Explain this," Gracie cried, motioning to the chaos surrounding them. "Was it your job to distract me so your accomplices could ransack my house?"

He stared at her. "You think I'm to blame for this mess?"

"What else am I supposed to think?" she replied, her voice rising. "You showed up at the reunion under false pretenses and played the part of Gilbert to perfection. That obviously took some planning."

"You're reading this all wrong," Zach told her. But he found himself reluctant to clarify it for her. Because in the light of day—and in the light of her anger—he saw himself through her eyes. It wasn't a flattering picture. He hadn't ransacked her house but he'd done something far worse.

"I'm sorry," he said, knowing it was too late for an apology. He'd manipulated her in the worst manner possible. It had been both thoughtless and selfish. He doubted she'd ever forgive him for it, no matter how noble his intentions.

She turned to the cop. "Are you going to arrest him or not?"

The cop looked between the two of them, then fished a notepad and pen out of his shirt pocket. "I'll need a few more details first," he looked up at Zach, "such as your name, sir."

Zach glanced at Gracie, hating that the truth had to come out this way. "Zachary Maddox."

"And how do you know Ms. Dawson?"

He hesitated. "We met last night."

"But it was all a lie," Gracie interjected. "He pretended to be Gilbert Holloway, an old friend of mine. He led me on and…"

"And?" the cop prodded, looking at her.

"And this is all just a big misunderstanding," Zach concluded. The cop didn't need to know about their night together. It had nothing to do with the break-in and would only embarrass Gracie.

But she didn't seem to realize he only had her best interests in mind.

"Misunderstanding?" she echoed, staring at him in disbelief. "That's how you describe what happened last night? A misunderstanding? Tell me, Mr. Maddox—if that is your real name—what exactly did I misunderstand? You introduced yourself as Gilbert Holloway to everyone at the reunion. You knew things about him—and me—that only Gilbert would know. You've obviously been planning this for a very long time. Now I want to know why."

"Perhaps we'd better take this downtown," the cop said, flipping his notepad shut. "We can run a check on Mr. Maddox, just to make sure he's clean."

"That's not necessary." Zach reluctantly pulled out his badge. It was the only way he could get rid of the cop and have a chance to talk to Gracie alone. "I'm with the Boston Police Department. You can call my chief, Thomas Brannigan, to verify. He'll vouch for me."

The cop studied the badge, then handed it back to Zach. "Looks legit to me."

Gracie looked shell-shocked. "You're a policeman?"

"A detective," he clarified. "I've been investigating a criminal case involving your friend Gilbert for the past six months."

She shook her head. "That's not possible. Gilbert would have told me."

Zach wondered if now was the time to tell her he'd been reading all her e-mails for the past three months. Instead he said, "There are a lot of things you don't know about Gilbert Holloway."

"Then why don't you tell me?" she challenged.

His gaze flicked to the cop, who seemed to be enjoying their exchange. "This isn't a good time."

The same passion that had flared between them

last night was in her eyes now, though stirred by anger rather than desire. Despite her animosity, he found himself aroused by her. He wished he could take her in his arms and turn all that energy into something much more pleasurable for both of them.

"I'm still waiting," Gracie said, making it clear that sex was the last thing on her mind.

He wasn't going to say a word. Not with the nosy cop standing between them, ready to spill their story to his fellow officers down at the station.

Gracie spun on her heel and disappeared down the hallway. He heard a door slam shut, the noise echoing throughout the house.

"That is one angry lady," the cop said, stuffing the notepad and pen back into his pocket. "So what are you really doing here, Detective Maddox? Texas isn't exactly your jurisdiction."

"I'm officially on vacation," he replied, aware he'd need the cooperation of the Kendall police if he wanted to pursue this case.

The cop arched a brow. "And unofficially?"

Zach met his gaze. "My partner was shot protecting Gilbert Holloway. So I'm not going to drop the case just because the desk jockeys in my department think it's time to move on. But I promise to stay out of your way if you'll stay out of mine."

The cop studied him for a moment, then gave a brisk nod. "It's hell when a fellow officer goes down. I'm Sergeant Bill Hayes. If you need any assistance, just give us a call."

"Thanks." Zach wished Gracie had been as understanding. But he only had himself to blame for her reaction. He just hoped she'd eventually cool down enough to listen to reason.

Twenty minutes later, Sergeant Hayes finished processing the scene and cleared out. He'd told Zach that the odds didn't look good for catching the perp or perps who had invaded Gracie's home.

Whoever had trashed her house hadn't left any fingerprints behind or other incriminating evidence, further proof to Zach that this had been more than a random break-in. Kendall was hardly a hot bed of crime. According to Sergeant Hayes, this was only the second break-and-enter he'd investigated in the past three years.

That convinced Zach it was connected to Holloway.

Gracie walked out onto the front porch. "What are you still doing here?"

Zach steeled himself for her hostility before turning around. "We need to talk."

"I don't want to talk to you," she said, bristling. "The only thing I want is for you to go away!"

Her words stung, but he didn't back down. Zach knew she'd probably hate him before it was over, but he didn't have a choice anymore. "Sorry to disappoint you, Gracie, but I'm not going anywhere."

GRACIE STARED at the stranger in front of her, feeling sick inside. She was still grappling with the fact that someone had invaded her home, her privacy. The last thing she needed was this imposter making things worse. It only reminded her of what a fool she'd been last night.

"Then I'll leave," she cried, turning away from him.

He stepped in front of her path. "Not until we settle this. You have to let me explain about Holloway... and about what happened last night."

The contrition in his voice made her hesitate, but she knew it was probably phony, just like everything else about him. She had no idea if Zach Maddox was a decent cop, but he was a hell of an actor.

"What about Gilbert?" she asked, purposely ignoring his reference to their night together.

He motioned to the house. "Why don't we go inside so you can sit down?"

She wanted to refuse but her knees still felt shaky and something told her this conversation wouldn't be a short one. Brushing past him, she walked into the house and took a seat on the battered sofa, drawing her legs up underneath her.

Zach sat down on the broken wing chair, an antique piece that had been upholstered in pink damask before a knife had ripped it to shreds. His hands smoothed over the damaged fabric, reminding her of the way they'd slid over her body last night. The memory set off a traitorous tingle deep inside of her.

"Well?" she prodded, hating the effect this man had on her. Despite his deception, there was something about him that still attracted her, something primal that she'd never experienced before. *And never would again*, she vowed to herself, at least not with him.

He met her gaze. "I'll start from the beginning—about six months ago, when we discovered Holloway was involved in an Internet fraud case."

She had no reason to believe him, not when he'd lied to her from the beginning. But she'd already agreed to hear him out. "What kind of fraud?"

"Credit card thefts, to be exact." Zach settled back against the chair, his obvious discomfort making her feel a little better.

"So you're calling Gilbert a thief?"

Instead of answering her question, he asked her one of his own. "Do you remember that cyber-consignment shop business Gilbert started about a year ago? He sent a mass e-mail about it to everyone in his address book, trying to drum up some customers. You were one of the names on the list."

Gracie nodded, remembering how Gilbert had always had one get-rich scheme after another, even back in high school. When they were juniors, he'd opened a savings deposit box at the Kendall State Bank to store all his riches. But all his inventions had ultimately failed, though she'd admired his creativity with the foot-massaging shoes and the talking trellis.

"That cyber-consignment store, as you call it, was legit," Gracie informed him. "Sort of like eBay, but on a much smaller level."

"We don't think Holloway initially intended to defraud people," Zach replied. "But we're not so sure about some of his vendors. We believe when customers bought items from certain vendors, with

Gilbert acting as the middleman, their credit card numbers were stolen."

She found it hard to concentrate while in the same room with Zach, especially when her feelings toward him were so conflicted. The man sitting across from her had lied to her and made love to her. One an act of intimacy, the other of betrayal.

Gracie took a deep breath, trying to maintain her equilibrium. "I don't understand."

"Say you wanted to sell this chair on Gilbert's consignment Web site." He patted the arm of the wing chair. "You'd list it, along with a price. When someone wanted to buy it, they'd send Gilbert their name, address and credit card number and he'd forward that information to you.

"Now, since you're a law-abiding citizen," Zach continued, "you'd handle the information for its intended purpose, then discard it. But we believe one or more of the sellers on his site made other, unlawful purchases with those credit card numbers or even sold them."

"So this is all about stolen credit cards?"

"That's part of it."

"But it's not Gilbert's fault if the people he does business with are crooks."

"We know that," Zach replied. "But he's the linchpin to solving this case. We set up a sting operation in his home, hoping to put it all together, but something happened..."

Gracie looked up as his voice trailed off. "What?"

Zach rose to his feet and began to pace across the

carpet. She couldn't help but watch the way his body moved, the way his clothes molded to the toned muscles she knew lay underneath.

"Gilbert must have tipped off one of the suspects to our investigation, because some thug showed up at the house while we had it under police protection. Things got out of control…"

She waited for him to finish, but his back was turned to her now and she could see the taut line in his broad shoulders. Apprehension fluttered inside of her and she found herself barely able to ask the question that hadn't occurred to her before.

"Was Gilbert…hurt?"

Zach turned around to face her. "No…we don't think so anyway. But my partner was hit. He took a bullet in the back. He almost didn't make it."

Gracie shook her head. "I can't believe Gilbert would ever be involved in something like this. It just isn't like him."

"No offense," Zach said, his voice hard, "but you haven't seen the guy for over a decade. You didn't even recognize the fact that I wasn't him last night."

His words brought all her shame and humiliation flooding back. Gracie stood up, her voice shaking. "Get out of my house."

"Look, I'm sorry," he said, obviously realizing his mistake.

"Not as sorry as I am."

He flinched, but she didn't care. Gracie had always gone out of her way to avoid hurting other people, but Zach was different. He was a cop. A man in a position of power. A man sworn to protect, not use and abuse.

That's why he'd slept with her last night. He'd used her to help him with his case. And that was the only reason he was here now.

He rifled a hand through his hair. "Look, I was wrong to keep my true identity from you last night. I'll admit that. But we're obviously dealing with people who are desperate to conceal their crime."

"What does this have to do with me?"

"Because they've escalated the situation by shooting a cop. Now they have even more incentive to shut Gilbert up—and anyone connected to him. You could be in danger."

"So that's the reason for your charade last night? To protect me? That's going a little above and beyond the call of duty, don't you think, Detective?"

Zach took a step toward her, then stopped. "You've got it all wrong."

"Really?" Gracie said. "So you just decided on a whim to crash a high school reunion a thousand miles away from home? Were you hoping to find Gilbert there? Or maybe you thought I was hiding him?"

He moved so close to her she could see the gold flecks in his dark brown eyes. "Understand this, Gracie. My showing up at the reunion last night had nothing to do with Gilbert Holloway and everything to do with you."

His tone more than his words made her skin prickle with awareness. He wasn't speaking to her as a cop now, but as a man.

"Yes, I lied to you last night," he admitted. "Hell, I've been lying to you longer than that. Holloway disappeared three months ago. Who do you think has been reading and replying to all your e-mails?"

"You?" she breathed, the floor shifting beneath her feet. "The past three months?"

"That's right."

Gracie closed her eyes, reeling from this latest revelation. It certainly explained the change she'd sensed in those e-mails, the intimacy. She'd never even considered a romantic relationship with Gilbert until the past couple of months. Because the Gilbert in those e-mails wasn't the Gilbert from her past.

"Just so you know," Zach said, his voice softer now. "Last night wasn't about Gilbert or about the case. It was about me. About my need to finally meet the woman who I can't seem to forget."

Despite everything, Gracie found herself wanting to believe him, wanting it so badly that it scared her. But she'd learned the hard way that this kind of longing meant disaster loomed ahead. All she had to do was look around at the chaos in her house—and her life—to realize it had already arrived.

Courtesy of Zach Maddox.

She walked to the door, turning to look one last time at the man she had thought was a dream come true, the man she'd thought was Gilbert. "I'm leaving now and I want you gone before I come back. Understood?"

She didn't wait for him to reply, walking out of the house before he could even open his mouth. Her head spun with everything he'd just told her and she needed time to sort it all out.

Time to bury another dream.

7

"I'LL TAKE ANOTHER cosmopolitan," Gracie said, pushing her empty glass across the bar.

Cat raised her eyebrows, but didn't say a word as
she started mixing another drink. Most of the Monday lunch crowd had already left, but a few strag-
glers remained seated throughout the bar.

"So what's Laine doing out in California?" Gracie asked.

"Running away from her problems." Cat laid
down a fresh napkin in front of Gracie, then set her
drink on top of it. "It looks like you're gearing up for
a little escape yourself without going anywhere.
What's up, Gracie? You never drink at this time of
day."

"There's a first time for everything," she muttered,
taking a deep sip. "Like Saturday night, for instance,
when I slept with a complete stranger."

Cat smiled. "So what's the problem?"

The fact that she wasn't horrified made Gracie
feel a little better. Then again, Cat didn't horrify easily.

"It's a long story," Gracie replied, hating to burden Cat when everything was falling apart around them. Not only were they losing the bar and the bookstore, but she'd found out that Tess and Laine were both taking off for parts unknown. Things were already changing and she hated it.

"I love long stories." Cat pulled out a stool from behind the bar and sat down across from Gracie. "Besides, you've always been so cautious—with men, anyway. I can't wait to hear what drove you to do something so spontaneous."

Cautious. The word bounced around in her head. Is that how Cat and the rest of her friends saw her? Cat Sheehan never minced words. It was one of the things Gracie liked most about her. But the image the word "cautious" evoked wasn't exactly flattering.

"How am I cautious?" she challenged.

Cat rolled her eyes. "Please. You never date, even when you have the opportunity. And there have been plenty of Saturday nights in here when you've had the opportunity. The only man you ever talk about is Gilbert and he's a thousand miles away in Boston."

Though she'd borrowed shoes from Cat for the reunion on Saturday, she hadn't told her about her plans to seduce Gilbert. Trina was the only one who knew—and Paul—but she knew they'd never talk.

"I date," Gracie said in her own defense. "I'm just…selective."

"You've been playing it safe," Cat countered. "So I'm glad to hear you finally took a walk on the wild side."

"Not by choice. The night definitely didn't go as I had planned."

Cat looked at her. "That's what spontaneity means, Gracie. Something you don't plan ahead."

"I know the definition. But I wasn't trying to be spontaneous—I was trying to seduce Gilbert Holloway."

Understanding dawned on Cat's face. "So Mr. Perfect was in town?"

Gracie had never called him perfect, but thinking back, she had talked a lot about him to her friends. Maybe she'd even gone overboard in listing his good qualities. Now she wondered if she'd built him up in her mind with the subconscious purpose of making it impossible for any other man to live up to him.

Except Zach had. That thought came unbidden to her mind and she shook it away. Zach Maddox was nothing like Gilbert. She should know that better than anybody.

"Gracie?" Cat said, breaking her reverie.

She blinked, then struggled to remember Cat's question. "Sorry, I was...daydreaming."

Cat smiled. "So I see. And something tells me it wasn't about Gilbert. So who is this mystery man?"

She took a deep breath. "He showed up at the reunion pretending to be Gilbert. He fooled everyone. Including me."

Cat leaned closer. "Oooh, this sounds good. Was it some kind of Cyrano de Bergerac story where Gilbert was trying to woo you through another man?"

"Nothing so romantic," Gracie replied, though

she knew that wasn't quite true. That night in the hotel room had been the most romantic of her life— until she'd discovered it was all a lie.

Gracie drained her glass, then told Cat everything, including the fact that she'd spent the night in Zach's arms. The alcohol made it easier, though she still blushed when she admitted to seducing the man when he tried to tell her good night.

"Wow." Cat shook her head in amazement. "That is unbelievable. So what happens now?"

Gracie played with her empty glass, feeling hollow on the inside now that she'd spilled everything to Cat. "Nothing happens. Zach goes back to Boston, so I'll never have to see him again. And I go back to life as usual."

Life as usual.

No, that wasn't quite true. Her house was a mess. Her friends were leaving. Her dream to be a lawyer was over. And her bookstore was about to be demolished.

Her life couldn't possibly get any worse.

"What about Gilbert?" Cat asked. "It sounds like he's in a lot of trouble."

Gracie realized she'd been so concerned about her own problems that she'd spent little time considering what he must be going through. "When he called me yesterday morning, he told me he'd be in touch again soon. But I haven't heard from him."

Cat took the empty glass away from her, without asking if she wanted a refill. "Sounds like you'd bet-

ter watch your back, especially after that break-in at
your house."

"Gilbert would never hurt me."

"I'm not talking about Gilbert," she clarified. "I'm
talking about the people that are after him. If they
know you're his best friend, they might use you to
get to him."

So maybe her life could get worse. She'd been so
preoccupied with her plans to seduce Gilbert, then
finding out that she'd slept with the wrong man
that she hadn't even pondered the aftermath, despite that Zach had warned her of the same dark
possibilities.

But if Gilbert needed her help, she'd be there for
him—just as he'd been there for her these past ten
years.

Zach was there for you, too.

Gracie pushed that unwelcome thought out of her
head. Zach's masquerade might have fooled her for
the past three months, but she wasn't going to be so
gullible again.

She also wasn't going let what happened Saturday night keep her from getting involved with Gilbert's problems. The way Zach had talked before
he'd left her house yesterday, he wasn't going to stop
until he brought Gilbert into custody, with absolutely
no mention of Gilbert's rights or what was best for
him in this situation.

Another David-and-Goliath scenario. Only this
time, Gracie wasn't going to let Goliath win.

Gracie fished the money she owed for lunch out

of her purse and set it on the bar. "Thanks for listening and for the cosmopolitans."

"Anytime," Cat replied. "Where are you going now?"

"I'm going to find Gilbert."

ZACH WALKED into Between the Covers, feeling as if he'd been there before. Gracie had described the place so many times in her e-mails that he could probably find his way around the store blindfolded.

The antique desk that had been in the Dawson family for three generations stood behind the counter near the entrance to the store. Rich oak paneling covered the walls, which stretched up to the twelve-foot ceiling.

Rows of towering bookshelves filled the store and he could glimpse a man seated in a small alcove. That had to be Paul Toscano, the writer she'd told him about who frequented the place on a daily basis. And the woman approaching him, wearing a sleeveless white shirt that revealed a tattoo of a phoenix on her upper arm, had to be none other than Trina Powers, her assistant manager.

"Welcome to Between the Covers," she said, smiling up at him. "Is there anything special I can help you find?"

"Actually, there is," he replied, his gaze still scanning the store. "I'm looking for Gracie Dawson."

"I don't expect her in today."

"Do you know where I can find her?"

Trina hesitated, sizing him up. "Probably. But I'm not sure I should. Who are you?"

The sound of a chair scraping against the wood floor echoed across the store and he looked over to see Paul emerging from his writer's nook.

"Need any help, Trina?" he called out.

"No, I've got it covered."

Seeing the expression on Trina's face, Zach realized that Paul wasn't the only one in the place with a protective streak—a fact he might be able to use to his advantage.

"My name is Zach Maddox and I'm a police detective."

She arched a skeptical brow. "I know everyone in Kendall and you don't work at the police department."

"I'm from Boston." He pulled out his badge, knowing she was the type of woman who would demand proof.

Trina took the badge from him and studied it closely before handing it back to him. "You're a long way from Boston, Detective Maddox."

"Please call me Zach."

"All right, Zach. Now why don't you tell me what's really going on?"

But before he could explain the door opened and Gracie herself walked inside. She stopped short when she saw Zach and for a moment he thought she was going to turn around and walk right back out again. Instead she squared her shoulders and approached him.

"Looks like I don't need to make introductions," Trina observed, glancing between the two of them.

Gracie didn't take her gaze off Zach as she spoke. "Will you please excuse us, Trina? I need to have a word with Detective Maddox in the back room."

"Of course," Trina said as Gracie turned on her heel and walked to the back of the store.

Zach followed her, his heart thudding in his chest. The heat of her anger enveloped him, just as her desire had in his hotel room. He'd accept her hate—accept any passion from her—since it was better than the alternative.

In his opinion, any emotion, even a negative one, was better than indifference. After his father had left, his mother had shut down her emotions, numbed herself to everything around her. Even him.

Zach had lived to make her smile—to evoke any reaction that showed she still cared. But those smiles had been few and far between. When she'd died five years ago, the emptiness inside of him had only grown.

Until Gracie.

He shook off thoughts of his past, telling himself to concentrate on the present. When they reached the backroom,

Gracie closed the door behind him, leaving them alone among the dusty stacks of boxes and old books. A lone lightbulb shone overhead, casting shadows over the room. The effect was oddly intimate.

He found himself wanting to tangle his hands in her silky brown hair and pull her to him for a kiss that wouldn't end until they were both naked on the concrete floor.

"Where's Gilbert?"

The question yanked him from his fantasy. He sucked in a deep breath and said, "That's what I was hoping you could tell me."

"If I knew, I wouldn't be here talking to you."

The fact that he deserved her anger didn't make it any easier to take. "Can we start over?"

"Why? So you can use me again to locate Gilbert? I'm not going to fall for it again, Detective. I want to find him so I can help *him*, not you. I wish I'd never met you."

"I know that," Zach said, hating like hell that she regretted their night together, a night he'd never forget. "But neither one of us can change what happened. The fact is that Gilbert is on the run from some very dangerous people. If you help me bring him in, I promise I'll do whatever I can to protect him."

Her gaze narrowed. "Why should I believe you?"

"Because I swear I'm telling you the truth." He knew his word would carry little weight with her, but it was all he had to offer.

Gracie stared at him, the moment stretching out so long that he didn't have a clue as to what she was thinking. "All right, I'll help you, Detective. Because I don't want anything to happen to Gilbert."

Zach chafed at the way she said the guy's name, remembering the way she'd called it out in his arms. But he was hardly in a position to complain. "Thank you."

"But just so it's clear," she continued, "I won't take orders from you. Understood?"

He gave a brisk nod, realizing he didn't have

much choice. If he wanted access to Gracie, it had to be on her terms. Even if that meant delivering Holloway to her. The man she'd wanted in the first place.

"What do you want to know?" she asked.

"Has Gilbert contacted you other than the e-mails and that videotape you received in the mail?"

Gracie hesitated, as if still not certain she could trust him. "He called me on my cell phone yesterday morning—at the hotel. That's how I knew you were an imposter."

Now Zach understood the reason she'd left the hotel so suddenly. Good old Gilbert had incredibly bad timing. "What did he say?"

"First, he had to convince me it was really him," Gracie replied. "When he found out there was someone impersonating him at the reunion, he got very nervous."

"I'm sure he did."

"I didn't understand what was going on," Gracie continued. "Gilbert promised to fill me in later, when I brought him the tape."

Zach's pulse picked up. "What?"

"The Burns & Allen tape. He wants me to bring it to him."

"When? Where?"

"He didn't say," Gracie responded. "He told me he'd contact me later to set up a meeting place."

There was no way Zach was going to let that happen. "You won't be meeting Gilbert or anyone else involved with this case. Just give me the tape and I'll handle it from here."

She shook her head. "I'm not taking orders from you, remember?"

Zach's duty to find Holloway battled with his fierce need to protect her. She was inextricably tied to this case in a way he didn't understand, a way that might put her in danger.

"Gilbert made contact with *me*," she reminded him, "and my house was ransacked. So I'm already involved."

She was right. But he didn't want Gracie in the middle of this mess. He'd already come close to losing a partner because of this case. He wasn't about to risk losing her.

"This could get dangerous," he told her. "I can arrange to have you placed somewhere safe, far away from Kendall until this is all over."

"Forget it," she replied. "I can't put my life on hold while you go on a wild goose chase. You know from reading my e-mails that I have to find a new location for Between the Covers in less than three weeks, plus manage the move and close up the old store. I don't have time to go anywhere—even if I wanted to."

It was clear to him that her loyalty to her dead aunt would prevent any of his arguments from swaying her. That left him with only one option. "Then let me protect you here in Kendall."

She took a step away from him. "No way."

"Just hear me out," he said, telling himself this was about the case and not about his feelings for her. "You want to find Gilbert—well, I can deliver him to you—with your help. We can accomplish more working together than we can separately."

He saw the uncertainty in her eyes and pushed even harder to convince her. "Let me stay with you— that way you can keep working at the bookstore while I monitor your house. Both bases will be covered in case Gilbert tries to contact you again. He's in big trouble, Gracie, and he knows it. That's why he's on the run."

Her brow crinkled. "Stay with me?" Then understanding flashed on her face. "You mean *live* with me?"

"I'll sleep on the sofa."

"Forget it."

"I'm not leaving you alone. Whenever you're at home or anywhere but work, I'm sticking with you." Zach needed to make it clear he wouldn't back down on this, even if meant she'd hate him for it. "It's either that or I contact the Kendall police and tell them to place you in protective custody. I think after what happened at your house, they'll accommodate me."

Anger flashed in her eyes. He wasn't giving her any real choice, but he still held his breath waiting for her answer.

"All right," she finally agreed. "I'll do anything to help Gilbert."

"I'll find him for you, Gracie," he promised, knowing he owed her that much. He'd let her seduce him, knowing she believed he was Holloway.

Now it was up to him to deliver the real thing.

8

SHE'D MADE A DEAL with the devil.

Only this particular devil had deep brown eyes and an unforgettable mouth that could melt away all her good sense. That had to be why she'd agreed to let Zach Maddox move in with her.

"You can sleep in Aunt Fran's room," she said, leading him down the hallway. "It might be a little frilly for your taste, but you won't be here long."

Better to set the boundaries now and let him know she considered this situation temporary. The sooner they found Gilbert, the sooner she could say goodbye to Zach Maddox forever.

"Look, I'll be happy to sleep on the sofa." He stood in the doorway of the second bedroom. "I don't want to intrude on you any more than necessary."

Too late. The last thing she wanted was to walk into her living room every morning to see Zach lying there, half undressed and disheveled from sleep. It would only remind her of their night together and she thought about that too much already.

"It's really no problem," she assured him.

All of her aunt's possessions were still in the room, since Gracie hadn't had the heart to sell them or put them in storage. Fran's complete collection of Harlequin Temptations were on an antique bookshelf next to her bed, their worn, creased spines evidence that she'd read them all numerous times.

Zach laid his suitcase atop the white chenille coverlet on the bed, then turned around to face her. "I'd like to take you out to dinner this evening, Gracie, if you're free."

The invitation surprised her. Then she realized he must be feeling guilty about lying to her. Good. She was in no mood to ease his conscience. "That's not necessary."

"I know it isn't necessary, it's just my way of thanking you for letting me stay here and assisting me on this case."

It was difficult to look into those brown eyes and remember he was the enemy. Okay, maybe not the enemy but certainly not her ally. Zach Maddox had shown her just how far he was willing to go to do his job. So she wasn't about to make it any easier for him.

"The only reason I'm doing this is for Gilbert," she replied, wanting to make that perfectly clear, "so you don't need to thank me. In fact, I'd appreciate it if we could just stay out of each other's way as much as possible while you're here."

"If that's the way you want it."

"It is. I'll be at the bookstore until late tonight." She turned toward the door. "Don't wait up for me."

Zach watched her walk out of the room, resisting the urge to go after her. She needed time to adjust to this situation and to the fact that he wasn't Gilbert. He needed time to figure out exactly how he was going to handle this relationship.

That wasn't his only problem. Brannigan would blow a gasket if he knew Zach was acting solo in going after Gilbert. But his boss was a thousand miles away in Boston. What Thomas Brannigan didn't know wouldn't hurt him or anyone else.

If he cracked this case, Zach was certain nobody would complain about it. Not when a fellow officer had been wounded in the line of duty. Besides, it wasn't costing the city of Boston anything for him to work the case during his vacation.

But what would it cost Zach?

He wanted Gracie—in his bed and possibly in his life. Hell, he might even be half in love with her. And now he'd promised to deliver Gilbert right to her door. The man she'd wanted all along.

What the hell had he been thinking?

Yes, he owed her. But she deserved more than a man like Holloway. And Zach could give it. The night they'd spent together wasn't just about sex. Zach had experienced enough one-night stands to know the difference.

He and Gracie shared a connection that was deeper than simple sexual chemistry. Yes, the attraction was still there and burning hotter than ever. But he didn't just want to go to bed with Gracie. He wanted to spend time with her, to learn everything about her. Even if sex wasn't part of the picture.

That was difficult for a man like Zach to admit. He had a powerful sex drive—one that had only increased since he'd met Gracie. But he'd be willing to put it on hold if it meant earning her trust again.

He'd almost blown it by deceiving her, but now he had one more chance. A chance to prove that *he* was the right man for her, not Gilbert Holloway.

Zach set his suitcase on the bed, then unzipped it and flipped open the lid. Despite the lavender and lace decor, the room had a cozy atmosphere that appealed to him. Maybe it was due to the fact that Gracie had told him so much about her aunt in those e-mails. Especially how much she admired Fran's strength and wit and gumption. All traits he could clearly see in Gracie herself.

Judging by all the framed photographs in the room, chronicling Gracie's life since she was a little girl, it was clear that Fran had loved and admired her niece just as much.

He removed a thick scrapbook from the top of the dresser, then stacked his clothes there. A fine layer of dust frosted the front cover of the album. Brushing it off with his palm, Zach saw the words Between the Covers inscribed in tarnished gold script.

Intrigued, he sat down on the end of the bed and opened the album. He found an old newspaper clipping taped to the first page and yellowed with age. Above the article was a photograph of two women standing in front of a brick building that looked familiar to him.

He scanned the short article, dated twenty-one

years ago, that announced the opening of two new businesses in that location, one a bar and the other a bookstore. His gaze moved to the caption beneath the photo, which identified the women as Fran Dawson and Brenda Sheehan.

He assumed that Brenda was the mother of Cat and Laine, since he knew they'd taken over the bar when their mother had remarried and moved to Toronto. Zach studied the photo of Brenda Sheehan, noting the determined set of her shoulders and the tilt of her chin.

His gaze moved to Gracie's aunt, surprised by how young she looked in the picture. Then he remembered that Fran Dawson had barely been fifty years old when she'd died, making her only in her late twenties when the picture had been taken. Close to Gracie's age now.

Fran had the same blue eyes as her niece, though she was several inches shorter. The same smile, too. Looking at her picture, so healthy and happy, he could understand Gracie's frustration with the insurance company that had caused her aunt so much stress. Gracie's desire to become a lawyer had been born from that experience.

Zach knew all about feeling powerless. He'd been unable to stop his father from leaving. Just like he'd been helpless to make his mother happy, no matter how hard he'd tried. That sense of helplessness was one of the reasons he'd become a cop. So he could stop some of the pain and misery and injustice in the world. So he could finally have a sense of control.

That was something he didn't have now, especially since Gracie had made it clear she wouldn't be taking orders from him. But he had no desire to control her, only protect her. He hoped she'd understand that in time.

Paging through the scrapbook, he found that it was a history of Between the Covers. The first dollar the bookstore had earned was in there, along with letters and autographed bookmarks from some of Fran's favorite Harlequin Temptation authors such as Jayne Ann Krentz, Carly Phillips and Jennifer Crusie.

There were pictures of book signings and book club meetings at the store, with Gracie appearing in most of them. As well as a book review column written by Fran for the local Kendall Tribune, until she'd become too ill to continue.

Zach sat there mesmerized, seeing a part of Gracie's life unfold before his eyes. Even after reading all of her e-mails, he'd never really understood why she didn't just sell the bookstore so she could go to law school.

All along he'd thought her connection to Between the Covers was the product of guilt. After all, Fran had taken her in as a teenager and raised her like her own daughter.

Now he realized he'd been wrong.

Gracie's connection to the bookstore was love. It was inexplicably entwined with her Aunt Fran—losing the bookstore would mean losing her aunt all over again. So despite that she hated working there, Zach knew Gracie would never let it go. Not without a fight.

He closed the scrapbook, realizing he was just the opposite. Nothing from his past mattered that much to him. His memories of his family were more about pain than love. Memories he'd rather forget.

The one memory he didn't want to forget was his night with Gracie. But he couldn't afford to dwell in the past or fantasize about the future, not when Gilbert was still on the loose and Gracie was at risk. Which meant he had to put his feelings for her on hold.

For now.

"You let him move in with you," Trina exclaimed after hearing the whole sordid story. "Are you crazy?"

"That would be a good word for it."

They both sat at one of the tables near the front door, watching the clock until closing time. Business had been slower than usual for a Monday night and the minutes had crawled by. Or maybe it just seemed that way to Gracie because she knew Zach was at her house, making himself comfortable. A fact that made her exceedingly uncomfortable.

She hadn't wanted to tell Trina about the high school reunion disaster, but Gracie couldn't have lied to her. Especially when Trina had asked to hear all about her night with Gilbert.

Trina shook her head. "So this guy lies to you, sleeps with you, then claims he wants to protect you. And you bought it?"

Her blunt assessment of the situation made Gracie bristle. "It's not that simple."

"Then explain it to me. Because the way I see it, this guy is just using you again."

A young man entered the store, giving Gracie a welcome reprieve from their conversation. She'd only given Trina the bare details of her encounter with Zach and their decision to team up to find Gilbert, not wanting to involve her any more than necessary. It was bad enough that she knew Gracie had seduced the wrong man.

As Trina walked over to assist the customer, Gracie returned to the inventory sheets on the table in front of her. The ones she'd been trying to ignore all evening.

According to her calculations, it would cost several thousand dollars to hire a moving company to haul all the store's books to a new site. *If* she could find a place in such a short time. She had some leads, but the few that were in her price range didn't have great locations.

Closing her eyes, she leaned her head back against the chair and indulged in a moment of wishful thinking. Instead of signing a new lease she could be signing up for her first year of law school classes. Her aunt Fran could still be alive, healthy and happy. And the man who had made love to her in the hotel could be the real thing, not an imposter.

Gracie opened her eyes and sighed. Reality sucked.

The truth was that night never should have happened. Law school wasn't in her future. Aunt Fran was gone forever. And now she was likely going to lose Cat, Laine and Tess, too. No doubt they'd all keep in touch for a while, but eventually they'd each drift off, pursuing their own lives.

Except Gilbert.

"Just a browser," Trina said, walking back to the table as the customer left the store. "Now where were we?"

"Talking about my recent insanity."

"That's right." Trina sat down across from the desk, adjusting her prosthesis at a more comfortable angle. "So this detective moved in, supposedly for your protection. My question is how do you know you're safe from *him*?"

"Because he hasn't made one move toward me since the reunion or one inappropriate comment about our night together." Gracie gave a small shrug. "It's not like I have much choice in the matter if I want to help Gilbert."

Trina's gaze narrowed on her. "Are you sure this is all about Gilbert? Because you sound different when you talk about this Maddox guy. You look different, too. So...alive. I know it sounds silly, but I can't think of any other way to describe it."

"That's ridiculous." But despite her words, Gracie could feel a warm blush creep into her cheeks.

The sound of a man clearing his throat made them both turn to see Paul standing near the door. He'd packed up for the day, the brown leather tote containing his laptop slung over his shoulder.

Trina glanced at the clock. "Leaving already? You've still got thirty seconds until we close."

"I'm having a few friends over tonight," Paul said, ignoring Trina's dig. "You're both welcome to come if you're free."

"Thanks, Paul," Gracie said, "but I'm planning to

check out a few rental opportunities I saw in the paper."

His gaze moved to Trina, who had been the real focus of his invitation. "The party should be a lot of fun. I'm having it catered by Hunan's. I know that's your favorite Chinese place."

"I've got to wax my legs," Trina said, rubbing one hand over her prosthesis. "But thanks anyway." Then she rose from her chair and walked to the back of the store.

Disappointment shone in his eyes as he watched her disappear between the stacks, and then he nodded toward Gracie. "I guess I'll see you tomorrow."

"Good night, Paul." When the door closed behind him, Gracie called out, "Okay, he's gone now. You can come out of hiding."

Trina emerged, carrying a book in her hand. "I wasn't hiding. I just need something to read tonight."

Gracie rolled her eyes. "Why sit home alone when you could go to Paul's party? It might be fun."

"I noticed you didn't accept his invitation."

"That's because I've got a new roommate, remember? He made it clear that he'll be tagging along whenever I'm not at home or here with you."

Trina grabbed her jacket off the hook, slipping it over her shoulders. "I can't wait to meet this guy. He sounds like a real piece of work."

But Gracie didn't want to talk about Zach anymore. She thought about him too much already. "I think you should give Paul a chance. He's a nice guy and it's obvious how much he likes you."

"Let's just drop it, Gracie, okay? I've got my reasons." Trina turned to leave, then stopped by the desk and picked up an envelope. "I forgot to give you this. It came in the mail today."

Gracie took it from her and immediately recognized Gilbert's handwriting on the front of the envelope. There was no return address. "Thanks."

She waited until Trina left to open it. Apprehension slid up her spine as she tore the back flap loose with her fingernail and pulled out the single sheet of paper inside.

Dear Gracie,
You're the only person I can trust right now. I know that sounds like something out of one of those old, corny thrillers we used to watch, but it's true. I don't know yet when I can see you. Things have gotten weird around here. In the meantime, please hide that tape I sent you until I can work something out.
I'm in big trouble, Gracie. Please don't let me down.

Love, G.

She read the letter again, hearing the desperation in each word. Gilbert was terrified. If only there was some way she could reassure him that help was on the way. Zach had promised to protect him—a promise she fully intended to make him keep.

But they had to find Gilbert first.

She turned the letter over in her hand, noticing the

small gray smudge on the back. When she rubbed her index finger over it, the gray substance adhered to her skin, fine and powdery. Her first clue to finding Gilbert.

And now she knew just where to look.

9

ZACH STOOD at the stove in Gracie's kitchen when he heard the front door open. He glanced at the clock, noting that she was later than he'd expected. Hardly surprising, since she'd been adamant about maintaining her independence during this investigation. A trait he admired about her—even if it did make him worry.

"Detective Maddox?" she called from the living room.

"I'm in here."

He didn't turn around, letting the anticipation of seeing her again buzz inside of him. He'd thought about her all day while digging up background information on Allison Webb and canvassing the Kendall area for any sign of Gilbert. Now she was home, safe and sound, and he could finally relax.

"What do you think you're doing?"

"Making us some dinner." He stirred the Spanish rice so it wouldn't stick to the bottom of the skillet. "I have chicken enchiladas in the oven and a pitcher of margaritas in the refrigerator. I hope you like Mexican food."

Gracie set her purse on the kitchen table. "Isn't it bad enough you have to invade my life? Do you have to take over my kitchen, too?"

Zach removed the skillet from the burner, then turned to face her. "I guess I didn't look at it that way. I used to fix dinner for my mom. She worked long days and was always too tired to cook."

His mother had never shown any gratitude for his efforts. She'd just sat down at the table and started eating. But at least she'd eaten, something that didn't happen if he didn't cook. So Zach knew she'd appreciated it without her having to tell him.

"Oh." Gracie looked contrite. "Sorry, I guess it's been a long day for me, too. Maybe I overreacted."

"No, I should have checked with you first."

He hated this stiff formality between them, especially after the very *informal* night they'd spent together. Part of him had hoped this dinner might dissolve some of the tension in the air.

"Look, I appreciate the thought, Detective Maddox, but this really isn't necessary. I can make my own dinner."

"This one is already made," he replied, pulling out a chair for her. "And don't you think it's time you called me Zach?"

She hesitated and he had to bite his tongue to keep from reminding her that they'd been intimate enough to be on a first-name basis.

"Fine," she relented at last. "Zach."

He smiled. "That's better. Now sit down and relax while I finish up here."

Gracie slid into the chair with a tired sigh. "It really does smell wonderful."

"And tastes even better." Zach pulled the enchiladas out of the oven, then dished up a plate for each of them. After he set them on the table, he poured her a margarita, then one for himself.

Gracie took a long sip, then set down her glass. "Almost as good as Cat's margaritas."

"That's quite a compliment," Zach said, seating himself in the chair opposite Gracie. "I'd like to meet her someday."

"Don't be so sure," she said, picking up her fork.

"Why not?"

She glanced up at him, a defiant tilt to her chin. "I'm afraid Cat doesn't have the best opinion of you, Zach. Not after I told her how we met."

He met her gaze. "I never wanted to hurt you, Gracie."

"Then you shouldn't have lied to me."

He winced at the pain he heard in her voice, knowing full well he was the cause of it. But he couldn't turn back time. All he could do was tell her the truth, no matter how it reflected on him.

"You're right," Zach said. "When I decided to come to Texas, I figured you'd realize I wasn't Gilbert the moment you saw me. I was going to come clean then, and just hope you'd give us a chance to get to know each other."

She looked skeptical. "Then why were you wearing Gilbert's name tag?"

He shook his head. "That's the crazy thing. Everybody there just assumed I was Gilbert without me even telling them. Then I got a break in the case." He set down his fork. "The first break in three long months. So I had a choice to make—continue the charade and the investigation, or tell you the truth."

"You couldn't do both?"

He shrugged, realizing he hadn't given her enough credit. "I didn't know how you'd react when I told you that I'd been reading all your e-mails to Gilbert. I thought you might be angry and give away my identity to everybody in that ballroom."

"Wait a minute," she said, her brow crinkling. "What break in the case are you talking about?"

"I met Allison Webb." He scooped up a forkful of rice. "She made it clear that she's been in contact with Gilbert and that she's somehow involved in all of this.

Gracie closed her eyes. "Oh, no."

He lowered his fork. "What?"

She opened her eyes and met his gaze. "Allison Webb was always Gilbert's weak spot. He was the smartest man I knew, except when it came to her."

"We all have our weak spots."

The way he said it made Gracie's stomach do a triple somersault, though she might have been reading more into his words than he'd meant. Had he really come to Texas just to meet her?

If she believed him, and part of her really wanted to, then his deception hadn't been planned. But it had clearly shown her his priorities. When the choice had come down to his case or her, he'd chosen his case.

Something she needed to remember. Especially when he kept doing things to lower her defenses, like making this wonderful dinner and looking at her in a way that made her itch to take her clothes off.

For one brief, insane moment she considered doing just that. Standing up and peeling off every piece of clothing, then straddling him where he sat. The thought made her squirm on her chair and she reached for her margarita, taking a long, deep drink.

"So tell me more about Allison," Zach said, oblivious to her thoughts. A good thing, too, since they were now living together and she needed to keep all those erotic fantasies to herself.

"I didn't know her all that well." Gracie set her glass back on the table. "Allison was different—a nonconformist. I think that's why she appealed to Gilbert. He always had a rebellious streak."

"So they dated?"

Gracie shook her head. "No. As I remember it, Allison barely even talked to him. He loved her from afar."

"Sounds like his taste in women was screwed up," Zach said. "Pining after Allison when he had you right by his side."

Now Gracie knew she wasn't imagining things. Zach Maddox was paying her a compliment. The only question was why? But instead of asking him, she decided it would be safer to change the subject.

"So did you cook for your mother a lot?" Gracie asked.

He shrugged. "She worked a couple of different

jobs while I was going to high school, so I always tried to have something on the stove for her. I liked trying out new recipes."

"Well, don't expect meals like this from me," she warned him. "Aunt Fran believed no woman should cook when there was take-out available."

He smiled. "I wish I could have met her."

Gracie suddenly realized this was becoming more like a date than protective custody. She couldn't let herself forget Zach's priorities. Or her own. "I received a letter from Gilbert today."

His smile faded. "Can I see it?"

She reached into her purse and pulled it out. "There's not much in it. But the postmark is local, so he must be somewhere in the area."

Zach took the letter from her, his brow furrowed in concentration as he scanned it. *"Hide the tape,"* he read aloud, then looked up at her. "What the hell is on that tape?"

She shrugged. "We watched it together in your hotel room. I didn't see anything unusual."

"Maybe we'd better watch it again," Zach said. "There might be something we're missing."

That was a definite possibility, since at the time she'd had nothing but seducing Zach on her mind. Gracie couldn't recall any details about the show, only details about Zach. Like the way his kiss had ignited a passion inside of her that she had never known existed. She'd done things that night, wonderful things, that she'd only read about, discovering how much better they were in real life.

The anger that had replaced that passion was burning away too fast, leaving her vulnerable to him again. She didn't want that to happen. But if her instincts were right, he wouldn't be around much longer.

"We don't need to watch the tape to find Gilbert," Gracie announced.

Zach looked surprised. "Why not?"

"Because I think I know where he's hiding."

THE NEXT MORNING, Zach rode in the passenger seat of Gracie's Miata, wondering why he didn't feel more excited at the prospect of tracking down Holloway. He'd been searching for the guy for the past three months, but there was a heaviness inside of him that he couldn't explain.

"How did you sleep last night?" Gracie asked, sunglasses hiding her beautiful blue eyes. Her window was half open, the wind blowing through her dark curls.

"Fine," he lied.

The truth was that he'd been up half the night tossing and turning, all too aware of Gracie sleeping close by in the next room. He tried to tell himself that if they hadn't already slept together, he wouldn't be suffering like this. But that was just another lie. He was more intrigued by Gracie than ever—sex or no sex—which blew his theory that coming to Texas would get her out of his system.

"How much farther?" he asked, telling himself to concentrate on the case. Her eagerness to find Gilbert dampened any hope that she might share his fantasies.

"About ten miles." Gracie rolled up her window, then switched on the air-conditioning. The Texas heat shimmered above the black top as they drove out of Kendall.

"The Holloways have owned this cabin for as long as I can remember," she continued. "It's very secluded. We'll have to park about a mile away and take one of the walking trails to the lake."

"Sounds like a good hiding place."

"It's the only place he could be," Gracie replied. "His parents moved to Florida several years ago and he doesn't have any other relatives around the area."

Zach knew if they found Gilbert there, he'd take him back to Boston before the day was over. Then Gracie would be out of danger. Once that was done, chances were depressingly good that he'd never see or talk to her again.

"I think I should go to the cabin alone," Gracie said, her words yanking him out of his lethargy.

"No way."

"Just hear me out." She glanced over at him, looking so incredible that she took his breath away. "Gilbert trusts me. He'll be more likely to open the door and let me inside if I'm alone. Then I can explain why you're here and that going back into custody is for his own good."

Zach didn't like the idea of Gracie alone with Gilbert—for more reasons than the issue of her safety. "I underestimated the danger of this case before and my partner almost died. I'm not going to make that same mistake again."

Gracie frowned. "How was his getting shot your fault?"

Zach sucked in a deep breath, guilt eating at him. He had no one but himself to blame for putting a rookie cop in charge of a situation that was more volatile than he'd ever imagined.

"My partner Ray and I were baby-sitting Holloway," he began. "It was a routine fraud case and we were assigned to gather more information for the assistant D.A. before she filed charges. Gilbert agreed to cooperate in exchange for immunity from prosecution."

Gracie turned the car onto a dirt road, the tires bouncing on the loose gravel. "But Gilbert didn't do anything wrong, did he?"

The trees along the road gradually began to thicken, soon blocking out the sun. "You have to understand how the police operate. Sometimes threats are necessary to achieve the desired outcome. We knew Gilbert was a dupe in the case, but he was involved up to his neck. If he had refused to cooperate, we could have made the charges stick."

She shook her head in disgust. "That is so typical. Pushing the little guy around until you get your way. What about his rights? Did he have a lawyer?"

"He never asked for one."

"And nobody suggested it might be a good idea, did they?"

"That's not my job."

She pulled off her sunglasses, setting them on the dash. "Of course not. That way the police have all the power. But it sounds pretty ruthless. No wonder he ran."

"He wasn't running from us," Zach clarified. "Whoever shot Ray was after Gilbert. A hired thug, most likely, who hadn't planned on bumping into the police. Ray panicked and pulled his gun. There was a struggle and the gun went off. If the neighbor hadn't heard the shot and called it in..."

"So how is that your fault?"

He turned to look at her. "I shouldn't have left Ray alone that night. He didn't have enough experience. Now he'll never walk again and I'll have to live with that for the rest of my life."

She kept her eyes on the road. "You can't change the past, Zach."

His throat tightened but he steeled himself against the emotions welling inside of him. "Maybe not. But I can keep from making the same mistake twice. That's why you're not going into that cabin alone."

A lake glimmered in the distance and Gracie pulled her car off the road, dry brush crunching under the tires as she slowed to a stop. "This is it. We'll have to go the rest of the way on foot."

He climbed out of the car, wondering if he should order her to stay here. But he knew it would be futile. She might not be a lawyer yet, but she had the instincts down pat.

Twigs snapped under their feet as they walked into the woods, the air around them fragrant with pine. Despite the narrow dirt path, Zach knew that if Gracie hadn't been in the lead, he would have ended up walking in circles.

"So did you and Gilbert come here often?" he asked.

"Only a few times," she replied. "He liked to fish and I liked any excuse to get away from the bookstore."

He was aware of her deadline for finding a new location for Between the Covers and knew that she was wasting precious time searching for Gilbert. That fact more than any other should have told him how important the guy was to her.

She stopped, a puzzled frown on her face as she looked around the path. "You know, I think I drove too far. Let's try going this way."

"Are you sure?" Zach said, as she veered off the path, deeper into the woods.

"No," she glanced at him over her shoulder, flashing a smile. "I guess you'll just have to trust me."

Zach found himself smiling back at her. "How can I be sure you're not going to ditch me here and go after Gilbert yourself?"

"I considered it," she replied and something told him that she wasn't joking now. "But I know you city boys can't handle the wilderness very well."

"I'm from south Boston. We're tough enough to handle anything."

Twenty minutes later, when Zach had almost given up hope, they walked into a clearing where a small cabin stood. All the paint had peeled off, leaving gray, weathered wood. Weeds surrounding the house, almost concealing the three crooked steps leading up to the porch.

"This is it," Gracie announced, turning to Zach. "The Holloway Hideaway."

Grime covered the windows and he saw a large hole ripped in the screen door. "Sure doesn't look to me like anyone has been living here."

"Oh, it's always looked like this. The Holloways liked the rustic charm."

In his opinion, it looked more rundown than rustic, but he had to admit the place would make a great hideout. He followed Gracie up to the front porch, then grasped her arm before she could knock on the door.

"Let me handle this," he said.

Gracie shook her head. "Gilbert won't run if he knows it's me. Just give me a chance to talk to him first."

Zach wanted to argue with her, but he knew she was right. He placed his hand on his shoulder holster, just in case.

After turning back to the door, Gracie knocked softly, then called, "Gilbert, it's me."

They both waited, but no reply came from inside the house.

"Try again," Zach prodded.

She knocked harder this time. "Gilbert? It's Gracie. Let me in." Then she moved over to a window and wiped the grime away before peering inside. The same grime Gracie had told him she'd found on the envelope sent by Gilbert.

"Is he there?"

"No, I think the place is empty."

Zach walked over to the door and tried the knob. To his surprise, it turned easily in his hand. "Looks like we can see for ourselves."

With Gracie behind him, Zach walked cautiously over the threshold. For a one-room cabin, it was much nicer on the inside than he'd expected.

There was an overstuffed plaid sofa and matching chair nestled around the fireplace. Colorful woven rugs on the hardwood floor. A small kitchenette with vintage appliances. The place was clean, if not modern. Clean enough to make him suspicious.

"Someone's been here recently," he said, swiping a fingertip over the top of the mantle. Then he showed it to Gracie. "No dust." He walked over to the waste basket. "And look at this."

She moved beside him, then bent down to pull out a fistful of empty candy wrappers. "These are Gilbert's favorite."

"I know," Zach said. "The guy's addicted."

"But we don't know how long they've been here."

He took one of the wrappers out of her hand. "You told me Gilbert hasn't been back to Texas for ten years."

"That's what I thought," she replied. "But as you said, it appears there's a lot about Gilbert that I don't know."

"Well, I do know that this particular flavor is new." He smoothed out the wrapper so she could read it.

"Watermelon-Kiwi?"

He nodded. "Gilbert preordered a case of it while we were set up at his house. That means he's been here recently."

She arched a brow. "You rely on a candy wrapper for evidence?"

He shrugged. "When you're a cop, you take what you can get."

Gracie turned slowly, studying the entire room. "So if he was here, where is he now?"

"Maybe he's just out for a while. We could wait."

She walked over to the kitchenette, opening the cupboards. "There's no food. I'd say he's cleared out already, if he was ever here to begin with."

"But where else would he go?"

Disappointment shone in her eyes. "I wish I knew."

Zach knew there had to be more clues here, but he just couldn't see them. All he could see was Gracie. She stood by the bed now and he wanted to lay her down on it and make love to her until nothing mattered anymore.

Not a smart move.

But he hadn't been feeling very smart lately. Better to leave before he gave into temptation. "Are you ready to go?"

She stood by the window, staring through the grimy glass. "Zach..."

The color drained from her cheeks as he moved toward her. "What's wrong?"

"I think there's somebody out there."

10

GRACIE STOOD looking out the cabin window, barely able to see through the layers of dirt coating the glass. But someone was moving out there. No, *two people.*

"Is it Gilbert?" Zach asked, reaching her side.

"No," she whispered, grabbing his arm as the images became clearer. "It's Allison and there's someone with her. But it's not Gilbert. I think it's a woman."

"Damn," Zach said, looking around the cabin. "I don't want Allison to see you here. She made it clear at the reunion that she resents the hell out of you."

"Why?"

"Who knows?" Zach looked under the bed. "No room there."

"They're getting closer," Gracie said, still watching them through the window. "It looks like they're arguing about something but I can't hear a thing."

He walked over to a small door and opened it, revealing a miniature pantry with shelves lining all three sides. "Think you can squeeze in here?"

She frowned at the tiny space. "Are you serious?"

"Completely." He glanced out the window. "We don't have much time."

Footsteps sounded on the porch steps and Gracie knew she didn't have a choice. She dove for the pantry, wedging herself inside. Zach edged in beside her, his large frame just fitting between the shelves.

It was so cramped they were barely able to get the door closed. Gracie tried to keep air space between her body and Zach's, but it proved impossible. Her back was pressed hard against the shelves, the edges cutting into her flesh. Her front pressed hard against Zach.

"Can you breathe?" she gasped, wondering how long they were going to have to hide in this small, pitch-black space. Even though the shelves were empty, it still smelled of cinnamon and cloves.

"Barely," he murmured and then his body tensed. "They're almost here."

Gracie could hear their voices now as the front door of the cabin opened, then closed again. "Are you sure we shouldn't confront them?" she whispered.

"Let's hear what they have to say first. We may learn something valuable."

She fought for breath, more a result of this intimate contact with Zach than lack of breathing space. She shifted slightly, finding a more comfortable position as the contours of their bodies fit more closely together.

Gracie swallowed hard, her heart racing in her chest. This little detour wasn't on the itinerary. But she couldn't do anything about it now—even if she wanted to.

"You've got some setup here, Allison," said an unfamiliar voice.

"Nice, isn't it?"

Even after all these years, Gracie recognized that faint Bronx accent in Allison's Texas drawl that had distinguished her from the rest of her classmates at Kendall High. Allison had hated Kendall and the "resident rednecks" as she called them, the moment her family had moved here from New York. A fact that she'd made plain to everyone she met.

Not exactly the way to win a popularity contest in high school, a place that had proved difficult for Gracie to fit in, too. The local students were big on football and tradition, resenting anyone who tried to make waves. And Allison loved making waves. She'd boycotted pep rallies and wrote scathing editorials in the school newspaper about the lack of culture and refinement in Kendall.

Gilbert had seen her actions as courageous, but Gracie had just thought she was a snob. That opinion had been confirmed the day Allison had laughed in Gilbert's face when he'd asked her for a date.

Now Allison was in his cabin, something that didn't make any sense to Gracie. When and why had Gilbert let that woman back into his life?

A cell phone rang and Allison said, "That's Gil. Come outside with me, Dorie. There's better reception."

Gracie heard them leave the cabin, their voices fading away. "Who's Dorie?"

"A cousin, I think," Zach replied. "I researched Allison's family at the library. There's a cousin named Doris Phillips who lives in Laredo. So it could be her."

"There's no way to find out in here," Gracie said, achingly aware of how good his body felt pressed against her own. "Now Gilbert's calling her and we can't hear a thing."

Zach hesitated, then said, "We've got to stay in here and hope they come back inside. If we go out now, we'll scare them off."

She knew he was right and nodded, bumping the top of her head against his chin. "Sorry," she whispered. "It's a little crowded in here."

"I noticed."

Gracie tried not to move, but her arms were trapped between their bodies and starting to grow numb. She wiggled a little, attempting to free them and heard a low moan emanate from Zach's throat.

"Please don't do that," he rasped.

"I can't help it. My arms are stuck."

He shifted slightly, the movement pressing her back into the shelves. Then he grasped both her wrists and brought them up around his shoulders. The change in position did give her more room. It also made her acutely aware of the intimacy of holding on to Zach in the dark.

"Better?" he breathed, his mouth so close she could feel his warm breath on her cheek.

Much better. "Yes, thank you."

"My pleasure."

She was so tired of fighting her attraction to him, so tired of just dreaming about what she wanted out of life. At this moment she wanted Zach and he was right here in front of her.

What was she waiting for?

Gracie knew she shouldn't move, but every nerve fiber in her body vibrated with the need to arch against him. To relieve the delicious pressure building between her thighs. She settled for sliding her hands around his neck and threading her fingers through the short, thick hair at the base of his scalp.

"Gracie," he said, his voice ragged. "This is… torture."

At least she wasn't the only one suffering. Neither of them could deny the sexual tension that had been sizzling between them since that night in the hotel room. She'd been fighting it ever since, but that just seemed to give it—and him—more power over her. Maybe it was time she took control.

"You're from south Boston, remember," she whispered against his ear. "Tough enough to handle anything."

Gracie remembered Cat's comment that she was too cautious and realized now that her friend had been right. Nothing like this had ever happened before and she found she was reveling in the excitement, the danger, the uncertainty. It heightened every feeling, including her desire for Zach.

She'd been numb for so long—putting her life on hold to care for Aunt Fran and run the bookstore. Zach made her come alive again. A prospect both terrifying and thrilling at the same time. But that was better than the inertia that had plagued her for so long.

Gracie brushed her cheek over his unshaven jaw

until he turned his head and caught her lips with his own. He moaned into her mouth and she held on as he kissed her with an intensity that touched her soul.

Zach slid his hands over her hips, pulling her so close she could feel the hard ridge of his arousal against the front of her blue jeans.

She stood up on her toes, bringing his hardness against the soft flesh between her thighs, the friction sending sparks of pleasure through her body. Gracie had never done anything like this before—never even imagined it. Now she couldn't imagine stopping. The fact that Allison and her companion could return to the cabin at any moment only added to the heated urgency of the moment.

Zach's hand slid over her hip, then around her thigh, until he was so close, but not quite touching the sweet spot between her legs. He held steady, silently asking her permission. She gave it by pushing against his hand.

Gracie closed her eyes as he began to move his fingers against her delicate flesh. Her head tipped back against a shelf as his fingers circled and pressed against the fabric of her jeans.

Heat spiraled inside of her, building into a flame that only his touch could extinguish. She writhed against him, wanting more, needing more, until the fabric beneath his fingers grew warm and moist.

"You're so beautiful," he whispered into the darkness, bringing his mouth down to nibble on her neck. Soft, tender kisses that heightened her desire for him.

The awkwardness of her position was soon lost to

her as he quickened the motion of his fingers, driving her higher and higher. She gripped his shoulders, hanging on as her breath came in quick, deep gasps.

"Now, sweetheart," he urged as her body tightened against him. "I've got you."

She barely heard him, losing track of time and space, unaware of anything except the magical movement of his fingers against her. Then she exploded, Zach catching her cries in his mouth with a long, deep kiss.

Her legs grew weak as the reverberations from her orgasm continued to wrack her body. A sweet, delicious ripple effect. Zach held her up, tenderly dropping kisses along her cheek and jaw until she could stand on her own once again.

Gracie was still trying to catch her breath when she heard voices inside the cabin once more. She had no idea how long they'd been there or when they'd come back in, aware that the solid wood door must have concealed the sound of her movements inside.

Zach held her in his arms as they eavesdropped on the conversation.

"So it's all set?" Dorie said.

"Only one more week," Allison replied. "Then I can kiss this Podunk town goodbye once and for all."

"Don't forget to hand over my share before you and Gilbert ride off into the sunset."

"That's up to Gilbert. He's still not too happy with the way you botched things up in Boston."

"That wasn't my fault!"

"You're the one who hired that cretin," Allison countered. "He was just supposed to cause a distraction so Gilbert could disappear, not barge in with guns blazing."

"Gilbert got away, didn't he?" Dorie said, her tone defensive.

"*After* that cop got shot. We still don't know if he's alive or dead."

Gracie didn't realize she was squeezing Zach's arms until his fingers gently loosened her grip. She couldn't believe what she was hearing. Allison made it sound as if Gilbert was to blame for everything. This had to be a ruse. Maybe she *did* know they were hiding in the closet.

"The cop's alive," Dorie replied. "I checked. He's in a wheelchair, but alive. So it's not like we'd be facing murder charges. And it's not like Gilbert hasn't screwed up, either. He's the one who sent that tape to the Dawson woman."

"He'll get the tape back," Allison assured her. "Don't worry about that. You just need to take care of everything on your end."

"No problem."

"Good. This thing should be wrapped up by the end of the week. If everything goes as planned, you'll get your share of the money."

Gracie heard the sound of footsteps and knew they were heading for the door. She resisted the urge to bolt after them and force Allison to admit she was lying about Gilbert's involvement.

The woman was setting him up. No doubt Gilbert was just as enamored with Allison as he'd been in high school, too blinded by his own obsession of her to see that she was trouble. Gracie knew she had to find a way to warn him before it was too late.

They waited several minutes before they finally emerged from the pantry. So much had happened since they'd taken refuge there that Gracie didn't know what to say.

Zach walked over to the window. "They're gone."

She straightened her clothes, noticing that Zach's shirt was half pulled out of his jeans. Then she saw the deep red finger marks on his arms. *Had she done all that?*

Her face warmed as she remembered exactly what he'd done to her. Something about that small, dark space had made her lose all control. Now she had to think rationally again, to put aside her feelings for Zach long enough to figure out what to do next.

He still stood at the window, his arms braced on the frame. "So what do we do now, Gracie?"

She wasn't sure if he was talking about their relationship or the case. So she answered his question with one of her own. "What do you want to do?"

He turned around, his gaze intent on her face. "I want to take you back home and make love to you. Hell, I want to do it right here."

She swallowed hard, but before she could reply, he continued.

"But we don't know if or when Allison is coming

back. The only thing we do know is that Gilbert is in this thing up to his neck."

Her warmth toward him chilled at the hard expression she saw on his face. "Don't tell me you believed her?"

"Didn't you?"

She shook her head. "Of course not. You said yourself that Gilbert was a dupe in this scheme. He was even helping the police."

"It doesn't look that way now."

"But you lived with him," Gracie replied, certain she could make him see reason. "You know he's not the kind of man to get mixed up in something like this."

"I've met all kinds of people who do all kinds of things for the craziest reason. Hell, look at us. I never imagined doing anything like what just happened in that closet." Zach moved toward her. "And I'm sure you feel the same." His words seemed to hold a double meaning.

She stared up at him, wondering if he was using her weakness for him to bolster his case against Gilbert. Just the fact that the thought had occurred to her proved that some part of her still didn't trust him.

Maybe it was her cautious nature taking hold again, but Gracie wasn't going to gamble with Gilbert's life or her own happiness to fulfill her sexual fantasies, no matter how tempting the prospect.

"We have a problem," she said, steering the subject back to safe territory. "You think Gilbert's guilty and I know he's innocent."

Disappointment flared in his eyes. "That's all you have to say? About this?" His gaze flicked to the closet, then back again. "About us."

"Yes." She turned toward the cabin door, not trusting herself enough to look at him, certain she'd falter under the vulnerability she saw in his dark eyes.

"Gracie, wait..." Zach moved beside her. "You're not going out there alone. In fact, after hearing what Allison had to say, you're not going anywhere alone."

"So you're going to help me prove him innocent?"

"No," he bit out, closing the cabin door behind him. "I'm going to prove once and for all that you've given your trust to the wrong man."

11

THE NEXT DAY, Zach was fighting the urge to hit someone, preferably Gilbert Holloway. Instead he settled for splitting wood in Gracie's back yard. It was hard work, normally hired out to the teenager next door, according to Gracie.

But Zach needed to relieve the tension that had been building inside of him since their interlude in the closet. He just wished the blisters on his hand would take his mind off the ache in other parts of his body.

Because she'd chosen Gilbert.

After coming apart in his arms, after hearing Allison name Holloway as the mastermind in the whole scheme, Gracie still preferred to give her loyalty—and her love—to a man who didn't deserve her.

Maybe Zach didn't deserve her, either. He picked up the ax and swung it over his head, bringing it down hard against the end of the log. A satisfying crack sounded as the wood split into two pieces. He tossed them onto the pile, then reached for another log.

The hot June sun beat down on him and he could

feel the beginning of a burn across his back and shoulders. He'd taken off his damp shirt an hour ago. Probably not a good idea to expose his Boston skin to these merciless Texas rays, but he'd been too hot to care.

The worst of it was that only a few steps away lay an air-conditioned house and a nice, ice-cold beer in the refrigerator.

Both tempting, but not as tempting as Gracie. She was in there, too, watching that Burns & Allen tape over and over again, looking for some clue that would lead her to Holloway.

Zach wiped the perspiration off his brow with his forearm, then attacked the next log. He needed to find some way to convince her that Gilbert wasn't the man she remembered. Words obviously didn't work—he'd been arguing his point since they'd left the cabin yesterday.

Which left him with one other option.

Despite her loyalty to Gilbert, even Gracie couldn't deny the physical connection between them. If he could make love to her again, break down her defenses until she was willing to listen to reason...

Zach split the last log, tossing the pieces onto the pile. Then he wedged the ax into a tree stump, his muscles throbbing in his arms. He'd be sore tonight. Hopefully, sore enough to drop into deep, dreamless sleep as soon as his head hit the pillow.

He sure as hell didn't want to spend another night awake and alone, not when he could smell the delicate scent of her perfume in every room of the house. It drove him crazy. Almost as crazy as the sight of her freshly laundered lingerie hanging from the shower rod in the bathroom. If he didn't know better, he'd think she was purposely trying to unravel him.

Wiping his damp hands on his jeans, he moved toward the house, ready to drown himself in a cold beer. He'd follow that with a long, cold shower— once Gracie removed her underwear from the rod.

He opened the back door, the hinges squeaking, then walked into the kitchen. The cool air hit him as soon as he stepped inside, a welcome relief from the heat. He just stood there, too hot to move, until he saw the note stuck to the refrigerator door.

Tossing his shirt over his shoulder, Zach headed for the refrigerator until he was close enough to read it.

> Had to run into work. Be back in time for supper.
>
> Gracie

Short. Impersonal. And directly against his orders. He swore under his breath as he yanked the refrigerator door opened and pulled out a frosty beer bottle. He'd made it clear to Gracie that she wasn't to go anywhere alone.

After twisting off the cap, he took a long swig, the icy amber brew washing down his parched throat. The way he saw it, he had two choices. Go after her or go take that cold shower. In the mood he was in, Zach knew going after her wasn't a good idea.

So after he finished his beer, he headed for the shower. If Gracie was lucky, he'd be in a much better mood by the time she got home.

IF ZACH WAS LUCKY, she'd be in a much better mood by the time she got home. At the moment, she was frustrated that he was too stubborn to listen to reason. She'd talked herself blue in the face since leaving the cabin yesterday, trying to convince him that Gilbert was one of the victims in this case. A victim who was about to be framed if Allison Webb had her way.

But Zach wouldn't listen to her. He was too caught up in his Tarzan routine to be rational. She'd left him chopping enough wood to last her for three Texas winters, all the while demanding that he know her every move so he could protect her.

"Right," she muttered to herself as she shelved the latest batch of book releases. "The only man I need protection from is him."

Trina popped her head around the corner of the bookcase. "That's the third time today I've heard you talking to yourself. Don't you know that's one of the first signs of insanity?"

"Then I'm a lost cause," Gracie replied, "because talking to Zach Maddox *is* like talking to myself. He's the most frustrating, bullheaded man I've ever met."

Trina grinned. "And that sounds like the first sign of a woman in love."

"Only if I really am crazy."

"Okay, so maybe you're only in lust."

Gracie sighed. "I hate to admit it, but that is a definite possibility."

"And the problem is...?"

"I already told you," Gracie replied, wiping a layer of dust off the shelf in front of her. "He's frustrating, bullheaded, bossy—"

"All unimportant traits when he's naked."

That was the real problem. It had been too long since she'd seen him naked. Four days to be exact. That time in the cabin didn't count since he'd had his clothes on. So had she, for that matter, which only made it more amazing that he'd been able to make her lose all control.

No man had ever done anything like that to her while she was fully dressed. So he did have *some* redeeming qualities. Most of them fully visible when he was naked.

"Naked just confuses things," Gracie said.

"Exactly my point." Trina pulled out one of the books that Gracie had shelved upside down and turned it over before sliding it back into place. "You claim he's bullheaded. I'm assuming that means he won't listen to your point of view."

"You guessed it."

"Then maybe you need a little naked *confusion.*"

Gracie stared at her in surprise. "You mean sex?"

Trina nodded. "It is the oldest method of persuasion in the history of mankind. Or should I say, womankind."

"You think my having sex with Zach will solve all our problems?"

Her smile widened. "Even if it doesn't, you'll have fun trying."

The prospect was more appealing than Gracie wanted to admit. Part of her frustration with Zach stemmed from her attraction to him. Even when he drove her crazy, she wanted to ravish him.

"I can't talk about this anymore," Gracie said, feeling even more flustered than when she'd left the house. One look at him chopping wood, half naked and muscles bulging, had driven her straight out the door.

"All right, let's talk about the bookstore. I've got a good lead on a new location."

Gracie brushed the dust off her hands, then headed to the front counter. "Tell me about it."

"Remember that realtor who contacted us when the highway deal went through?"

"Barely. That was months ago."

"I know. But he must have kept tabs on us and heard the Kendall Historical Society rejected the building. Apparently, he's been calling all over town looking for empty spaces for us to lease."

"Why would he do something like that on his own?"

Trina shrugged. "I suppose he wants the commission. Face it, Gracie, we're not getting anywhere trying to find a place on our own. Time is running out."

Trina had a point. Gracie had been too distracted by Zach and too worried about Gilbert to give all her attention to the bookstore. If she didn't find a new place for Between the Covers soon, she'd have to pay double the moving costs—once to haul the books in storage and again when she leased a new space.

"Here it is," Trina said when they reached the desk. She handed Gracie a sheet of notebook paper with the address scribbled on it.

"Parvey Road?" Gracie read aloud. "Where's that?"

"On the other side of town," Trina replied. "The real estate guy said it's a new development that's looking for tenants, so it's in our price range."

Gracie tucked the paper into her purse. "I'll head out there now and take a look. Do you want to come along? Paul can watch the store."

Paul often stood in for them for an hour or two when Gracie and Trina both had to be away from the bookstore at the same time.

"No, I'm expecting a call from one of the girls in my support group. She's having a rough time, so I'd better be here."

"Okay." Gracie knew how important Trina's volunteer work was to her. She ran a support group for people who found themselves suddenly disabled, either through an accident or a medical condition.

Gracie headed for the door. "Wish me luck."

"Good luck," Trina said. "I'll slip over to Temptation and buy a bottle of champagne—just in case we get lucky."

Gracie walked out the door, relishing her freedom. Zach had been like her shadow these past few days, never letting her out of his sight. But even on her own, she couldn't seem to stop thinking about him.

Or about the old-fashioned method of persuasion that Trina had put into her head.

ZACH WALKED into the bookstore refreshed from his cold shower and ready to lay down some ground rules. Gracie might not be ready to admit that Gilbert was guilty of his crimes, but she needed to know that helping him could put her in legal jeopardy. A risk Zach wasn't about to let her take.

"Hello, may I help you?"

He looked up to see Paul Toscano standing behind the counter. "I hope so. I'm looking for Gracie."

Paul smiled. "Sounds like you have a hard time keeping track of her. I was here the last time you were looking for her."

"That's right. My name's Zach Maddox. And you're Paul, aren't you? Gracie's told me about you."

"Really?" His expression grew guarded. "What did she say?"

"Don't worry, it was all good. She told me you're a writer. And that you're very talented."

Paul shook his head. "My only talent seems to be handling rejection well," he replied, "in my writing and my life."

"Sorry to hear it. Maybe that will change soon."

"Oh, I'm sure it will," Paul said cryptically, "one way or the other."

According to Gracie's e-mails, the guy had it bad for Trina Powers, the bookstore's assistant manager.

Zach had thought it amusing at the time. Now that he found himself agonizing over a woman, he could definitely sympathize.

Unfortunately, he didn't have the time or the patience to play Dr. Phil. "Do you have any idea where I can find Gracie?"

"Not a clue. All I know is that she left here about half an hour ago."

Zach bit back an oath, wondering how he was supposed to protect her when she kept disappearing. "What about Trina? Would she know where to find her?"

Paul shrugged. "She got called away, too. That's why I'm working desk duty. I'm sure one of them will be back soon."

Zach reached for his cell phone on his belt, but found the clip empty. "Damn."

"Something wrong?"

"I forgot my cell phone."

Paul pointed to the desk behind him. "It looks like Gracie forgot hers, too. So lending you my phone probably wouldn't do you much good."

He was right. But that didn't make Zach feel any better. Not only was Gracie out there alone, but she didn't even have a way to contact him if she got into trouble.

Zach knew the odds of that happening were slim, but he didn't want to take any chances. Not with Gracie. He just wished she didn't have the power to distract him so much—like making him forget his cell phone. Zach never did things like that back in Boston.

He was spending so much time focused on Gracie that he hadn't been thinking straight.

Lust could do that to a man. But Zach knew that it was more than lust. Living with Gracie these past few days had shown him what was missing in his life. Someone to cook for and talk to and worry about. A real relationship.

A real home.

Paul cleared his throat, breaking Zach's reverie. "Do you mind if I ask your opinion about something?"

"Go ahead."

He pulled a small black velvet box out of his shirt pocket, then flipped open the lid to reveal an emerald and diamond ring. "What do you think?"

"Nice," Zach replied. "What's the occasion?"

"I'm going to ask the woman I love to marry me."

Zach wondered if he'd missed something in one of Gracie's e-mails. "Are you talking about Trina?"

Paul nodded. "You've met her. She's an incredible woman, isn't she?"

It was the kind of question that didn't require an answer. "I didn't realize you two had started dating."

"We haven't," Paul replied. "But we've been seeing each other every day for over three years. That's got to count for something."

It looked like he got to play Dr. Phil after all. Zach just wished he knew what to say. "Sure, but do you know if she feels the same about you?"

Paul shrugged. "All I know is that she thinks that prosthesis she wears will keep any man from falling in love with her. I thought if I proposed, she'd realize that I was really serious about her."

"A form of shock therapy?"

Paul grinned. "Exactly."

"What if she turns you down?"

"What have I got to lose?" Paul caressed the ring with the tip of his index finger. "I love Trina more than anything and this is the best way I know how to show it. If she turns me down, at least I gave it my best shot."

Zach stared at him, certain a stinging rejection was in the man's future. But Paul didn't seem to care. No, he did care, he was just willing to risk it, willing to put his heart on the line for the woman he loved.

A risk Zach hadn't taken yet.

"I've got it all planned out," Paul said. "I know Trina's working tonight, so I'm having a gourmet dinner delivered here right before closing time. I've got a bottle of Cristal cuvée chilling in the mini-fridge in the backroom. When the time is right, I'm going to pop the question."

"Well…good luck," Zach said.

"Thanks. I'm scared shitless. But better to feel scared than nothing, right?"

The words hit him like a sledgehammer to the gut. Without realizing it, Paul was the one who had taken on the role of Dr. Phil, making Zach realize what was really holding him back from admitting his feelings to Gracie.

He'd grown up with a mother who had numbed herself to relationships and to the world, forming a protective shell forged from too many broken dreams. A shell he'd never managed to break through.

What he hadn't figured out until now was that he'd followed her example. Zach had always pushed people away, using the excuse that his line of work had the potential for too much heartache. But the truth was he'd been trying to protect his own heart.

Now he knew that simply wasn't possible. He'd thought he'd been playing it smart when all he was really doing was playing it safe.

But no more. Starting tonight, he was going to engage in a form of shock therapy himself.

12

THE CLOSER Gracie drove to Parvey Road, the more she wondered if the real estate agent was playing some kind of practical joke on her. The neighborhood grew more dilapidated with each turn. A view of rundown and abandoned buildings, surrounded by trash, wasn't exactly the atmosphere she wanted for Between the Covers.

It was almost dusk, making it difficult to read the addresses along the street. The area was more industrial than retail, but the agent had said the neighborhood was undergoing revitalization. Maybe the trash lining the gutters meant they were still in the demolition stage.

The paved road led to a dead end, where Gracie saw a warehouse made of gray steel siding with an address that matched the one Trina had given her.

She pulled into the empty lot and parked near the door, keeping the engine running as she debated whether to go inside. There was no way she'd ever move Aunt Fran's bookstore to a place like this, no matter how desperate she was.

Then she saw a shadow move behind the glass

door of the warehouse. Startled, she shifted her car into reverse, ready to peel out of the parking lot. But the door opened and a man stepped outside.

It was Gilbert.

She cut the engine, then opened the car door, surprised to find her knees shaking. Despite his claims of weight loss and Lasik surgery, Gilbert looked much the same as she remembered him.

He still had shaggy dark hair that hung too low on his brow, Coke-bottle bottom glasses and a stout frame. Had he posed as the real estate agent and made the call to bring her here? Or was there someone else, besides Allison and Dorie, in on this scheme?

Despite her confusion, she didn't hesitate to enter the warehouse. She knew she had nothing to fear from Gilbert.

He held the door open for her, then followed her inside. Without saying a word, he enveloped her in a big bear hug. His clothing stank of stale sweat and she could feel the rough graze of his whiskers against her cheek.

"I'm so glad you came," Gilbert said.

"Why all the secrecy?" she asked, taking a step back for a better look at him. She would have recognized him anywhere, making her wonder once again how she could have ever believed Zach was Gilbert.

"Sorry about that," he replied. "I just can't be too careful these days."

"Gilbert, what's going on?" she asked, looking around the dank, empty building. There were water stains on the ceiling and insulation jutting from holes in the wall.

"It's a long story," he replied, steering her toward a small vinyl card table and two chairs, all scarred with wear and splashed with different colors of paint. "How much time do you have?"

"Time enough for you to tell me you had nothing to do with the Internet fraud—or that cop's shooting."

"Cripes," Gilbert said, staring at her in amazement. "How much do you know?"

So she told him everything—from Zach's appearance at the reunion to the break-in at her house to overhearing the conversation at the cabin between Allison and Dorie. The only thing she left out was her night with Zach and the fact that she was living with him now.

Gilbert kept shaking his head as she relayed her story, reinforcing her belief that he truly was innocent of all the charges Zach had laid at his feet.

"I can't believe this is happening to me." His face grew mottled and panic shone in his eyes. "What the hell am I going to do now?"

"Let me help you," Gracie entreated. "We'll go to Zach and you can tell him your story. Between the two of us we convince him that you're not to blame for any of it."

Gracie wished she could be as confident as she sounded. Zach hadn't listened to her yet. But she had to try. She couldn't leave Gilbert alone in a place like this.

"That's the problem, Gracie." Gilbert stood up and began to pace in front of her. "I *am* to blame."

Disappointment welled in her throat, but she still couldn't believe her best friend from high school would hurt anyone. He'd even refrained from killing spiders whenever they'd cleaned out the cabin every spring, preferring to catch them in a glass and release them outside.

"Tell me what happened," she said softly, "from the beginning."

He took a deep breath. "It all started when I sent out those mass e-mails about my Internet consignment store. You got one, didn't you?"

She nodded. "I even tried to buy some rare books you had on sale there, but someone outbid me."

"That was me," he admitted. "By that time, I'd figured out what was happening with the credit card thefts and I didn't want you involved."

"If you knew, why didn't you go to the police right away?"

"Because of Allison."

His voice softened when he said her name and Gracie recognized the same glazed look he'd had in his eyes back in high school whenever Allison Webb had walked by. What she couldn't figure out was how the woman could still have this effect on him after ten years.

Then she thought about Zach and knew a hundred years could pass and she'd still feel the same sizzle when he walked into the room, as well as the same spiritual connection.

But Gracie hoped she'd never compromise her values because of him. Or worse, betray the people around her. Gilbert had done both.

"Look, I know you don't understand." Gilbert knelt in front of her chair. "But you've got to believe me. I never wanted anyone to be hurt."

She didn't know what to believe anymore. "What am I doing here?"

"I need you to do one favor for me," he entreated. "Then I'll never ask you for anything again."

Apprehension skittered up her spine. "What?"

"Bring the videotape to me tomorrow night. Same time. Same place."

She rose to her feet. "What does that videotape have to do with any of this? I've watched it over and over again. There's nothing on it but a bunch of old comedy routines."

"It's better if you don't know." Gilbert used the table for leverage to pull himself off the floor. "Just bring me the tape, then this entire mess will be over."

"How?"

He hesitated. "I've got the information the police want, but I need to be the one to give it to them. I sent the tape to you for safekeeping while I was on the run."

"Let's go to them now," Gracie suggested. "I'll drive and we can pick up the tape at my house on the way. You know I'll vouch for you."

He shook his head. "Not without Allison. She has to be there, too."

"Gilbert…"

"No," he interjected. "I mean it. I won't turn my back on her now."

Gracie rubbed her hands over her arms, chilled by the dank air and by Gilbert's blind devotion to a woman who didn't deserve him. "Where is Allison?"

"I can't tell you."

She blinked. Gilbert had always told her everything. "Why not?"

"Because I promised not to tell anyone. I'm sorry, Gracie, but I gave her my word."

"Then give me your word, too," she said, taking a deep breath. "If I bring you the tape, promise me that you'll go to the police right away."

"I promise," he said without hesitation.

She looked around the warehouse, hating the thought of leaving him here. "Do you need anything, Gilbert? Food? Some blankets?"

He shook his head. "I'm not staying here. Don't worry, I'll be fine." Then he glanced at his watch. "Time to say good night, Gracie."

Her throat tightened. He sounded so much like the old Gilbert and looked like him, too. But he'd changed and so had she. The man she'd built up in her dreams, comparing him to every other man she'd ever met, had never really existed.

Gracie walked to the door, sensing that there was still something that Gilbert wasn't telling her. But she didn't want to linger in this creepy place any longer than necessary.

Especially when she only had twenty-four hours to decide whether to tell Zach that she'd found his prey.

GRACIE ARRIVED HOME that night to find the house dark and empty. She flipped on a light in the living room, surprised that Zach wasn't there waiting to rip into her for leaving without telling him.

A twinge of apprehension rippled through her. She walked down the hallway and opened the door to her aunt's old room. The bed was neatly made and she didn't see his suitcase anywhere.

Zach had left her.

No goodbye speech, not even a note. Disappointment thickened in her throat and she felt a ridiculous urge to cry. He'd driven her crazy these past few days, but now that he was gone there was an emptiness inside of Gracie that threatened to overwhelm her.

The Burns & Allen videotape still sat on top of the television set. He hadn't taken it with him. Maybe he'd already gotten a tip on where to find Gilbert. He might have even followed her to the warehouse.

But before she could make sense of any of it, she heard music emanating from the back yard.

After walking into the kitchen, she pulled back the curtain on the window above the sink. In the darkness, she could just make out a tent and one of those outdoor patio heaters shaped like a round chimney. Puzzled, she walked out the back door, the squeaking hinges announcing her arrival.

Zach stood at the grill, marinating two steaks with a brush. The aroma of sizzling meat made her mouth water.

"What are you doing out here?" she asked him.

"Well, I'm supposed to be on vacation," he said,

flipping over one of the steaks. "And I've always wanted to camp out, so I thought I'd give it a try."

"Camping?" She looked at the tent, then the stone chimney. It had a small fire burning in it, just enough to cast a romantic glow over the lawn. "Here? In my back yard?"

He fixed his gaze on the grill. "I figured we'd both have a little more room this way. I was going a little stir crazy in the house."

His face was flushed, though she couldn't tell if it was from the heat of the grill or something else.

"Besides," he continued, "Texas is a lot different than Boston. I can actually see the stars out here."

She looked up at the sky, impressed with the glittering canopy above her. After living in Kendall so long, she'd taken sights like that for granted. "It is beautiful, isn't it?"

"Breathtaking," he agreed. But Zach wasn't looking at the sky—he was looking straight at her.

Relief that he hadn't left her mingled with guilt that she wasn't telling him about finding Gilbert or about her plan to meet him tomorrow night. But something told her now wasn't the time.

"Are you hungry?" he asked, taking off the steaks.

Famished. But for more than food. That was something else she didn't tell him as he led her to the tent, carrying the meat on a platter. He had cushions on the canvas floor with small table set up between them.

Two place settings of her aunt's fine china were set on the table, along with a neatly folded linen napkin. Merlot sparkled in the wineglasses and a taper candle burned in the center of the table, casting a flickering golden glow inside the tent.

"Looks like you've thought of everything," she said, taking a seat across from him, "except silverware."

He smiled, then pulled two forks and two steak knives out of his pocket. "Hey, I used to be a Boy Scout. I'm always prepared."

She laughed, realizing there was something different about him. He was more relaxed, the tiny tension lines erased from his eyes and mouth.

"Dig in." He handed her a linen napkin, then laid his own across his lap.

She picked up the knife and fork, eyeing the steak in front of her. "There's no way I can eat all of this."

"Just make sure you save room for dessert," he replied. "We're roasting marshmallows."

She picked up her fork. "So were you really a Boy Scout?"

"For a couple of years," Zach said, cutting into his steak, "until my dad left and I had to find a job. But I never did get to go on any campouts."

Gracie found she enjoyed talking with Zach about something other than the case and Gilbert, two subjects that had dominated their every conversation for the past few days. She wanted to savor this moment, make it a special memory she could keep forever and dust off once in a while whenever her life got too mundane.

"More wine?" He refilled her glass before she even had a chance to reply, then topped off his own.

They ate and talked, oblivious to everything but each other. Zach told her about growing up in south Boston and why he'd decided to become a cop. Gracie talked about her parents and how abandoned she'd felt when they'd left her—something she'd never even confided to Gilbert.

She never wanted the evening to end. Looking around her back yard, Gracie felt as though she and Zach were alone in the world. *If only it were true.* "I've never done anything like this before."

"Neither have I," he admitted. "Paul gave me the idea."

"Paul?" she echoed. "Paul Toscano?"

He nodded, then pushed his empty plate away. "He's a nice guy. I like him."

"When did you see Paul?"

"At the bookstore today when I went looking for you."

"About that..." she began, still uncertain how much to tell him.

"Later," he said, then held out his hand. "It's time for dessert."

She let him pull her to her feet. They just stood there for a moment together, their shadows touching on the tent wall. Gracie looked up at Zach, suddenly hoping that he'd kiss her.

Instead he handed her a stick with the bark peeled off. "Made especially for you."

She laughed, then stuck a marshmallow on the end of the stick while he carried the small table, the dishes still on top of it, into the kitchen. When he emerged from the house, Zach peeled a stick of his own before joining her by the stone chimney.

"How much did all of this cost?" she asked, standing next to him as they roasted the marshmallows.

"The sticks were free," he replied. "I pilfered them from your yard."

"And the rest?"

He turned to look at her. "The rest doesn't matter. It was worth every penny."

Something in his eyes told her this night was just beginning. A thrill of anticipation shot through her and Gracie knew exactly what she wanted for dessert.

"You're marshmallow's burning," he said softly. Zach pulled her stick toward him and blew out the fire. Then he carefully pulled the marshmallow off and held it to her mouth. "Be careful. It might be hot."

She grasped his hand, bringing it closer to her mouth. Then she lightly blew on it before taking a tiny nibble of the charred surface. The gooey, warm middle oozed out and she caught it with her tongue.

She saw Zach watching her and noticed his eyes darken when her tongue flicked over his thumb. Taking her time, she took small bites of the marshmallow, enjoying both the sweet flavor and Zach's reaction. When it was gone, she brought his fingers to her mouth.

She'd been wanting to touch him, to taste him, since that day in the cabin. Now, she circled her tongue around each fingertip, her gaze never leaving his face. Then she drew his index finger deeper into her mouth, simulating an act that made his breathing grow heavy.

She slid her tongue around it, easing his finger in and out of her mouth until every last trace of marshmallow was gone. Then she repeated the act with each remaining finger, ending with his thumb. By that time, Zach's arousal was evident in the glow of the fire.

"That was delicious," she said, feeling a little stickiness on her lower lip as she spoke. She reached up to wipe it off, but Zach stopped her.

"Let me," he rasped.

He leaned forward, nipping her lip with his mouth until the stickiness was gone.

"We still have mine," he said, pulling his marshmallow from the fire. It was charred almost beyond recognition, but neither one of them seemed to mind.

Gracie pulled it off and brought the marshmallow to his lips, then replaced it with her mouth. Zach moaned low in his throat, his arms coming around her.

But she placed her hands flat on his chest, pushing him gently back onto the blanket inside the tent. He pulled her with him, her body sprawled on top of his. She could feel the hard ridge of his erection between her thighs and the rapid beat of his heart beneath her hands.

"Now I have you exactly where I want you," she breathed.

"The question is," he said softly, "what are you going to do with me?"

"You'll see, Zach," she promised. "You'll see."

13

ZACH STARED up at Gracie, wondering if she had any idea how exquisite she looked in the light of the fire. The glow made golden highlights shine in her hair and made her eyes such a deep blue that he could happily drown in their depths.

He watched her reach up and start opening her blouse, one button at a time. She moved with excruciating slowness until every nerve fiber in his body vibrated with anticipation. After what seemed an eternity, she slipped out of her blouse, her breasts almost spilling out of the top of her lacy white bra.

The urge to reach out and touch them almost overwhelmed him, but he made himself wait, wanting to see what Gracie was going to do next. She sat up on her knees, braced on either side of his hips, then popped open the top button of her slacks. She wriggled out of them, rising to her feet and lifting one leg, then the other, to pull them off.

Zach's breath caught in his throat as she towered above him, still straddling his hips, but wearing nothing except her bra and panties. From his vantage

Kristin Gabriel   165

point, her slender legs seemed to go on forever, stretching up to that thatch of white silk that concealed his ultimate destination.

But before he could begin the journey, she lowered herself once more, her face now hovering just above his waistband. He groaned as she bent her mouth to his groin, feeling her warm breath through the denim fabric of his jeans. Then her lips made contact and he knew the meaning of paradise.

The sensation almost undid him. He grabbed fistfuls of the blanket beneath him as she moved up and down, creating a friction so hot he thought he might explode.

When he couldn't take it anymore, he sat up and grasped her shoulders, pulling her up for a soul-wrenching kiss. Her hands pulled his shirt out of the waistband of his jeans, buttons flying as she tore it open.

He cradled her face in his hands, showering kisses on her mouth, her nose, her cheeks. Savoring the feel of her soft skin and the heady taste of her that he knew would leave him craving more.

Sometime in that vortex of desire, he shed his jeans and underwear, then watched her remove her bra and panties while he rolled on a condom. Then he lay with her on the blanket, her skin feeling like silk against him. Zach caressed her cheek with one knuckle, ignoring the pounding need in his body to savor this moment together.

"You are so beautiful," he breathed.

Tears gleamed in her eyes, but she smiled at his

words. "I'm glad you weren't Gilbert. That night at the reunion. I'm glad it was you."

"Me, too," he said, settling into the warm cradle of her body. He intended to take his time, lowering his head to nuzzle each breast. His tongue circled one nipple then the other, drawing sweet whimpers of desire from her throat.

Then her hands moved on him and he knew that time was something he didn't have. As if sensing his need, she opened her legs for him. An invitation he couldn't resist.

The next moment he was inside of her, relishing the way she enveloped him. Her warmth. Her acceptance. Then she moved her hips, arching upwards, driving him to the brink of ecstasy. His body began to move of its own volition, driven by a need that almost scared him

He needed Gracie. A fact he embraced now, just as he embraced her, catching her mouth in a kiss as their bodies moved together, harder and faster, until they both reached a crescendo that made them cry out into the night.

"Zach!"

This time she called out *his* name. Satisfaction, deep and primal, flowed through him. His woman. His love.

His Gracie.

THE NEXT MORNING, Gracie awoke in her bed, the sun slanting through her window. She lay wrapped in Zach's arms, his warm body spooned around her back and his head nestled in the crook of her shoulder.

He'd carried her inside the house when lightning had flashed across the sky in the middle of the night. Then he'd made love to her again as the thunder boomed and raindrops pattered against the windowpane. She could still taste marshmallow on her tongue. And Zach. A thrill shot through her at the memory of their night together.

A night that had burned away her last remaining doubts about trusting him.

"Are you awake?" she whispered.

"Hmmm," he murmured against her neck.

"Zach," she said, turning in his arms to face him.

His eyes were half closed, his face slack with sleep. "I'm awake."

She smiled, hating to rouse him from his relaxed state. But this was too important to wait. "It's about Gilbert."

His eyes opened at the name, tension lines forming around his mouth. "What about him?"

Gracie wasn't sure how to broach the subject without making him angry, so she just decided to tell him straight out instead of trying to sugarcoat it. "I saw him, Zach."

"You what?" He was wide awake now, rising up on one elbow. "When?"

She placed one hand on his shoulder, smoothing it over the taut muscles there. "Last night. Right before I came home. I met him at an abandoned warehouse on Parvey Road."

He stared at her for a moment, then pulled her tight against him. "Promise me you'll never do that again, Gracie. He could have hurt you or...worse."

Her eyes stung at the anguish she heard in his voice. "I'm fine," she assured him. "Gilbert would never hurt me. He just wanted to talk to me."

Zach held her a few moments longer before finally pulling away far enough to look into her face. "So what did he say to you?"

She sighed, part of her feeling like she was betraying her friend. But she couldn't keep this secret from Zach any longer. Not after what had happened between them last night.

"He wants me to bring him the videotape."

Zach sat up at that news, muscles flexing in his chest at the movement. Gracie couldn't help staring at his body, honed to perfection. He seemed oblivious to the effect looking at him had on her. Or maybe he was used to women ogling him in bed.

She shook that unpleasant thought from her head. He was with *her* at this moment. That's all that mattered. She couldn't let herself worry about yesterday or tomorrow, not when she knew how often life interfered with her plans.

But part of her couldn't help but dream about a future with Zach, making love with him every night, waking up with him every morning. A dream that seemed impossible with so many obstacles in their way—but that didn't make it any less precious.

"That damn tape," Zach muttered. "What's on it that could be so important?"

She shook her head. "Gilbert wouldn't tell me, though he did say that he intended to take it straight to the police."

Zach arched a skeptical brow. "And you believed him?"

A chill passed through her at his expression. "Of course. He'd never lie to me."

He tossed back the covers and climbed out of her bed. "I don't believe this. Why didn't you tell me all of this right away?"

She pulled the sheet up to her chest, hating the tension forming between them once more. The same tired argument. Zach vilifying Gilbert while she defended him. She didn't want any more walls between them, but he had to at least meet her halfway.

"I wasn't going to tell you at all," she replied, watching him get dressed. "But…"

"But?" he prodded, then his face softened. "But you thought I wouldn't be such a jerk about it." He walked over to the bed and reached for her hands. "Look, Gracie, I'm not really upset with you. Just the thought of you alone with that guy…." He grasped her hands tighter. "Anything could have happened."

"Don't you trust me?" she asked, really needing to know the answer.

"Yes," he replied without hesitation. "It's Holloway I don't trust."

"But I've told you over and over that Gilbert would never hurt me. If I matter to you at all," she said, meeting his gaze, "then you need to know how important it is for you to believe me."

"You matter," he said firmly. "You have no idea how much. Gracie, I…" The phone rang, cutting off his words. He huffed out a breath, then said, "I'll get it."

When Zach walked out the door, Gracie climbed out of bed and got dressed. She could hear his voice in the other room, surprised the phone call hadn't been for her. Who would be calling Zach at her house?

She discovered the answer to the question when he walked back into her bedroom. "It was the Kendall police. They have Dorie in custody. Apparently she wants to cut a deal."

"In custody?" Gracie said. "How did that happen?"

"She stole a car and was headed out of town when it broke down. The police caught up with her before she could get away."

"She was leaving Kendall?"

"Looks that way."

"Then Allison's plan must have fallen through. That means Gilbert could be in trouble."

"Forget about Gilbert," he bit out. "I want you to promise me to stay away from both him and that warehouse until I get back from the police station."

"But—"

"No, Gracie. We have to do this my way. If we're lucky, Dorie will spill everything and we'll be able to wrap up this case today."

After everything she'd said, everything that had happened between them, Zach was still acting solo. He didn't really trust her. Didn't believe in her. And it was starting to seem likely he'd never be able to do either. So much for fantasizing about a future with him. It was just another dream that wouldn't come true.

"Promise me," he prodded, his gaze intent on her face.

She looked at him, something breaking inside of her. "All right."

He leaned over to kiss her, his hands gripping her shoulders. "I'll be back as soon as I can. Then we'll talk about everything. About us."

Gracie watched him walk out the door, knowing nothing would ever be the same between them.

Because she was about to break a promise to the man she loved.

ZACH DIDN'T realize until he entered the Kendall Police Station that he'd forgotten the videotape. He'd been too distracted by the expression on Gracie's face to think clearly. Something was wrong, but he wouldn't be able to resolve it until he cleared up this mess with Gilbert.

Holloway was the problem, as always. Coming between them just when they were about to make a connection. Like this morning, when he'd awakened to find himself in Gracie's bed. For a moment, he thought it had been a dream. Then she'd smiled at him and he'd known it was real.

That's why this uneasiness roiling around inside of him bothered Zach so much. He felt as if he were being pulled in two different directions, forced to choose between doing his duty as a cop and making Gracie happy.

It was also the reason he needed to close this case before it broke them apart. He wanted Gracie to be his first priority. Wanted to give her his full and undivided attention.

But that wasn't the only reason. Despite Gracie's promise to stay away from Holloway, he couldn't really be sure she appreciated the danger she was in. She was so confident in her ability to judge people, especially Gilbert. His partner had been the same way before he'd been shot. So sure he could handle any situation.

But he'd been wrong.

And Zach had been wrong to ignore his own instincts just to make Ray happy. He'd lost a partner because of Gilbert Holloway. So he wasn't about to take the chance of losing Gracie.

"Detective Maddox?"

He turned around to see Sergeant Hayes walking toward him, wearing wrinkled gray slacks and a white shirt with a blue tie. He carried a cup of coffee in his hand, along with a chocolate donut wrapped in a paper napkin.

"Glad you could make it on such short notice," Hayes said, stopping beside him.

"I just hope this won't take long."

"We're still waiting for Dorie Phillips's lawyer to show up." He held up the doughnut. "I figured there would be enough time for me to have breakfast."

Impatience wafted through him. "She lawyered up already?"

"She's a smart one," Hayes said, taking a sip of his

coffee. "Smart enough to know she's got information we can use. I think you'll be happy you came down here."

But Zach was already regretting it. Lawyers were notorious for causing delays, not only in criminal trials, but in every other aspect of the justice system. He'd always figured Delays 101 was a required course in law school.

Now he'd have to bide his time here while Gracie waited for him alone at the house. At least she'd promised to stay put, so he wouldn't have to worry about her.

Thirty minutes later, Hayes tracked him down at the coffee machine. "The lawyer finally showed up. He and Dorie are in conference right now, but that shouldn't take too long. Then you can talk to her."

Zach had waited six months for this case to be over, so he figured he could wait a few minutes more.

But it was more than an hour before he was finally called into the interrogation room. Dorie sat at the table beside her lawyer, looking tired and sullen. Her attorney was a young man, fresh out of law school, judging by the new leather aroma of his briefcase.

"My client is willing to offer information in a criminal case in exchange for a plea deal," the attorney said. "I think you'll find it worth your while."

"Let's hear what she has to say first," Zach said.

Dorie's head jerked up at the sound of his voice. "Are you from Boston?"

He nodded, surprised his accent was that noticeable. "That's right. I've been working on the Holloway case for several months now."

Her mouth thinned. "Gilbert Holloway is to blame for all of this. He roped us in, making us believe he was legit. Then it was too late to back out."

"Who's we?" Zach asked.

"My cousin Allison and I," Dorie replied. "She'll back me up if my word's not good enough. I know she will."

Zach pulled out a chair and sat down, ready to get down to business. "Then tell me where she and Holloway are hiding."

Dorie snorted. "They're not together. Gilbert doesn't trust her enough to let her hide out with him. He doesn't trust anybody."

Except Gracie.

Zach's instincts told him she wasn't safe, no matter how much she protested to the contrary. Or maybe it was the thought of losing her that made him refuse to believe her about Holloway. She was so damn loyal to the man.

"Here's the thing," Dorie said, glancing at her lawyer. "I don't want to do any jail time. I've made too many enemies, inside and out. If I agree to testify against Holloway at his trial, then I want full immunity."

"I think you're getting ahead of yourself," Zach said. "We're not making any deals until both Holloway and Allison are in custody."

She shrugged. "Fine. I just hope you don't keep

wasting time with that Dawson woman, because Gilbert is planning to leave the country today."

That Dawson woman. The way she said it, like acid dripping from her tongue, made his skin prickle. "How do you know about Gracie?"

Dorie rolled her eyes. "Allison doesn't take any chances. She knows Gilbert has a soft spot for the woman. So she's been watching the house and knows you've been staying there. The only thing she doesn't know is that you're a cop. She figured Gilbert brought Gracie in on the deal and you were just another guy who would get a split of the pot."

Zach hesitated, wondering how much he should reveal to Dorie. Then again, she wasn't going anywhere. "How can Gilbert be leaving today if he's got a meeting set up with Gracie tonight?"

Dorie laughed out loud. "You people are so dense! This is why he's still on the loose. There is no meeting tonight. It's all a scam."

Zach stared at her, certain Gracie wouldn't lie to him. Still, there'd been something in her eyes this morning…. "How do you know?"

"Because I was there, in the warehouse, when Gilbert's little Gracie came calling. I heard everything. He set her up, making her believe the tape had some secret message. It's simply bait for Allison. She's the one he wants to frame for all of this."

"So Allison's the one meeting her tonight?"

Dorie nodded. "Why else would he make it so easy for you?"

She had a point, though Gilbert hadn't known

Gracie would tell a cop about the meeting. *Or had he?* Maybe Gracie had told him all about Zach staying with her. He raked his hand through his hair, uncertain what to believe.

The lawyer rose to his feet. "Sounds like my client has given you more than enough information for that plea deal."

Zach looked at Sergeant Hayes. "This isn't my jurisdiction, so it's not my call."

Hayes hesitated for a moment, then gave a brisk nod. "You've got a deal, but we won't make it official until we bring this Webb woman into custody."

"Just send me the paperwork," the lawyer said. Then he left the interrogation room along with Dorie, who was escorted by a guard.

Hayes turned to Zach. "So what can our department do to help you?"

It was a sticky jurisdictional problem. Gilbert Holloway hadn't broken any laws in Texas. Yet. But they had enough evidence to suspect him of a possible conspiracy, along with Allison Webb, and she did live in this jurisdiction.

"Nothing until tonight," Zach replied. "That's when Gracie's supposed to meet Gilbert at the warehouse, although it sounds like Allison is the one who will show up. Maybe you could send a couple of unmarked cars out that way to intercept her."

Hayes nodded. "No problem. Is there anything else you need?"

"As a matter of fact, there is." Zach stood up and

moved toward the door. "But let me buy you lunch first. I'm starving."

Hayes laughed. "I never turn down a free meal. Lead the way."

Zach glanced at his watch, hoping to make it a quick meal. He wanted to get back to Gracie. And if everything proceeded as planned, he'd never have to leave her again.

14

GRACIE WORKED on autopilot that morning at the bookstore. She shelved the latest arrivals, assisted customers, and caught up with the paperwork while her mind was somewhere else. On Zach, to be exact. And on the videotape in her purse.

If only she knew what was on it.

"Earth to Gracie," Trina said, a sharp edge to her voice.

She blinked, then looked up from her desk. "Oh, sorry. What do you need?"

"The stapler," Trina snapped. She'd been in a bad mood all morning, snarling at customers and even avoiding the phone.

"I've asked you for it three times already."

Gracie plucked the stapler off the desk and handed it to her. "I guess I'm not quite with it today."

"Not getting enough sleep these days with that sexy cop living at your house? Must be rough."

Her mind flashed to making love with Zach in the tent, then later in her bed. She'd been so sure everything had been resolved between them. But obviously good sex, no *great* sex, couldn't solve everything.

"Do you want to tell me what's bothering you?" Gracie asked, finally confronting Trina's attitude. "Or do you want to just keep growling at me and everybody else who walks through the door?"

Trina's mouth thinned, then she turned away. "Sorry. I've just remembered that my life sucks and I can't do a damn thing about it."

That didn't sound like Trina. She was not a woman to feel sorry for herself.

"What's wrong?" Gracie prodded. "Maybe you'll feel better if you tell me."

"What's right?" she countered, then heaved a long sigh. "Forget it. I'd rather hear what's going on with you. Why are you so out of it today?"

Gracie knew Trina was avoiding the issue, but she also knew better than to push her. Trina would confide her problems when she was good and ready. Gracie, on the other hand, needed some answers now.

"I can't stop thinking about Zach," she began. "I believe he cares about me, maybe even loves me. But he hasn't been able to rely on anyone but himself for so long that he doesn't know how to trust—or how to admit when he's wrong."

Trina winced. "Not exactly the best basis for a relationship."

"I know." Gracie glanced over then filed an invoice. "The worst part is that I still want him in my life, inner warts and all."

"So go for it," Trina said.

Gracie wished it was that easy. But Gilbert was still standing between them. As much as she loved

Zach, she couldn't compromise her values. And one of those values was loyalty. Gilbert had been her best friend for over a decade and even though they'd gone their separate ways, he needed her now. She couldn't turn her back on him.

Something that Zach would never understand.

"Not to change the subject," Trina said, looking around the store. "But have you heard from Paul today?"

"No. Isn't he here?"

"I haven't seen him all morning."

"Maybe he's sick," Gracie ventured.

"He's never sick. The guy hasn't missed a day here for the past three years." Trina shuffled a stack of receipts in front of her. "Besides, I called his house. There was no answer."

Gracie smiled. "So you do have a soft spot for him after all."

Trina grimaced. "Please. I'm just concerned, that's all. Something happened last night and, well, I may have said some things that hurt him…" Her voice trailed off and she pressed her lips together.

"For two people constantly surrounded by romance books, we both certainly seem to have trouble in that department. You'd think we'd have learned something by now."

"None of those books have anyone with a disability for a hero or heroine," Trina retorted. "They're all perfect. You talked about Zach's inner warts." She pointed to her prosthesis. "Well, I have an outer wart that no man can overlook."

At least now Gracie knew the cause of Trina's mood. Despite her denial, Paul did mean something to her. Trina just wasn't ready to believe that any man could love her.

"First of all," Gracie said, "you're wrong about those perfect heroes and heroines. There's a Harlequin Temptation called *Out of the Darkness* with a hero who is disfigured by a fire. And another one called *Tongue-Tied*, that has a heroine with a speech disability."

"They're fiction, though, aren't they?" Trina said wryly. "Not real life."

"Second of all," Gracie continued as if she hadn't spoken, "Paul does care about you, despite your 'wart.' That's obvious to anyone who sees you two together."

Trina set her jaw. "He just feels sorry for me. Why else would he offer to help me so much? I'm not going to be with any man out of pity."

"You know, I saw one of his poems once," Gracie said softly. "It was about you, Trina. He compared you to the sun and how he needed to orbit around you to feel light and warmth in his world. It was beautiful."

Her face softened. "A poem? Why didn't he ever show it to me?"

"I don't know," Gracie replied. "Maybe he was afraid of your reaction. Sometimes dreams are safer than reality."

The truth of her own words hit her in the solar plexus. How long had she dreamed of law school, yet always found some excuse not to pursue it? Yes, she had obligations, but so did most people. They still found a way to make their dreams come true.

"I need to get out of here for a while," Trina said, grabbing her purse. "If you need me, I'll be over at Temptation having a drink or three."

"All right." Gracie watched her walk out the door. The limp was more pronounced than ever today, but she knew Trina's real handicap was the way she saw herself.

Maybe Gracie had the same problem. Seeing obstacles where none really existed. Was it possible for her to go to law school and run the bookstore? Had she been holding back not out of necessity, but out of fear?

There was certainly a basis for that fear—like racking up big debts and juggling her life around. Yet, part of her was ready to throw caution to the wind and just go for it, knowing full well there wouldn't be any guarantees.

The fact that she was even considering such a thing surprised her. But deep down Gracie knew she was more than considering it. She was going to do it.

The bell on the door jingled and she looked up to see Paul walk inside. She almost didn't recognize him. He'd shaved his beard and wore a new gray suit.

"Well, look at you," Gracie said as Paul walked up to the counter. "What's the occasion?"

A grin prefaced his announcement. "I sold my book."

"You did?" Gracie rounded the counter and embraced him in a hug. "Paul, that's wonderful!"

"I still can't believe it. The editor called me this morning and gave me the good news. I've been pinching myself ever since."

"So that's why you were a no-show when we opened today. Trina and I were wondering what happened to you."

His grin faded. "I'm surprised Trina noticed. In fact, I thought it would be less uncomfortable for both of us if I stayed away from now on. But I had to come in and share the news."

Trina had mentioned something happening between them last night, but Gracie hadn't thought it actually serious enough to drive Paul away. "What's happened?"

He looked surprised. "She didn't tell you?"

"Not specifically."

"I proposed to her last night."

Gracie stared at him, waiting for the punch line. "Proposed...marriage?"

He nodded. "She had the same look on her face that you do. Best described as stunned disbelief."

"You two have never even dated. Don't you think a proposal was a little premature?"

Resolution darkened his eyes. "You know what, Gracie? I've been hopelessly in love with that woman for the past three years, as she was well aware. I thought it was time to declare myself and see where I stood. Now I know."

Gracie wanted to shake both of them. "Paul, I'm

sure your proposal came as a shock to Trina. Give her some time to think about it. She might not be ready for marriage, but…"

He shook his head. "Look, I'm not here to talk about my disaster of a love life. I have an offer I hope you can't refuse."

"What kind of offer?"

"I'd like to invest in Between the Covers, if you don't mind taking on a partner."

She stared at him, shocked into silence.

"I've got a big advance coming my way," he said with a wide grin. "So, what better way to invest that money than in a business that showcases my work? Between the Covers is like a second home to me. I won't be coming here anymore, but I'd still like to be a part of it."

"I don't know what to say."

"Say yes," he insisted. "I've already found a prime spot for us to relocate. It's a little pricey, but I'd like the lease to be my investment. We can work out all the financial details later. I'm willing to defer the return on my investment until the new store is up and running."

Gracie had never subscribed in mystical mumbo-jumbo, but this almost made her a believer. Only moments before, she'd made the decision to pursue her dream of becoming a lawyer despite the obstacles in her way. Then Paul had walked in the door and removed the biggest roadblock.

"Just think about it," Paul entreated. "We can go look at the site tomorrow and you can give me your decision then."

"I don't have to think about it," Gracie replied, holding out her hand. "Partner."

"You mean it?" he exclaimed, then let out a whoop as he grabbed her hand and pumped it up and down.

"On one condition." Gracie hoped she wasn't overstepping the bounds of her friendship with Trina and Paul.

Paul beamed at her. "Just name it."

"Don't give up on Trina yet. Talk to her—at least one more time. She's over at Temptation right now having a drink."

He looked more resigned than perturbed by her suggestion. "It will just be a waste of time."

"Just go." She pushed him toward the door. "I'll start drawing up a rough draft of our agreement while you're over there."

"This shouldn't take long," Paul said, walking out of the bookstore.

Gracie stared after him, still awed by the sudden turn her life had just taken. She'd never imagined that Paul could hold the key to solving her problem with the bookstore. And he'd been right in front of her eyes the whole time.

Right in front of her eyes.

Maybe she'd been looking at the videotape the wrong way, too. She walked back to her desk and pulled it out of her purse. After watching it a hundred times, she still had no clue why it was so important to Gilbert. But what if the reason wasn't *on* the tape. What if it was *inside* the tape?

There was only one way to find out.

ZACH WALKED into Temptation, his eyes adjusting to the dim lighting inside. The cool air was a welcome respite from the hot afternoon sun. A beer would taste even better.

He walked over to the bar and took a seat on a barstool. A young woman stood at the door of the kitchen, talking to a man in a white apron that read Hot and Spicy.

From the color of her hair and eyes, Zach guessed she must be Cat Sheehan, one of the bar owners. No doubt the older man standing in the doorway was Zeke Watson, who worked the grill.

Strange how he knew them so well when he'd never met them before. Their physical attributes matched Gracie's e-mail descriptions perfectly. With such strong communication skills, she'd make a damn good lawyer if she ever got the chance.

Zach wanted to help her have that chance—and more. But he had to find her first.

"May I help you?" Cat said, moving toward him.

"I'd like a Michelob on tap if you have it," Zach replied, "and some information."

"The beer I can handle." Cat grabbed a frosty mug from the cooler and walked over to the tap. "The information depends on the subject."

"The subject is Gracie Dawson."

Her eyes grew wide, and then she looked him up and down. "Let me guess, you're the cop who's been staying at her house."

"That's right."

She nodded. "Gracie's told me a lot about you."

He wondered just how much, but the expression on Cat's face made it clear that she wasn't going to tell.

"I was just over at Between the Covers," he began, "but it's closed. I was hoping you might know where I could find Gracie."

"Closed?" Cat crinkled her brow. "That's odd. I can't ever remember the bookstore closing in the middle of the afternoon. Somebody is always there."

"That's what I thought," Zach took a deep sip of his beer. "Paul was there the last time I stopped by."

Her brow cleared as a smile teased her mouth. "Well, that could explain it."

"What do you mean?"

"Paul and Trina were in here about an hour ago. When they left, I should have guessed they weren't going back to the bookstore."

"Why do you say that?"

She leaned over the counter, lowering her voice. "Let's just say they barely made it out the door with their clothes on. First they were talking, then they were arguing, then they were kissing. I'm talking H-O-T. I never knew that Toscano guy had it in him."

Score one for Paul. Zach smiled into his beer mug before taking another sip. At least that explained why the bookstore was closed. Gracie probably had to run out for a few minutes and had no one there to run the place.

"Oh, by the way," Cat said, wiping the counter in front of him. "If you hurt, Gracie, I'll kill you."

Zach set down his beer mug. He admired her loyalty, even if he was at the receiving end of her threat. "I have no intention of hurting her."

"Glad to hear it."

He finished his beer, then fished his wallet out of his back pocket.

"The beer's on me," Cat said, picking up the empty mug. "Just tell Gracie to stop in sometime soon. I have a lot to tell her."

He nodded, putting his wallet away. "Thanks."

When he emerged from the bar, he glanced at Between the Covers, hoping to find it open once more. But the Closed sign was still on the door, evoking a twinge of anxiety deep inside of him.

Gracie was right. He worried too much. The Holloway case was almost wrapped up and his life was finally on the right track. All he had to do was nab Gilbert and the man would be out of Gracie's life forever.

Leaving plenty of room for Zach to step in.

15

GRACIE STOOD outside the Kendall State Bank, staring at the silver key in her hand and wondering if she should continue to follow her instincts.

She'd been right about the video, finding the key taped on the inside of the cassette case. Now the question was where this key would lead her. Gracie needed to know the answer before she met with Gilbert. The tape was ruined now, since she'd been unable to put it back together after prying it open. And she wasn't about to just hand over the key.

Especially since she had a good idea where to find the lock that it opened.

Twelve years ago, she'd been with Gilbert when he'd leased a safe-deposit box at this very bank. He'd just started a computer repair business and planned to keep the income separate from his checking account so he wouldn't be tempted to spend all his earnings.

Gracie had forgotten all about it until she'd found the key. It was smaller than a house key, looking almost identical to the one kept by her aunt for her safe-deposit box at the same bank.

Even after all these years, she hadn't forgotten the

number to Gilbert's box. He'd laughed when the bank clerk had assigned the number to him, saying all he had to do was think of Gracie's June tenth birthday to remember the number.

Gracie swallowed a sigh, realizing how different Gilbert was then from the man she'd seen in the warehouse. More open and easygoing, less paranoid and tense. The years hadn't been good to him.

Though, she supposed hiding out from the police, as well as the people who wanted to shut him up, could do that to a man. Gracie just wished he'd confided in her sooner. Maybe she could have found some way to help him.

She still might have that chance now.

Taking a deep breath, she walked inside the bank, wondering how she was going to convince them to let her have access to that safe-deposit box when she didn't even have an account here.

Then she saw her old classmate Sandra Atley standing behind one of the teller windows. As a new employee, she probably didn't know all the bank's customers yet. As an avid gossip, she might be willing to bend the rules in exchange for some juicy information.

"Well, hello there," Sandra said as Gracie walked up to her window. "You disappeared from the reunion the other night. What happened?"

"Gilbert and I wanted to reminisce in private."

Sandra heaved a wistful sigh. "Lucky you. I was hoping for a chance to *reminisce* with him myself, but I guess you had first dibs."

Gracie leaned closer. "Actually it turns out he wasn't Gilbert."

Her eyes widened. "What?"

"He was a policeman from Boston impersonating Gilbert as part of a criminal investigation."

"No way!"

"It's true," Gracie said. "I don't know all the details, but Allison Webb is involved."

"Well, that's no surprise," Sandra replied. "That woman never was up to any good." Then she reached for the cordless phone in front of her. "I've got to call my mother. She'll just flip when she hears this."

Gracie held up the key in her hand. "I need to check a safe-deposit box."

"Oh, sure," Sandra replied, handing over the prep key that fit in all the boxes.

Gracie knew a safe-deposit box couldn't be opened by one key alone. That was part of the bank's security feature. The prep key had to be inserted first, then the key she'd found in the videotape could open the box. *If* her instincts were right about it.

"Just bring back the prep key when you're through," Sandra said, already punching in the numbers on her phone.

It had been easier than Gracie had imagined.

A moment later she stood inside the vault, her gaze scanning the rows upon rows of safe-deposit boxes until she saw the number she wanted: 610.

She walked over to the box, a knot in her stomach, then inserted the prep key into the lock, followed by the key she'd found in the cassette. A soft click sounded, then the box popped open.

She pulled it out and set it on the table, her heart thudding in her chest. Was there cash in there? Precious jewels? Drugs or other contraband? Ready for anything, she opened the lid. But Gracie wasn't prepared for what she saw inside.

It was a computer disk.

The flat, gray 3.5 inch floppy disk looked like any other computer disk. She picked it up, turning it over in her hand. Another mystery. But this time she knew it wouldn't take her as long to figure it out. All she had to do was go home and fire up her computer.

And figure out what she was going to tell Zach.

But her time ran out when Zach met her at the door of her house.

"Where have you been?" he asked, pulling her into his arms. "I was starting to worry."

Her traitorous body savored his warmth, despite knowing she might never trust him enough to be someone she wanted in her life. Zach seemed perfect for her in so many ways. But the greatest test was yet to come.

"I stopped by the bank on my way home." She stepped out of his arms. "I figured out the secret of the videotape, Zach."

He smiled. "I know how hard you've worked on this, Gracie, but there is no secret. Dorie Phillips confessed that it was all a ruse."

She pulled the computer disk out of her purse. "Then why did I find a key inside the tape cassette?

A key that opened a security deposit box at the Kendall State Bank with this disk in it?"

His brow creased as he took the disk from her. "What the hell is this?"

"It's proof that I was right about Gilbert. Allison and Dorie are the ones pulling the ruse, trying to set him up to take the blame for everything."

Zach shook his head. "We don't know that for sure."

"Then let's put this in my computer and find out. I have a feeling that everything we need to know is right here."

Thirty minutes later, Gracie was proven right.

"Holloway's got it all," Zach said, scrolling through the pages of information the computer screen. "Everything we need to file charges. Names. Dates. Every transaction that's connected to the credit card thefts. Gilbert must have saved it all to this disk before erasing it from his hard drive. We've spent months looking for this stuff."

Gracie couldn't believe it was almost over. "It's pretty clear that Allison and Dorie were the ones stealing the numbers. Either to use for themselves or to sell to the highest bidder. Gilbert was the gullible middleman."

Zach turned in his chair, taking her hands in his own. "All this proves is that Gilbert wanted some insurance. Dorie told us that he's the mastermind behind this entire scheme."

Gracie wanted to scream. After everything that had happened between them, he still wouldn't budge from his misconception about Gilbert. He still wouldn't believe in her.

"You're wrong," she told him. "But the only way I can prove it to you is by going to that warehouse tonight and confronting Gilbert."

Zach's face softened. "Sweetheart, Gilbert's not even going to be there. It's all a setup. Allison is supposed to arrive at the same time you do. It's not safe, Gracie. That woman hates you."

"Gilbert wouldn't do that to me." Gracie cupped Zach's face with her hands, entreating him to believe in her. "If you care about me at all, you'll let me do this. Maybe Gilbert isn't completely innocent in all of this, but I want to help him. As his friend, that's the least I can do."

Anguish shone in Zach's dark eyes. She knew she was putting him in a difficult position—making him prove his love for her by letting her do something he thought might be risky. But Gracie didn't have any other choice. She couldn't plan a future with him if he couldn't agree to meet her halfway.

"Damn it, Gracie, don't ask me to do this. I can't let you go in there alone. Not after what happened to Ray."

"I'll be fine," she promised him. "I'm not Ray. And Gilbert's not the one who shot him. You've got to trust me on this, Zach."

He didn't say anything for so long that she almost gave up hope. Then he met her gaze and the expression in her eyes told her that she'd won.

"You have to wear a wire," he bit out, "so I can

hear what's going on inside. The second I think it's too dangerous, I'm coming in. Understand?"

She leaned forward and gently kissed his lips, aware of how difficult this was for him. "Perfectly. Do you understand how much this means to me?"

He pulled her to him, his embrace so tight she could barely breathe. "I must be crazy to let you do this."

For the first time, Gracie wavered in her conviction of Gilbert's innocence. If he was guilty as Zach believed, then she was putting her loyalty to him above the man she loved. But at this point, she didn't have a choice.

"I hate to say it." Zach pulled away from her. "But we'd better go."

She nodded, then took a deep breath. Soon she'd know which one of them was right about Gilbert. She just hoped their relationship could survive the outcome.

A LIGHT RAIN FELL as Gracie stood a few blocks from the warehouse, letting Zach adjust her jacket around the wire she wore to record her conversation with whomever showed up—either Gilbert or Allison.

Four other Kendall police officers stood nearby, talking quietly to each other around their unmarked cars. They were parked between two buildings and behind a row of pine trees, well hidden from view.

"Keep it short," Zach instructed her, gently untucking her hair from the collar of her jacket. "Let Al-

lison do most of the talking. Just enough to incrimi-
nate herself on tape. Then get out of there."

He still wasn't ready to admit that Gilbert would
keep his word to her. But she had no doubt about
who was meeting her tonight. "I'll be all right."

Zach met her gaze. "I'm counting on it."

She wanted to tell him how much she loved him.
That he was the man who mattered most to her in the
world, not Gilbert. But this wasn't the time or the place,
not with those other cops close enough to hear her.

Thunder rumbled in the sky, threatening a down-
pour at any moment. Gracie suppressed a shiver,
though the night air was still hot and humid.

Sergeant Hayes walked up to them. "Are you
ready?"

Gracie nodded, her throat too tight to speak.

"It's not too late to change your mind," Zach said.
"You don't need to do this."

"Yes," she replied softly. "I do."

He stared at her for a moment, then gave a jerky
nod, turning away as she climbed into her car.

Gracie switched on the engine, then pulled onto
the street, feeling more vulnerable than ever now
that she was on her own. Zach and the other officers
would move closer to the warehouse once she was
inside. She just hoped she didn't blow it.

Lightning flashed when she reached the warehouse, as if warning her away. She shook herself, realizing she was letting Zach's fears for her safety
infect her. This was Gilbert, after all. Her best friend.
The man she'd always been able to trust.

The rain spattering on her windshield multiplied and she knew if she didn't get out of the car soon, she'd get soaked. Taking a deep breath, she tipped her chin toward the wire and said, "I'm going in."

She could feel the wire move when she reached for her purse and hoped she hadn't dislodged it. Then she opened the car door and made a run for the warehouse. Rain dampened her hair and eyelashes, blurring her vision.

The door opened before she got there, Gilbert standing on the other side. She breathed a sigh of relief that he'd been the one to meet her.

"Hey, you made it," he said. "I was starting to worry."

"Sorry, I'm late." Gracie wiped the moisture out of her eyes.

"No, problem." Gilbert smiled. "I knew you'd come."

He trusted her, not knowing she was wired and that the police were only a short distance away. But she wasn't doing this to trap him, only to help him. If Zach *was* right and Gilbert was more involved than she believed, he'd need all the help he could get.

"Did you bring the tape?" he asked.

She pushed her damp bangs off her forehead. "No."

He frowned. "But Gracie, I need—"

"I found the key," she interjected.

Gilbert froze. "What?"

As soon as she saw his reaction, something inside of her withered. Zach was right. Gilbert wasn't an innocent dupe in this case. "Inside the video cassette. The key to your old safe-deposit box at the bank."

He rubbed one hand over the back of his neck, obviously buying some time to think. "So…do you have the key with you now?"

"No." She didn't elaborate, wanting him to explain exactly what was going on, to make her understand how the boy she'd known so well could have changed so much in the past ten years.

Gilbert met her gaze. "Don't look at me like that, Gracie. You don't know what it's been like."

"Then tell me."

He got up and started to pace across the dusty concrete floor. "We both had such big plans back in high school. I was going to get a full scholarship to MIT and get a job at NASA. Rub elbows with the astronauts…" Gilbert turned to face her, bitterness turning down the corners of his mouth. "Well, we both know that neither of our dreams came true. I ended up doing IT work like a million other guys, barely making ends meet."

"But you went to Boston College and got a degree," she said, amazed at the self-pity she heard in his voice. "That's a great school."

"Yeah, but I bombed out with the women there just like I did in high school. *None* of my dreams ever came true. Nobody ever really cared about me except you, Gracie."

She rose to her feet, wishing he'd confided all of this to her sooner, before he'd gotten in so deep. "I still care about you, Gilbert. That's why I want to help you now. It's time to turn yourself into the police. You know I'll stand by you all the way."

One of the cardboard boxes stacked around them tumbled to the floor, startling them both. Gracie looked over to see Allison appear from behind the stack, a gun in her hand and an implacable expression on her thin face.

"That isn't going to happen, is it, Gilbert?" Allison said, moving beside him.

He looked between the two of them, clearly torn. "Allison, this isn't necessary. Gracie's not the enemy."

"The way I see it, she is." Allison's cheeks grew mottled with anger.

Gilbert shook his head. "Gracie's just a friend. You're the only woman I love."

"Then why did you send her the tape with the damn key?" Allison exclaimed. "You've delayed leaving this hick town until you could explain everything to her. Now she's the only one who can stop us." She trained the gun on Gracie. "Unless I stop her first."

"Look, I—" Gracie began, wanting to defuse the situation.

But Allison wasn't going to give her the chance. "Say good night, Gracie."

Then she pulled the trigger.

16

ZACH'S HEART LURCHED in his chest when he heard the
gunshot echo over the headset.

Gracie.

Fear clutched at his throat and cramped the muscles in his gut. He tore off the headset, then raced toward the warehouse, his legs as heavy as lead.

Why had he ever let her go in there alone? He'd
known it was dangerous. Known she didn't understand how desperation could drive people to do
something crazy. Now Gracie had paid the price for
his bad judgment.

Voices and footsteps sounded behind him, but he
didn't take the time to turn around. He knew the
other officers had no idea why he'd taken off on a
dead run for the warehouse.

When he reached the building, he made himself
stop, knowing he had a duty to protect the officers
even as he ached to be with Gracie.

"Shots fired," he said hoarsely, pulling his gun
from his shoulder holster.

They followed suit, then took the standard positions for a raid. Zach led the way to the door, mov-

ing faster than procedure allowed but too desperate to find Gracie to care.

If he lost her…

He swallowed hard, knowing he wouldn't be able to function if he even considered that possibility.

He kicked open the door, shouting, "Police!"

The first thing he saw was the blood running on the uneven concrete floor. His gut clenched and a small moan escaped from the back of his throat. His gaze followed the stream of blood until he saw the body lying on the floor.

It wasn't Gracie.

Relief made his knees buckle, but he managed to remain upright as he hurried to her side. She sat on the floor with Gilbert's head cradled in her lap. The guy was alive, but woozy. From his vantage point, Zach couldn't tell where or how badly he'd been shot.

Tears glistened on Gracie's cheeks as she looked up at him. "I love you, Zach. I almost didn't get the chance to tell you that. I love you."

"Shh," he murmured, emotion welling up inside of him. He fought it back, determined to stay professional.

She started trembling as the other officers attended to Gilbert, one of them calling dispatch for an ambulance.

Hayes arrived at his side. "What happened?"

Gracie sucked in a deep breath. "Allison showed up and pulled a gun. She was going to shoot me, but Gilbert dived in the way. He saved my life."

Zach's chest tightened until he had trouble drawing breath. He'd come so close to losing her, the only person in the world who really mattered to him.

"Where did Allison go?" Hayes asked Gracie.

"She panicked when Gilbert went down and ran out the back door."

Hayes waved his arm at his men to go into pursuit, then looked at Zach. "You take care of her. I'll handle the other two."

Zach shrugged out of his jacket and placed it over Gracie's shoulders. She was shaking violently now. He picked her up in his arms, never wanting to let her go.

"I thought you were shot. I thought…" He let his voice trail off, unable to form the words that had almost shattered his heart.

Sirens sounded in the distance as she wrapped her hands around his neck. "I'm all right, Zach. Really. Just a little shaky."

His grasp tightened around her. "You're in shock," he told her, moving toward the door. "You need to see a doctor."

"I'm fine," she protested.

But this time, he wasn't going to be dissuaded. He forced himself to hand her over to the care of the paramedics. They took her vital signs, then placed her on a stretcher and put her in the second ambulance. The first one containing Gilbert had already left, the siren screaming into the night.

"We got her," Hayes said, coming up behind him. "Allison Webb is in custody. Looks like you closed the case, Detective Maddox."

He nodded, too choked up to speak. This was the danger of letting someone into your heart. He'd let Gracie in and almost lost her. Now part of him understood his mother's choice to wall herself off from the world. It just hurt too damn much.

Maybe it was time for him to make that choice as well. For good.

THE NEXT DAY, Gracie walked into Between the Covers to find Trina packing books into one of the many boxes scattered around the room.

"What are you doing here?" Trina asked. "Shouldn't you be home in bed?"

That was the last place she wanted to be. Her bed held too many memories of Zach. She could still smell his aftershave on her pillow, making sleep impossible for the few hours she'd been able to rest last night.

After the doctor had declared her perfectly healthy, Gracie had stayed at the hospital long past midnight, until she was assured Gilbert would be all right. He'd suffered a superficial gunshot wound in the gluteus muscle. Or as he'd wryly put it, his big butt.

She'd expected Zach to show up at the hospital, but one of the officers told her that he was at the police station arranging for Gilbert's extradition and trying to explain events to his irate captain back in Boston.

Though she'd tried calling him on his cell phone, Zach hadn't picked up. Maybe he was avoiding her. Gracie didn't want to believe it, but she couldn't come up with any other explanation.

Had her declaration of love scared him off?

After coming within a few inches of that bullet, Gracie had been so grateful for the chance to tell him her feelings she hadn't even considered his reaction. But she wouldn't take the words back. She loved Zach Maddox and nothing would ever change that.

"I'm perfectly fine," Gracie said, pulling an empty box toward her. "And ready to get some work done."

"Good, because I have some news."

"What?"

"Remember that great location Paul told you about? Well, he sealed the deal yesterday. It's downtown, in the same building as The Bean Tree."

Gracie tried to feel excited for Trina's sake, but inside she just felt numb. "That's great."

"It's more than great," Trina exclaimed. "It's fantastic! The Bean Tree is the most popular coffeehouse in Kendall. We'll have a huge customer base ready and waiting for us."

Despite Gracie's lethargy, she found Trina's enthusiasm contagious. Every part of her life was going well—except one. But if she couldn't be with the man she loved, then what was the point?

"Even better," Trina continued, "Paul's made arrangements with the owner to construct an open archway between the two businesses. That will guarantee us a great customer flow."

Gracie thought about her Aunt Fran and knew her legacy would live on. Now it was time for Gracie to begin her own legacy. "How would you like a promotion, Trina?"

Trina looked up from her box. "What are you talking about?"

"I've decided to go to law school this fall in Austin and I need someone to run the bookstore. Are you interested in the job?"

To Gracie's surprise, tears sprang into Trina's eyes. "This is too much. First I get Paul and now I get to run the bookstore. That's been my dream for as long as I can remember."

"A dream that's going to come with a lot of hard work," Gracie reminded her. "I'll be busy taking classes and studying again, so I probably won't be in much. Are you sure you don't mind handling all of this by yourself?"

"Positive," Trina replied, packing books with a renewed vigor. "In fact, I've got some great ideas for the new store. I'll outline them for your approval and—"

"Not necessary," Gracie interjected. "Paul's a partner in the business now. His approval is good enough for me."

"Me, too." She laughed. "Especially since I'm sleeping with the boss."

Her joy for her friend's happiness was tinged with envy. "So everything's working out between you two?"

"Oh, Gracie," Trina said with a sigh. "I've never been happier in my entire life. Paul may seem quiet around here, but once he starts talking he's spellbinding. The man knows everything. He's just... wonderful."

She laughed. "And it only took you three years to figure it out."

"Paul told me I was worth the wait," Trina chimed, and then her smile turned mischievous. "Of course, if I'd known how good he is in bed, I never would have held out for so long."

Gracie smiled, knowing no man could ever compare to Zach. Or perhaps it was her love for him that made him so perfect in bed. She just wished those feelings had been able to sustain them *out* of bed.

They packed books until noon, saving Aunt Fran's Harlequin collection in the back of the store for after lunch. Trina left to meet Paul at a downtown restaurant, but Gracie chose to run over to Temptation for a quick order to go.

When she returned to the bookstore, she wondered why she'd even bothered to buy lunch. She didn't have much of an appetite, even though Cat had told her that Laine and Tess would be back in town next week and the four of them would be getting together. Cat didn't say why she'd planned the mystery meeting and Gracie didn't want to get her hopes up.

She wasn't ready to say goodbye to Tess and Laine and Cat. They, along with Trina, were the sisters she'd never had, the only women who really understood her. But all their lives were changing now. They each had their own dream to pursue.

Her mind drifted back to Zach. There was still no word from him and Gracie was beginning to give up hope. For all she knew, he could be on a plane to Boston by now and she'd never see him again.

She set the takeout bag from Temptation on her desk, deciding to save it for later. Maybe she'd have an appetite after she'd packed up some more books. But the sound of footsteps in one of the aisles told her she'd have to wait on a customer first.

Gracie swallowed a sigh, wishing she'd locked the door before running over to Temptation to pick up her lunch. She walked over and flipped the sign on the door to read Closed, knowing she needed some time alone.

But first she had to get rid of her latest customer. She just hoped it wasn't a browser, one of those people who spent hours hanging around reading the merchandise.

Gracie moved toward the aisle. "May I help you…"

The words died on her lips when she saw Zach standing there. He looked dangerously sexy with the dark shadow of whiskers on his jaw. Though he'd showered and changed from the day before, her intuition told her he'd been up all night.

"I hope so," he replied. "I'm looking for a story with a happy ending."

She swallowed hard, too stunned to think straight. "What kind of story?"

"Oh, it's definitely a romance. I don't know the title, but the main characters are an aspiring law student and a Kendall city cop."

Hope mingled with the fear that she might be reading him all wrong. "I don't understand."

"Don't you?" He moved beside her, taking both

of her hands in his own. "I love you, Gracie Dawson. Simple as that. It just took me a while to figure it out. Cops are dense that way sometimes—and stubborn."

"I noticed," she breathed, telling herself this wasn't a dream. It was real. Beautifully, wonderfully real.

He reached out to caress her cheek. "Do you think you can stand having a dense, stubborn guy like me around for the next forty or fifty years?"

"Is that all?" she asked, joy bubbling up inside of her. "I was hoping for a lot longer."

"I'm glad you feel that way." His gaze softened on her as he moved closer. "Because I've just accepted a job with the Kendall Police Department. I want to be as close to you as possible for as long as possible."

"Oh, Zach," she exclaimed, wanting to laugh and cry at the same time. But part of her still held back. She didn't want him to have any regrets. "Are you absolutely sure about this? What if you miss Boston? What if you don't like living in Kendall? What if you're bored—"

He silenced all her worst scenarios with a kiss that convinced her that life wasn't going to be boring at all.

When he finally pulled back, she looked into his dark brown eyes and saw the promise of more happiness than she'd ever dared to dream of.

"I love you," Zach said hoarsely. Then he pressed his hard length against her with a groan of desire. "I want you."

"Then what are you waiting for?" Gracie whispered, pulling him to her for another kiss. This one was even hotter than before, with an urgency that neither of them could deny.

Gracie leaned against a bookshelf as Zach's fingers began to work the buttons of her blouse. She helped him, pulling her blouse open so she could feel his hands on her skin.

Zach obliged, dropping his head to her breasts and suckling them through the thin silk of her bra as his fingers lifted her skirt past her waist.

Then his hands were sliding into her panties, pulling them downward. She arched against the solid oak behind her as he dipped his fingers inside of her, finding her wet and ready.

Gracie heard the rip of a condom package, followed by the rustle of clothing. Then he was finally inside her. She moaned at the exquisite sensation, wanting it to last forever.

But it only got better.

She grasped his shoulders as he lifted her legs on either side of his hips. He filled her completely, making her cry out in ecstasy as he began to move. The bookshelf quaked behind her, but all she could feel was Zach. His strength. His desire. His love.

His cry of satisfaction ripped through the air, compelling her own as her body clenched and rocked with pleasure. The motion caused all the paperback books to tumble off the shelves above, raining down on them as they found their completion.

When she finally caught her breath, Gracie gazed at all the Harlequin Temptations scattered around them. "Here you go, Zach. Now you can take your pick of happy endings."

Zach looked at the books surrounding them, then met her gaze, a forever kind of love shining in his eyes. "I pick you."

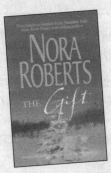

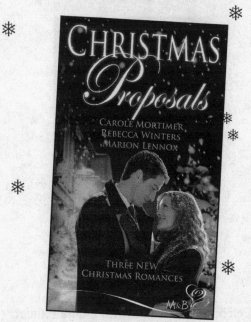